A LONG STEM ROSE

To Ja
love From Mom . Dad
Christmas '95 - XXX

A LONG STEM ROSE
BRIEGE DUFFAUD

POOLBEG

Published in 1995
by Poolbeg Press Ltd
123 Baldoyle Industrial Estate
Dublin 13, Ireland

© Briege Duffaud 1995

The moral right of the author has been asserted.

The Publishers gratefully acknowledge the support of
the Northern Ireland Arts Council.

A catalogue record for this book is available from the British Library.

ISBN 1 85371 502 6

Cover photography by Gillian Buckley
Cover design by Poolbeg Group Services Ltd
Set by Poolbeg Group Services in Garamond 11.5/13.5
Printed by The Guernsey Press Ltd,
Vale, Guernsey, Channel Islands.

A note on the author

Briege Duffaud (nee Finnegan) was born near Crossmaglen in County Armagh, Northern Ireland. She has lived in England and Holland and now lives in France. She has worked as a freelance journalist and a short story writer. Previous books include *A Wreath upon the Dead* and *Nothing Like Beirut* both published by Poolbeg.

Acknowledgement

With sincere thanks to my sister Bernadette
and her word-processor.

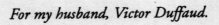

For my husband, Victor Duffaud.

Everybody talking to their pockets.
Everybody wants a box of chocolates
and a long-stem rose.
Everybody knows.

(Leonard Cohen, *Everybody Knows*, 1987)

Part One

❧

It happened in Arles, outside one of those sprawling tourist cafés whose tables overflow off the pavement into the pedestrian part of a square. They flowed right up, these graceless metal tables and awkward scraping chairs, to the immense statue of Frédéric Mistral on his pedestal. And it was there, that Saturday, as she crossed over past the café with her loping self-possessed French walk, (her consciously grown-up walk), that Hélène unexpectedly, miraculously, saw him again, Christopher Milton, after more than twenty years. There he stood among the scurrying shoppers, in his authentic Burberry and longish hair and his interesting lined face battered by experience, wrapped tightly in his solitude (as he always had, she remembered, even in a room full of talking laughing people, stood wrapped in watchful solitude), staring up at the statue of Mistral with that quizzical, slightly bewildered, expression she'd once known so well. Had he been expecting it to be Van Gogh?

"Our other local celebrity," she said helpfully, "Your man up there, I mean. How are you, Christopher?"

For a second he looked even more bewildered. As well he might, she thought smugly. The difference there must be, after all, between the naive Belfast teenager he'd known and rejected and this, well this sophisticated Frenchwoman for want of a better phrase, she thought, as if the two words necessarily . . . But she knew she did look coolly sophisticated and was glad of it, silk shirt loosely draping the throbbing heart, cream linen trousers covering other longings.

"We've met . . ." Christopher said, not sounding at all sure.

"Yes," she murmured, smiling. "But that was in another country and besides, the wench . . ."

His face came alive with recognition, with appreciation. The murmured quotation had been so apt, so worthy a gift to offer him. He wasn't to know she'd prepared it years earlier, soon after she'd managed to kill off the ignorant wench, soon after she left Belfast, and kept it in readiness for just such a meeting. She'd never once doubted that there would be such a meeting. Christopher Milton might have despised her, might have rejected her, but could not have vanished completely out of her life unless he was dead. And she would have heard if he'd died. Her mother would have mentioned it. (Would certainly have mentioned it, spying on her with a sideways look, or with one of her significant silences on the phone.)

"I've thought of you often, Eileen," he said. "It's strange how we just vanished out of each other's lives after all that . . ."

All that. That summer. She looked him straight in the eyes for a second, struck, bouleversée, her eyes for that one instant deliberately expressing . . . Everything, she hoped, that could be expressed in something as limited as a look. Just for that one instant. Long enough to let him understand, if he chose to, that there always had been, that summer, underneath it all, under the masks she wore to defend herself, just such a face of complete vulnerability.

2

(Or so she recalled it, driving back in tears from Arles, between the terraced vineyards.)

They moved together to a table, choosing one with extreme care though they were all alike, the tables, all empty because of the weather, because the tourist season hadn't really got going properly.

She thought: remember a table in the Club Bar, Chris, the very first evening? I came back from work in the café and you were there, as miraculously as now, standing on my doorstep. You'd just pushed a note under my door. And when I opened the door you retrieved the note, wouldn't let me read it, said it didn't matter now since I was there.

I could have kept that note, Chris, it would be worn away by now from being read, from being kissed. Would have been my souvenir of you. Might have been a clue to you. I never even knew your handwriting. So you asked me out for a drink and seemed pleased when I didn't go off coquettishly to change, just went with you happily as I was. We sat at a table and you asked me what I'd drink and I didn't even know, I had no idea what grown-ups drank, with Chaz I always had a Coke. And you said why not try a Pimms, Eileen, it's a fun drink, you'll like it. You said you'd worked it out through months of painful experience that in the social desert called Belfast there were only three kinds of women; the Babycham kind, you said, with Disney eyelashes and Bambi brains, and the pint-o'-Guinness buy-your-own-round lot, we all know what *they're* like, and it struck me, you said, it struck me Eileen when I was talking to you that evening at Mitzi's party, it struck me that you're far from being either of those two. I interpret you, you said, as one of the very rare young Irish girls worthy to be offered something more exotic. You're a Pimms lady in embryo, you said. Still in the bud. The last bit in that flat defiant Belfast accent you were so good at imitating: stoll on the bodd. And I laughed and stopped being shy of you.

"You're forgetting there's a fourth kind now," I said, "What about our newest MP? Not much Bambi about that one!"

"Ah yes," you agreed in that lovely dry voice of yours, "Miss Devlin and Company. I should imagine they'll be Ulster's alternative to Germaine Greer and the brave new permissive society. And have you been on any of dear Bernadette's marches yourself, Eileen?"

"Only at the very beginning," I said, "Way back last autumn. Mitzi and her parents dragged me with them to that one in Derry. Never again! Talk about being petrified! And I went with Mitzi to the Tariq Ali meeting in Queen's, actually I noticed you there, standing on your own at the back, imagine you going to something like that and you not even a student!"

"Aren't you the great little observer," you smiled. "Imagine you being there yourself. And what did you make of all that revolutionary chic, Eileen? Was it your . . . uh, scene . . . at all?"

"Well to tell you the truth," I confided, "I couldn't really follow what he was on about half the time, could you? I mean he seemed so. So foreign, I suppose. I mean it didn't seem to have much to do with *me*, what he was saying, like."

"Isn't that terrible," you said seriously, "After the poor wee fella coming all the way from Pakistan just to entertain us! And did your friend Mitzi follow what he was on about?"

"Oh Mitzi!" I said, "Mitzi's different from me. Mitzi's really involved in all that, she takes it all dead seriously. Mind you I suppose she has to, it runs in her family. They

4

keep trying to educate me, Mitzi's ones, they speak Irish in the house and everything. Imagine!"

And then I heard myself rattling on like a ten-year-old, boring you stiff, nothing *like* a sophisticated Pimms lady, but you were very kind and very gentle, pretending to be deeply interested in Mitzi and her parents.

"Oh really?" you asked, speaking to me as if I was a grown-up, as if it really mattered what I was telling you, "What about Mitzi's family? Is she related to de Valera or someone?" So I told you all about Mitzi's famous family and we laughed and you said: "A proper little Pasionaria, your friend!"

If we'd but known at the time, if we could only have known what would happen to poor Mitzi, we mightn't have laughed, Chris. And you asked me about my own family, did they go in for that sort of thing at all, hadn't you heard something, oh just something vague? About my father wasn't it? And so I told you about daddy, only making it far more interesting and romantic and leaving out all the squalid bits about drink. "And of course Mother and Gerald, Gerald's my stepfather, well *they're* just boring do-gooders. The unemployed, you know. Discrimination. The homeless. All that sort of."

That was the very end of the Sixties, Chris, a whole lifetime ago. A whole other age. The Club Bar was brown and beige, empty because it was June and most of the students gone, and you wore a battered old beige Burberry and drank a mug of brown and beige Guinness and smiled at me with your crooked ironic lips and I was in heaven. When you left me back at my door you said you hadn't enjoyed an evening so much in a long time and I went to sleep that night dizzy with Pimms, imagining myself pampered in beauty and in love like an Edna O'Brien heroine. There were all those other bars and all those lovely summer evenings. There was Kelly's Cellars and the Stagecoach and the Regency and the Crown Hotel and the Turfstack.

There was the Turfstack. Hélène ached with shame and with memory, thinking of that last disastrous evening in the folksy old Turfstack Inn.

"You're over on a holiday, Eileen?"

"I live here. Well not exactly here, not in Arles, we're spending the weekend with my in-laws. I've been living up in Brittany for the past sixteen years actually. I'm called Madame Bourjois now. Hélène Bourjois." As she said it she was wondering if some vulgar side of him would be thinking it suited her. France, legendary land of tarts. Of frivolity. Of futility. But then, nice wise public-school Christopher never had a vulgar side, and hadn't that been part of her problem back then, before she'd managed to outgrow the wee abandoned country gawk whom all her mother's irritation and Gerald's grey pedantic tolerance hadn't succeeded in killing off.

"Oh that's a coincidence," he said, "That you chose to change your name, I mean. I've just been reading a novel by an old Sixties acquaintance of mine who did exactly the same thing. She chose a name so glamorous and so alien that it lifted her right out of her generation and religion and social class, changed her utterly. *A tarrabull byutty*, so to speak," he quoted suddenly in a Belfast accent, dragging her achingly back across all those years. "So had you always felt uncomfortable as an Eileen, then? Had you been mal dans ta peau, unknown to us all?"

"Oh not at all!" she laughed, "I'd never have dreamed of changing my name, it was my mother-in-law's doing. I think it was the only way she felt she could decently accept me. And actually I was really outraged at first, it seemed such a violation of the person I'd always been seeing myself as. Until I discovered it was just something the French do. I mean it's no big deal, it's just that they can't leave foreigners' names alone. Can't leave foreigners alone, as witness Monsieur Le Pen, my daughter's big idol! They're great ones for integration. For knocking the corners off."

"Sixteen years. That must be why we've never run into each other since that summer."

But that's wrong, she thought, driving back, we met twice afterwards. Would Christopher have forgotten that night in the dance-hall, or the ghastly Saturday in October when she turned up on his doorstep with Teresa? Would he possibly have kept quiet about that, not to embarrass her?

"I was desperately in love with you that summer," she said, suddenly blurting it out because it hurt her too much not to. Meaning: I'm desperately in love with you still, but not quite daring to be that vulnerable.

He pulled down the shutters of his face exactly as she'd seen him do that other time. "Then perhaps you'd tell me," he said coldly, "Maybe now, when it doesn't matter at all, you'll tell me why you deliberately brought your lover to the Turfstack when you knew I'd be there?"

But would he have said 'lover', she wondered, driving back in tears along the road from Arles, going over every detail. Recalling a party she'd been to when she was over in Belfast years ago with Jean-Hubert, where this married actor had brought his mistress, a gawky girl she'd been at school with.

"Imagine!" she'd said when they got back to Finaghy, "Just imagine Mary Flanagan having the neck to turn up with a lover!"

"You're not in France now," her mother said shortly, "We don't use words like that here. We call it an 'escort'".

Well, Christopher would hardly have said 'escort'. Or would he? How well had she ever known him?

"He wasn't my lover," she protested, "Well of course Chaz McCreesh wasn't my lover, he was just Anny and Patrick's nephew, just a nephew of that old nurse of mine. How could you have thought he was my lover, Chris? How could you have thought I'd be bitch enough to do that to you?" And how could he have thought that some, some redfaced plouc like Chaz McCreesh . . .

It ended there of course, because what other conclusion could it have? She told him the truth, all of the truth, and he understood and pardoned and they wandered off hand in hand through the grey old streets of Arles. But would that, she wondered, have been a possibility anywhere outside of a Mills and Boon novel? And then, wandered off to where? To a squalid rented hour in a slimy old Hôtel de passe? Arles had always struck her as the sort of traditional French town that would still have Hôtels de passe lurking away up narrow sidestreets for the local notables to deceive their wives in. To a romantic interlude on a park bench? Christopher had a certain dignity and besides he must be getting on a bit by now; he'd been The Older Man even then, though younger than Chaz. How old had he been? Thirty-five? Older? Younger? How can you tell adults' ages when you're seventeen and a half, what have you to go on? Too old now anyhow to play at young lovers on a park bench. And what about Hélène herself in her famous cream linen trousers and silk shirt kissing on a tatty old park bench among the screeching French children and their knitting mums? Wander off perhaps to confrontation with Jean-Hubert, and lawyers and divorce and fights over who'd have the twins? And would Christopher Milton even want the twins? Or the twins him?

No, Hélène thought, driving along with the tears blinding her, no it wasn't like that, it was nothing like that. Rewind the whole film, you poor cow, take it from the beginning. Tell it how it was. You drove into town, right. You parked the car. You short-cutted across the. And there he was. There he stood. Christopher Milton, miraculously standing there among the scurrying Saturday shoppers on the grey June afternoon, staring up at the statue of Mistral with that quizzical, slightly bewildered etcetera you once knew so well. Or knew hardly at all, if you can bear to be strictly truthful about the thing. Right. There Christopher stood n'est ce pas, twenty years on into Hélène's history, into the world's if it comes to that, and what did you do? What did this cool sophisticated Hélène you've been imagining, what did she do? Well I'll tell you what she did, she ran. Hélène Bourjois, instantly shrunken back down into that naive Belfast teenager, into the wench from another country and another age, Eileen gaped at him for a stunned second and then took off panicking between the tables, across the square, and into the sanctuary of this shabby little bureau de tabac on the corner of a sidestreet. The square was his, the statue was his, the whole town of Arles belonged embarrassingly, shamingly, to Christopher Milton, as the Turfstack had belonged to him on that summer evening long ago, and she was an intruder, a blushing outsider, a scrubby wee teenager from up the Falls lurching into his elegant life, trying to force her cheap little stammering attentions on him as if he was only poor Chaz McCreesh or someone. She needed to hide for a minute, she needed to breathe, to turn her back on him for an instant as she'd done that evening, before she could dare confront him. By the time she'd bought *Midi-Libre*, paid for it, exchanged a few courteous banalities, and received the accustomed male homage from the shopkeeper's greasy admiring little eyes, she was able to be Hélène again, stepping longlegged back between the tables in classy silk shirt and linen trousers, an acceptable greeting ready upon her lips. "Our other local celebrity." she would say helpfully, "Your man up there I mean. How are you, Christopher?" And then he'd . . .

Only Christopher was no longer standing beside the statue. Christopher was gone. Looking wildly, desolately, around the square she saw him walking away quickly, Burberry swinging, in the direction of a battered-looking black BMW with GB licence plates.

"Christopher!" she called, running towards him, "Christopher!"

But he'd already got in on the front passenger door, the car was sliding out of its parking-space and heading off towards Centre Ville and Toutes Directions, and Hélène stood there, jostled by all the miserable grey people who were not Christopher, in the slight drizzle that had begun to fall, unable even to catch a glimpse of him at the lights because there were two other men in the back seat. And then they were out of sight. Christopher Milton had been there, as she had often daydreamed he would be, standing once again in the very centre of her life, and once again she'd panicked and he'd walked away, not recognising her, having no idea who she was. Or had he recognised her? Had he recognised, not Hélène, but the ignorant teenager that was all he'd been able to perceive of her twenty years earlier? And had he simply walked quickly away again from anticipated boredom? Or embarrassment? Or pity?

("So what did you do then?" Pierre asked, "Did you run wildly after the car? Hire a taxi and have yourself ferried round all the tourist sites hoping he'd turn up waving a guidebook at you? Throw yourself weeping at old Mistral's stony feet?"

"I'm not mad, Pierre! And in spite of everything I'm not Eileen. No, what could I have done? I simply finished my shopping and then I drove back to Jean-Hubert's cousins' place and helped them prepare dinner. They were expecting me, after all.")

But, driving back, she found herself daydreaming it, daydreaming in detail how it might have been if she'd not had that moment of panic. Foolishly planning to return tomorrow, Sunday, when the streets would be empty of shoppers and it might be possible to find him again wandering through the grey town alone. And I've become exactly the kind of woman he'd accept now, she told herself, driving back along the narrow roads below the vineyards, a sophisticated Pimms lady. A champagne lady, if it comes to that.

And the joke of it is, she said aloud in English, needing to say it aloud, confident that no peasant spraying his vines above the roadside could understand her, the joke of it is that I'm exactly the same woman as I was twenty years ago underneath the masks and the mimes and underneath the fear. Why couldn't Christopher, with all that famous wisdom and understanding they all used to go on about, why couldn't he have seen down to my very young panicky fear of being rejected again?

But the vineyards, totally uninterested in her woes, skipped away happily towards the blue horizon and she knew, quite coldly, that Christopher was probably no longer even in Arles, had probably just been passing through, could be anywhere by now, might even be driving up through France on his way to the ferry. No use looking for him there tomorrow. No use dreaming that he was staying in one of those golden farmhouses and that when she got back to the cousins' he would be miraculously standing beneath the acacia tree on the patio asking for directions to somewhere. She'd missed her chance with Christopher Milton, once again.

The man beneath the acacia tree would be Jean-Hubert, waiting for her to come back from her afternoon's shopping so that they could eat another duty dinner with his boring relations, and she was Jean-Hubert's wife and she would sleep with Jean-Hubert that night between lavender-smelling sheets in the creaking old bed in the room where his father was born. And, in spite of Christopher, (and in spite of the small village boy who wore, so shockingly, her husband's face), she wouldn't really mind sleeping with Jean-Hubert, as she never did really mind. Jean-Hubert had inherited none of the solid Bourjois chunkiness. If he had, she would certainly not have married him, might indeed never have met him: if he'd been shaped like a Bourjois cousin (those round important bellies, those majestic backsides!) would it ever have entered his head to hitch-hike to Amsterdam, let alone marry some beautiful Irish vagrant he met there? She thought with sudden thankfulness how tall and dark and slim Jean-Hubert was, with his long legs and his neat aristocratic little bones. Which was more than could ever have been said about Christopher Milton so why, after all the years, was she still languishing?

When she got back to the house they were sitting round a bottle of Pernod, talking about Tante Ruby's party.

"Well sooner you than me!" Simone was saying, "Hou la la the idea, Jean-Hubert! I don't even know what you can find to say to those people. Nobles, generals, diplomats, ben dis donc! Your poor papa was a hero of the Resistance but he never frequented people like that. In spite of your

12

mother he stayed faithful to the class he was born into, le pauvre!"

Neither did Hélène and Jean-Hubert frequent them very much, but they seemed to be moving that way more and more, especially now that Tante Ruby was on the point of astonishingly, magically, coming into what she'd always regarded as her birthright. *Ludicrously* coming into her birthright, Hélène thought, recalling all those years since about 1986 when the old lady had taken to boring everybody with the famous sepia-coloured photograph of a group of Chekovian-looking young people sitting round a samovar on a landscaped lawn – long since swallowed up by a collective farm – with the remark: "Great-uncle Boris's place near St Petersburg," as if it was still there only a dose of jet-lag away and might even yet be handed back as the ultimate perestroikal gesture.

"St Petersburg doesn't *exist*, Tante Ruby!" Jean-Hubert used to shout when she'd worn his bourgeois courtesy down to its peasant roots with endless teeth-grinding evocations of sleigh bells and troikas and sumptuous evenings at the opera, "You're living in a dream, aunt! You got all that rubbish out of *War and Peace*!"

But St Petersburg *had* existed, and so had the estate, miraculously preserved as in aspic under the piles of rotting beetroots in the collective farm and it was, almost certainly, about to be handed back. Tante Ruby had contacted the Mayor of that faraway village, elderly residents had remembered Great-uncle Boris (and happily they had all been far too young at the time to participate in his massacre), old yellowing papers had been unearthed from safes, lawyers contacted. A jokey young reporter had come from Ouest-France, Tante Ruby's photo had appeared in the paper along with that of a Grand Duke, heir to the

Romanoffs, who'd been living quietly all these years in a modest villa near Dinard, he too patiently waiting his hour, he too nostalgically passing round photos, boring his entourage . . . All sorts of notable neighbours discovered that they'd always held Tante Ruby (and indeed, in spite of two centuries cold-shouldering, the whole Ploudel de Medeu family) in high esteem; Jean-Hubert, with his children's future in mind, was moved to consolidate all this esteem with a grand party in his aunt's honour. A party Tante Ruby deliberately chose to have on the eve of the Fourteenth of July – a thumbing-one's-nose party the old lady wanted, aimed at teaching a lesson to all those foolish tenants and villagers who would be holding their own brash Republican party that evening, letting off their noisy vulgar fireworks, still foolishly celebrating outdated ideas of Liberty, Equality, Fraternity . . .

It stuck Hélène that Tante Ruby, leafing faithfully through all those royal old faces who stared arrogantly out every week from the pages of *Points de Vue – Images du Monde*, might by now be seriously expecting the glorious overthrow of the French Revolution, and the dawning of a bright new Bourbon day. Since Our Lady of Fatima had done her bit so efficiently, Tante Ruby was possibly thinking, might not Jeanne d'Arc be about to do hers as well?

The party. The reality of the party was suddenly there in Hélène's mind, blotting out Christopher Milton, blotting out her flippant little speculations, terrifying her with the idea of failure, of inferiority, of being once again totally unable to live up to what was expected of her. Nobles, generals, diplomats after all? With awkward little Eileen as their gracious hostess? A bit hopelessly she forced back into her mind an image of Christopher driving steadily through

France towards a place where, this time, she'd be serenely awaiting him. Driving wifeless, she saw him, with his three companions, in the battered old black car, wearing his battered old Burberry, smoking a battered old pipe – a bit Tolkien perhaps, a bit C S Lewis – civilised man of a certain age driving from chaos towards order, towards culture, towards tradition. Towards the mature sophisticated Hélène. A bit of a joke really, an exorcism. And it worked. I am mature. I am sophisticated. I am able to cope. Eileen O'Neill is dead. So is Eileen Campbell. Today was an aberration, it was the shock, it was . . . Yes, but you won't *get* another chance, she thought bleakly, today was it, you're not likely to accidentally run into him another time, are you? It doesn't ever work like that. Life doesn't work like that.

"Oh you know," she shrugged, "I've always found our local aristocrats quite easy to talk to. They're exactly like the rest of us," she told the cousins, as dismissively as if she was in the habit of crunching a viscount for breakfast every morning.

They drove up to the house on Monday afternoon past the fallen branches and headless tree-stumps that were still lying desolately there six months after the big winter tempests. The avenue looked shabbier than ever after a pampered weekend in the kitsch comfort of the Bourjois cousins' country cottage.

"I simply can *not* imagine what Hervé Le Moal finds to do with his time," Jean-Hubert grumbled, "I intend to speak to him a bit sharply about this, I expressly ordered them both before we left . . . "

They came on Le Moal about fifty metres farther on. Bent double like a Millet painting, he and his stout grey-haired wife were slashing away with old-fashioned sickles at two monstrous clumps of brambles on either side of the avenue. Jean-Hubert's serfs, Hélène thought, feeling a sudden democratic irritation at the sight of their archaically up-ended bums as the poor old things sweated away painfully in the service of the Big House. Jean-Hubert slowed down and stopped the car between them.

"Bonjour madame!" Hélène called merrily, "Bonjour monsieur!", filling her voice with a big neighbourly smile, all God's creatures together because after all, she thought, Tante Ruby or no Tante Ruby, Louis the Sixteenth has been dead a brave wee while now and maybe it's about time someone let the tenants know . . .

They straightened up slowly when she spoke (guard of honour with sickles at ease? mad peasants poised to attack?), and nodded very slightly with straight dignified faces. Instantly her smile was far too much, was a pathetic clown's mouth, was a custard pie plastered unto her very being and she sank back and let Jean-Hubert speak as sharply as he liked to them. She wondered uneasily if she'd looked as grotesque as Rosalind Bouchon always did, scrambling madly round in circles courting the village's goodwill.

"Your smile is an act of foreign aggression," Pierre once teased his wife in Hélène's presence, "It is a way of colonising us. There we all are, living peacefully inside our own egos, cosily wrapped up in our little cocoons of anxieties and lusts and neuroses, and along comes old Rosy with her Great British Grin insisting that we all love her, that we join her in some universal street party, jumble sale, animals' rights crusade. We don't need it, Rosy," Pierre said, "Nobody needs this jolly castrated love of yours. All anyone wants of anyone is sex, Rosy. Or money. And why are you English always so scared to admit that?"

16

Hélène had felt sorry for Rosalind at the time though the poor woman was, one had to admit, a walking soup-kitchen of smiles as far as the villagers were concerned. Breton villages, unlike the Gloucestershire one Rosalind grew up in, do not readily welcome outsiders and Hélène guessed that the promiscuously offered smiles were as resented, and as ridiculed, as soup would have been. Pierre may well have been right: even safe and contented inside her own little cocoon as she was (as she'd been), Hélène was often aware that ordinary everyday friendliness was rather thin on the ground in Plouch'en. That, after all, was why Pierre was doing so well for himself. He listened. He'd set himself up as paid friend to the friendless, and the village had come flocking. Not because the only other doctors were a Jew and a woman (as Jean-Hubert insisted), but because Pierre understood that the only sure way of finding chaleur humaine in Plouch'en was to pay for it. And have your fee reimbursed by the Securité Sociale of course – without that incentive the villagers might well have chosen to stay friendless. She thought: Rosalind and Pierre! Well that's it of course. That's what I need, that's what I'll do, that's the solution. This house exchange thing they've been boring us with for months, Pierre's famous drinking mate from the Irish pub in Paris, I can travel over with them. Pierre the great expert on everything from Bewley's coffee to the Twelfth parades, Pierre the great shower of snaps and of slides, a right pain in the ass, but I can go to Ireland with them in September if I can coax them to invite me, Jean-Hubert won't think it strange the way he would if I wanted to go to my mother's. Christopher Milton will be there, Belfast will be there, Saturday only proves that he still exists. That the city, like St Petersburg, still exists beneath the piled-up years of my exile, that Upper Crescent still exists and his neat little booklined flat. I could seek him out if I chose to, throw myself in his path, waylay him behind the dusty dark shrubs of the Crescent. Or not. I could go to Belfast if I liked and deliberately choose not to seek him out. Go there and just walk freely and calmly in the steps of my past, without longing and without pain.

She settled back in her seat and listened with amusement to Jean-Hubert ridiculously and uselessly scolding the Le Moal couple. Hervé Le Moal was a big farmer now, thanks to the European market, still a tenant of the château but no longer a serf, so the weeds grew high and the branches lay rotting and Hervé put in the few days annual duty labour that his lease obliged him to and strictly no more, and in the end Jean-Hubert would be forced to engage the usual team of unemployed village teenagers who would spend most of their time democratically trying to chat up a contemptuous Clémence and talk football to an uncomprehending Henri . . . EuroDisney, she thought, reality is over there in Belfast and we're all wandering like kids through Disneyland here, with our Mickey Mouse problems and our Mickey Mouse snobberies. I'll talk to Pierre this evening, she thought.

The long avenue finally decanted them into the pale formal garden Hélène had created around the ugly old manor house. That, and a kitchen garden, were all that remained of a landscaped park once extensively planted with exotic specimens brought back by various Ploudel de Medeus from their foreign travels. Cut off from the flowers by an electric fence, Hervé Le Moal's cows grazed now among a few banyans and tulip trees, the rest having fallen victim to years of hostile Breton winters, and to Uncle Vladimir's occasional pressing need to turn his timber into hard cash.

Michel Le Borgne was deadheading roses in one of the white and cream beds and straightened up slowly as they approached. His expression changed slightly, flatteringly, when he realized it was her. A small dim light bulb switched itself on somewhere behind the cool blankness of his everyday face as he nodded to them, the villager's stiff nod. Hélène waggled her fingers in a minute unsmiling wave, cordial but not too familiar, no point in being snubbed a second time.

"Et voila un cocu!" Jean-Hubert muttered with a salacious chuckle, "They say Nathalie Le Borgne has had four different lovers since she discovered WeightWatchers last year. Let's hope, for the sake of your anaemic flower-beds, ma chère, that the wronged husband doesn't take to drowning his sorrows. Or, in true Plouch'en style, himself."

To Hélène's surprise, Clémence and Tante Ruby were waiting on the steps to greet their return with faces of sad circumstance.

Tante Ruby was Jean-Hubert's rich aunt, the twin sister of his dead mother, Elsie. In the Twenties (Rosalind once quoted out of some book or other,) it had been the height of chic for aristocrats to name their baby daughters after their English housemaids and indeed the Ploudel de Medeus, mad to be chic, seemed to have rushed in so enthusiastically where real aristos ever after feared to tread that Hélène, when she first came to France, had found herself clutched, though none too warmly, to the sixty-year-old bosoms of assorted Millies and Pearls and Rubys and Elsies, Jean-Hubert's horde of terrifying relations.

They were waiting on the steps not only in welcome but also to announce a domestic catastrophe.

"The servants have run away!" Tante Ruby trumpeted, her voice quivering with well-bred outrage. "Poor little

19

Clémence was actually obliged to neglect her studies and prepare our luncheon this afternoon. And I, Ruby Boulanger de Ploudel de Medeu, have spent the afternoon scraping dried omelet off yesterday evening's plates. This would never have happened in my poor brother Vladimir's time," she accused, "I do not know what La France is coming to!" All these foreigners was implied in every outraged quiver of her voice.

"Tante Ruby rang up the gendarmes this morning and they actually laughed at her, imagine!" Clémence said, wide-eyed, "With ten bank robberies in as many days, they said, they had more to."

"The gendarmes?" Jean-Hubert interrupted in alarm, "Why, did they take anything?"

"Take anything? *Take* anything? What is there in this baraque for them to take? Servants are not fools, mon pauvre neveu, they do not steal whitewood furniture and aluminium teaspoons!"

"They weren't servants," Hélène protested. "We don't have servants, Tante Ruby, who does nowadays? Apart from yourself. They were a very nice young Dutch couple, theatrical people actually, who helped me a bit in the house. Why did they leave, Clémence, they seemed perfectly happy the other day when we were going?"

Clémence shrugged, and Hélène recognised the stubborn expression of family solidarity she'd inherited from her father. All this, the shrug implied, was a private affair taking place among Ploudel de Medeus and Hélène was a spare part, a commoner, an outsider engaged to perform odd little tasks they weren't capable of doing themselves. Like childbearing. Or so Hélène interpreted it. With Henri she felt perfectly at ease: with his freckles and his jokes and his enthusiasms he might almost have been an Irish boy, but she occasionally felt herself overpowered by this very superior young demoiselle she'd so unaccountably created. A battered black car drew up in her head and Christopher Milton stepped out, smiling with his crooked ironic lips. Only why should he be there? Even daydreams require a little logic to hold them up. A sketching tour of Brittany with his old friend Louis Le Brocquy? A pilgrimage to the spot where his dad parachuted down to hound Hitler in '44? Impatiently she shook his smile out of her mind, grabbed Clémence by the arm and dragged her in to face the chaos of the kitchen.

Alone with her mother, Clémence became quite human. "C'était tordant!" she shrieked, once out of earshot, "Only of course one couldn't really laugh out loud. Tante Ruby didn't even realise the Happy Pair were gay, imagine, so she asked little Joop to run her a bath last night, well she'd been strolling around all day in her skin, you know how she does, and then of course she'd had a good bit to drink at dinner, you and Papa not being there to share the bottle. So just as the honest servitor was bent over testing the water she came up behind him and pounced. Well I don't know what she actually *did* but it must have been pretty startling because he let out this tremendous shriek and came rushing out of the bathroom just as I was going to my room and practically knocked me over. He just hurtled by me and up to his attic and locked himself in. So when we got up this morning they'd both gone, just fled into the night as it were. Folded their tents like the Arabs and as silently stole away. And wouldn't we all be happy if the Arabs ever did decide to . . . "

"Spare me the facist politics, darling!" Hélène snapped, "It's a bloody nuisance, I mean I knew they couldn't stay forever but I had been counting on them for this party.

Can't *think* what I'm going to do now. Village charladies I suppose, handing round the canapés with red swollen hands, what that will do to your poor father's ego! God she ought to be put away that old tart, why doesn't she go back to her husband or find herself another gigolo? And why aren't you at school by the way, did she really keep you home to make the lunch?"

"Toy boy is the state-of-the-art expression, maman. And really I should think that's exactly what she was trying to do, wouldn't you? Oh school? Well there was yet another demo planned for today, all the pimply leftists trying to raise their feeble heads again, so she absolutely refused to drive us there. Quite right too. Henri's gone over to that B & B where there's the Irish yobbos, he said they were going to teach him a new folksong, quel horreur! By the look of them I expect they're showing him how to make bombs. *Why* did you have to be born in a Third World country, maman, why couldn't you have been French like everyone else?"

"If I'd been French, young lady, I'd have boxed your ears for that! You don't know how lucky you are that I'm Irish and evolved. Look at your schoolmates, dressed in navy blue from head to toe and only let out of the house to put flowers on the altar! Now shut up and switch on the oven."

Hélène wiped four Arcopal cups and threw some tea bags into a stainless steel teapot. As Tante Ruby said, there wasn't much in the house to steal. When Uncle Vladimir died, Jean-Hubert and Hélène were living in a squat in Amsterdam and by the time his solicitors found them the château had been ransacked several times over by former tenants presumably hailing a brave new era. Uncle Vladimir had been such a bad-tempered old recluse in his final years, refusing to let the outside world look on his infirmities, that none of his relations had any idea what furniture and fittings might have been in the house at the time of his death and it was assumed that, like many a straitened country squire, he'd been selling off his possessions all along to antique dealers. It was only when Hélène, at her mother-in-law's bidding, started doing good works in the village that she began to guess what had happened. She kept coming across bits of priceless-looking porcelain and great lumps of carved oak furniture with the family crest on, rubbing shoulders in garish new bungalows with mass-produced Louis Seize from mail-order catalogues. At the beginning, she couldn't find the words to make an accusation or the courage to tell Jean-Hubert and plunge them all into a great big drama with heaven knew what repercussions. She'd recently seen Jean Gabin in *The Dominici Affair* and was uneasy about the sullenly murderous capacities of French peasants when it came to revenging themselves on outsiders. Later on, after she'd heard a few stories about the Ploudel de Medeu's behaviour to their tenants, she wished the poor sods joy of Uncle Vlad's bits and pieces. They'd earned them, she considered, over the centuries. It was one of the small secret revolts that kept her from being entirely swamped by Jean-Hubert and his family.

Or so she'd seen it at the time, still fresh from Amsterdam and the squat and all those years of sneering at material possessions and bourgeois values. Now, when it was far too late to do anything about it, she wondered if she'd been totally mad to let her husband's inheritance stay tranquilly in the hands of plundering villagers who couldn't possibly appreciate it as anything more than a way of slyly getting back at the Big House, while she and Jean-Hubert had to struggle so hard to make ends meet.

They filled up the spaces in the cold empty rooms with

nice solid pieces of modern pine furniture from the *Trois Suisses* catalogue, and bought quite presentable cups and saucers from Catena, the hardware store in Seulbourg. Recently however, Jean-Hubert had begun to linger (with whole layers of haughty ancestral portraits grafted on to his own handsome twentieth-century face) in front of every antique shop window from Dinan to Quimper. Soon now, Hélène knew, it would become intolerable to him to continue living without all the outward marks of his position, even if he had to plunge the family back into debt to acquire them.

Clémence warmed up the cousins' homemade beignets and called her father and great-aunt in for *le five o'clock*. Tante Ruby was in a good humour again so Hélène assumed Jean-Hubert had been entertaining her with a detailed account of their weekend with the down-market end of the family. Jean-Hubert had this treacherous side to him. It used to disturb Hélène, knowing that her own shortcomings and vulgarities were being very certainly spread out at intervals to be chuckled over by his mother and aunt. She even went so far as to consult Pierre Bouchon about it. Pierre told her not to worry, Jean-Hubert's was a very typical case: feeling himself to be not completely a Ploudel de Medeu, he was impelled to seek the love and approval of his tribe by betraying those elements of it which seemed even more alien than himself. And in fact, said Pierre, on a deeper level it is not really a betrayal, it is a craving to have you, and incidentally his dead father, accepted in all your exotic difference. All of which, when Hélène thought it over, sounded very like Jean-Hubert. And probably very like Pierre himself, when one remembered the exotic differences *he* had to live down.

As if she was a mind-reader, Tante Ruby said: "Your

great friend, Madame Bouchon, euh, dropped in, I think that is the correct expression? On Saturday. N'est ce pas, Clémence?"

"Heavens!" Hélène remembered, "I'd asked her to come up and have a coffee with us, completely forgot to tell her we were going away!"

"Oh maman!" Clémence groaned, "She is awful. I know you once made the mistake of engaging her as my nanny (and whosoever shall scandalize one of these my little ones!), but that's no reason to make a *millstone* of her. She came clumping up the avenue like a poisonous little glow-worm in a bright green velour tracksuit with matching eyeliner and mascara, with Mujah and Din tearing along in front of her demolishing all before them. She addressed me as *Clem*, asked if my mum was *indoors*, and said she'd seen this darling bit of Artemisia vulgaris growing at the end of the drive and if you didn't mind she'd come with a trowel and trug and fetch it away before Hervé Le Moal got his murdering hands on it. That's exactly what she said. And then, how disgusting, she only went and had a hot flush right there in the middle of the lawn, bee-urk!"

"Rubbish!" Hélène said, "Rosalind's younger than I am, she's hardly thirty-five yet. And what's come over *you* so suddenly? You were the best of friends only the other day."

"She is not menopausal," Tante Ruby agreed, "She is only Anglaise. Though perhaps to be menopausal would be less of a trial, poor thing. The English blush at everything . . . No, it was that she spotted me following the sun across the terrace, I do want to get a perfect all-over tan before I return to Paris, (not that Gustave, poor fish, is likely even to notice!), and Madame Bouchon's good Protestant soul was overcome at the sight of the naked human body. When the English come to France they are in a continual state of hot flush. They blush at breasts, they blush at bottoms, they blush at zizis. She had the temerity, your friend, to point out to me that young Michel Le Borgne was working nearby and could see me. She actually believed it mattered! In my dead brother's garden, do you realize? If poor Vladimir was alive she would not have dared! Ah mon dieu, mes enfants, I cannot become accustomed to all this democracy, it appears we must cover up our bodies nowadays in case we give the servants erections. In case the gardener's boy has the impertinence to rape us, perhaps? The Le Borgnes have served our family faithfully for two centuries and now they must notice we have bosoms? Enjoy the sun for ten minutes in one's own garden and Egalité oh Egalité what crimes may be committed in thy name!"

It was not her own garden. Jean-Hubert was allowing her the run of it while she recovered from her latest bout of adultery and waited for her husband to take her back. Unaccountably, he always did take her back. Hélène supposed that even in these democratic times her name was a considerable help to him in his business.

"So she blushed," Tante Ruby continued, "She blushed and she blushed, and then she trundled off down the avenue behind these two pretentious Afghan hounds of hers, looking exactly like a stout little peasant driving two cows. Mujahedin indeed! When the immigrants invade Plouch'en as they've invaded everywhere else in France, that young lady will find herself crucified for blasphemy!"

"Talking of peasants," Jean-Hubert said, "You'd better go down to the village tomorrow, Hélène, and engage Nathalie Le Borgne to come and cook for us. I remember Michel mentioned she was looking for a job. Apparently she did some sort of poor woman's *Cordon Bleu* course at evening classes, so she may be just what we need for our reception.

And her sister's a waitress. Find out what she's earning in the Hôtel de la Poste and promise her fifty francs extra. If they haven't both been snapped up already by the du Bois-Fleuris."

Hélène knew they wouldn't have been: the du Bois-Fleuris, Count and Countess as they were, had enough self-confidence to be above the servant problem. It was only Jean-Hubert who was terrified of being seen to be without domestic help by the local notabilities. He could never afford anything but amateurs – runaway teenagers, single parents, struggling actors who seemed to have been granted eternal rest – but he put as much energy into the finding, hiring and overworking of them as the president of a multinational would into the engaging of top executives. Inferiority complex, Pierre explained, caused by your husband's sense of shame at his petit-bourgeois upbringing.

"Why not employ Madame Bouchon?" Tante Ruby suggested, "After all she was in service with you before her marriage, n'est ce pas? And she looks as if she needs the money to clothe herself, poor thing."

"Oh yes, do let's have Rosalinda Vulgaris!" Clémence crowed, "That should really make our party swing!"

"Rosalind was our au pair girl, Tante Ruby. It's something quite different, even in France. And she'll be coming to the party anyway, as our guest. Her husband is our local doctor, after all."

"Oh mon dieu, mon dieu! Ça, c'est le bouquet! Now the son of old Blanche Bouchon can call himself a doctor! The offspring of my brother's cook is at liberty to read the secrets of my body and to be received into the home of my childhood. Ah ma pauvre France! Quelle siècle! But he shall not be presented to me at this reception, you understand? You will make no attempt to present him. That at least you will spare me, Jean-Hubert, for your poor uncle's sake, and your dead mother's!"

"Actually I think I'll take a stroll down there now," Hélène said, "To Bouchon's, I mean. I must apologise to Rosalind about Saturday, you know how sensitive they always are about being neglected."

A long-legged gawk of a child standing alone in the twilight of a Belfast drawing-room, that's the image Hélène invariably saw when she allowed herself to look nostalgically, or bitterly, back down the winding staircase of her adult years.

"And it's not just me, Pierre," she said, "I mean don't think I'm going all maudlin or anything just because I happened to run into a ghost from my past at the weekend! No, it's just the sort of soggy old memory we all love to wallow in. All us Irish. Can't stop ourselves!" she told him brightly that Monday evening, smiling at him across his wide oak desk, must ask Rosalind where they picked it up, how much they.

"Now you are being flippant," Pierre said and she laughed.

"Well of course I'm being flippant. I'm just dead scared you're about to point me towards that red plush couch over there. I assume that's what you use when you're playing shrink to the village?"

"I do not use a couch," he said seriously, "And I am not a psychiatrist. The people of my village like to confide their problems in me because I am not a bourgeois, I rose from the ranks, I am one of their own. My wife put that sofa there. To take the bare look off the place, she said. She would have had china ducks flying up the wall if I had not forbidden it. And it was you insisted on coming to the surgery, madame. We could have chatted far more easily about this suggestion of yours over a drink in the living-room, Rosalind is out walking the dogs. Though of course it is her decision too, about inviting you to join us in Ireland. Not that she won't be delighted of course . . ."

"I like it here," Hélène said, "Nice and austere, the idea of talking across a desk in a surgery. Perhaps I ought to pay you a fee, pour faire plus vrai? And, flippant or not, it's true that we do all love a good wallow in the past. Old Paddy O'Proust," she said, "I mean dip a soda scone in a mug of stewed tea and we're instantly back whinging over our poor old granny's rosary beads or whatever." Though say what you like, it was their fault, she thought bleakly, if it hadn't been for them I'd have, I'd have . . . Well for a start I'd have Christopher wouldn't I? I wouldn't even be here. I'd be Mrs Milton now. Though again . . .

Sitting there in the converted byre that was Pierre's surgery, and could it possibly have been one of Uncle Vladimir's tables, she couldn't really see either Rosalind or Pierre in some antique shop choosing a, would his old father have had the *neck* on him? Right on their doorstep? Sitting there in the vile pink tapestry chair, (and that wasn't stolen, that was pure Rosalind), she allowed herself, and Pierre too of course, to look back down into the drawing-room where it all began, recalling how the brown velvet curtains moved gently and eerily in an invisible draught, flames stretched narrow little tongues in a prim beige fireplace, two brown leather armchairs and a sofa crouched in dark forbidding masses, saving themselves up, it seemed, for the broad authoritative backsides of adults. Of *Them*.

"Backside," the ten-year-old Eileen whispered, "Bum. Behind." In Clonaville Primary, with a punishment looming, they crouched in giggling trembling corners muttering bad talk to diminish the threat, Teresa and herself. Alone, she saw her words flap about miserably and fall to earth in the muffled brownness of the room, diminishing nothing at all. "Hen's cack," she whispered bravely to the beige walls, to the Sacred Heart, to Pope John the XXIII, "Cats' piss." Nothing happened. The strange tall room refused to shrink down into anything she could easily deal with.

The woman had left her there, Mother had left her there, alone in the drawing-room, saying she had the tea to get ready and Eileen could burrow around to her heart's content and make herself at home. *He* was in his study, the woman said, Gerald, writing up lesson notes for Monday and don't on any account run in disturbing him, she said, Mother said, or there'll be murder done. How could she have imagined that Eileen would, or could, run in to disturb a strange man in a study? What was a study? "Arse," Eileen whispered, looking fearfully and defiantly up at the holy pictures, but nothing happened. The Pope kept on beaming with his fat old face, the Sacred Heart stared at her with hurt disapproval – but then he'd almost certainly been staring like that already: he gazed with those same big wounded eyes out of a different frame in Anny and Patrick's kitchen, filling her with uneasy guilt even when she was in the state of grace and as good as gold.

She moved timidly across the brown carpet to a sideboard that had one immense mirror reaching to the ceiling, and two sets of small narrow mirrors incrusted behind carved wooden pillars. Six times over she was reflected, white and serious, with her straight face and her short pale hair scraped back with two grips. She thought: so that's what I'm like. The mirrors glinted back mockingly in the firelight: that's what you're like.

In Anny and Patrick's there was one small looking-glass

high on a nail, only taken down when Patrick was shaving. She never really remembered seeing her reflection before, except when she glimpsed it in darkened windowpanes. Ever since she learned to read she'd been giving herself the features of girls in books – prim Alice, and Wendy, and poor adopted Hetty Grey, and Georgina in the Famous Five; sometimes with a secret thrill the beautiful gigantic witch in the *Narnia* books who demolished whole cities with powerful snarling words. Well now she knew exactly what she looked like, and she realised she wasn't about to demolish Belfast, or even demolish this cold strange drawing-room, no matter how many curses she uttered. The drawing-room resembled drawing-rooms in books, with its velvet curtains and its flickering fire; *she* resembled only herself, frightened and strange and alone. She looked what she was, something pulled up by the roots. She recalled *his* hurry to get them into the car and away, her mother's tight little smiles, Anny crying her eyes out on the doorstep, Patrick's old white face: sure you'll come back and see us, Eileen, in the holidays, we'll never feel till the holidays, darlin'. "What did they feed her on anyway?" *he* asked in the car, the Gerald man, "Potatoes and salt? She's the shape of a knitting-needle!"

In the long sideboard drawer, silver forks and spoons and knives lay still and bored and unexpectant in a velvet box. "Family treasures," she whispered, trying the words on her tongue, imagining with excited dread the ceremony of eating in this vast strange house. Would there be a dining-room? A breakfast-room? Or would they eat here, the three of them spread out around the dark shining table by candlelight, silver spoons glittering in their hands? She shivered, and quickly pulled out one of the smaller drawers. It was a mess of a drawer, friendly and disappointing with its tangle of Christmas cards and rosary beads and broken garlands. But underneath the rubbish, a miracle, she came on this long lovely string of pearls. She took it out and, cautiously, wonderingly, ran it through her fingers. So her mother was rich now. She owned a pearl necklace and a sideboard and high carved mirrors and a drawing-room. What else did she own? A big fur coat and a whole team of curtseying servants? Was she in the kitchen now supervising the bustling red-faced cooks preparing tea in white aprons, cutting up dainty cucumber sandwiches, arranging them on a heavy silver tray? A line out of *Hetty Grey* (her favourite book, a book out of Anny's own childhood dug up out of the dust on the head of the dresser) used to fascinate Eileen, and discourage her, every time she read it: *"Mrs Rushton shrugged her shoulders."* Shrugging of shoulders had seemed to her a gesture so elegant and so alien that she'd never been able to imagine anyone even attempting to make it at home in the cottage, and the one time she'd tried it herself Anny had shamed her in front of Chaz and his wife: "What has you shaking yourself like that, Eileen, is there fleas in your shift or what?" Now, in this room, holding in her hands the cool creaminess of pearls, she could see that there were endless possibilities of shoulders being shrugged, eyebrows raised, laughs tinkled, cocktails sipped, hands kissed . . .

Anny in this room, she thought, or Patrick? She pictured them, frightened and shrunken, huddled by the door while the woman, while Mother, strode about in her straight navy skirt and stiletto heels, saying neat sharp things with the pointed edge of her voice, changing them into two shabby little heaps of dust. They'll never dare come to see me, she whispered, and I have to live here without them for ever and ever now. That was unimaginable.

She danced the necklace up and down in the firelight:

pearls ran wildly off the end of their string and went hop hop hoppity over the carpet; it was catastrophe. When the woman came in and switched on the light Eileen was on her knees on the carpet, crying. "I broke your pearls, I lost your good pearls all under the furniture."

Her mother took her by the shoulders and forced her up, sat her at the table and pulled a chair close: "Sure it's nothing. Just a broken old thing I used to wear to the dances. A pile of old junk I shoved in that drawer till I have time to sort things out. It wasn't a *treasure*, Eileen!"

If she had crushed Eileen beside her in one of the big armchairs as Anny would have done, pretended the pearls *were* a treasure but Eileen was more important . . . Or if she'd shouted and given her a clout around the lug as Anny, in a different mood, might have done . . . But she was cool and friendly and reasonable, like a teacher in a classroom. ("Well what could you expect?" she asked, years later. "I was twenty-seven years of age, Eileen, I hadn't exactly a lifetime's experience as a mother! I wasn't a child *psychologist*, for heaven's sake!")

"I want to go back now," Eileen said, "I want to go home."

"But this is your home from now on, Eileen dear, you know that well! And we want you to settle down and be happy with us. This is where you live now. But we'll drive you down surely for a few days in the holidays, they'll be glad to see you contented and settled. They want the best for you, Eileen."

"They didn't want me to go," she sobbed, "They were crying their eyes out."

"Well of course they were crying, anyone would after six long years! But they always knew that you'd go some day, that was the arrangement. And be sensible, they couldn't have looked after you much longer, an old bachelor and spinster, they were getting too old for it, Eileen. This is your home now and we are your parents. Gerald is your new daddy so he is, and he loves you as much as I do and he wants you to love him. You have a family now, Eileen, you have a mammy and daddy both now."

"Anny's my mammy!" she cried, "I'm not calling *you* mammy!"

"Did she used to make you call her mammy?" the woman asked in a hard jealous voice, "An old maid of sixty that no man ever as much as looked at, used she pretend you were her own child?"

"She is my mammy and I want to go home."

"She wouldn't want you back. She looked after you for six years because she was well paid to. She wouldn't have looked after you for nothing. What did you expect me to do for God's sake when your poor daddy died? I had my way to make and my living to earn. I couldn't just stay there in Claghan and take care of you, much as I'd have liked to. I had only myself to depend on, I was hardly going to ask *his* people, I was hardly going to ask the Campbells for anything, that's why . . . But it's finished now. You're here with us now. We're not strangers, for heaven's sake, who stole you away! I'm not a witch, Eileen, out of one of those books you're always stuck in! Who bought you those books anyhow? Did you think it was old Anny Maguire? I've been visiting you for years in that wee house, every Christmas holidays I came over to see you and this last couple of summers as well, I sent you toys and books and lovely clothes, you know that well, I thought you'd have . . ." She sounded furious.

She's a witch, Eileen thought, she's a witch, she's going to turn me to stone in a minute.

"Sitting in that smelly little house listening to their country nonsense, drinking mug after mug of stewed tea so as not to offend them . . . Do you think I liked it? My poor mother's old servant girl and her daft brother, did you think I left you there for fun? I had my way to make, Eileen, I was only twenty-one, I couldn't afford to just sit and be a sorrowing widow for the rest of my days!" Her fingers dug into Eileen's shoulders, her face was hard and frightening, and Eileen tried to pull away. The woman let go of her shoulders and smiled. "It's all right, Eileen," she said, "Don't you worry about the old pearls. Or about anything. You'll go back and see them again. Often. In their little house."

Their little house. But all houses had been little, before Belfast. Ned Maginn's and old Maggy Connor's and the house where her best friend Teresa lived. There had been no drawing-rooms and no velvet curtains before Belfast. ("Nonsense," her mother said, years later, "Your first four years we lived in a lovely big house in a decent street. And Anny was our maid, she came to us when your Granny died. You're only letting on to forget. You think you have to punish me for something. You like to think you're hard done by!")

"Is there anything you want to ask me now, Eileen? Is there anything you'd like to know? About your . . . About anything?"

There was something the woman wanted her to ask. It was there in her mother's hungry insistent eyes, but Eileen had no idea what it was. She had no idea at all how to please this strange smart woman whom she hardly knew. She searched hard in her mind for a suitable question, something as shocking and momentous as the occasion was.

"Are yous ones Protestants?" she asked, "You and him?"

"It's 'you', Eileen," the woman corrected, "Not 'yous

ones'. Protestants? Why, you funny little thing! Why on earth would Gerald and I be Protestants?"

"Yous . . . You talk like the Prods, all pointy. And Patrick said God help you darlin' you're going to a Protestant hole of a town."

"Well you won't meet any non-Catholics in this area, I can assure you! And wait till you see, Eileen, in a few weeks you'll be speaking with an educated Ulster accent just like us."

"I'll never talk like you," Eileen said, "I'm always going to talk like the ones at home so I am!"

"Well I'm sorry to hear that, Eileen, because they're only going to laugh at you and call you a country gawk at school. You have to go to school on Monday, you know. To my school. I'm going to be your teacher as well, you see. As well as your mammy. That's why I went to England. That's what I was doing in England all those years, I must have told you a hundred times. Supply-teaching just to pay Anny your keep and put clothes on your back, waiting for a place in a training college, it took years, that's why I couldn't . . . I wasn't exactly gallivanting, Eileen, I wasn't being a selfish bitch, whatever your father's crowd may have spread round the town about me. And look at me, I'm far better able to take care of you now, amn't I? And I've found you a good home and a nice kind man to take care of us both. And you're going to fit in as nice as anything with Gerald and me when the strangeness wears off you. Just wait till you see, you're going to grow up to be one of us in no time at all!"

"I'll never be one of yous!" Eileen began fiercely, but the door opened and the man called Gerald was there, tall and grey and slightly stooped.

"The kettle, Margaret . . . Is the tea . . . ?"

They took her by the hand to a white clear kitchen and sat her between them at a scrubbed pine table no different from the one in Anny's, with her own Peter Rabbit mug that they'd remembered to bring from home. The sight of her mug there on the scrubbed table between their flowery cups and saucers set her off crying again, and her mother and Gerald looked at each other helplessly and patted her shoulder over and over and had no idea at all how to make her stop.

"Pure Radio Eireann!" she told Pierre, "Bring on the wailing pipes! Of course that unfortunate youngster was me, stumbling about like an idiot among the big lumps of Falls Road mahogany. Is it any wonder I never knew what to say to someone like Christopher? Never knew how to cope? I tell you, Pierre, I've spent whole decades of my life just trying to kill that ignorant wee brat off!'

"You've succeeded beautifully," Pierre said, looking at her appreciatively as she faced him across the wide desk, "Not much of old Anny's cottage about you now, madame! Or the Falls Road either. So is that what you are eating you heart out about? That you spoiled a beautiful friendship, what, twenty-three years ago, because you tried to shrink this Christopher down to your size with four-letter words as you did with that stiff strange house, daring it to reject you? Would your Mr Milton even see the symbolism, I wonder? Is he that intelligent? Or have you perhaps been building him up all these years into something infinitely wise, infinitely divine? Have you considered that he is probably just a dreary pedantic old professor by now waiting for his pension, taking his dreary pedantic little dose of French culture every year as professors do? You have perhaps transformed him by your nostalgia, madame, and by your discontent."

But he *was* infinitely wise, she thought wistfully, he was Aslan the lion, he was old Mr Badger, he was Gandalf the wizard, he was Santa Claus, he was . . . "Oh do please call me Hélène, Pierre, why are you being so formal? Discontent? Yes," she admitted, "If I'd seen him three months ago, if I'd seen him when I was still a happy contented wife I might just have walked up and said hello, fancy seeing you here. Like anyone. Or maybe I wouldn't. No, of course I wouldn't have. I still remember what it was like that summer. It was magic. I mean it was like magic for me those few weeks before he. It's never been like magic since, Pierre. I have a feeling I chose mediocrity. Since Saturday I just want to drop everything and. It's like being eighteen all over again."

"So you want to go over there and do a Great Gatsby on him," Pierre said, "Dazzle him with your new-found wealth and beauty? Except now you've a husband and two kids. And what are *they* to do, may one ask, while you go sighing through Belfast in the steps of your old love affair?"

"Oh the children! *They're* all right, they're quite self-sufficient by now, they never even seem to notice whether I'm there or not, let alone need me!"

"Less than fifty kilometres away, madame, a young boy, a boy of the age of your twins, a brilliant student at a public lycée, was the victim of a savage shooting on Saturday evening. Hadn't you heard, didn't you read about it in Ouest France? What mother can ever say with confidence that her children are 'all right'?"

"Oh how terrible, Pierre, no I hadn't heard . . . But I'm glad to say mine don't risk running into that sort of situation, they're nearly too respectable! Henri sits around playing the guitar and listening to old Dubliners' records of all things! And Clémence has got herself a steady boyfriend. Great little French patriots the pair of them, and so holy with it, they hold hands at Mass! I expect it was a drugs quarrel, that poor boy, they say there's a lot of it even in Brittany."

"The boy was of Algerian origin, Hélène. Third-generation French, but of course the wrong colour to please our little local patriots. That is the fourth murder of its kind in France this year. And, have you noticed, all committed by quiet respectable middle-aged people. Not thugs, not drug dealers, not the Mafia! Ethnic cleansing as a cottage industry. Can any of us afford daydreams or nostalgia, madame, when this kind of behaviour can produce itself in our midst?"

"Oh indeed I know it, Pierre. But sure nothing ever changes in the world does it? There's always something . . . That summer I knew Christopher, Belfast was going mad with civil rights meetings and elections and violence of all description. But I mean it never came anywhere near us, it never touched us at all, we all lived our lives in spite of it . . . So can I not come to Ireland with you and Rosalind, then? You sound all cold and disapproving! But anyway the twins will have gone to Paris by then, to Tante Ruby, she's getting them into one of the top lycées you know, they certainly won't be needing my apron-strings to cling to!"

Pierre looked very tired for an instant, then he shook his head comically and smiled at her: "Come if you wish, Hélène. Of course. If Jean-Hubert agrees. But do not expect too much. Do not expect to rediscover your innocent past. And your Christopher may not want to be rediscovered, he will not be sitting there like the wreck of the *Titanic* waiting for you to dive in and plunder him. He too is certainly married with a family, had you thought of that? About thirty-six youngsters if I know the Irish."

"Oh don't be futile, Pierre. He's a Protestant. No, I don't believe he's married, why would he be travelling round France with a carload of other fellows? Actually there's lots of intellectual men over there who don't ever feel like marrying, I mean it's no big deal, it's not like here . . . "

"An ageing Ulster Presbyterian and a confirmed bachelor en plus! Much better stick to Jean-Hubert, ma fille! Let your old lover stay an exile's fantasy. Don't we all need our secret gardens to keep us going. If you knew some of the things *I* dream about, hou la la!"

"He's not a fantasy, Pierre, he exists. And I know where to find him. My mother mentioned him when I was over for Gerald's funeral, she said he was teaching in the University." ("That journalist you made a fool of yourself over," was what her mother had said, "he's got a job in Queen's now. No qualifications that I know of, but trust them to look after their own! And when you think of all the Catholic teachers and writers that have to emigrate, poor Seamus Heaney for a start . . . " Eileen looked him up in the phone book: Christopher Hamish Milton, and the same address in Upper Crescent. It hadn't even occurred to her to try and see him then; he seemed to have receded into some sad and mythical past, beyond any possibility of resurrection. Only now, since Saturday, had he come alive again.)

"All right then, come to Carrickfergus with us as you suggested. Take a bus in to Belfast every day and look for him, it's nothing to me. Get him out of your system."

"But I may not get him out of my system, or Belfast either, I may decide to stay over there. I do have good grounds for divorce after all. I could stay in Belfast and make myself useful the way my mother does, working for peace. Far better then vegetating in France as a rural housewife, with a husband who deceives me into the bargain!"

"Hélène, do not talk nonsense! You are not a housewife. You have no intention of divorcing Jean-Hubert, and no grounds at all for even considering it. No, I am certain that if you manage to see this decrepit old professor of yours, shorn of whatever pittoresque may have been conferred on him by Arles and by your nostalgia, tottering through his dreary battlefield of a town (I have been to your Belfast, hou lala!), all you will long for is to return to civilisation and to your handsome husband who adores you."

"Who adores me? Funny adoration!" she snapped, achingly picturing Christopher Milton, far from decrepit, striding romantically in his Bogart trenchcoat across the grim media-land battlefields of Belfast. "Funny adoration, with that little brat flaunting himself around the village."

"But are you sure about the little boy, Hélène? I myself have never remarked such a child in Plouch'en."

"God, I'm not imagining him, Pierre, I'm not one of your village depressives. He was there. I saw him. Tenez, old Mother Balavoine saw him too, she was right beside me, it sort of clicked with her that I noticed him. She probably added it to her stock of local gossip."

Two months earlier she'd got out of her car in front of the little village post office, her hands full of letters to post, and been buttonholed by poor garrulous Madame Balavoine from the schoolhouse, eager to spill her grotesque headful of gossip over anyone polite enough to listen. The post office was on a corner, the mairie on the opposite side, and between the two an open grassy space led into the housing estate. Some children were kicking a ball around the space. Hélène watched them idly while Madame Balavoine's extraordinary tide of words ebbed and flowed through her ears and, suddenly, among the anonymous heads scrumming around the ball, was one with the distinctive Ploudel de Medeu face. Jean-Hubert's face. It didn't register for a second or two: when she first came to Plouch'en Jean-Hubert had often entertained her by pointing out village people whose features were evidence of just how intimately the notorious Uncle Vladimir had known their mothers. To Hélène it had been another example of the way France was a caricature of all the picturesque legends you'd ever heard about it. As amusing as the village brothel where a respectable elderly widow and her four matronly daughters plied their trade in a neat little bungalow that was as hung about with lace curtains and Calvaries and pots of geraniums as any in Plouch'en.

So Hélène had glanced indulgently at the little boy thinking, aha another of old Vlad's little indiscretions, before remembering that Uncle Vladimir had been dead seventeen years, and that in any case the child didn't resemble any photos she'd seen of him, it was the image of Jean-Hubert. In the same instant she'd noticed Madame Balavoine watching her watching the child and was careful to smile and look casually away.

She'd said nothing at all to Jean-Hubert or to anyone: what was there to say without making a complete fool of herself? Her life continued as busy as ever, the house, her children, her garden, the upkeep of the gîtes, Mass on Sunday (where she once saw the boy, but sitting with the other schoolchildren next to Madame Balavoine, who by no stretch of paranoid imagination could be his mother). She continued to be gratified by invitations to dull little dinner-parties where the village's immorality was clucked over

('Much worse, ma chère amie, since those Socialists took over!'), and family marriages were commented on with cooing satisfaction ('Timothée found himself a rich girl, Aymeric found himself a rich girl, but Jean-Vianney! Oh that lucky boy! Jean-Vianney he married a money-bag! Un veritable sac, mes amis!'). If anyone else knew about Jean-Hubert's little bastard it didn't seem to be doing any harm – the Bourjois couple was being slowly but steadily assimilated into the ranks of the local notabilities at exactly the same pace as before.

"Ah. Madame Balavoine was nearby, was she?" Pierre became evasive. "But maybe it was not a village child. A little holidaymaker from Paris, perhaps, with finer features than the local boys? Your husband's looks are classical after all, rather than very original, you might well have been mistaken . . . "

"You're talking nonsense, Pierre. I tell you it was Jean-Hubert in miniature. Has he ever talked to you about any woman he fancied?"

At which Pierre became very stuffy and French.

"We are hardly on those terms, chère madame. And even if he did tell me his little secrets, I should certainly not be tempted to pass them on to his wife. No, you are tired, Hélène, that big house is too much for you, and all your tourists to look after . . . By September you will need a little holiday. Come by all means with us to Ireland, telephone this old celibate of yours if you must. If you are sure it would not be an embarrassing indiscretion? Drink a glass or two together of cold disgusting beer in a sandbagged pub where you are body-searched at the door (so very very erotic n'est ce pas), eat a meal of fried food with gravy and custard, endure a puritanical kiss if le pauvre petit vieux still remembers how to kiss, and after one such evening together

I am sure you will find yourself longing for the little chefs-d'oeuvre that are French wine, French cuisine, and French lovemaking. No no, I am joking, Hélène! But if I remember Belfast it is exactly the place to throw a healthy little chill on your daydreams!"

She hadn't been over to Belfast since Gerald's death. Mrs O'Neill much preferred going to France now and then to see her daughter; it was an excuse for an outing, and then there were so many lovely holy places to visit and pray at. The old lady was expected in a month or so: "I'll take advantage of the Diocesan pilgrimage to Lourdes," she'd written, "And I'll be able to nip across to Brittany on the way back to say hello to my grandchildren." Luckily the party would be well over by then — because imagine a salon full of nobles, generals, diplomats getting politely but thoroughly pissed, and Margaret O'Neill with her good tweed suit and her Pioneer pin striding piously through the midst of them!

Pierre was being clever now, showing off to her in a pseudo analyist's jargon that he had no right to, pretending to find all sorts of dark symbolism in her love for Christopher Milton. He always goes just that much too far, she thought as he walked her to the door, always has to demonstrate that he's the local boy who made it. She thought of Tante Ruby and her snobbery: I'll have to invite them to dinner, she thought, as soon as the old thing goes back to Paris, it's the least I can do.

"Rosalind doesn't seem to be back yet," she said, trying to get away, "Tell her I'll drop in tomorrow morning . . ."

"But surely it didn't begin there," Pierre swept on, ignoring her, "That's what I don't understand, you've been talking as if you suddenly sprang into life at the age of ten in a Falls Road drawing-room. But I mean, even you must have been born, Hélène, like the rest of us?"

It didn't begin there, of course. No, it certainly didn't she thought, walking back up the avenue when she'd finally managed to get away. It began in a mist farther off than memory, the nice big house in a decent street, Anny busy in the kitchen, her mother's warm scented knee, and do you think he'll come home in any sort of a shape Anny, honest to God I'm living in pure dread every evening this last while, bubbling of tea towels bleaching in the big boiler on top of the Aga, don't ever say you weren't well warned, Margaret, troth and I mind your poor mother lord a mercy on her all that Easter holidays and you running out mad like a tramp round the ditches with him! Her father. My young truant of a father is clean anonymous bones now lying at peace under the Campbell tombstone, whatever linked him to us long dissolved into the clay. What linked that dead man to me, she wondered? A laugh, a song, a voice that shouted. Loud voices cursing in desperate fury up the stairs in the middle of some half-dream: who pays the rent here anyhow? The anger and the pain. Anny's broad rough hands smoothing her into sleep again. Suddenly another house, a small strange house with a different smell, dog with a rough warm back, old men and women with slow voices dandling her on their knees, this is the way the farmers ride, soft damp grass, and hens with jabbing beaks peering curiously, threateningly into her eyes. Then Anny in the walled garden again fixing clothes-pegs on to sheets, sing a song of sixpence a pocket full of rye, chestnut trees lifting high their candles, look at the lovely big candles, Eileen, look at the lovely white roses. On hands and knees she galloped the clean red tiles of the kitchen floor, hands seized her at the waist, swung her high in the air laughing, threw her across a shoulder, held her close against a warm

face, she's into everything, you'd want never to lift your eye
off her, wait till she's walking out here and it'll be far worse .
. . She walked, and the world cowped suddenly into another
shape. Walls and dresser were parallel with her now; the two
chestnut trees, attached to the ground, no longer loomed
like rafters. They had black limbs now, the world was in
winter, she had no conscious memory of leaves and white
roses. Her three people were separate from her, no longer a
knee, swinging hands, a shoulder for her convenience. They
moved about the place doing things that had no connection
with her needs, but always ready at a cry to come running,
with a song, with a cake, with a ribbon for her hair. The
house was hung with coloured tinsel, lights winked in a stiff
dark tree, they held her up to tie a star on its summit, just
wait Eileen, wait till you see what you'll get! Night behind
the windows, the street door opened bringing snow in gusts,
her laughing father filled the narrow hallway, when Oi came
home on Christmas night as dhrunk as dhrunk could be,
say daddy Eileen, come on now be a sport and say daddy for
me and you never know what Santy might take you! Come
away into the kitchen now, Eileen, your poor daddy's worn
out so he is after a hard term at school, leave him to rest
himself now. Whispers and sighs and the smell of pudding
steaming away in the boiler, if we can manage to keep him
away from midnight Mass, please God the Canon . . .

  Spring again in Anny's house, the vertical world
conferred power; with both hands she turned the bellows
wheel and the flames jumped and shivered; sparks flew up,
converged, took themselves off into a dark nothingness: I'm
telling you, Eileen, there's a big black Protestant man hiding
above in that chimney with three heads and a hundred
teeth, he won't make two bites out of you so he won't! She
believed it was true because Anny said it, lies had no

existence for her, and she left the bellows alone, wandered unsteadily out into the Easter street.

Patrick's hand waited: come on and we'll feed the wee chickens, darlin', we'll give a drink to the calf, move the goat down the meadow. Hens, transformed from last summer's grey jabbing beak, round suspicious eyes, became flat squat backs to look down on, raggedy tails with bits of cinders and cack stuck to fluffy square backsides that wagged with foolish impertinence as they scratched nervously complaining och-och-och-och in the street's thin dust. Round yellow chickens with bewildered faces, a new staggering calf shivering in its wet black hair, a goat dancing at the end of her tether while she was pegged farther down the meadow where the long grass grew: don't ever come this far on your own, Eileen, I'm warning you, there's men standing in them bogholes there with scythes and graips in their hands waiting for you, there's a wild dog in the drain, a weasel at the back of Ned's ditch. Everywhere things to maim her, to steal her, to drag her away and live under the water, everywhere Anny and Patrick to protect her, don't ever walk out of this street on your own, Eileen, don't ever . . .

Voices up the stairs again, deed and I'll take the job if I see fit so I will, you're not the one that can afford to stop me! And her father: who says I'm not earning enough to keep my family? You that has a good house and a servant girl at your backside, troth and you have little to complain of! Aye earning it and spending it, her mother's voice shrieking, filling the dark empty spaces on the hall and landing, well fit to earn it and spend it! Tell me when was the last time poor Anny here got a ha'porth of wages? I'm taking this job since Canon McGinty offered it so I am, I'd be a trained teacher by now if it wasn't for you! Eileen crawled shivering into Anny's bed, was lulled by prayers and

kisses, wakened to loss. Her mother wasn't there, suddenly
wasn't there to wake her in the morning, it's all right darlin',
it's only away out to school she is, she'll be back home to us
at lunch-time.

Her mother got her hair permed, bought a nice new
pink skirt that sat round her like an umbrella, asked other
teachers home in the evening. They sat in the front room,
marked copybooks together, tried on each other's lipsticks
in front of small round mirrors, skiggled and laughed
among themselves. It's only for this one term, Anny, now
give my head peace Eileen dear, I have to concentrate on
what I'm doing, away off and play with your blocks now,
and are you are going to this dance in St Ronan's, Kathleen,
God you don't know how I envy you, what it is to be single
and free! C A T spelled cat, P A T spelled Pat, A N N Y
spelled Anny, mind you I'm not saying it's all that bad, like
it's not always bad, we dump the child on old Anny when
she goes home to Cross for her fortnight's holidays and
away with the pair of us to Bundoran, the laughs we have! It
was in Bundoran I met him you know, one Easter holidays,
I was still in the flippin' old Convent imagine! And before I
knew it I was married. The best was when they played
records, Joe Lynch and "The Whistling Gipsy", and "The
Green Glens of Antrim". I'm clean mad about Lee Lawrence
so I am, her mother said, God is that the time and this big
eejit of mine not home yet, and then Anny came in with a
face on her and carried Eileen yawning up to bed, teachers
aye! In my day schoolteachers had a bit of respect for
themselves and their profession, so they had!

Her father wasn't there, didn't come bursting in through
the singing doorway, the house was filled with tall people
and quiet voices and her mother was crying, would you like
to go away on your holidays, Eileen? And Anny: I have to

go home for a wee while darlin, to look after Patrick and I'm taking you with me, there's a new wee calf and the black cat's after kittening. Her mother walked them to the bus, I wish to God you'd just stay with me Anny, till it's all over! And Anny stretched her neck and pulled the collar of her black coat tight together, indeed and I'd stay if I could darlin' but sure you can see for yourself I'm not wanted there, it would only cause an awkwardness for you. It's their house and sure they have a right to lay down the law in it, God help the poor creatures in their trouble.

"It's my trouble too," her mother snapped, "and it's my house and the child's just as long as I'm willing and able to pay them the rent on it. They're going round hinting and whispering behind my back Anny, did you hear them, they're hinting that it was my fault, that I drove him to it."

"Don't talk nonsense now, Margaret, nobody's hinting anything. And for God's sake now don't go causing any whillabuloo with them people, not at a time like this, think of poor wee Eileen and her future if you can think of nothing else."

And then the bus came and Mother hugged Eileen, and then Anny kissed Mother and said: "I'll be praying for you every minute, darlin'. And I'll just get her nibs nicely settled in with Patrick and I'll be back here to be along with you on the day of the. If your poor mother had to live, lord a mercy on your mother, if she had to be here to advise you now."

And they settled themselves in the front seat behind the driver and her mother waved and waved, standing there in her black costume, till the bus turned the corner into Lockhart Road. Eileen was too big now for the cot in Patrick's kitchen, and they gave it back to the neighbour who lent it. She slept in the big bed beside Anny, with lilac branches tapping at the two small windowpanes. Patrick slept alone, rose early for the spring labouring. They joined him in the April fields, bearing tea in a lidded can, thick cuts of soda bread and butter. The holidays went on and on and Anny made no move to pack her clothes in the suitcase and go down the pass to the bus. Her mother came instead, and slept in the big bed with her and Anny. When Eileen turned in the night she was entwined with one or other of them, she was part of them both. In the evenings their voices rose and fell endlessly, low and grave and arguing through the kitchen wall when she was alone in the big bed before they tiptoed in with their candle. Then one day her mother kissed her and said be good now and don't forget me, Eileen, and waved from the green bus at the foot of the pass. "She's away over to her auntie Catherine in London, sure she'll be back to us in no time!"

Eileen was made much of by Jem McCabe and his hired boy who gave Patrick a hand dropping seed. Patrick was joined with Jem that year. Sometimes he was joined with Paddy Connor or Ned Maginn. Being joined meant they shared labour, shared implements, turned work into friendship. She ran in her flowery dress along the sunny headlands asking the names of things and being patiently told: buttercup and fairy flax and day nettle and hardihead, and sloe blossom high upon the bushes.

Ned Maginn spoke across the ditch from his own field: "It's off that bush they took the thorns for Our Blessed Lord's crown, Eileen, that's why they call it blackthorn, that's why the berries be's so sour. Gall and vinegar," he said sadly, "Gall and vinegar." They called him holy Ned Maginn when they talked round the fire of an evening. He borrowed Patrick's rake and wouldn't give it back, said he never seen sight nor light of it. His wife was a crushed little woman, scurrying across the street bent double with big buckets of meal, his daughters were beaten into sullen submission. Now he stood with his foot in a gap and joined the crack.

"That's a fact, Ned, that's a fact," Jem McCabe said and winked at Patrick.

"Troth and they were glad to eat them long ago," Patrick said, "Don't I mind my grandfather saying it."

"I heard on the wireless they make wine out of them beyond in England," the hired boy said, "and out of the fruit of the boothery. Elderberry wine," he said with a laugh, making light of his knowledge.

"Hawh England!" Ned Maginn said, "England! From the boothery came the wood of the Holy Cross," he intoned.

"That's a fact, Ned, now that's a fact. I mind Master Quigley lord a mercy on him . . . "

"But sure you wouldn't think they'd have boothery bushes out in the Holy Land," the hired boy said, "More like palm trees maybe." He was reproved for making little of his faith and fell into a scarlet muttering, all eyes upon him. He said he was fed up to the teeth among all these old-fashioned people, fed up sleeping on a straw mattress in a loft, up at six winter and summer, fed up of soda bread and porridge; when his time was served he was heading for England and a good job in Ford's motor factory. *"You load sixteen ton,"* he hummed, *"and whaddya get? Jest another day older and deeper in debt, Saint Peter don't ya . . . "*

"And the wee one's mammy, any word lately?"

"Doing well, or so she says. Subbing in different schools. There's a training college might take her next year or the year after. If she manages to save enough to keep herself, the poor aunty can't help her much, she has only her bit of a pension . . . "

Briege Duffaud

"And the child. Can she not . . . "

"No. No it seems the old woman's very particular, won't hear tell of a child about the place. A retired oul' schoolmistress. And sure isn't she as well here, among them she's used to. Please God when Margaret's trained she'll be able to get a school near hand . . . "

Eileen was lifted across a stile and led past rocks and whin bushes to a long slated house where an old woman and a young one were busy sewing lacework. Anny handed in a white parcel, tea was made, they were given thin slices of bread and butter. The old woman opened Anny's parcel, examined the twelve lovely lace handkerchiefs, counted out money, silver coins that Anny rattled into her deep pocket.

The young woman drew patterns, baskets of roses and snakes with two heads, cut net and muslin, said: "Do you know, Miss Maguire, I'm delighted you're back in the country, tragic and all as the circumstances are. My mother says when you were a girl you were the best hand at the sewing she ever came across, and I can see you haven't lost your touch!"

The things they talked of were strange and had no connection with Eileen; they repelled her with their alienness. She started fingering the pretty white materials, the young woman spoke sharply; Anny looked annoyed and slapped Eileen's hand away. Immaculate, nothing less than immaculate, the young woman said. She talked about rejection, said the lace would be rejected for the least little stain, talked about returned Yanks with dollars, the English gentry, debutante frocks and ball dresses, the Royal family . . .

Back in the house, Anny washed her hands carefully, pinned a big white apron over her flowery overall, tacked net and muslin on the oval of paper where the woman had drawn lovely baskets of roses in blue ink, then sat on the sunny doorstep, inch by slow inch turning the drawings to lace: look Eileen, the wee leaf with its veins, the petals, the basket, but above all never let your wee hands near it or you'll get me slaughtered! She stopped at intervals to wipe the sweat of her own hands; she kept spools of white thread immaculate inside shiny red tea packets: the needles and scissors were the finest Eileen had ever seen. She stood beside Anny while she sewed and Anny taught her to say her prayers: oh angel of God my guardian dear to whom God's love commits me here, and God bless mammy and send her success in her work and studies, and send her home soon, and God bless my grandmother and grandfather and pour forgiveness and mercy into their hearts if it be Thy holy will. And lord have mercy on my poor daddy and my granny and granda and send them eternal rest amen.

Anny had to rise to make Patrick's dinner and their own. She rolled the lace in its white sheet and put it on the windowsill out of harm's way. She said she was teetotally blinded walking into the dark house after sewing all morning on the bright doorstep and she was never in a hundred years going to get accustomed to sitting at the lace again; after a lifetime in service she was used to being on her feet all day and going from one wee turn to the next but sure a body had to pass her time some way and earn a few shillings where she could, and everything that happened was the will of God if we could but understand it. She said since she was on her feet now she'd take Eileen for a wee walk round the field and meet Patrick and get a lawk of nettles for broth. The nettles grew along the cornfield ditch, a whole richness of them, with dockens and big fat dandelions on their outskirts. If you stung your hand on a nettle, Anny said you only had to take a docken and crush its sap on the sting, that's why God made them grow together. The light green nettles, the young shoots, were the tastiest for broth. Dandelions were good too, to eat in a salad, the leaves, the roots, the fat milky stems. And sorrel. She took Eileen down where the field was swampy and picked her a bunch of sorrel leaves. Cuckoo sorrel it was called. "Cuckoo Sal! Cuckoo Sal!" Eileen chanted, taking a mouthful of leaves. She liked the taste and she didn't; it made her tongue feel rough and there were tears crackling away behind her eyes. Anny said that believe it or not it wasn't until she went away to service in Belfast that she knew you could even use dandelions and nettles to cook with: your poor granny lord a mercy on her was a domestic science teacher and a great one for natural ingredients. The country people were too swanky now to eat the good nourishment that came out of the fields, mushrooms and herbs and wild chives; it was all tins now and dainties from out foreign.

Patrick came across the kesh with his cap on one side and the spade over his shoulder: what are yous pair colloguing about at the back of the ditch? Oranges and lemons, Anny said, oranges and lemons like the bells of Saint Clemmens! They went into the street laughing and Eileen laughed with them, she was happy and warm and loved, nothing had ever existed before this bright sunny day in the blossoming field with Anny and Patrick joking her and McCabe's hired boy sauntering up singing along the dandelioned ditch, *ah wuz born one mornin when the sun didn't shine, well ah picked up ma shovel and ah walked it a,* "Cuckoo Sal!" she called to the hired boy, "Cuckoo Sal!" and he took off his cap and waved it at her singing away and she was in heaven.

Anny and Patrick went away to a funeral and the two

Maginn girls came to keep house. Outside it was teeming down; they piled sods of turf on the fire and sat with their feet in the ashes skiggling and laughing under their breath, whispering about boys. Eileen came up close to listen, to be noticed, to be petted, and Meg said look at big lugs with the ears flapping, she'll slabber it all out to the old ones, Nancy gave her a push and said go way ye wee skitther ye, go way and play or I'll shut you in the barn so I will. The barn door was up a step beside the bellows. When she went in with Anny to get meal for the hens the window was matted with cobwebs and the light was all grey. Two calves moved in their stall at the far end, rustling straw in the half dark. There were bags of meal and seed potatoes and a heap of oats in the corner. Oats moved through your fingers as hard and shiny as rosary beads. There were mice, and there were mousetraps everywhere that you could put down your hand without thinking, Anny said, and get the finger took off you. The snap of your finger caught in a trap, the way your insides would jump! She went quickly away from Meg and Nancy and played quietly with her bricks beside the dresser, but the time was long. Sheets of grey rain blew past the window, the galvanize rattled on the roof, flames leaped and jumped and made shadows on the ceiling; it wasn't her house, there was no one in it belonging to her, it was a strange house and she cried for the clean red tiles of the kitchen and the smell of bread baking and her mother's scented dress and lipstick and her father throwing open the door on to the bright singing town and the street lights and the cars whishing past. Meg and Nancy laughed and whispered and hoked in Patrick's old jacket for cigarette butts and said this is the life, man this is the life and you're talking! Eileen needed the po but when she came up close again to whisper it to them Meg gave her another push and said ye telltaling wee skitther ye, did ye not hear me tellin ye to go way and get lost? She tried hard to hold herself in, concentrated on her wooden building blocks with letters on them, trying to remember the names of the letters, but she felt it coming coming coming and made a desperate race for the door but she couldn't reach the latch and crying and sobbing she let go in her knickers. "And you over four years of age! Dirty dirty! You must be the dirtiest child in the world. The smell of ye! It's not a bit of wonder nobody wants you, it's not a bit of wonder yer oul mother took off for England and dumped you on this pair of oddities!"

The roses came back, bloomed and died, smells of cut hay and clover drifted up from the meadow, wild raspberries ripened at the foot of the pass. Gipsies in plaid shawls came wheedling round the door, you'll be rewarded missus, the good God'll reward you. Tinkers came over the pass, put patches on damaged buckets and milk cans, a travelling handyman set working an old clock that had belonged to Anny's poor mother lord a mercy on her and that had lain silent for years on the head of the dresser: the miracle when it started ticking! Two priests came round the doors, gathering money for the missions; they had no car, were walking the country, they said, to do penance to Our lady of Fatima that Russia might be converted and bring peace to the world. Holy Ned Maginn took them in and gave them their dinner, a big feed of bacon and cabbage and new spuds. I noticed they had no word of fasting, them same lads, Paddy Connor said later when the truth came out, but at the time, like everyone else, he envied Ned his initiative. Nancy Maginn swore one of the priests got a feel of her leg while she was dishing out the potatoes and her father gave her a blow that sent her flying. Next day the news came that they weren't priests at all but a couple of rogues dressed up in soutanes to cod the people. They collected a fortune in the town from the shopkeepers and publicans before heading out round the country, and the police and Guards were going mad looking for them on both sides of the border. Jem McCabe said he noticed something odd about them from the start, someway they hadn't a right look of missionaries about them, but he gave them the few shillings anyhow because he didn't want to look mean in front of Ned Maginn.

Paddy Connor and Ned Maginn took a short cut home through the fields one Sunday evening coming from the Sodality, and caught Ned's daughter redhanded at the back of a ditch with McCabe's hired boy. If Paddy Connor hadn't been there they could have kept the thing quiet but Paddy went round the country with a full and outraged description of Nancy Maginn sprawled out among the cowslips with her knickers down and her dress thrown over her head. Ned Maginn leathered into his daughter with the belt of the bellows, threatened to kill her out and out before he was done with her. Only that the mother went over in hysterics and got Paddy Connor to come and talk sense to him he'd have left the girl crippled. Troth and yon fella was loading more than sixteen tons of number nine coal, Paddy said with a bit of a laugh, and Jem McCabe said could you not for once in your life Paddy shut that dirty big mouth of yours, y'ignorant gulpin ye, and he said he'd guarantee it that the gasson married her in double quick time, poor Ned and the woman God help them they'll never get over it, the so-and-so will have to keep a wife now on them big wages he was planning to earn in Ford's factory. Patrick said but sure they're only a couple of children and Paddy Connor said haw haw bejaburs it was no child's play they were playing at when me and poor Ned came on them at the back of that ditch. Jem McCabe said he was ashamed of his life to think that he was any way responsible, hiring a shameless sort of an eejit like that from across the border, it was the last time he'd take on any fellow that he didn't know the pedigree of.

Maggy Connor came up the pass with her sewing and sat down on a chair on the doorstep with Anny. She asked Eileen a riddle: long legs short thighs wee head and no eyes? Eileen couldn't even think what she meant, it could be anything, it could be nothing, and she stood with her eyes wide open in surprise and they laughed and said sure it's tongs, it's a pair of tongs, Eileen! And then suddenly they forgot all about her and put their heads together and let the sewing lie on their laps and talked, with their voices down low och-och-och-och, and their hands in front of their mouths, and the hens ran in and out through their legs and into the house and Eileen chased them out and nobody paid a bit of heed to her till Maggy Connor got up and stretched herself and said she was as well be making tracks for home and she smiled at Eileen and said: *Humpy Dumpy sat on a wall, Humpy Dumpy had a big fall, All the king's horses and all the king's men couldn't put Humpy together again?* It's an egg, Eileen, they said, it's an egg do you see? But Eileen didn't see, she didn't see at all that it could be an egg, how could it be an egg? And then Anny hugged Eileen tight and close and said God a God the dangers there be's the dangers, and sure nobody's safe from sin and shame no matter how high up they are and this thing is upsetting me now, it's five years ago all over again, it's taking the whole business back to my mind the way that skitther of a Margaret one threw away her good home and her education, and the poor mistress the state she was in lord a mercy on her, there's no girl safe from temptation these days no matter how many convents you put her in. She warned Eileen to be always pure and good and never forget even when she was on her own that Our Blessed Lady was looking down at her and watching every move she made and she was never to do anything bad or say any bad talk, it was a shocking shocking world altogether, Eileen! Eileen understood none of it but it sounded cold and strange and menacing and she hid her face in Anny's overall and prayed to her guardian angel never to let it happen, never to be crippled with the belt of the bellows and her dress thrown over her head, to keep her always there in the sunny street with Anny's arm around her, and with Patrick strolling up the pass for his tea with the scythe over his shoulder. Anny said well it seems the wedding's on, they were in seeing the Canon and everything. Sixteen years of age, Patrick said, and the wee fella barely seventeen and them to be pushed away over to England in such a hurry, could Maginn not have waited a bit? Anny said they brought it on themselves and it's not the first time she saw it happening, her ladyship Margaret in her last term at the convent no less when she sprung the awful news on them, and didn't it kill the poor mistress, she was dead within the year lord a mercy on . . . Patrick said that's all in the past, Anny, and it's not for us to pass judgement on anyone and now before we sit down to bite or sup let us go on our knees and say a decade of the Rosary for that poor girl and her family and let us ask God's blessing on this wee child that was put in our care that He may keep her away from shame and disgrace.

Eileen knelt down in front of her own wee stool and buried her head in the smells of paint and wood and said Holy Mary Mother of God ten times, counting on her blue glass rosary beads that had a relic of Our Lord's cross behind a glass diamond on the crucifix. When she was big and going to school and able to count past ten she'd be let stay up for the whole rosary, they told her.

Maggy Connor came nearly every day after that; she said it was lonesome sewing away on her own and she didn't like to be in and out too often to the Maginns; the Maginns was being quiet and keeping their heads down and letting the scandal blow over. But sure it won't blow over, Maggy said, when did anything ever blow over in this place? They're right forcing the pair of them across the water, Anny said, what class of a life would they or their children ever be let have round here?

Eileen stayed close to them, surveyed the street, learned its contours by heart. Joined to the house on one side was the barn with its red outside door, its cobwebby square of window; then the flat-roofed byre, then the henhouse. In front of the byre the dunghill was enclosed from the street by a low wall where yellow weeds flourished richly. To the right of the dunghill a space with two high ricks of hay and two of straw, dog-daisies and gilgowns, dandelions and presha, a pad leading to the cornfield, a hawthorn hedge. The pighouse had two pigs with rings in their noses, the byre had two cows now. They came in bawling every evening around bedtime, big frothy cans of warm milk arrived morning and night. The goat had disappeared. She didn't notice it going, its absence grew on her unawares, as did the absence of the dog. One day she suddenly remembered him and he wasn't there. When she asked they were amazed, said but you were only a wee baby when we had that dog, it was the first summer you ever came here, he died shortly after you left. To think of you remembering old Nero! There were two calves in the meadow; they nuzzled at her with damp curly faces looking for milk, then suddenly loomed large and stared at her over the gate with swinging horned heads and insolent eyes: she ran. Patrick drove them away one day, came back without them in the evening, said not too bad, not too bad at all. He brought home a paper bag of caramels. Another time he brought a honeycomb. There was always some small treat: damsons from Jem McCabe's tree, currants and gooseberries from Maggy Connor's plot, once a bag of apples from Anny and Patrick's brother that was a gardener in a big place near Armagh, fresh butter from off the top of the churn. Anny fed it to her in spoonfuls to make her grow. They said she was thin for her age, a puny wee thing, your mother will think we're starving you. She didn't know. She had no idea what she looked like, what shape she was. She existed only in relation to things and people. Sometimes she strode like a giant around hens and daisies and the black cat's kittens; other times, unnoticed among the big people's legs, she was nothing at all. She knew the lines of other people's faces, she had never seen her own. Patrick shaved at the small framed looking-glass, Anny straightened her hat there of a Sunday; otherwise it stayed high on its nail. She had never seen her naked body. She was washed bit by bit with a facecloth, standing straight up on a sheet of newspaper beside the table where the Lifebuoy soap and the basin of water were, lifting one arm then the other, one leg then the other, never looking down at herself. Once she touched the two wee pips below her shoulders, they were like grains of oats, like the beads of her blue rosary, and Anny slapped her hands away: dirty dirty! Quit examining yourself like that, you're making God's mammy blush. She had never seen her clothed body either. She had no image of herself as a thing apart. Dresses came in a parcel from the postman, swung briefly above her head in Anny's hand, look at the nice wee frock your mammy sent you, then were passed over her head and arms and shoulders and disappeared, existed only in bits and pieces, a sleeve held out to be examined, a skirt to spread round her like petals when she sat down: shame on you, Eileen, pull down that skirt over your bare knees now! When she thought, when she questioned or observed, she looked out of her mother's body or Anny's, sometimes out of Meg's or Nancy's or Maggy Connor's, never out of Patrick's or Jem McCabe's or her lost father's. She was a wee girl: she would never grow up to milk or plough or dig a field, would never stroll across the kesh with a spade over her shoulder, never burst loud and singing through a Christmas doorway. She assumed that her eyes were brown, her face round and dimpled like her mother's in the bedside photo, was surprised when she gathered that she was in fact blue-eyed and thin-jawed, favouring her father's side. She had never seen her father's side: some day you will, darlin', sure they'll soften to you as nice as anything; their grandchild, it'd only be natural . . .

I wouldn't be putting them notions in that child's head, Patrick, if I was you, sure that Campbell crowd has no nature and no softness. Big town shopkeepers and them with their fill of grandchildren besides Eileen, don't set her going on me about grandparents now! Eileen sat quiet at their feet on her wee stool, listening and listening as their soft blurred voices blended gently with the whirr of the bellows wheel or the sounds of the autumn street. The words soaked into her with the sun and the fire's warmth, things to be absorbed without question.

Anny was always busy now, feeding the hens, gathering eggs, washing the cack off them and packing them in a big basket for Mick the Kipper to sell in his shop: "Six dozen of eggs the day, Maggy!" "Troth and isn't it great, Anny, isn't it a help, Patrick's on the pig's back since you came home! And they're a powerful price now; with the help of God it'll last a wee while."

Everything was a powerful price that year, the berries were a terror, six or seven shillings a stone and the ditches hanging with them. The whole country was out gathering, old and young. Anny took the big can and took Eileen by the hand over along the cornfield ditch. Eileen had a bean tin and at first the berries ping-pong-panged on the bottom, red and green and everything she picked to fill it quick, but after a while she lost interest. Butterflies lit on the hardiheads, a wasp incessantly followed her intent on the berries, she dropped the tin in the stubbles. Anny was away on ahead, half climbed into the hedge like a briar herself, nothing in her eyesight only berries. Pale violets grew in among the stubbles, and the tiniest of red flowers. Close to Eileen, insects buzzed minutely, chirped and crawled and gave mad races here and there intent on their own small business. They were no part of her or she of them: she had an instant's awareness of her own isolation, standing on her feet in the stubbles, part of nothing. Why? Why am I? What am I? She buried the question in a mad panic: Anny Anny look at me, see me, make me exist! She was terrified. Anny stepped down off the ditch with a full can, fingers stained with juice, arms scratched cruelly up to the elbow: look at that now, Eileen! The berries moved on the surface of the can, a grey spider ran here and there in rings, maggots reared up bringing some hidden memory of terror. She stayed close from then on, holding Anny's skirt.

At Ned's gap, Agnes Quinn blushed bright red to find herself caught out gathering blackberries like the ordinary seven-eighths. She didn't really need to, was above all that with her man a factory foreman in England sending home money every week. she had her hair in a feathercut and always wore lipstick and high heels.

"They're a great price this year, thanks be to God," Anny said.

"Oh I wouldn't know anything about that, Miss Maguire, I'm just picking a few for bramble jelly."

A plump little girl with a tartan bow in her hair looked coldly at Eileen and stuck her tongue out as far as it would go. It was the first time Eileen was close to a child of her own age: why did she hate me? Why? Going back home along the headland she felt small and lonesome and anxious and wondered what she did to offend the little fat girl.

"Bramble jelly!" Anny snorted, "Did y'ever hear the like of that?"

"Hawh, they're destroyed with the swank that crowd and always was," Patrick said, "But if you had to look right you'd have seen the big bucket of berries hid in the ditch. Grandeur or no grandeur that one wouldn't let pass the chance of a few easy shillings! We're nothing to the likes of her, nothing," he said. "We're the dirt under Agnes Quinn's feet, with all he's earning beyond." He looked cross and sad, as if he was going to cry.

"Ach sure aren't you far better off without her," Anny said, "She'd have had your heart scalded so she would. Haven't you a bite to eat and a roof over your head, thanks be to God, and the health and strength to enjoy them."

"Still and all," he sighed, "Still and all. I'll never amount to nothing now. This wee shanty of a place, for two pins I'd sell out and away over to England like the rest of them." He stayed cross and worried and Anny shook her head slowly behind his back and Eileen couldn't understand any of it, why Patrick was nothing and why the girl stuck out her tongue and why the girl's mammy laughed without laughing.

Jem McCabe got a new hired boy for the harvest. He was big and slovenly and red in the face and he whistled all day at his work. The Whistling Gipsy, Patrick christened him, and Eileen was enchanted: the name made her think she'd known him always. When he came to Patrick's to help with the threshing she followed close behind him as he humped bags of oats from the hagard to the barn, and had to be ordered into the house for safety: many a wee child lost life or limb, Eileen, through carelessness on a threshing day. When the men were sitting round the kitchen table and Anny and Maggy Connor were dishing up the dinner, Eileen edged round to where the Whistling Gipsy was sitting and someone said there's your wee girlfriend looking for you, Nicholas, and the Whistling Gipsy took her on his knee and gave her a piece of crispy bacon and she said sing! sing a song, gipsy! And the men all clapped and the Whistling Gipsy, redder than ever, started a song that Eileen never heard before, and everybody around the table suddenly started to look uneasy but he didn't even notice and kept on singing in his clear high voice. *"No more he'll hear the curlew cry,"* the hired boy sang, *"O'er the lonely Shannon tide, For he lies beneath a Northern sky, Bold Hanlon by his side,"* and Eileen gazed into his big shiny red face as he sang, and the men were whispering a bit and shuffling their feet, *"He has gone to join the gallant band, Of Plunkett, Pearse and,"* and the hired boy's eyes were very wide and blue and full of dreams, and then Anny banged the big heavy teapot down on the table and said for God's sake and for God's sake over again has that fellow neither common sense nor decency and is there not a man among yous that'd shut his big ignorant mouth for him and that poor wee child sitting there on his knee listening? And the Whistling Gipsy stopped singing and looked bewildered and stupid with his mouth and eyes wide open and all the men looked embarrassed and he said haw bejaburs I'm sorry missus, I'm sorry, sure I didn't right think, I didn't remember, and he put Eileen down very gently on the floor and ruffled her hair with his big rough hand and said will I sing you a song of sixpence instead, Eileen? But Jem McCabe said there was enough singing and more than enough and why in the name of God did every thick labourer that ever came about his place start taking himself for a bleddy blackbird? And then all the plates were filled and the men put down their heads to say grace and Maggy Connor took her by the hand and said will we go for a wee walk Eileen and maybe we'll get a nice big tin of berries for Anny to sell in the shop maybe.

Agnes Quinn and her daughter crossed Ned's ditch one day and walked over the headland to the house. Eileen saw them coming: Anny Anny it's the girl with the ribbon, she's coming! Anny sat with her sewing on the doorstep and watched Mrs Quinn pick her way daintily round the hens and chickens.

"I'm just after making a nice batch of rock buns, Miss Maguire, would you and Eileen like to come over and have tea with Teresa and myself?"

Anny looked doubtful for a minute but then she said sure I might as well, it'll do me no harm to take a wee dodge over the field for once in a while.

Mrs Quinn couldn't stop talking. She set out china cups and saucers and arranged the rock buns on a doiley. "Do you know, Miss Maguire, you and me's the only two women that ever set foot outside the townland, I can't talk to any of them in this dump, they're all about a hundred and ten and headed straight for canonization, how do you stick it after all your years in town, how do you put up with it, does it not drive you halfway round the bend? When I think only a few years ago I was running to the dances over in London and spending every penny on clothes, that's what they used to say about me, every penny Agnes earns she has it on her back they used to say, and would you look at me now, amn't I a sight, wouldn't I scare crows? If they could see me now, the ones in Lyon's factory, they'd have a heart attack!"

"But sure you're grand," Anny said when she could get a word in. "Aren't you grand and stylish, your hair in the latest fashion and everything."

"I bet you they be talking about me, the old Connor one and that poor wizened creature of a Maginn woman, I'll bet you the old tongues does be wagging. Tell us, Miss Maguire, what do they be saying about me?"

"I never heard anything bad," Anny said cautiously, "They be admiring you, I think."

"Go way outa that with you, I'll bet you they'd have me strung up if they could get half a chance. Afraid their poor wee runts of men would look sideways at me."

Anny burst out laughing: "Oh go way, Agnes, is it Holy Ned or wee Paddy Connor, sure they're ages old!"

"Old or no old!" Mrs Quinn laughed and laughed and Anny looked worried and said maybe these wee girls would like to go out and play in the field, they don't want to be stuck here listening to old people's talk.

Teresa pulled Eileen by the arm and said come on you and I'll let you push me on the swing. The swing was on the branch of a big tree. Teresa made Eileen push and push and wouldn't let her have a go herself. "You can swing away to your heart's content at home in your own house!"

"I haven't a swing," Eileen said miserably.

"You haven't even a house!" Teresa swung high up

among the branches, cackling. Eileen could see her pink knickers with a lacy frill on them. "You haven't even a house. Is Miss Maguire your grandmother or what?"

"Anny's our servant girl," Eileen said, "She's here on her holidays and my mammy and daddy are away to Bundoran so they are."

"Well, deed and they're not. Your daddy's dead so he is and your mammy's away working in England. Like my daddy. Are you starting school next week? We can be up the road together, Mammy said."

"Knickers," Eileen said, "I can see your dirty pink knickers. Your dress is over your head so it is like Nancy Maginn."

"They say she's half daft, "Maggy Connor said, "Not that I ever had much to do with the woman, she's a bit too uppity in her ways for me."

"She's going mad with the loneliness," Anny said, "Would you believe what she asked me? She asked me would I look after Teresa some Friday night so that she could go down to the dance in the hall!"

"In God's name! And what did you say, Anny?"

"Well sure I told her out straight she'd be destroyed if she was seen running to dances with her man away in England. I promised I'd go to the pictures with her some night. I was sorry for her, Maggy. But she says they'll be moving up to Belfast soon, she says the man has the offer of some great job in a factory and there'll be work for her too."

"She's dreaming. Do you know, it's well over two years since he was home at all? Whether he sends money or not I don't know, but he doesn't come home to see her. He was only over once or twice since the wee one was born. That's what has her lonely."

"God help the creature," Anny sighed, "Maybe she's

sorry now she turned up her nose at Patrick a lawk of years ago when he was mad about her. She couldn't have found a steadier man even if he was that bit older than her!"

"Isn't Patrick far better off without her? And she can't be any chicken herself either."

"She's thirty-nine, there was just the fifteen years between her and Patrick. A fine age to be thinking of the dances, even if she was as single as myself!"

"She'd be as well off going back to her own people with the child till she knows what the man's going to do. They're only renting that house from Ned."

"Do you know, Maggy, I don't believe she has anybody left to go to. There's a couple of brothers in America but."

Anny and Patrick had people in America too, four sisters and a brother. They wrote often and sent parcels and dollar bills, lovely frocks for Anny and bright check jackets that Patrick wore round the fields in winter. They sent fat shiny magazines, *The Sign* and *Saint Anthony's Messenger*, that Patrick read out loud in the evenings while Anny sewed beside the lamp and Eileen sat on her stool at their knees.

The frocks hung in a press unworn, sparkling with sequins and blue and green stones and big splashy bunches of roses: the sisters had lost contact with Ireland and the way people lived. Anny continued to wear her flowery overall, and her decent black coat to Mass: the lovely dresses in the wardrobe smelt of fungus and turned mildew, were occasionally spread out in the meadow to air. The day Teresa came over to play – the first Saturday after they started school – she and Eileen took the scissors and cut out the big cobweb made of sequins with the blue glass spider in the middle. Eileen had yearned for it, been dazzled by it, ever since it was shaken out of its tissue paper the day the parcel came. When the deed was done and they saw the big crooked hole in the good blue dress they were horrified, ran in terror and hid the cobweb in a hole in Ned's ditch, knew they would never dare to take it out, never in all their lives see it again. Nothing was said to them, though they lived for days in expectation of chastisement, from time to time at school caught each other's eyes in accusation and looked away, shunning each other in the shame of their shared guilt. But nothing was ever said to them: the Yankee dresses were not real clothes to be worn, though they could not be given away or thrown out because of the affection that had crossed the Atlantic with them.

"Do you know," Eileen wrote years later to Teresa, "That cobweb must be still there. Not the material of course, but the stone and the sequins. You could go back and dig it out sometime, like an archaeological find, a relic of a golden age, to show your children. And mine. I'm sure Henri would be delighted, he's mad keen on his Irish heritage, though Clémence is so French she frightens me!"

"Not a chance!" Teresa wrote back, "Old Ned's son-in-law flattened all those humpy little fields and ditches into one huge prairie years ago. Try looking for your cobweb there! And what do you mean, golden age? It was awful, my mother always in tears and yours God only knew where and that old Anny of yours never done grumbling, some golden age!"

Every single relic of my life has been flattened, Hélène thought, rereading Teresa's letter that Monday evening, every room that I ever lived in, every field or garden where I played: all flattened to nothing! The nice big house in the decent street in Claghan was turned into a furniture store by one of my Campbell uncles and got a bomb in it in 1974; Gerald's old house on the Falls Road was burnt out years back by person or persons unknown; Anny and

Patrick's cottage was bulldozed along with the humpy fields by Ned Maginn's son-in-law who bought it all from Patrick's heir. Old Sixteen Tons himself, a solid farmer now, and the sinning bullying Nancy a respectable big mare of a farmer's wife, according to Teresa. Meg entered the Convent shortly after her sister's hasty wedding, went out to the missions and died of malaria. If she hadn't been in such a hurry, Hélène thought, she might have made something of big slobbery Nicholas the Whistling Gipsy, the first big love of my life, and they'd have bulldozed my home and fields anyhow – there was no way that warm little world could have survived into the grasping cruelty of the Nineties. Nothing remains, no place that I can go back to weep a few tears the way people do, and say: I used to live here one time; I lived, breathed, was human here. Even the house where we lived in Amsterdam, the lovely big cracked house where the children were born, was due to be flattened no sooner had we left it.

Nothing remains except Christopher Milton and the queer tormented city that I loved him in, and the memory of a failed relationship that those first years of my life could never have prepared me for.

71

Part Two

꩜

Rosalind really didn't know where to put herself coming away from the château, honestly that disgusting old hag wandering round the garden as nude as a worm and Clémence lying there topless on the lawn reading, with Michel Le Borgne working away only a few . . . I ought to have said something to her, the daft little cow's only seventeen after all, and I was her nanny, I suppose I have a responsibility. Only what the blazes could I have said, it was quite embarrassing enough having to stand there and be polite, exchanging bilingual nonsense about the weather and the dogs and the, tell your mum I called, Clem, no it doesn't matter a, anyone can forget, enchantée madame I'm sure. I stood there like a sausage smiling and smiling with embarrassment, say what you like but the French really! Bet they were looking after me and all, staring in that mocking way they do, as I legged it down the avenue and those bloomin' dogs, "Mujah! Din! Come here would you!" lolloping along as sloppy as mongrels, lifting their legs against Hélène's precious rosebushes, snuffling after some rabbit or whatever in among the, why the hell didn't I put them on a leash, happy as pigs in Périgord they looked,

"Mujah! Din! Come here blast you!" And there again typical wasn't it, just typical Frog crassness, make you quite ashamed having to call them in public, imagine if any unfortunate immigrant heard you. So insensitive, but they weren't exactly pups when Pierre bought them and they'd always refused to answer to anything else. But you couldn't go round explaining that, you couldn't very well tie labels on them disclaiming responsibility. And anyway there weren't any immigrants to hear her, what would an immigrant be doing in Plouch'en? *No Muslims Here* someone painted on the road last week. Lucky old Muslims. Probably that skinhead fellow of Clémence's . . . Should she drop a hint about that to Hélène? Or not? Would it be interfering, would Hélène put her in her place? You never knew with old Hélène, one minute all chatty and smiling and the next straight face nose in the air lady of the bleedin' manor. My only friend, if you could call her a friend. Friends used to be different before I got married, before I settled in this hole . . . She was realizing lately that she'd never been so alone in her whole life as she was since she married Pierre. Not that it was his fault, not always his fault, not really his fault until old Loulou moved back to Brittany. And even now, even pining for Loulou as she often knew him to be, even now (whenever his patients gave him time) he managed to be sometimes as matey and entertaining as he'd been before they got married. As for sex, after all that wasn't so very . . . No, it was just the way being a married woman in France seemed to automatically cut you off from everything. It's like joining the bleedin' Carmelites, she thought, this whole village is probably lonely, and what about all that famous joie de vivre they were always rabbitting on about, all that fantastic sun-soaked, wine-soaked social life? *A Year in Provence* my foot, that Peter Mayle ought to be strung up, he wants to try living in Brittany for a bit. Whole village huddled behind their net curtains all day long obsessively scrubbing and dusting. And knitting, the poor cows actually knitted every stitch they wore, in this day and age, no wonder they had to keep running to Pierre with their hang-ups, or else suiciding themselves at the rate they did. You feel a bit down in the dumps in old Plouch'en, you don't drop in on your best mate for a drink and a nice little chinwag, bien sûr que non! You just reach for the rope or the nearest shrink, vive la France! How to have a Meaningful Relationship with a Temesta Tablet . . . No of course it's not all that bad, she thought, it's not really bad at all, great little place for a holiday they all say, bit of a rest from the twentieth century, just think of it as an extended holiday, Roz, a whole long lifetime away from it all! Anyway you're just huffed aren't you because you were done out of the one bit of social life you were going to have in weeks, an after-lunch coffee up at the château no less, and the bitch didn't even think of letting you know. Oh go on Rosy, that's all that's biting you, France isn't exactly the flames of hell, people are basically the same the world over aren't they, and don't you start getting all racist and neurotic my girl or you're never going to survive it here for the rest of your life. The words sprang up in front of her, bleak as a tombstone – the rest of my life! – and she hurried on down the avenue towards, at least, the nice friendly shelter of her home and her garden and her big broad smiling husband.

"Another prudish foreigner!" Tante Ruby sniggered, "She is worse than your poor mother, that one!"

"My mother is not a foreigner!" Clémence snapped, "She has been a French citizen for ten years now. And you have no right to criticise her, Tante Ruby. Henri and I may laugh at her because we are her children, but you are only a guest here, it is not your home and you have no right to make fun of any of us. Now I am going to spend the rest of the day with Madame Bouchon at her house; she has just invited me to."

Rosalind hadn't got far when Clémence caught up with her on her bicycle. To Rosalind's relief she'd put on a T-shirt and shorts. "I told Tante Ruby you'd invited me to your house, Rosalind, I hope you do not mind? Sometimes I have to use you as an alibi. And today it is most important, Maurice and I have to meet some friends in Seulbourg. You are sure you do not mind?"

"Oh yes, I do mind!" Rosalind snapped. "You needn't think you can count on me, young lady, if you're going where I think you're going. Another of your fascist meetings, isn't it? I happened to see you the other week didn't I? On the local news of all places. You didn't even try to hide your face, anyone may have seen, the whole village must have recognised you. Your poor parents might have . . . You looked obscene, Clem. Standing there holding that banner. France for the bleedin French, yet, who do you think you are! The expression on your face. Gaping up at that stout repulsive old man as if he was . . . "

"My parents do not watch television. And what if they did? My father, he has a great respect for Monsieur Le Pen. How could he not? Someone who has beliefs and who fights for them, not a slimy greasy politician like the others. So why should I have hidden myself, Rosalind? I am proud to have gone to that meeting. To have helped carry the banner of Jeanne d'Arc. And I am proud that I was able to stand so close to our leader. He actually noticed me and smiled, imagine!"

"If you could see yourself, Clem! If you could just see

what you look like standing there. Do you know you look like one of those teenage Nazis out of old films, out of *Cabaret* or something, who the blazes do you think you are anyway, Unity Mitford or someone? I'm going to have to tell your mum, Clem, she'd never forgive me if."

"Unity Mitford? Who is that? I do not know of whom you speak. And it is not necessary to tell my mother. I am only going to Seulbourg with my boyfriend. She knows I go out with Maurice, she does not like him but she tolerates it. We are not going to a meeting today, we are only going to stick posters on walls for the by-election. It is perfectly legal."

"God! And you're seventeen! I must say when I was your age I could think of plenty more exciting things to do with a fella on a Saturday afternoon. What is this anyway, the sexless generation? What are you all so scared of? AIDS? You only have to buy a packet of. Taking safe sex a bit far innit, all this National Front chastity!"

"I think you are as disgusting as Tante Ruby! Why have grown-ups all got such filthy minds? Oh yes, when you were my nanny I often heard you recounting your squalid little adventures to my mother. Giggling over them. If you think that sort of thing interests me! My generation has better things to do, for a start we have to clean up the mess you and your Socialists have made of my country."

"Not guilty! I haven't even got the vote in France. And if I had I'd vote ecologist. Speaking of which, the ozone hole's going to make a right mess of you and your precious aunty long before the Socialists get a chance to if you will insist on lying around in your buff in the middle of the day. It isn't even sexy any more, for Christ's sake!"

"Ozone! I am not a fool, Rosalind, if you are. We have a right to enjoy God's good sunlight. Everybody knows this ozone scare has been invented by the leftists to take people's minds off all their corruption and wickedness."

"Oh yeah? Well say what you like about the Socialists, luv, but at least they're halfway human, they don't go round stirring up hate and inciting all the yobs to go round killing poor immigrant workers!"

"No, they have only murdered half the country's haemophiliacs with contaminated blood transfusions because it saved them money. And why do you love immigrants so much, Rosalind? Is it because you are only a foreigner yourself? But will all you English be so happy living in la Belle France I wonder when it is invaded and colonised by Muslims? Will you like it when you cannot walk through Plouch'en without a veil for fear of being raped by an Arab?"

"Oh come off it pet, you're delirious, Arabs don't go round raping, they leave that to the civilised Europeans. And there's none of them in Plouch'en anyway, I don't suppose you ever as much as saw an Arab except on telly."

"Oh yes, there is already at least one family in Seulbourg. And they are literally everywhere in Dinan and St Malo and St Brieuc, it is the thin end of the wedge."

"So what? They're human aren't they? Listen I'm not going to argue with you, Clem, it's just not worth it but I did help bring you up so I feel I've got some sort of a duty. I'm going home now to ring up your aunty and tell her all about your National Front meetings and your poster stickings and."

"Tante Ruby would laugh her head off at you, she would think you'd gone crazy. She and my uncle quite often have Monsieur Le Pen to dine in Paris, everyone does, he is received everywhere. After all, it was the Marquis de Cuevas who launched him when he was starting in politics."

"A great thug like Le Pen! So why do you need me as an alibi then? If your little friends are so acceptable to everyone?"

"Tante Ruby disapproves of me frequenting Maurice, that is all. Because his father is only an estate agent. She is a dreadful old snob, my aunt, she would like me to marry into the nobility. As if any of them would have me, little petit-bourgeois mongrel that I am!"

"You see, you can sound quite human, Clemmy, when you get down off your soapbox and giggle a bit. Oh come on now, confess luv, wouldn't you rather tart yourself up and go out to a disco with this Maurice of yours instead of wasting your time at dreary old political meetings?"

"No, I would not, madame! I have always thought I could depend on you for support because you were kind to me when I was a baby and my mother did not have time for me. And because you yourself seemed to believe strongly in something, even if it was only feminism. But now I realize that you are just a foolish frivolous old Englishwoman. I am afraid I will have to think of you as one of the enemy from now on. Goodbye madame!" And she pedalled off furiously towards the village.

I made a right mess of that one, Rosalind thought, just as well maybe I haven't got kids of my own. But what could I have said to convince her, what could anyone have said? What can anyone do? She tried to take her mind off it by bathing the dogs and combing out their endless tangled hair, but she was in tears by the time Pierre came in from his surgery.

"That poor misguided child! Whatever's going to become of her, Pierre? She used to be so sweet and funny and affectionate, if you only knew, and you should have heard her just now, so stern and sort of humourless, she sounded like some kind of middle-aged fanatic. It's Hélène's fault you know, the way she neglected those poor kids! Too busy with her château and her tourists to . . . "

Pierre only laughed and said he wouldn't be losing any sleep over the fate of la petite Clémence: if he knew that young lady she was certain to fall firmly on her feet in the long run. Probably end up as the power behind the throne if that madman ever got elected President, probably have Rosalind herself locked away as an undesirable alien, if not worse, doesn't do to antagonize that lot, ma pauvre fille, especially when you've not had the good fortune to be born in the Hexagon like the rest of us!

"It's not a bit funny, Pierre. And that crowd will never get into power, the French aren't completely mad, it would be unthinkable."

"I agree that Monsieur Le Pen himself may not get into power, he is already an old man after all, but those in power are going to adopt the ideas of the National Front one after another, oh very gradually, very discreetly, but they will be obliged to if they are to survive. The fashion for ideals is dead, my child, and we are basically a racist people, as you may have noticed over the years. Xenophobic, even! It is not only the Arabs and Jews – we do not like anyone, we suffice unto ourselves. Actually that is the reason for our unique charm, it is what gives us our identity. No nation could have developed a culture and a cuisine and a fashion industry like ours if it was continually pandering to the inferior and eccentric needs of foreigners, pasteurizing itself, making itself politically correct! I myself do not say that this is a good thing: some of my most amusing meals have been eaten in MacDonald's, after all! And I did choose to marry you, an Anglaise. But you will find, Rosy, that the little Clémence's parents are more than prepared to think the unthinkable if they believe it will profit them. Not to mention old Madame Rasputin! Voyons, the whole Eastern bloc has suddenly fallen to pieces, the cold war is ended, democracy, whatever that is, is feebly trying to establish itself, the weak are thrown out of the window, small nations are savagely tearing themselves to pieces, Cuba is being starved to slow death, the famous nuclear threat has flown off in a thousand different directions like creatures out of Pandora's box, refugees by the millions are staggering with dazed faces all over our television screens – and all Madame Ruby and her kind can see is: what is in it for them? Where are the pickings? Such charming people you frequent, my dear!"

"Clémence was saying he dines with old Ruby, Le Pen does."

"Of course he does! They are not like us, the grande bourgeoisie, they will always see to their own advantage. That is why they are where they are and why we are paying them rent. And I should imagine that Monsieur and Madame Bourjois are perfectly au courant with their dear daughter's activities."

"Oh nonsense, Pierre, Hélène and Jean-Hubert would be shattered if they even suspected the things Clem got up to. And don't talk about Hélène as if she belonged to some rarefied upper class that wasn't fit to breathe the same air as us. She's just an ordinary decent woman, just like any of our neighbours. Only friendlier. And I mean she was Eileen from the Falls Road when I first met her. Probably still is, underneath it all."

"Yes but she engaged you as a nanny, didn't she? I mean they didn't exactly invite you to stay as an honoured guest in their nice new château, did they, that day they first met you hitch-hiking in the village? They offered you a job as a servant, they must have seen that as your level. And look at today – she asks you up for a coffee, the first time in months I'd remind you, and then she only arranges to be a thousand kilometres away when you arrive at the house to drink it!"

"Oh don't go all 1789 on me, Pierre, it's depressing! You know quite well I often stayed there as a guest before I married you, that's how we met after all. And they have occasionally been known to invite us to dinner, you know."

"Ah yes, but never when there's been any beau monde present. Have we ever been invited to eat there when the Last of the Romanovs was in residence?"

"Would we want to?"

"Not after all you've told me about her. I do not think I would relish the sight of the lady's great naked bosoms splashing about in the soup tureen! Though I suppose she does dress for dinner? I must say, Madame Ruby throws a whole new light on the expression! But it is the thought that counts, and they have rarely thought of us. And now, ma chère épouse, if you remember, I have invited Paul and his wife to supper this evening: might it not be as well to start preparing a meal? Do not grimace like that, Rosalind, you will enjoy the evening if you put your mind to it. You are forever complaining of the lack of social life and then when I invite my family you make faces. What have you against Paul and Maryvonne? At least they are people of our own kind, des braves gens, we will be at ease with them. It is always best to stay among one's own kind, my dear, as your château friends so invariably do. That way there are no problems and no disappointments."

In-laws, Rosalind thought, why has my social life withered down to the odd weekend meal with my boring brother-in-law? Where are all these charming witty

Frenchmen you hear about, sparkling with life and wickedness and savoir-vivre? These elegant bitchy women in fantastic clothes and Givenchy perfume? They're sparkling snobbishly in châteaux according to Pierre, she thought savagely, while I'm stuck with Paul's little paunch and Maryvonne's button-through polyester from the *Trois Suisses* catalogue and her schoolmarmy conversation. Des braves gens. Yeah! La France profonde, that's where you've ended up, mate! After all your famous hitching around Europe. Well at least Maryvonne does use a deodorant, I suppose that's one blessing to be counted, she might so very easily not do, in Plouch'en.

She dug four helpings of boeuf bourguignon out of the freezer to thaw, pondering on her husband's extraordinary inferiority complex. Pierre had lived fifteen years of his life in Paris, he was a very successful man of forty-two, an excellent doctor, much respected in the village, yet after all this time he was still seeing himself as a cringing shoeless little tenant, son of and now presumably husband of, poor oppressed servants of the Big House. Why, she wondered, did upward mobility take so many weary generations to accomplish itself, in France?

They were going to dine in Le Tour d'Argent that evening and Margaret O'Neill, tangled luxuriously though she was in silky hotel sheets, was already beginning to worry. "But imagine it if we bumped into anyone that knew you, Gustave! I mean what on earth would you say, how would you explain me away, like?"

"But we are certain to meet whole multitudes of people who know me, my dear; where would be the interest of dining in total obscurity like a married couple in from the suburbs? I am an important man, and it is Saturday evening after all, we shall see and be seen by any number of my acquaintances. You and I will utter the usual courtesies, we shall explain nothing, and nobody will dream of obliging us to. This is Paris, after all, ma très chère, not Belfast. Those who know me will simply envy me for being accompanied by such a beautiful and elegant lady."

"Elegant maybe, since you've taken me in hand, but sure I'm as old as the hills, Gustave! I honestly don't know what you see in me, so I don't."

"You really must learn not to say bad things about yourself, Marguerite, it is an Anglo-Saxon habit that we in France find quite incomprehensible and très très vilaine! No French woman would ever permit herself to say 'I am old.' Especially not to her lover! You are the woman with whom I wish to spend the rest of my life, my dear, thus you will always be young and very very beautiful to me."

"The rest of your life's all very fine, Gustave, but supposing somebody tells your wife on us?"

"Et alors? My wife is at this moment busy cuckolding me in Corsica. Unless the young man has grown tired of her by now, in which case she will have thrown herself on her nephew's hospitality and may well be en train d'emmerder your daughter and your abominable grandchildren. She is certainly not in Paris."

"Why Corsica? It must be like going to Crossmaglen for a dirty weekend, I mean isn't it full of autonomists and bandits, South Armagh with the sea all around it, I'd have thought the Bahamas would be more in her . . . "

"Oh but Corsica is renowned, it is the Isle of Beauty, I must bring you there one day. And then my wife likes to entertain her little fantasies. She enjoys treating herself to un petit Corse from time to time, so delightfully brown and muscular, she says. A bit of rough trade I believe you would call it?"

"Indeed and I'd call it nothing of the sort, Gustave! I'm not exactly used to this sort of. And I don't know how you put up with it, I think it's disgusting so it is, you should have left her long ago!"

"Oh course you are not used to it! And I find your little coté puritain so very very attractive. It is something unusual in my life. And I have put up with my wife's little fantasies until now because until now it has not been important to separate myself from her. Now of course I ask for a divorce. I demand a divorce. You and I have been growing close to each other for years, summer after summer on those dreary visits to Plouch'en; we have already wasted too much time. I am not growing younger, Margaret. So you will put aside your scruples and for the first time in your life you will think of yourself. Not of your daughter, or of your church, or your pupils, or those miserable ghetto children you so vainly try to help. Remark, I have nothing against helping the poor, I myself send cheques to UNICEF and to Médécins sans Frontières, do not think me an egoist. Only . . . did you ever really believe you could change the minds of bigoted adolescents by obliging them to camp together at the Giant's Causeway for two weeks a year? Come now, Margaret, I know you are not a fool!"

"Of course I knew it wouldn't help for all of them. Only it seemed worth it if only two or three . . . A beginning. A sort of a wee spark of hope. You know? There's not too many sparks of hope over there, I can tell you! To be honest, Gustave, I'm feeling a right traitor over that as well as everything else. I was supposed to be taking a group of them to Corrymeela this summer you know, when I got back from Lourdes. I mean I'm not even going to Lourdes, it's the first year I missed since donkeys ago. I can't go to Lourdes, I can't even go to Mass, I'm living in sin, do you realize that?"

"Only until you marry me. It is a blessing for you, Margaret, that I did not marry my first wife in church! Very few people know that, it was during the Occupation, you understand, when everything was a bit ambiguous, one could get off with murder, among other things! But even His Holiness the Pope, if he knew I existed, would be forced to agree that I am an old bachelor. At my age, imagine! Quel horreur!"

"Honestly you're like a wee boy sometimes, Gustave. Nothing ever worries you!"

"Why should anything? I am a very rich man, I am still handsome, in perfect health, I play tennis every morning, I hunt regularly in winter, and I am at this moment drinking Scotch in a most luxurious bed with the woman I love. Think of it, I can manage to appreciate you even when you scold me, Margaret. I think it must be your beautiful strong assertive voice. So sexy, this strange defiant Belfast accent of yours. And believe me, Margaret, I have been in my time an expert on such matters. I have in the past loved so many women uniquely for their voices. Eartha Kitt, aah if you had heard la petite Eartha when she came on her celebrated tournees in France long ago. Quelle merveille! How I used to adore her. The orchids, the diamonds . . . And Nina Simone. And Juliette Greco. And of course Piaf, the one great love of my life! You have heard of Piaf, Margaret?"

"Pee aff yerself! No no it's just a wee Belfast joke, must be all this whiskey, don't be cross, Gustave. Well to be sure I've heard of Edith Piaf, where do you think I was dragged up? So go on with your wee litany of pop stars why don't you, you're a right old cliché do you know, with your orchids and your diamonds. You'd nearly expect you to be plastered with Brylcreem so you would!"

"Ah your little iconoclastic side is adorable! I have

noticed it too in your daughter, is it perhaps a national characteristic? Though less attractive in Hélène, I think . . . Yes, I was telling you that once, in my youth, I was so in love with la petite Piaf, so very despairingly in love, that I thought I would simply suicide myself if she did not allow herself to be conquered."

"And did she?"

"Ah, these are things one does not tell! But you need not worry, it was far in the past, Margaret, the poor little sparrow has been dead for a long long time. Now there is only you. And I am so happy, you cannot imagine, now that I have succeeded in persuading you to fly away with me from your dreary suburb and your boring school and your so so depressing political activities! Tell me, are you not perfectly happy to be here with me at last in Paris?"

"Indeed and I am, I could hardly believe it that day you turned up on the doorstep in Finaghy, I mean I'd got into the way of thinking I was there for life, just waiting for my pension. Talk about powers of persuasion, no wonder you're such a great businessman! Only I'm dead scared of us being found out, I'm dead scared of Eileen finding out for a start, I mean I'm still supposed to be in that school, she thinks I'm still in Belfast teaching away, I'm supposed to be going to Lourdes at the end of July, I mean she'll be sitting there expecting her wee postcard of the grotto! And my God, when she gets a look at me, these clothes you made me buy, and my face! She'll throw me out, Gustave, so she will, she won't let me in on the door!"

"So we will go and sleep elsewhere. But why are you so afraid of your daughter? I myself have children of her age, I rarely see them. They certainly do not wish to interfere in my life! Have you not made enough sacrifices for this middle-aged child of yours?"

"She's never thought they *were* sacrifices, that's the trouble. She thinks I ruined her life on her that time, going away to England to train. And I mean I only married Gerald to give myself and her a home, but try telling her ladyship that. She's just sitting there waiting for her chance of getting back at me. Unless I'm paranoid. Och maybe I'm paranoid, maybe the woman never gives me a thought. Some hope! No but she's as odd as two left boots and that husband of hers the same, I can't say I ever liked the fellow but they're well met! Look at them I mean, the way they live in that freezing old manor house that's falling to bits, it's not what they make out of their tourists that's going to put a coat of paint on that barrack of a place! Wouldn't they be far better off selling it to some institution and buying themselves a nice wee town house, better for those unfortunate children too? I mean it's not healthy, stuck there in that village is it, I mean all they think about is keeping up appearances and licking up to the local aristocrats, I mean *nobody* lives like that nowadays!"

"Tens of thousands of people do, my dear, in crumbling old manors all over France. Counting the centimes and keeping up appearances. They are still a power in the land, I'm afraid. Not that I mind: they have a certain pittoresque after all, these impoverished country squires, they are amusing to contemplate for a tough old crocodile like myself. Especially as I married one of them. A black sheep but still . . . It is true that the little Hélène may be shocked by our liaison, but she will survive it. She has after all survived my wife's little escapades."

"I'm her mother!"

"So you have no right to be happy? Come, my dear, she will have to know very soon. Next week we are going to travel down together to this ridiculous party of theirs. They are certain to suspect in any case, so why not confront them proudly with the truth? Then, hey presto, my divorce will arrange itself, we will be married and live very happily indeed ever after, respected by all who know us. Where is the problem?"

"I can't travel down in your car, I'd die of embarrassment, I'll go on the train on my own. I'll have to break it to her gently, I wouldn't know where to put myself if they saw us arriving hand in hand like, I'd die! And do you honestly believe your wife's going to smile nicely and agree to divorce you just like that, I know that woman, she's as hard as nails, she'll try and hang on to you for all she's worth."

"For all *I* am worth. No, but the whole of Paris knows that Ruby has been cuckolding me for years, I can have all the evidence I need. And then she has so many other interests at the moment, this motheaten old Russian estate she is trying to recuperate, her interviews in the papers . . . She will not wish to hang on to a husband who has always bored her."

"But *you* were cuckolding *her* all the time too. Piaf and all those lovely sexy ladies. Not to mention me."

"But how ignorant you are, ma petite Marguerite! There is no such thing as cuckolding one's wife! In France it is perfectly acceptable for a married man to have his mistresses; indeed it is expected of him, if he is as rich as I am. You might say it comes into the realm of philanthropy."

"Oh is that the way it is? Maybe I might be better off getting up out of this bed and going to Lourdes after all."

"No no, you need not worry yourself. I was speaking of the customs of my youth. Now that my wild oats have been scattered and my four hundred blows struck (four hundred, you understand, is merely a symbolic figure), now I am preparing, like Louis XIV, to settle myself down with a sensible widowed lady of a certain age who will love me and be faithful to me and take good care of me in my declining years."

"Well as long as you won't be expecting me to start up a boarding school and recruit whole harems of wee teenage girls to keep you amused."

"How repressive you are, Margaret. And what a sad little chronicle Irish history must be. All war and no love. I am sure your Gaelic kings, when you still had some, were respectable pillars of society who got drunk and ritually beat their wives on a Saturday night but would never have done anything as amusing as deceiving them! Are you not lucky to have in the end found yourself a wicked old Frenchman who teaches you so many wonderful things? About history and about love?"

"Indeed and I am lucky, Gustave, you're a real wee miracle so you are! I honestly don't know how I survived it up till now without even knowing all these fantastic things existed. Where must I have been dragged up?"

"You were dragged up, my dear, on the Falls Road, Belfast. Your pious old Gerald would be turning in his tomb if he could see you now. Is it not good at last to be learning how to enjoy your beautiful body?"

"Aye it's great but you can leave Gerald out of it, lord have mercy on him, he may not have been a bundle of laughs all the time but he was a good kind man and I was fond of him so I was. I can tell you I was glad to find someone like him after a wastrel like poor Brian Campbell."

"Do not be boring, my dear. You sound like tweed suits and Finaghy, not at all like my new happy Marguerite! And now, my little Child of Mary, shall we perhaps get dressed and prepare to go out and eat a very delicious dinner under the indulgent eyes of all my disreputable friends?"

"Aye why don't we; do you not feel it's a wee bit odd, Gustave, lying up in bed in the middle of the day, like? In a four-star hotel too, I mean what must all the chambermaids be thinking?"

Michel Le Borgne took the long way home that Saturday evening through the château woods. With his denim jacket hooked over one shoulder he stepped lightly down into the tunnel of trees. A pheasant trotted a few friendly steps alongside him trailing its tail, he could have reached down and caught it no problem, tame as chickens those beasts, raised expressly for the slaughter. His mind slid away sideways from the tame woods and he was galloping, galloping, reins in one hand, gun in the other, and the game was away out there in front of him savage and snarling and desperate, and the mountains swayed and swung above him, beside him, below him . . . Some old film he saw on the telly.

September they'd all be out shooting again, not in these woods they were private but in the balding scrubby copses around the village, pigeon, rabbit, anything that moved. All the neighbour men in boastful khaki uniforms, hung about with game bags and cartridge-belts and hunting-horns, a pack of half-starved dogs yapping at their heels. Farmers, plumbers, shopkeepers disguised as keen-eyed predators, hunting down imaginary prey. Stalking imaginary enemies, he wondered? Jews, Arab immigrants, common market competitors were they thinking, lurking in the undergrowth armed to the teeth? Defending la belle France were they, those paunchy old men, in their Sunday morning dreams? His father's generation, after all, had been sent off to fight in colonial wars, his grandfather's had known the Resistance and the German occupation: ageing quietly now in the oil-fired boredom of housing estate and bungalow, were they still on autumn Sundays trying to recapture the lost glory of those few youthful years? At this distance they would be seeing it as glorious wouldn't they, would have transformed the cold and the heat and the fear and the disgust and the blood into a moment of glamour and significance, one patch of sunlight to illuminate the dim tunnel of their lives. Think of the Monument des Morts even, on the eleventh of November – if you bothered to look you could still see half a dozen pairs of youthful daring eyes flashing proudly out from smashed decrepit faces, the owners of those eyes having long since edited their own pathetic far-off trot to the slaughter into a thing of worth and beauty: last few survivors of the Ladies' Road.

Nathalie would be at him again this year to go out shooting like the neighbours. All that lovely equipment in the catalogues, she'd say, those lovely khaki uniforms and why couldn't he be like everyone else, not even a gun she'd say, not even a shotgun in the house and you never know these days, quite apart from shooting and making a man of yourself you never know nowadays when you might need a gun in the house to. Nathalie, don't think of Nathalie, not here in the lovely woods, don't spoil the peace of the. Of the leaves moving and sighing above his head, quieter than silence. Beneath his feet, whole autumns and winters of leaves rustled and splashed and gradually sank in on themselves, turning peacefully back to earth. Leaf-mould. Your only lad for the garden his father used to say, that and horse manure for the roses. They always used to get a load of free manure long ago when Monsieur Vladimir kept horses, and then on Sundays he and his father used to go to the woods for leaf-mould while his mother cooked the dinner singing along with the transistor she used to in the tiled kitchen, *Tous les garcons et les filles de mon age* she used to sing, his mother, long ago when he was a child, before his parents moved out to the housing estate. His father gardened out of plastic bags these days, his mother in her fitted formica kitchen still listened to Françoise Hardy. Except that Françoise Hardy, when you saw her on the telly, still looked young. Different and harder and tougher, but still young, while his mother had long ago withered into just another lumpy old village woman with a grey perm. Was it money that did it? Intelligence? Education? A life without everyday little worries? Madame Bourjois must be near forty by now but she still looked young and all, still as beautiful as that day he was asked to show her over Monsieur Vladimir's garden and she drifted around beside him in her long flowery skirt and Indian beads, smelling of sandalwood, looking dazzled and bewildered and a bit frightened, who could blame her, those two terrifying old hags, and he had fallen in love with her immense blue eyes full of uncertainty as she tried to come to grips with the kind of life they'd be expecting her to live. "I never imagined it would be this sort of a place," she said, "Jean-Hubert never really described it properly," in her timid little voice, in her slow correct school French. Run, he'd wanted to say to her, get out of here quick before they lock the doors on you, run away back to whatever commune he must have seduced you out of. But it was not the sort of thing you could easily say when you'd lived the whole nineteen years of your life in the shadow of a place like that, of people like that. He'd seen her change over the years, grow a cool beautiful shell over the uncertainties, learn to speak French in a high clear voice of command, learn to wear the clothes they all wore, utter the same polite formulae. But still . . . When that summer holiday ended he'd stayed on working there, not bothering to go back to university in the autumn, because anyway it was acceptable, in those years, to choose to drop out of college even if you were a brilliant student with a great future ahead of you. Especially if you were a brilliant student with. It was acceptable to choose to live one's life among the simplicity of trees and flowers and tranquil kindly village people. It was even acceptable to imagine that a shy young foreign woman with long tangled blonde hair and hippy clothes might easily choose to leave her rich husband and stifling existence and drift off with him towards adventure in a rose-covered cottage. It was the spirit of those years. And he still, in daydreams, sometimes imagined it might even now be possible: she was not a happy woman, Madame Bourjois, it was plain for anyone to see. Anyone who cared. "Mais quel con!" he thought, "Quel con je suis! We are living in the real world n'est ce pas Michel, and they are a rich successful married couple. And it is no longer the nineteen seventies." And in the end, because he had to live in the real world, he'd married Nathalie. Almost absentmindedly married Nathalie. Because she was a big healthy good-looking girl, and because she'd always fancied him, and because a man can't live in a dream, can't exist on a few kind words and a brief bewildered smile thrown at him from time to time just because he happened to be there, happened to be passing the window when that bastard Bourjois was in one of his moods . . . Some day I'll be there and I'll be needed, he thought, I'll be able to do more than comfort her with an exchange of feeble little smiles, I'll be able to . . .

"Do you know, Michel, there's books about fellows like you," Rosalind Bouchon told him, "Fellows that go round pining obsessively over some woman that's happily married.

They're mostly murder stories, I'd have you know! Patricia Highsmith. Ruth Rendell. So take care you don't set about poor old Jean-Hubert some day with the digging fork! Not that I'd complain," she laughed, "That man was one right shit to work for. Still, she did marry him, no one twisted her arm, and she has stayed married to him what's more, and she has a nice cosy life of it. Everybody wants the box of chocolates and the long-stemmed rose, n'est ce pas? As the man said. So I wouldn't give much for your chances of future bliss, mon ami! Cheer up and come round for a drink one evening, why don't you?"

And why not, this evening? He could talk about her, not obsessively, not romantically — he'd read those books too — but just casually drop her name into the conversation now and then. Even if Pierre and Rosalind only laughed, at least they laughed nicely. Except that Nathalie would probably want to go out somewhere. Some bar where they'd sit with other married couples and drink too much and talk nonsense. Talk grown-up nonsense about cars and petrol consumption and building societies and interest rates and. *You're* grown-up, Michel, he reminded himself, you're well over thirty. It seemed like a joke. It always seemed like a joke, that he was a grown-up married man like the rest now.

But the one time he did bring Nat to the Bouchon's for a drink she'd sat stiff and silent with her handbag square on her lap, as if she was totally unable to see a room in a doctor's house as anything other than a waiting-room, a place you sat stiffly waiting your turn for a pregnancy test or something.

"The poor girl was just shy," Rosalind said, but you could see she was relieved when he came on his own next time.

"Well, what could I have talked about?" Nathalie

snapped, "I'm not educated like you lot, I don't know anything about medicine!"

"We never mentioned medicine the whole evening," he said wearily, "People don't usually, when they're just having a few beers with a man who happens to be a doctor. Bon dieu du merde, Nathalie, he's only an old mate of my brother's! And I used to work along with Rosalind, up at the château."

"Oh well anyway, you know I can't stand educated people, they're always trying to make me feel inferior. And you can't really have a good laugh with them can you, I mean they're not really like the rest of us are they, admit it?"

Which was why she'd refused to go to Denis and Lindi's wedding anniversary last Sunday. And that was probably what had inspired Denis into making his Big Offer, and inspired too the brotherly heart-to-heart that followed.

"But what's so wrong with living the way I do?" he'd asked finally, "Can you see me, Denis, living here in some street in town, managing one of your shops? Do you think that's the sort of thing would satisfy me? A bachelor flat in a provincial city, nine to seven in a little shop selling somebody else's ancestors to a shower of jumped-up pig breeders, and then back home to my wife at the weekend like some commuter? Because Nathalie certainly wouldn't leave the village. Is that honestly how you see me?"

"It might be the solution to a lot of things," Denis said, "You're fooling yourself, Michel, you're living in some sort of a dream that might have been OK about twenty years ago but nowadays Jesus . . . Listen mon vieux, you're thirty-five years old, you've had some sort of an education even if you did choose to throw it away halfway through, you're far brainier than I ever was and look at you, just look at yourself living in that village, drifting round half a dozen little jobs that mostly pay only joke money. Working the odd day for me, the odd day for the château, for the curé, for the notaire – my God you could have been a notaire by now if you'd wanted! Where is it all supposed to be leading? Imagine when you're forty-five, Michel! When you're fifty! An ageing handyman living in a tied cottage in Plouch'en. Why? I mean I wouldn't mind if you were even happy."

"Years ago you both of you said I'd made a wonderful choice. Remember how you used to come to the cottage at the weekends your nerves in a frazzle, or so you said, after slogging away all week in the city, and how you used to go shrieking around about how intensely satisfying my way of life was, how significant, how authentic, what a fantastic choice I'd made, all the old jargon of back then. So what's changed? Is it just that it's not fashionable any more? Is it just that human greed's won out, with you too?"

"We always thought back then that you were on the point of doing wonderful things," Lindi said gently, "All of us, our whole crowd thought that. You were so talented, Michel! You used to be full of dreams and wit and life and poetry. We were actually waiting for you to get off your backside and start to paint, or to sculpt, or even to dig French literature out of its grave, for heaven's sake! It really did seem possible that you could do any of those things as soon as you were ready to seriously put your mind to it. It never occurred to any of us that you'd just marry Arabella Donn and settle down to be a villager!"

"Her name's Nathalie," he said coldly, "And I am happy with my life, Lindi, at least it's clean. I'm not constantly grabbing and climbing and cheating and."

"Don't mind Lindi," Denis soothed, "My wife did English literature in evening classes and she's never quite recovered. But think it over won't you, petit Mic? Talk it over with Nathalie if that's what you want. The offer stays open for as long as you need."

Talk it over with Nathalie? She'd jump at it. Five whole days and nights of freedom every week while he was working, and enough money coming in to start building a little bungalow. "A family? If you think I'm even going to consider having kids in a tied cottage, I'm not your old mother you know! Find us a nice modern pavillon like everyone else and then I might start thinking about kids!"

I'm happy with my life, he'd told Lindi, because what else could you possibly tell her? Because what could he do, what choice had he now only to drift quietly on in the path he'd chosen? He loved the village, and everyone in it was his friend, it was the place he was comfortable in, it fitted him like a warm old sweater. But he was bored, yes, and he was dissatisfied, and he was becoming more and more aware that the quiet leafy road he'd chosen had somehow over the years transformed itself into a narrow dusty lane leading nowhere. Leading to a cheap and garish shopping centre full of things that Nathalie wanted. A modern house, mass-produced furniture, terrace with a barbecue, her horde of relations shrieking and gossiping . . . His mind slid away sideways to the image of a slim foreign woman with tousled hair and big dreamy eyes lying quietly beside him listening to Bartok in an overgrown garden. A dream and, as Denis said, it was long past the time for dreaming. But what? What could he even begin to do, at his age? Just walk out on Nathalie and start all over again? With Denis and Lindi in the shop? Sod that! No way was he going to take a salary from Denis, be the poor relation, turn up in Rennes looking for charity, with nothing to offer but the fact of being Denis' brother. Do a university course? He could still train as a teacher, there was still time for that, the age limit was forty-five or something. Or become a social worker. He knew that was the last thing he wanted. And would he have the neck on him to walk out on Nathalie, what would she do, what would she live on? Where would she even live? The cottage was theirs only as long as he put in a few days every week in the château gardens, Monsieur Boujois would turf Nathalie out before he was gone five minutes, that's all the bastard was waiting for, tart it up and fill it with foreign tourists. He felt a pang as he thought of his lovely cottage and garden overrun by a succession of English and Germans and Dutch. He'd lived all his life there, it was all he knew apart from those two years in Rennes; the village people were all the friends he had, he liked them and respected them and he was sure that they liked and respected him. But that would all change if he smashed up his marriage and left his wife homeless for no reason, for boredom, for a whim. They'd see him as irresponsible, a selfish bastard, a real salaud. A nutcase. He might never try to come back to the village even for a visit if he walked out on poor Nathalie. And Madame Bourjois? If he left the village he would leave her behind him as well as everything else, it would be the end of all his dreams, the end of his youth. It was not to be thought about, Denis and Lindi were not to be listened to. Not now. Not yet. Something would happen, something must happen to change things. He walked on quickly, fearing that nothing would happen, that he was drifting quietly on towards middle-age and a bungalow in the village and a life like his father's. He must not think about that. Not yet. Not now. Not here in the lovely tranquil woods.

Over there to his left the château showed through the spaces where the trees blew down a few years ago in the big tempest, its battered green shutters a sicklier shade than the leaves. They'd have to do something about those shutters and that ugly cement-wash if she ever intended opening the garden to the public. You couldn't ask people to pay twenty francs to walk round a beautiful garden with that eyesore stuck in the middle. It would cost money though.

"Going to take them a good thirty years to restore that place," his uncle Hervé said, "at the rate Monsieur Bourjois is prepared to spend money. Paper a room here, replace a window frame there, slate a few centimetres of roof, it is not serious, that!"

"In the old days," Hervé's father-in-law croaked from his chair in the corner, "In the old days they wouldn't have stopped to count the cost, they'd call in a team of skilled workmen every few years regular, do the whole place over in one go from roof to cellar. Put bread in the mouths of them that needed it. Before the war," he sighed nostalgically, "Before the Occupation, that was."

"Well if people can't afford to keep up a place like that," Hervé's wife snapped, "then what business have they setting themselves up above the rest of us to live in it? Clear up that avenue he told us, Thursday when he was leaving, get rid of all those brambles for me over the weekend! Neither a please nor a thank you. Servants they want, they don't even realise that the likes of us are not serfs any more. In a few years we'll be able to buy and sell them if things keep on the way they're going."

"I doubt it, woman," Hervé grumbled, "Not if the bloody English and Dutch keep on flooding the market with their lamb and their pork and their."

When Michel was a child, the château had been like a dream palace, the place where his father went to work as head gardener and came home on magic evenings with his pockets bulging cherries and apples and nectarines. A place you could see at night sometimes all lit up and glittering, with Beatles music pouring out of the windows, girls in miniskirts and men in coloured evening suits dancing down the avenue, sprawled giggling in Uncle Hervé's haystacks smoking big fat loose cigarettes nobody knew were called joints. Set the place on fire les salauds, Grandpapa grumbled, cheeky young blackguards, I'll tan their hides for them so I will if I catch them! But when he caught them he raised his cap and shuffled his feet and addressed them humbly as Master, which made them giggle even more, fall about giggling and snorting in among the tousled hay: "Notre maître! Did you hear him? He's an antique, the old man, un vrai pièce d'antiquité!"

In the daytime, coming from school, you could see the tall chimneys and spires growing out of the tops of the trees, sometimes big foreign cars overtook you and turned in between the chestnuts on the long avenue. There were no weeds then, and Uncle Hervé never had to be reminded to cut back the brambles. Years ago, that was, in old Monsieur Vladimir's time. And before that, people said, it had been even more splendid, balls and parties every weekend, Mademoiselle Ruby and Mademoiselle Elsie and their friends, galloping along the village roads on their ponies and God help you if you happened to get in their way. And worse, the old man chuckled, it wasn't only the ponies they were riding hou la la! A hot rabbit, that Mademoiselle Ruby, will you ever forget the time we were mowing the five-hectare field over by Bourins'? Two fine birds we startled out of the wheat that day! Young Jacques Bourin, he wasn't a notaire then, must have been still at school . . . Just before the Germans came, that would be, just before the Occupation. And then the uncles and the neighbours dropped their voices and trailed into uneasy silence because, even fifty years later, it was wiser to be discreet about how life had been lived in Plouch'en while the Germans were in possession.

Now the château had lost all its mystery. It was as familiar to Michel as his own cottage. Well, the outside was as familiar, because he had never been allowed inside the house, not even as far as the back hall. He could have gone inside, he could have joined the neighbours who went with tractors and trailers to plunder the place when Monsieur Vladimir died. He had not wanted to join them, it would have seemed like sacrilege. It still did seem like sacrilege, but for a different reason – often he was on the point of telling her, of putting her wise, because finally it was she whom they'd robbed and not a dead old man, but when it came to the bit he could never quite bring himself to form the accusation.

Every summer holidays since he was twelve he had gone to work in Monsieur Vladimir's breathtaking garden, and even after the old man died he had continued going up there without pay, just to keep the flowers from being overgrown. It had been a shock when Madame Bourjois ordered him to dig up all the magnificent old climbing rosebushes that must have been there for a century at least, and plant stiff white flowers in their place. He supposed it was more sophisticated, more modern, but he didn't much like it. And it certainly didn't go with the decrepit old château, didn't take your mind off the peeling paint and the damaged walls the way the savage old-fashioned garden had done. Above all, it wasn't *his* garden the way Monsieur Vladimir's had been; you couldn't throw yourself down in the long grass with a book and be dazzled and drunken with colour and scent the way he'd been that long hot month of June when he was revising for his baccalauréat.

With old Monsieur Vladimir, last legs or no last legs,

shuffling out as beaky and arrogant as ever: "But what are you going to be, boy? What is the point of all this studying for someone like you? Can you not be content with a decent manual job like your father and grandfather? Be a plumber, my boy, be an electrician, the country is crying out for good tradesmen. I never heard the like of it, every peasant child is doing his bachot nowadays, these diplomas will soon be worthless. And we saw the result of it, in '68!"

The old man had been terrified in May 1968, when Paris was in turmoil and it must have seemed, to the likes of him in his country estate, as if the tumbrils were about to start rolling again. He had distributed a lot of his valuables for safe-keeping among those tenant families whom he considered loyal and trustworthy. All the things had been given back, of course, when the danger of revolution was over, but it must have been the sight and feel of those lovely Chinese vases and the Aubusson tapestries and the Persian carpets and the Limoges porcelain that inspired half the village to go up there and help itself that year when the château stood empty. From now on, the villagers must have been thinking, those objects were not fixed there, immutable as they had been for centuries, in their traditional places in the château: they could be moved, be displaced; a Ploudel de Medeu, shaken for a moment out of his ancestral arrogance, could actually fear for their security. The events of May had called the bluff of old Monsieur Vladimir and his kind. His treasures were no longer inviolable. They could easily become the property of anyone. And, when the old man died, they did. It was certainly the big trunk full of beautiful and delicate objects, stored for months in their own attic, that had inspired Denis to borrow books on paintings and furniture and ceramics and start haunting antique fairs while other kids were haunting record shops. Just as it was probably those long warm scented days in Monsieur Vladimir's garden that had inspired Michel himself to his lazy sensuous appreciation of getting through life with as little effort and as little aggression as possible. Just do enough work to live, drift through beautiful places, listen to music, drink wine, chat to your neighbours, laugh and read and make love . . . And yearn hopelessly over an unattainable woman.

Nathalie was sitting at the kitchen table when he got home, in her pink gingham miniskirt with lace at the hem, though God knows, he thought, she hasn't lost *that* much weight that she can . . . She was sitting in front of a mail-order catalogue reading it as if it was a novel. She read all the catalogues straight through from cover to cover, well everyone *does*, Michel, all my friends do that, you never know what you might find. There are women, he thought coldly, who don't ever read mail-order catalogues, who probably don't even know they exist, who don't automatically get a dozen of them through the post twice a year, who just walk by them, imagine, in the newsagents the way they walk by the cheap magazines and the. There are women who don't read cheap magazines. I used to belong to a world where women don't . . . His mind slid away sideways and he was free of Nathalie, lying in the long warm scented grass with a slim warm scented woman who never read cheap magazines. And why did you strangle your wife, Monsieur Le Borgne? I strangled her, Father, because she started reading the love stories in *Nous Deux*. Bless you, my son, now say three Hail Marys . . .

He looked down at her neat curls, childishly blonde like a dandelion clock. I'm a bastard to her, she's basically only a kid isn't she, a mind like a teenager and that's what I wanted wasn't it, somebody simple and pretty and ordinary, I never wanted to marry some great intellectual, what would I have done with old Simone de Beauvoir? Yes, but Madame Bourjois left school at sixteen too, and still she . . . Forget Madame Bourjois.

"Why don't we go out someplace, Nat? Just by ourselves for a change? Don't bother making a meal, why don't we just take the van and go over to Seulbourg? Walk by the sea, buy a cooked chicken to eat on the beach, a nice bottle of wine. Just the two of us . . . "

"You crazy? What would people think? Anyway I've got to go out this evening. Going to give a hand in the hotel again, they're short-staffed. Might be very late back. Don't worry, I've left you something in the fridge. Actually," she added casually, "I might even stay overnight there, with Séverine."

"Don't be ridiculous," he laughed, "I can easily come and pick you up, you don't have to sleep in the hotel when we don't even live a kilometre away! I'll come and get you."

"Better not, I don't exactly know what time I'll finish. They're having this farewell party after work, it might go on a bit. For Gabriel. It's to say goodbye to poor Gabriel, he's been given the push did I tell you?"

"Oh well, if you're not going to be here there's no point in me staying in, then. I might as well drop over and have a few jars with the Bouchons, Rosalind's been at me to call in. "

"Rosalind, eh? Still frequenting the doctor's wife are we, and calling her by her first name! Imagine his face if I called him Pierre next time I go down with flu. Salut Pierre, Ça va ti bien? I can just see myself! You're making a right fool of yourself, Michel, running after the bourgeoisie. Oh but I forgot, Madame use to be a domestique like yourself, didn't she. I suppose you can amuse yourselves for hours chatting about the good old days when you were both licking the nobles' boots up at the château! Never thought doctors married women like that."

"You don't have to be unpleasant just because you feel guilty, Nathalie. *I* don't mind if you stay overnight with your sister, I was just trying to be helpful. I mean I've never exactly been the heavy husband. And *I've* stayed over in Denis's many a night so now it's your turn so where's the problem?"

"Well, you should mind, shouldn't you? Any normal man would at least yell at his wife if she just suddenly announced she was staying out all night."

"OK, so what do you want me to yell? I'll yell if that's what you want, I just thought we were civilised. You know, Nat, you should have married The Incredible Hulk or someone, some big brute with biceps who'd keep you chained to the leg of the bed, and beat you once a week!"

"Maybe I should. Maybe that's just where I made my mistake! You're too complicated for me, Michel, with your famous civilisation!"

But when he got to the Bouchons' he could see they had visitors, the brother and his wife just getting out of their car, carrying wine and flowers so they must be staying to dinner, Pierre on the doorstep with a whisky in his hand, social kisses and chatter and Rosalind, all pink, hastily tearing off the apron she'd forgotten and shoving it under a cushion on the hall chair. He waved, gave her a thumbs-up sign, the poor cow was going to need it with an evening of Paul and Maryvonne, *brave* types but . . .

Anyway, not much point in going home, big anti-climax, she'd be rushing round the place busy with the eyeliner and the lacquer, getting ready to go out to the hotel. He thought of Madame Bourjois with her straight pale hair above her shoulders, her cool pale face and large eyes. A thousand kilometres away, in every sense of the word.

He turned into the village street, one might as well have a drink all the same, what else can you do on your own in Plouch'en on a Saturday evening, and pushed open the heavy glass door on to the smells of cider and bodies and pastis and Gauloises. Into the familiar sweaty friendliness you could wear like a warm overcoat, like an armour to shield you from the slings and the arrows. If that's what you wanted, to be shielded from them. He was no longer quite sure that he did. Wasn't that what Denis and Lindi reproached him for, wasn't that what he reproached himself for? But give me an alternative, he thought, Jesus, folks give me an alternative! Should I go home and switch on the telly and watch the Serbs and the Croats and the Muslims and the Jews all busy tearing each other to bits, should I sit and gape at the Somalis starving, would that be a more significant way of passing a warm June evening?

He shouldered his way to the counter.

"Hé, Georges, un Ricard s'il te plait," nodded to the neighbours, shook hands with the neighbours: "Salut Didier, Joseph, René, Ça va?"

"Ça va. Et toi, ça gaze?"

The nice warm accepting clichés. He shook more hands, he smiled at more faces. Over in a corner, Gabriel the waiter from the Hôtel de la Poste was hunched over a table frowning, painstakingly picking winners for tomorrow's Tiercé, oiling himself up with pastis to face his last evening at work, wonder why they sacked him? The bottle, too many little glasses? Hands in the till? Poor sod, might as well be civil I suppose, colleague of Nat's, push my way over with the condolences, hi Gabriel mon vieux, but why's he looking so scared all of a sudden, does he owe us money or what? Looks as if he's expecting to be hit.

"Salut, Gabriel, what's this I've been hearing then?"

But why is everyone looking scared? Why have they all suddenly stopped talking, all the copains? You'd think I'd grown horns and a tail all of a sudden. Grown . . . Jesus no . . . Grown *horns*?

"I want to kill that woman! Do you realise, Maurice, that soulless pedestrian old cow actually brought me up until I started going to school? What can my mother have been thinking of? To engage a thick slut like her?"

"What should she have engaged, a nun? A doctor of philosophy? Nobs like you are always brought up by servants, aren't you? Most of them are far thicker than Madame Bouchon so what are you complaining about?"

"You're in a right mood, aren't you? Is it something I've done? Did I say something? Maurice?"

"It's not you, idiot, it's me. It's my dad again. He never even came home last night, he went out with that tart of his after dinner, he's been with her ever since. He wants to marry her, Clémence, what am I going to do, she's going to move in here and be my stepmother."

"He can't want to marry her, he's only known her a few weeks. Did he tell you he wanted to marry her?"

"He doesn't have to. She was here for dinner last night. She *cooked* the dinner. And she never stopped going on at me. She calls me Mo-Mo and Moumouche and Moumoune do you *realize*? Like a nasty sugary mummy person in a soap. My mother's only been *dead* two years. I'm going to leave home, I'm not living here if they get married. I'm going to run away to Paris."

"Yeah, well better wait till September when I go to stay

with Tante Ruby, I'll smuggle you in the back door and Uncle Gus will give you a job slicing ham or something."

"It's not funny!"

"Of course it's not funny, but it would astonish me if your father actually married her. She's ancient, she must be at least forty."

"The very first day she came to his office he went out himself and drove her round looking at these old ruins she wanted to buy. He came home that evening with this silly smile on his face and told me there was a famous artist had bought a weekend cottage nearby."

"A lady watercolourist. I wouldn't exactly call that a famous artist."

"Another thing he told me was that she was old doctor Bouchon's first wife. She was born in Plouch'en, they were childhood sweethearts. She left him because he wouldn't take her painting seriously, he wanted her to be just a doctor's wife and arrange flowers. That's what she told Papa."

"She's *Loulou*? You mean this Korrigan woman's Loulou?"

"I don't know. My father calls her Mary-Lou, it's her nom de guerre, it's what she signs the old merdes she paints. What are you so excited about?"

"But apparently old Bouchon's still mad about her! It's her your papa wants to marry?"

"He can't still be mad about her. They haven't seen each other for centuries."

"Still. Bouchon must have been talking about her to Papa, because I heard Papa saying the other evening that he wasn't a bit surprised Pierre couldn't stop going on about Loulou. He said no one in his right mind would have thrown over a lovely big sexy lady like that to marry a banal little tête de dactylo like Rosalind. And Mummy got all prim and said there was more to marriage than sex, well she would have to stand up for Rosalind, and my father gave one of his laughs, you know how he does, I was really sorry for Rosalind, the *cow* if I'd but known! Imagine, oh imagine, Maurice, if they got back together again. Think what it would do to Rosalind, she'd probably have to leave the country, even!"

"How could they get back together again? When she's not in Paris this old Mary Lou Korrigan spends every second of her life shacked up with my father in that cottage of hers. Even if she ever did think about Bouchon and why would she, I bet she's had a hundred men since him, I bet she's had a thousand the sow the revolting old tart, how could she ever even meet him?"

"Maybe we could arrange it?"

"Us arrange it? What could *we* arrange?"

"I'll think of something. Actually I've thought of something brilliant already, I've only got to work out the details. Just you wait, Maurice, nobody's going to marry your petit papa chéri unless you want them to. And just think what it's going to do to Rosalind! Listen, I thought we were meant to be going to Seulbourg this afternoon, I thought that spotty cousin of yours was coming to get us with his mates?"

"Look, I don't think we'd better go over there, Clémence, he's changed his mind, he's got something else on today, I think we're better out of it. A crowd of those thick fellows with motorbikes, I don't think we."

"But they were just going to stick up posters, I thought?"

"No they've got something else on, they're going to beat up this boy from Cyril's school. Cyril's always bullying him because he's a skinny little nerd apparently. See? It's not our sort of thing is it, Clémence? Not exactly class, is it?"

"Nah, you're right. Your big thick virile working-class cousin beating up the little ones. Virile Cyril. It's gross. I thought it was something political. Something relevant. Oh look, there's our dishy gardener staggering out of the bistro, didn't even know he drank did you, I always thought he was too Green and holy. Oh he's crying, the poor man's only crying, Maurice!"

"He's laughing, you twit, he's actually holding his sides laughing. I always said you were all crazy up at that château. Wonder what he's got to celebrate? So what shall we do instead this evening? Fancy going over to Seulbourg anyway? Go on the beach? Just the two of us?"

"Yeah, sure, OK. I don't mind. Wonder what old Michel's found to laugh at, though . . . "

When the grandparents came they brought, shamefully, the bidonville and the couscous and the mosque and the poor put-upon immigrants: Miloud was glad, finally, that he didn't have school-friends who called at the house to listen to Guns 'n Roses and talk about girls.

"You're not glad so stop pretending," Layla told him viciously, "You're eating your little heart out to be accepted by the yokels and they know that and that's why they give you a hard time. So you can leave our grandparents out of it. *My* friends don't worry if Grandpapa chews tobacco and Grandma wears a veil, they think they're quite sweet actually and if they didn't I'd soon let them know how their own grandfathers stink of pig-dung and garlic and have paunches swinging round their knees, the whole world *knows* about the French working class, the whole world sees them making clowns of themselves on telly blocking up the motorways and frightening the tourists, so why are you so *humble*, Miloud, why are you such a slave to them?"

Why indeed? His marks were good at school, the teachers liked him, but that was hardly his fault: would there be any point in pretending to be as thick as Cyril Delamotte and his crowd? Could you pretend to be that thick if you weren't? Would they have accepted him from the beginning if he'd been thick? But then, Luis hadn't been thick and yet . . .

"I don't know what you're on about," Layla said, "*I* had no efforts to make to be accepted and I'm as bright as you are, I mean you're no Einstein! Nobody makes fun of me for my good marks."

Girls were different, they had no special efforts to make. Because they were less important? Because they changed nothing, ruled nothing, had no real responsibility beyond prettiness? Because . . .

"You talk like an ayatollah!" Layla snarled, "Petit con de mullah! We're *French*. I'm a liberated French girl, with a brown skin and a cosmopolitan culture. I'm going to university and be a barrister, or a doctor. Or a tycoon if I feel like it. And when I'm rich and independent and successful my snotty little brother will still be there disgracing me, still running whining to SOS Racism because the ploucs don't accept him. Petit con de merde!"

If Mother heard her language, if Father, she wouldn't be so liberated. And sisters were supposed to help. To help you find friends. Find girls. Help you get asked to parties.

"Help you to practise your male superiority on, I suppose! Well you can practise it this afternoon can't you, sit with the men talking big while Mother and I are run off our feet filling you up with mint tea and loukoums."

"Actually I'm going out this afternoon," he said.

"Actually Cyril Delamotte and his crowd said I could meet them down the beach. He's going to let me have a go on his moto, Delamotte said. I'm going to leave now, to be gone before the old ones arrive."

"Not today you're going on no beach!" Layla snapped, "Not with our grandparents coming! Be serious, Miloud, you can't *do* that to them, it's their one big thing they have in their lives, coming down to Brittany to see us. We're their big success story."

"My name is Milo. And I don't intend to sit here one more Saturday listening to yet another monologue on the cruel colonists and the Algerian war. You say we're French? Well right, so I'm going to be French. Who cares about the rising in Sétif and the revolt in Constantine and Uncle Boujimah tortured and cousin Beni massacred? Who cares if Grandpa was shitting himself with fright when they started the reprisals in Paris? All that was over and done with thirty years ago. It's old people's talk, Layla, it's ancient history, I've had it, his blessed Guerre d'Algerie! I'm off out."

Because they had, miraculously, asked him. Oh no big deal, no big forgiveness drama, just a word slung casually at him after school as if he was anyone: "You coming down the beach tomorrow then, Milo?" Down the beach was where they revved up their motor-bikes on a Saturday afternoon, you could hear it all over Seulbourg, see them roaring black and arrogant up the Boulevard de la Mer, through the narrow folksy streets with their shops full of lace for the tourists, in and out among the neat new villas, up and down the shaded alleys between the holiday homes. Like kings, like heroes, like devils. Like the Guns. Conquering the town and the beach and the tame little hard-earned houses where adults cowered and kids longed to be out there, how often he had longed to be out there demolishing the silence and the smugness and the reminiscences! Demolishing the couscous and the mosque and the hammam and the white dazzling streets of Constantine and Sétif! Crashing and roaring through his parents' little bungalow, through their fitted kitchen with its varnished cupboards, their three-piece salon from Monsieur Meuble, their beige moquette, their flowered curtains. Smashing through their dream-come-true, their integration.

"We go up, and up, and up," he said, "That's what we think n'est ce pas? Grandpa cringing round the building sites for decades, licking boots. Brickies' boots. Foremens' boots. Landlords' boots. For *what*? Did he really imagine that was a worthwhile life for a man?"

"You know nothing, petit merde! Grandpapa may have had to act humble but that was the fault of the French, it was no sin of his. Behind it all he had dignity, he worked hard and he saved his money and he brought his family to France. He sent Father to school, let him stay on and do his baccalaureat, do you realise what it must have cost him? It was another world, it was a cold hostile world and yet he made his children succeed in it. *I* call that a worthwhile life!"

"And Father worked hard and succeeded in life, yeah sure! You know, Layla, there used to be a group called the Beatles. They were famous, they were known literally all over the world, I bet you in Timbuctoo and Patagonia and Outer Mongolia even there were little kids running around teaching all the monkeys to sing 'Yellow Submarine'!"

"Mais bien sûr! Everyone knows about the Beatles, petit con!"

"*Father* didn't. That's the point. Papa was a kid back then, in the sixties, but he never even heard of the Beatles.

Or of Johnny Halliday. Or Françoise Hardy, or Mireille Matthieu. Papa was too busy learning by heart the names and dates of all the kings of France from Clovis the First on down. Just so that he could grow up and be a little brown bookkeeper in a little grey office and build a little villa in Brittany and tell himself that he's integrated."

"Et alors, petit con? You'd have preferred us living in a council flat on the twenty-fifth floor with pools of other people's piss on every landing and Papa a trendy labourer playing his old Beatles records to make up for the awfulness of life? While we sat there waiting for the National Front skinheads to come battering down the door?"

"You understand nothing. Yeah sure you're right, Layla, you'll make a great little bourgeoise, and have a little villa of your own. You'll not get to marry a *French* barrister, though. It'll have to be a barrister whose grandfather also cringed round the building-sites and whose father never heard of the Beatles."

"T'as une frite sûr l'épaule, as the English say! If that's the way you go on at school I'm not astonished that they don't pick you for their football teams."

At school he didn't go on like that. He smiled and spoke gently and was obliging to everyone. He didn't know how to do anything else. He had not the self-confidence to do anything else. His mother spoke gently and smiled at everyone in the shops. His father too, no doubt, was gentle and obliging with his colleagues in the office. It had been like that when they lived on the council estate in Trappes, now it was like that in Brittany. Except that in Trappes there had been others like themselves. Other families to come to the flat and eat couscous and tabouleh and sweet honey cakes. Other boys whose grandfathers chewed tobacco and spat great brown spits on the pavement. Other veiled housewives to smile humbly at the blank-faced cashiers in the supermarket. He hated his parents for their obliging smiles.

The first week at school in Seulbourg he had almost made a friend. A small brown boy whose father was a Spanish architect. (And why had the teacher automatically sat the two brown boys together?) At recreation they had stayed together talking about music, listing their tapes and making plans to swop, since neither was interested in kicking a football. In class again, Luis let him try his new black-and-gold pen. It was called a Mont Blanc and he'd had it for his birthday. It was the most expensive pen in the world, he explained, it was cool to have a Mont Blanc. Miloud had not known that; at his previous school no one could have afforded an expensive pen, they wrote with just anything, felt-tips mostly and Bics. And in fact, in the classroom at Seulbourg nobody but Luis seemed to have a pen of that mark. Later, in the Technology room, when they were all working in groups, the Mont Blanc had gone missing. The teacher obliged them all to turn out their satchels and pencil-cases. Miloud had searched carefully everywhere, even his pockets in case he had absent-mindedly put the pen away. It didn't turn up and Luis got into a state, he was white and shaking. The pen had not been a birthday present, he confessed, it was not even his, he had taken it from his father's desk and brought it to school to show off. His father would half kill him; a pen like that cost the earth, it had been a present from a rich client. They had lunch and recreation; Miloud tried to console him. They went together to the Technology room and painstakingly took the place apart, searching desks and corners and cupboards. After lunch the class went to the Salle de Permanence for silent study. When Miloud arrived he found, surprisingly, Delamotte and all his gang standing round his desk looking, for the first time since he'd been there, friendly and jokey and eager to chat. It was unbelievable, all these big rough popular boys wanting to be his friend. Even in Trappes, though he had not been unpopular, he had not had many friends, he had belonged to no gang. Perhaps it was because he'd shown such concern for Luis that they'd decided to accept him, perhaps it was a beginning? The boys hung around in a friendly way while he got out his books, oh is that how you spell your name, Miloud Abdallah, what's that an American name or what, ha ha? He laughed with them, feeling warm and wanted. And then he opened his pencil-case and there was the Mont Blanc, right there on top in full view of everyone. He was amazed, incredulous; it could not be real, it could not be there, he had looked carefully in his pencil-case, he had looked several times. The pen could not possibly be there. But it was real, and it was there.

"Come here, lads!" Delamotte shouted, "Come over here everyone, venez les gars! Seems we've got a thief in the room. The Arab's a thief. The dirty little bicot only stole poor Luis' pen!"

Miloud felt that he might vomit, as if someone had thumped him hard in the stomach. Luis was staring at him with a blank face. His accusers were leaping up and down, yelling. Then the prof came in and the noise died down, though the whole class remained around his desk. What would be done to him? Would he be beaten? Expelled? Would the police be called? Reform school? "But I didn't steal it. I don't know how . . . I didn't . . . Delamotte gave it to me!" he blurted out in a panic and instantly knew that it was true. It was Delamotte who had put the pen into his pencil-case, he must have done it at lunch-time while

Miloud was away with Luis searching the Technology lab. That's why they'd all hung round his desk, pretending to be friends. Waiting. They were all in it, all Delamotte's gang. And he knew that he could never prove it. Nobody could possibly have believed him. That was two years ago, a week after they'd moved to Seulbourg. Nobody had ever tried to be friends with him again, though he didn't think they held it seriously against him. He had not been punished, it was his word against Delamotte's. People stole all the time in the lycée at Seulbourg, stole and lied; it was no big thing. Luis had always behaved politely to him, though they never spoke again about listening to each other's tapes, and soon his family moved back to Spain.

Now, surprisingly, Delamotte had as much as invited him to join his gang. Cyril Delamotte was powerful, a leader. Miloud admired him, though he did not think he could ever grow to like him as a friend: how could he, after all? Sometimes, when he woke in the night, he would see himself again, a small thin brown boy cowering bewildered at his desk while his accusers leaped and danced, and Luis looked at him with a hurt blank stare. How could you like Delamotte? But if you were in Delamotte's gang . . . Once you were allowed into his gang it meant you were accepted, you weren't an outsider any more. You weren't an Arab. You'd be just one of Cyril Delamotte's big tough crowd in leather blousons and Doc Martens, roaring up the Boulevard, smashing through the humble obliging smiles, knock knock knockin' on Heaven's door. You'd be the best. You'd be the Guns . . . You'd be *French*, and that was the important part. Finally you'd be French, in a way your gently smiling hardworking parents never could be. Never could have been, no matter how many decent little seaside villas they built for themselves.

Monsieur Balavoine picked up his empty lunch plate, held it against his face, and licked it clean with long efficient silent licks. A tribute to my cooking perhaps, his wife thought, keeping her face deliberately straight and expressionless. Years ago the habit had revolted her, in the early days of her marriage there had been protests and rows and tears and screams; she had found it almost impossible to accept his body in bed, picturing as she always had at the crucial moment the licked plate, the too-large portions of apple and orange and cheese and bread that had to be shoved into his mouth with the heel of his hand, the tiny pieces of meat that sometimes, when he spoke, flew across the table to land perhaps in her wine glass. Now she had learned silence. She could see a licked plate as merely a licked plate, (finally unimportant since the children were gone and they never had guests), not as part of some general awfulness, not as another symptom of the squalid failure her life had been since she left her village to live with him in the flat above the school. She could laugh silently about it behind a carefully straight face. A tribute to my cooking perhaps, she would comment to Doctor Bouchon on Wednesday, not a single drop of sauce wasted! It was a help in survival, this ability to laugh and detach oneself.

"That Bouan child," he said, one eye suddenly swivelling round the side of the plate, "Son of little Matthieu Bouan the plumber." He licked again. "He used no less than four foreign words in his essay this week. An outrage! Influence of television, of course. Our own glorious French tongue, the tongue of Molière and Racine." His own tongue licked and licked. "Is no longer found to be sufficiently expressive for the young people of Plouch'en! Skateboard, the boy wrote. And Walkman. And weekend, and fast-food."

"What should he have written?" she enquired mildly,

118

"Should he have said: établissment de restauration rapide? A bit heavy, non? For a ten-year-old's essay?"

"Imbécile!" he roared, "pauvre imbécile! I ought to have learned by now! It is impossible to discuss intelligently with you. You know nothing. You have learned nothing. You came out of nowhere. A fishing village among the rocks and whins! I could have married a teacher like myself and I had to choose you. A woman of no education and no background and yet she dares to comment on my teaching methods and on the French language! Poor fool, you who were unfit even to pass your baccalaureat!"

"I was never given the chance to try," she said, "How many girls were, in my day? We were brought up to be pleasing to men and to find husbands as soon as possible. Which I did," she said without expression, following the renewed progress of his tongue around the raised edge of the plate.

"But you could have left him and got a job," Doctor Bouchon said, "When you were in your twenties and thirties for example, there was plenty of work to be had, France was in full expansion. Did you never consider it?"

"What do you think?" she sighed, "Of course I considered it. I considered it all the time. I was never done picturing a nice little life for myself. Hundreds of nice little lives, in different places, without him. But I would have had to leave my children behind. He saw them as his children, you know, the fruit of his loins, they had very little to do with me. His wife gave him two children, that is the usual expression n'est ce pas? And that is how he literally saw it. I had given them, they were not mine to take away again. He would have felt that he had every right to forbid me, a runaway wife, any access to them. And I loved Magali and Jean-Marc, they were everything in the world to me."

"But the courts would certainly have given you custody . . . "

"The courts? Why should they? I had no real reason to divorce. He was a faithful husband, he did not drink or beat me or squander his pay. He saw our marriage as a success, he still does. And then it seemed to me, perhaps I was wrong, but he has always seemed to me a man of potential violence. It is only an impression, he has never done anything . . . But it seemed to me that if I left he would have made our lives impossible. I was afraid of him then, doctor, I was afraid of what he was capable of doing to me and the children."

"I'm going over to Seulbourg after lunch," Monsieur Balavoine said, "To the villa. I want to check up on those painters. I may stay the night again, one never knows what . . . "

While she washed up he went into the living-room and took his revolver from its case. Once, in the new villa, he had found traces of squatters or of tramps. An empty Coca-Cola tin, sandwich wrappings, cigarette ends. "Kids," she told him, "Just a few kids probably, having a picnic. They always do, on building sites, it's a little adventure at that age, I always used to, with my brothers."

"It is no longer a building site. It is my house. The home of my retirement. The rooms are almost habitable now, there is glass in the windows. No one has the right to picnic in my house without my permission, it is a criminal offence. I would be well within my rights if . . . " He had installed a camp-bed and a little gas stove and he spent most weekends there now, dozing off to the sound of the sea. One more year of teaching and they would be in Seulbourg for the rest of their lives. He would enjoy his retirement, would go for long walks by the shore, would roll up his trouser-legs and collect shellfish on the beach after a high tide. Meanwhile,

the empty villa had to be protected. There was no security
in Seulbourg. Gangs roamed and wrecked on Saturday
evenings while the gendarmes stayed tranquilly playing
cards in their barracks. He'd reproached them for their
nonchalance when he applied for the revolver permit and
the brigadier had laughed: "Seulbourg is hardly Chicago,
Monsieur Balavoine!" But he had been given his permit,
and he was not the only one. Many people in the village
kept guns in their houses, shotguns, revolvers. People were
increasingly worried for their own safety. He would have
liked to spend every night at the villa, watching, but the
schoolhouse had to be protected too. It was his duty, the
council expected it of him. Everywhere there was chaos
nowadays, even in a small village; old standards of decency
had been abolished, there was no security in everyday life.
There was theft and vandalism and muggings and murder.

"Nobody's ever tried to attack us yet," his wife protested,
"As that gendarme said, Plouch'en is not Chicago!"

But in Seulbourg gangs of young men rode their motor-
bikes up and down the Boulevard in front of the holiday
homes, black shapes masked and menacing, revving and
roaring and racing: an insult.

"They do it to anger us," he said, "It is their vengeance
on the decent middle class, it is their envy. For now they are
content to insult us and destroy our peace; soon they will
find courage to break in and demolish our homes and our
persons."

"They are mostly middle-class themselves, his wife said,
"Those kids with their motor-bikes. They are only having a
bit of fun is all, taking advantage of being young. Making
men of themselves for a few hours a week."

Imbécile. Pauvre imbécile de bonne femme! Pauvre

optimiste! He looked coldly at her and gave a quiet snigger. Tu te rends compte! Do you realize what the prettiest of girls can come to! If only a man could see forward in time . . .

She pictured him lying helplessly in the roadway, a team of Hell's Angels riding back and forth viciously across his broken body. She pictured him lying snoring in his camp-bed in the raw new villa that she hated, while a grinning monster with stocking mask and iron bar stood over him, waiting. She pictured him at the living-room table, cleaning that disgusting gun of his, a forgotten bullet laughing its little head off in the chamber . . .

("We all have our violent fantasies," Doctor Bouchon said, "To help us survive. If you knew some of the things I imagine, hou la la!")

"There's Arabs," he said, "There's Algerian immigrants in Seulbourg now. Nothing is safe, nothing is sacred any more, even a quiet seaside town in Brittany. My poor France has been delivered over to them lock, stock and barrel!"

"One family!"

"The thin end of the wedge," he said, "By the time we've retired there will be a ghetto, the marketplace stinking of their spices, women in veils, bidonvilles along the coastline. The dirt, the smell, the noises. We shall be allowed no tranquillity in our old age."

She hoovered the living-room carpet around him. Nothing he did or said could touch her now. She was an old woman, in some years she would be dead: Better to let life slide tranquilly towards its finish. She had chosen her destiny without sufficient thought, she had suffered, but it was too late now for regrets or rebellion. The children, in spite of him, had grown up to lead safe happy lives; he could no longer bully them as he had done in the past. Magali was forbidden the house but even without the interdiction she would not have wanted to see him again: the life Magali had chosen was a complete negation of all his values. She herself would survive as long as she had to.

"I've become a tough old skin, doctor," she said, "Over the years. I've made an art of surviving. But I cannot forget that without him my children might have done something great with their lives . . . If he had not killed their imaginations, their spontaneity. My son, after all, is only a village electrician. My daughter . . . My poor Magali . . . "

"Your Magali seems to be well and happy," Doctor Bouchon said gently, "From what you have told me, she is living exactly the life she chose for herself. What else is happiness?"

She would phone Magali after he left for Seulbourg, and Magali might be able to come to Jean-Marc's for the weekend, with the little Sebastian. If she didn't insist on bringing Claude as well. Increasingly now, Magali insisted that they be all three of them received openly as a family. And was she not right to insist? They were a family, like any other. If only Jean-Marc and his wife could learn to accept Claude as an in-law. Was it too much to ask for, in this day and age? Was she herself, uneducated imbécile from an obscure fishing village, the only really enlightened person in Plouch'en? The only one who could accept her daughter's warm happy love affair?

Rosalind knew it would be a catastrophe to joke about it but she couldn't stop herself. "It's like," she blurted between giggles, "It's just like trying to squeeze toothpaste back in the tube isn't it, Pierre?"

Pierre fell back on to the bed, furious. "How dare you, you bitch!" he roared, "Garce! Salope! How dare you cut my effect like that? How dare you bring down the curtain on my . . . "

"Oh come on, Pierre, you're not on a stage, you're not performing to an *audience*. Cut your effect! We're both supposed to be enjoying this, it's meant to be fun. You know: Sex as Fun. Sex as Adult Amusement. Didn't they teach you that at medical school, then?"

"You're a crass insensitive English bitch. You deliberately set out to destroy my effect. You want to demolish me, don't you, that's what you're after n'est ce pas, you frigid feminist cow!"

"Your effect? Pardon me, mon vieux, but your effect was well and truly cut already. That's why I mentioned toothpaste, remember? Christ, if we can't even laugh about this. If we have to turn every little incident into a Greek tragedy. Old Loulou popped into your head again, didn't she? That's all that happened, come on admit it, you were lying there on top of me just yearning for Marie-Louise weren't you?"

"If you must know, Rosalind, if you *must* poke your nose into the privacy of my mind, I suddenly recalled that today is exactly the fifth anniversary of my divorce. It simply entered my head that is all, and if you had even a minimal idea of the techniques of lovemaking you would have obliged me to forget it again instantly. Instead of which."

"Instead of which the ghost of Loulou's opulent backside rose up before you in all its glory and everything else fell, as usual. It's not dramatic, Pierre. It's not some big significant failure of your manhood. All the same, it's been happening most of the time since I went off the pill so . . . "

"So your technique is deficient! You are unable to keep me aroused. You have never, I may add, approached your marital duties with sufficient seriousness. Ma pauvre femme, you are hopelessly irreverent, you laugh like an

English sitcom all through the act. Where other women have erogenous zones, my poor wife has tickles, how do you expect me to accomplish lovemaking?"

"Thousands managed. I was just going to say, isn't all this maybe significant? Is it not maybe a symptom of, oh I don't know, I'm not the psychologist here, but it looks like you don't maybe want to commit yourself that far with me? I mean have kids together. I mean I think you might have had the idea that I was OK as just some sort of temporary painkiller after Loulou let you down but not . . . "

"Is this a chapter out of a feminist book? Or is it a rehearsal of some merde you're trying to write for one of your magazines?"

"Calm down Pierre, and stop blustering. When I first mentioned wanting a baby you immediately rushed out and got me these two dirty great dogs to look after. When I said they weren't a real substitute and told you I'd gone off the pill you instantly stopped being able to make love at all and started drooling about Loulou all the time. So do you not think it's time we maybe considered splitting up? You know where the dear departed lives after all so what's to stop you getting on the phone one weekend and. Well people *do* all the time, with their exes, I mean if you're yearning all that much . . . "

"You bitch, you bitch, you've been leading up to this haven't you? Three years married and Madame has had enough. Madame wants to go whoring off around the world again! Don't you dare leave me, don't you dare walk out on me. Two divorces in five years, what do you think it would do to my reputation? It would ruin me that is all, I would become the laughing-stock of France, I would lose all my patients. Two sets of horns in five years, don't you dare do it, Rosalind!"

"I want children, Pierre. I can't go on like this, that's why I got married after all, to have a family. Ten years looking after other people's kids, I mean I'm over thirty, if I wait any longer I'll be."

"We'll have children, Rosie, just give me time would you. I don't even think of her all that often nowadays, just when things remind me . . . Don't leave me Rosie, please. Promise?"

"All right, all right, relax. I'm not about to leap out of bed and on to a plane. Maybe when we get to Ireland for this holiday it will be different," she added soothingly, "I mean there won't be much over there to remind you of sexy Parisiennes, I shouldn't think."

Though she'd thought that when they went to her mother at Easter. Surely, Rosalind had imagined, in a remote Cotswold village reminders of this sexy first wife, this, this *character* from a Feydeau farce, would be few and far between. She'd thought it last summer as well, in the Corsican mountains, where the only other women besides herself had been heavily shawled peasants with holy put-upon faces. But Loulou's ghost was pretty resilient. She surged up as incongruously among the black-clad bulky old grannies as she did months later amidst the chirpy liberated housewives of Gloucestershire. Pierre kept insisting that he was full of affection and desire for Rosalind, desperate to make this marriage work, but he seemed to be helpless. Between the desire and the reality, between the motion and the act fell, always nowadays, this shadow that Rosalind had long since identified as the very substantial phantom of big sexy lost Marie-Louise. And now the bitch, as if by some disgusting frog telepathy, had only bought a cottage two miles away . . . Should I leave, she wondered, should I just walk out and let them get on with it?

126

"If you'd be more co-operative, Rosie," he coaxed, "If only you'd . . . "

"No way. Once again, Pierre, I have no intention whatever of sitting down in front of a pile of dirty books."

"Manuals of sexual instruction, Rosalind!"

"Dirty sex manuals then, and learning off a whole range of techniques to help you forget your first wife, for God's sake! You've got a bloody nerve, Pierre. I mean if I sleep with someone it has to be because I fancy him or because I'm feeling friendly about him, it's got to be *spontaneous*. Christ, imagine learning off all this list of mechanical tricks like some, some fucking *juggler*!

"If you were French, Rosalind, you would know by instinct how to please a man. These . . . tricks . . . as you so coarsely call them, would come naturally to you. You would make it your whole vocation in life to satisfy my sexuality. Why else does a man marry?"

"Yeah well I'm English aren't I, you thick bastard, so I'm getting up now to make myself a nice cuppa tea, I've had quite enough of this discussion thanks. The old cliché, right? Frigid Englishwoman hugging the teapot instead of performing all these acrobatics with her master's drooping ego! A bloody virtuoso no doubt your old Loulou was, I can just see her falling on her knees begging to get in a bit of practice every time the postman came up the path. Do you want a cup?"

"No, I do *not* want a cup. And there's no necessity for these unpleasant fits of hysteria, Rosalind. *I* don't scream insults at *you* do I, even though I am the one who has been let down. *I* am the one who will lie awake all night in frustration while my insensitive wife calmly drinks tea. No need to shout like that, Rosalind! If you are suffering from premenstrual tension, ma pauvre fille, go and help yourself to a tranquilliser from the surgery and stop screaming at me like a virago."

Rosalind, trembling, went down to the kitchen and brewed herself up a pot of strong tea. She sloshed cognac into the cup and drank it at the kitchen table, with a pile of old gardening magazines at her elbow, *Rustica* and *L'Ami des Jardins* and *Le Jardin Biologique*. She'd begun keeping a stock of them in the table drawer for such occasions. Soon she stopped trembling and poured out a second cup, leafing through the magazines and contentedly making plans for the autumn. Next time she saw Michel Le Borgne she would ask him for some cuttings from the lovely old rosebushes he'd rescued from the château. Lately she was beginning to feel that wild flowers on their own were not quite enough . . . That gardening wasn't enough. Maybe I should get a job, any old job, use up all that energy, work off my frustrations. Dead right I've got frustrations. Did other marriages have these problems, she wondered? Or is it his age? He's forty-two after all . . . Don't be a nit, that guy in Brussels a few years back, that Dane, he was well over fifty and he. Maybe I shouldn't have laughed at Pierre, shouldn't have got that fit of the giggles, they're not really like us, fellas, they never see the funny side, they've always got their little dignities to consider . . . Anyhow not to worry mate, it'll all work out, no point in sitting up half the night brooding is there, he hasn't the slightest intention of going back to old Loulou, people don't, do they, you never hear of men going back to their. Liz Taylor yeah but that was. Bet he'll feel daft in the morning, bet he'll feel a right sausage . . .

She rinsed out the cup and teapot and went calmly back upstairs. Pierre was spread out, snoring, over most of the bed. He'd had a few too much to drink at dinner that was all, well so had she been leaning on the old vin rouge a bit and no wonder what with Maryvonne and Paul, no joke the famille française! Especially when you have to ask them home and feed them. Tomorrow he would be as hearty as ever, the row forgotten. In the daytime he was easy to live with, breezy and simple and full of big brash laughs. Uncomplicated as anything, when the little worm wasn't having trouble wriggling. And a hell of a lot easier, after all, than nannying other people's spoiled kids.

She manoeuvred a small quiet place for herself on the edge of his noisy sleep and curled up contentedly, planning out her next year's flower garden as she drifted into dreams.

"I know it's your life, Nathalie, I know this is your choice but why do it like that? The whole village knows about it, the whole village is talking. My old dad knows about it even, he was up here last night saying I ought to take this Gabriel fellow apart and then sling you and your belongings out on the road. I mean just turning up like this on a Monday morning after . . . "

"Why don't you then? Why don't you go for Gabriel? It's what any man would do. You're scared, aren't you? Oh yes I heard about you in the bistro Saturday evening, any other man would have knocked Gabriel down but not our Michel, our Michel just walks out like a coward, makes a laughing-stock of me!"

"There's such a thing as being civilised, I'm not some big brute that thinks he owns you body and soul. I thought we were more evolved than that, Nathalie."

"Evolved, is that what you call it? I can think of better names and so can everyone in the village. Other fellows go to university and they get educated and they come out and they get a good job from it and a nice car and they put a roof over their wife's head, but not Michel Le Borgne. All Michel gets out of it is, he learns to be evolved. What did you marry me for if you're so evolved you don't give a shit when I stay out two nights shacked up with someone else? I mean go on, what did you marry me for, I'd be interested to know!"

"I thought you were different. I thought you were simpler and kinder. I suppose I just thought you were somebody else when we used to go out walking in the woods and all . . . "

"Yeah. Thought I was your poor mother who'd bring up your kids for you in a tied cottage. Or some sort of schoolmarm who'd be all happy sitting in every evening listening to old people's music with you. I'm young, Michel, and I'm good-looking and I like nice clothes and going out places. I like a good time, I like a bit of a laugh, I want a man that's got a bit of life in him, I . . . "

"So you've found him and that's great. I'm happy for you. I mean that, Nathalie. But you don't have to sleep with him in the Hôtel de la Poste, like some tart. Tarts bring their customers there, you know, to the Hôtel de la Poste."

"Where do you suggest I sleep with him then? In his parents' place, sharing a room with his kid brother? We can't exactly afford to go to Paris and stay in the Ritz, you know!"

"You can bring him here if you like, it would be decenter, more discreet. I don't care. I can always go camping in the woods while I decide what I'm going to do with myself. Bring him here anyway till you find some place. Honestly I don't mind, I'm quite happy about it."

"You don't *mind*? What are you anyway, Michel, you don't even mind when your wife tells you she's going off with somebody else? You don't even pretend it bothers you? You ask him home to meet the family!"

"It doesn't bother me, Nat! Doesn't bother me at all. I couldn't care less what you do, it's been over for ages, hasn't it, so let's not make some big drama, let's not put on an act to each other, we don't have to. Only whatever you do it's maybe not such a great idea to go doing it in the Hôtel de la Poste in front of all the neighbours. So I'll move out whenever you like. I used to camp in the woods all the time when I was a kid, I'm quite looking forward to it actually. Come on, Nat, this is the nineteen-nineties, it's no big tragedy, people are allowed to do what they want. People are allowed to choose their lives nowadays, even in Plouch'en!"

"Evolved, he calls it. I know one thing, the village is going to be doubled up when it hears about this. It may be the nineteen-nineties while you're watching American soaps on telly, Michel, but you can take it from me Plouch'en has a different calendar. Still! Quite convenient for me, your old evolution n'est ce pas!"

131

Part Three

❧

Rosalind lived with her tall broad husband and her tall narrow dogs in their rented farmhouse at the end of the avenue. It was one of the five farms belonging to the château; Hervé Le Moal's was the only one where crops were still grown and animals reared; three others had become gîtes ruraux, and were let to foreign visitors every summer. Pierre, who was making a good living, had offered many times to buy the home of his childhood from Jean-Hubert, and at a very good price, but Jean-Hubert like his ancestors before him refused to sell a square centimetre of the patrimony that had been accumulating since the first Ploudel de Medeu grabbed all the other farmers' land to add to his own in the chaos of the Revolution, and that he hoped would accumulate even more when Clémence and Henri got married. (Where now, Hélène often wondered, was the bearded moody young man who sat at a bare wooden table in the Akhenaton café eating natural yoghurt and telling her how far-out it was going to be when the pair of them were wandering round in holy poverty from one crushing patch of Eastern sunshine to another, like Brahmins holding their begging-bowls? The timid young exile who'd begun hastily patching her broken heart together again as she sat listening to him seemed, on the contrary, to be increasingly present these days.)

So Pierre continued to pay rent, as generations of his ancestors had done before him. It is true that his father was a tenant farmer and his mother Uncle Vladimir's cook, but that was over twenty years ago and Hélène supposed that only people like Tante Ruby and the Comte Joffroy du Bois Fleuri would see it as something to blush for. The village of Plouch'en seemed to have evolved at an alarming rate even since they'd first come there and its inhabitants, far from being ashamed of their peasant beginnings, were aggressively proud of having risen from the cow-claps of their dead past (as Jean-Hubert put it) to higher things.

The Bouchons' house was full of books and dried flowers and dust, and was surrounded by herbaceous borders of buttercup and foxglove. Rosalind complained that she lived in a state of undeclared war with Hervé Le Moal who, every spring, prowled round the hedgerows wearing a spraying-hose of weedkiller like some great aggressive tool to rape the environment with. Every year he attacked the backs of her elder bushes with glyphosate (which he was legally entitled to do as they abutted on to his fields) but in doing so he usually allowed the deadly hose to snake casually through the branches and shower mullein and meadowsweet, buttercup and poppy. The elder bushes fought back but the meadowsweet over the years had taken heavy losses. Soon it was extinct around Plouch'en, except for a few diminished patches in l'Anglaise's eccentric garden.

Rosalind was not at home on Wednesday morning when Hélène called in on her way to welcome the English visitors who were renting the last of the gîtes. Pierre said she'd find her at the library. Hélène thanked him and tried to leave quickly, before he had time to become flippantly professional about Christopher Milton. Now, in the sober light of day, she regretted her confidences of Monday evening: it had not, surely, been necessary to tell him all that? To *wallow*, like one of his depressed patients? And, to judge from his joking allusions as he'd shown her out of the surgery, he'd taken the whole thing far too lightly. The despair, the sense of loss which, she realized now, had always been with her even in the happiest days of her marriage were apparently nothing more to Pierre than symptoms of her quite natural foreign refusal to face up to the realities of French sexuality. A way of escaping back into your Puritan childhood, he'd said her longings were. The very fact, he said, that this man is an Ulster Protestant is *most* significant: the famous bowler-hatted righteousness, the denial of the pleasure principle. Well what else could he be, Hélène had retorted, in Belfast it was either that or an Ulster Catholic which is even worse, I mean I wasn't meeting many gorgeous Latin lovers when I was seventeen. Pierre had ignored that. Rosalind's just the same, he swept on cheerfully, only with her it comes out in wild flower borders. My poor wife doesn't go round meeting exotic old lovers, not as far as I know, but mention sex to her and she instantly starts getting lyrical about couch grass lawns or whatever. Nice for me, he'd said, because as long as she gets a buzz out of her little obsessions *I* don't risk getting cuckolded do I?

"So how is *your* secret garden today?" he asked her as she was examining Rosalind's latest acquisition, the admittedly rather pretty clump of Artemisia vulgaris she'd planted where any ordinary person would have put a climbing rose.

Hélène was suddenly furious at hearing her tragic tale of

love and loss and childhood traumas so flippantly reduced to the level of a piece of common mugwort.

"I'd love to know how *you* escape the realities of French sexuality!" she snapped, "I mean setting yourself up as an amateur psychiatrist you must have to wade through it all day just to earn your crust."

"But how foolish you are, ma pauvre Hélène," he said pityingly, "I am a *Man*, voyons! C'est moi la sexualité française!"

She looked at him, startled, pondering the thin line that divides perfect mental health from perfect crassness. She decided not to comment however. Hélène had a horror of resembling one of those strident women who make a vocation of cutting men down to size. Rosalind would have retorted, probably did many a time. She smiled sweetly and deferentially, which was what Pierre, French sexuality in person, expected of women and got from all of them except his wife, and set off down the road towards the gîte.

A whole procession of English cars met her as she walked, coming from the eight o'clock ferry at St Malo. Most of them were on their way to the pretty tourist towns of Seulbourg, Plouchmad and Plancoet, only a few were bound for Plouch'en itself. Drivers and passengers wore the expressions of near-orgasm she'd become accustomed to after years of letting houses to English holidaymakers. Gazing ecstatically out of the car windows, they were allowing their souls to be caressed and ravished and penetrated by the luxurious Frenchness of it all – the little slated houses with their neat marigold gardens, the crumbling grey farm buildings, château spires above the chestnut trees, the pots of mauve and scarlet geraniums plastered thick on every cottage wall, the pungent scent drifting on the morning air from Hervé Le Moal's pigsties. La belle France, quoi!

Hélène wished she was capable of seeing it all with a tourist's delighted eyes. Never having known France other than from under the wing of Jean-Hubert and his family, she'd been absorbed into it from the start without the thrills, without the bliss of discovery – a dull old in-law rather than a tourist or an ex-pat.

One of the cars, a little red Fiat, turned in on the lane ahead of her, and by the time she'd reached the farmhouse swinging her bunch of keys there they were, standing about in the yard, looking exactly as she'd been hoping they would. An amiable, rather chubby, couple in their mid-thirties, the man in a maroon leather jacket and jeans, the woman in a bright blue track suit, and a small boy and girl in baggy T-shirts and shorts. The back of the Fiat was stuck all over with baby seals and man-eating tigers and endangered elephants and the Brooke Hospital for Sick Donkeys in Cairo.

Hélène greeted them happily, knowing in advance that this lot would be courteous and friendly and easy to please.

"Isn't it super here!" they exclaimed, "Isn't it just like Cornwall! Bet you're Irish aren't you, with that nice soft accent, what part are you from?"

When she said Belfast their smiles never wavered, they expressed neither anger nor commiseration nor mourning for a dead soldier friend.

"Matthew! Kate!" they called, "Don't be so rude, come here and be introduced to our landlady."

But Matthew and Kate had discovered a squirrel – or was it a rabbit, or a serpent – rustling busily through the undergrowth, and their parents shrugged indulgently and followed Hélène into the house. They exclaimed again over the high granite chimney piece, the massive beams supporting the ceiling, the immense feather beds and carved wardrobes in every tiny room.

"Yes, original farm furniture," Hélène said, "The family who lived here moved out to a housing development and built themselves a modern bungalow full of formica. Don't they all! They were our tenant farmers, well my uncle-in-law's tenants, and we got all this lovely rustic furniture for next to nothing, just one step ahead of the antique dealers."

The English couple exclaimed again, at the folly of people who could leave all this for a modern bungalow. "Though again, think of it in winter," the wife shuddered, "But I must say it's super for a holiday, the ideal place for three weeks away from it all."

Hélène told them where to find the shops and post office. "We've Germans at the moment, and a French couple," she said, "Though there are some more English in those little cottages just behind you. Those were the farm labourers' cottages, tiny compared to this, not really suitable for children . . . " She had an instant picture of herself growing up warm and happy and loved, in Patrick's cottage, far tinier than any of these. "I expect you'll all get to know one another before long," she smiled. She knew they wouldn't. The last thing any of them wanted was to make friends with people from home. Otherwise they'd have gone to the Costa del Sol, wouldn't they?

She occasionally saw the other two English couples drifting amiably around the shops, smiling at everyone, buying dried sausage and camembert and oceans of supermarket rosé. This group would be the same. She'd never been to England herself, but over the years she had built up an identikit picture in her mind of the kind of English people who would rent the cottages and farmhouses; they were interchangeable, they all exactly resembled this gentle chatty family. For three weeks they'd picnic on bread and wine and sausage and paté on a trestle table in the old farmyard with its climbing roses, they'd lie in the sun and sightsee and take photos, they'd do no housework whatever. When they left, the place would be a tip by French standards. Hélène and Madame Le Moal would spend a whole day with brooms and mops and dusters, getting it ready for the next lot, Madame Le Moal raising her eyes to heaven and muttering: "Eh ben dites donc madame, ces feministes anglaises! What sluts!"

Sluts or not, Hélène infinitely preferred them to the unsmiling Parisians in the gîte over the lane, who'd be sure to leave the house spotless when they went – the woman indeed seemed to have come to Brittany for no other purpose, if one judged by her endless demands for extra floorcloths, Ajax, lavatory brushes, Harpic, clean dish-cloths and Windolene. *They* hadn't commented on Hélène's accent or asked where she came from, they'd shown no interest in her at all beyond a sort of blank-faced assertiveness when they saw the house she herself lived in. "Robespierre rides again," Clémence commented. The day they left, Madame Le Moal would be all smiles: "Impeccable!" she'd exclaim, "Now that's what I call nice people!" And Hélène would consult her bookings list and smile with relief that all the next batch were English.

Sometimes, on a Tuesday, when Jean-Hubert made his weekly visit to Rennes and brought back the English Sunday papers, Hélène would realise that this identikit vision of hers bore little relation to the reality of life in Britain: logically the next lot of visitors ought to be football hooligans, rapists, sex-killers, con men, paedophiles, drug dealers, bomb-makers, or just an average crowd of big-bellied lager drinkers who'd not only not pay their rent but smash up the cottage and probably Plouch'en as well. It never happened. Time after time she turned up at the gîtes in welcome and trepidation to hand over the keys and was met by yet another smiling mum in a velours track suit, another vaguely amiable husband in a worn jacket, a couple of nice Peter-and-Jane children who within seconds had discovered, and were miraculously cuddling, two of the snarling half-mad farm cats one occasionally saw stalking their prey around Le Moal's fields. She would sigh in contented relief, her husband and son would sigh in exasperation. Henri wanted glamour, adventure, international terrorists. Jean-Hubert longed for sexy foreign women with submissive eyes and pulpily promising mouths . . . And all either of them got were carbon copies of Rosalind Bouchon.

Looking at the very ordinary family cars driving from the ferry, Hélène recognised that little Plouch'en with its smelly farms and its windy inaccessible beach was not likely to attract either fabulous crime or jet set glamour. Or for that matter, she decided sadly, mysterious intellectual Ulstermen like Christopher Milton.

Making her way back down the leafy July lane, she hugged to herself the idea of Belfast in September. A whole summer to wait and then . . . I'm going back home, she thought, back to my youth, I'm going to look for Christopher Milton. The words filled her, possessed her, like the lyrics of a lovely romantic song, as she walked down the lane and into the village's main street.

"I'm going to see Anny and Patrick again!" The words possessed her at the start of every school holidays, transfiguring with joy the few uneasy duty days she had to live through with Them first, with the woman and Gerald. With Mother and Gerald.

The Falls Road house had never been the mansion she took it for that first evening. "And the drawing-room wasn't a drawing-room," she'd told Pierre on Monday, "It was a good front parlour, with a few sticks of mahogany furniture that must have dated back to Gerald's grandparents. Oh and the velvet box of cutlery, now you're never going to believe this, that cutlery was a wedding present to my mother. From Anny and Patrick. Bought out of what she paid them for my keep, I suppose. Gerald's famous study was squeezed in between the parlour and the kitchen, must have been a dining-room once. There were three bedrooms upstairs, and an attic. Oh it wasn't a bad house by any means, it wasn't a slum. But it was no mansion. I suppose I used to read too many books, I used to have a habit of illuminating everything. "

"You illuminated Christopher Milton?"

"No, Christopher was reality. Christopher was exactly what I thought he was, he was what I aspired to. It was me that was all wrong . . . "

"How unlike you, Hélène, to confess yourself in this way! But tell me, why am I honoured with your confidences? Is it to Doctor Bouchon that you are speaking of these things? Or are you merely chatting idly to the husband of your friend?"

"I'm speaking to someone that I think's in the same boat as myself, Pierre. Let's not be hypocritical, I know your first wife has bought a cottage nearby, I know you've been running to her exhibitions in that gallery place. Rosalind told me you were still . . . "

"So? I was married to Loulou for over ten years. We did not part as enemies, it is natural that I go to look at her pictures, voyons! And actually she was not in the gallery the times that I went. It is true that I was most unhappy when she decided to leave me, but that was some years ago. I do not exactly know what I feel about her now. I am certainly not pining for the lady, I am perfectly content with my little English Rose."

"Maybe your little English rose isn't so content, though. She swears you are pining."

"Rosalind is unhappy because she sees the years passing. She is over thirty and she longs for a family. I do not. I have never wanted children, even in my youth when I was married to Loulou. I believe that it would be an act of unwarranted egoism to reproduce myself in this world that we live in. Rosalind is not a complicated soul, naturally she sees the situation in woman's magazine terms. She persuades herself that I refuse to give her children because I still love my first wife. Brutally simple, as always, our dear Rosalind. But how does my private life concern you, Hélène? What connection can it have with your little crise de nostalgie?"

"Forgive me. None at all, I suppose. Only I thought you might understand better since you yourself . . . "

"I understand that since this apparition of Saturday you are in a mood to reflect on the realities of your life. On the shortcomings of your marriage. It is the business of apparitions, after all, to make their public more reflective and more spiritual. At least for a time. Lourdes, Fatima, Knock . . . they induced a temporary little spirit of gentle self-awareness in their respective nations . . . Medjudgorje, unfortunately, does not seem to have been so efficient in this respect, but then of course the Vatican never."

"God you're a right old cynic, Pierre, you have to laugh at everything! I can't imagine why half the village comes to you with their problems!"

141

"My patients are generally too self-absorbed to even notice my cynicism. Too busy listening to themselves weep. I'm glad it was not a mansion, though. It would have been sheer carelessness, Hélène, to have allowed yourself to be exiled in a hostile château twice in your relatively short life."

"No, it certainly wasn't a mansion. Not poor Gerald's house."

And the string of precious pearls had turned out to be only a chain store necklace, worn to parish dances by a nice young middle-class widow with a tragedy in her past who still dolled herself up and went out hunting for a nice middle-class husband. All she found was Gerald O'Neill, a shy widower in his fifties with grown-up children in America, who taught Latin and Irish in a boys' school in the city. Though maybe there had been younger, more inspiring, men before him who'd backed off hastily when they heard about the grotesquely-dead husband and the fatherless child in the country? Her mother never mentioned it.

She never mentioned anything till Eileen was twelve, about to set out for boarding-school. They'd decided to send her to Mrs O'Neill's own old school in the country rather than St Dominic's just down the road, because her friend Mitzi was there and also it wasn't too far from Anny and Patrick's house. The old couple could come to visit her on Sundays. Patrick did call once wearing, for some reason, not his Sunday suit, but his ordinary working clothes, and the nun in charge made Eileen receive him outside the day-girl's entrance instead of inviting him into the boarders' parlour like all the other visitors. Neither he nor Anny ever attempted to come again and Eileen, for the rest of their lives, was forced to carry an obscure guilt for the insult the old man had so inexplicably brought on himself.

"Would you come in here a minute, Eileen dear," the woman said on that last evening at home, leading her into the brown room that was not a drawing-room but an ordinary Upper Falls parlour with heavy old-fashioned furniture. "There's something important I have to tell you."

"If it's the curse I know all about it already," Eileen snapped, distrusting the brown room and its disclosures. That's where she'd been told the first evening that she was never going to live at home again. That's where she'd been told about Santa Claus the following Christmas in the woman's hateful assertive Belfast voice: "But good heavens! A big girl like you, Eileen, I'm surprised you didn't guess it all for yourself!"

And finally ("No it's not about periods," the woman muttered, turning bright red) that's where she was told, like some dramatic disclosure out of *Tales From Shakespeare*, that her father had not died the peaceful natural death she'd always imagined when she was praying for his soul. "But didn't it ever occur to you, Eileen? Did you never even wonder about it? Had you no curiosity at all about your own father's death?"

"People do die," she muttered, "It was no big thing to start wondering about."

"They don't usually die in their beds at the ripe old age of twenty-six!" her mother snapped, "that's what you should have wondered about."

How could she have wondered, any more than she could have wondered about Santa Claus? There were things far too big to come into one's doubting. Life had begun with Anny and Patrick and the warm nest of a cottage between the meadow and the hagard, it had been solidly there, there had been nothing to wonder about. How could it have entered her head that a father whom she barely remembered might have died lying up stocious in a van that was carrying a bomb?

"Like Sean South of Garryowen?" Eileen asked, shaken, recalling a crowded dinner table and the Whistling Gipsy, and Anny banging the big brown teapot down on the blue oilcloth.

"*Not* like Sean South! Not a bit like Sean South, the fellow was a drunken wastrel, he was on the bottle since he was sixteen, I never should have married him, they all warned me, I should never have had anything to do with him. No, he saw the van parked outside the public house at closing time and he must have crawled into it for a bit of a kip and a lift home the way he often did before. He was banned from driving of course. It belonged to a crony of his, Johnny Kerr another right hero, they often went on the booze together. Brian mustn't have realized that . . . Whether he touched the thing or not, it went off anyhow. Kerr was within in the pub, couldn't even drive a couple of miles to blow up a customs hut without filling his fat kag first. That's your Sean South!"

Life was crumbling apart bit by bit in the ugly brown sitting-room. A drunkard and a wastrel, ignominiously dead. That bright laughing father, singing in a Christmas hallway . . . What would they disclose to her next? She had no idea what might be in store for her, and never felt safe from her mother's beckoning finger till she escaped at sixteen to the little haven of a room beside the university and to her job in the Lilac Room café, where nothing too difficult was ever expected of her.

Years later, half-joking, she told Jean-Hubert she'd stopped believing in God at the age of twelve simply to forestall being called to the brown room one day and flatly, shatteringly, told that He'd never, after all, existed. ("But good heavens Eileen, all that nonsense about miracles! Did you never even wonder? And rising from the *dead*, yet! A big girl like you!")

"And did Gerald ever know my father?" she asked, hoping that Gerald would be able, somehow, to soften this news, as he managed to soften so many things in her life.

"Well of course he didn't, how could Gerald have known your father, he's from a different background altogether. Gerald is a kind good-living man who agreed before we were married that he'd take you in and make a good home for you. It's not easy for him, Eileen, at his age when he could have expected a bit of peace and quiet in his life instead of. You owe him a huge debt of gratitude, we both do, it's not every man would have taken on with the pair of us!"

The Falls Road house was Gerald's house; it had been his parents' home and his grandparents'. There had been teachers, nuns, and priests in his family for generations, as there had been in her mother's. The house was semi-detached and had a stiff little garden in front, too small, Gerald often regretted, to put a swing in. He taught her to play Scrabble instead, it would give her a decent vocabulary, and he could correct her pronunciation as they went along.

Their neighbours were elderly Catholic doctors and civil servants and teachers, the odd solicitor. It was considered a nice area, that part of the Falls Road, but younger professional people moved out to more fashionable suburbs as soon as they could afford to, so there were few children of Eileen's age.

Gerald and her mother moved out too, later on, but that was because with the troubles the whole of the Falls area had gone completely downhill. By then Eileen was in Amsterdam. The summer she knew Christopher Milton her family still lived on the Falls Road. That was where he came to call for her one Sunday afternoon, and came back oddly enough the very next evening to see her mother and Gerald, though he must have known she was back at work in the café and wouldn't be there. He'd stayed for hours apparently, talking, taking an extraordinary interest in everything about them. An inquisitive sort of a man, Gerald said, though tactful with it, you'd hardly even notice you were telling him all your sins and your sorrows! A journalist of course . . . And a non-Catholic, her mother added suspiciously, where did you fall in with him, Eileen?

"But you mustn't tell anyone," her mother said, "Don't ever let on about it at school. The way your father died. We'll keep it a wee secret between the three of us, won't we?"

"Between the five of us," Eileen said coldly, "Anny and Patrick knew all along, didn't they?"

"They couldn't have told you. How could they have told you, Eileen, it would only have unsettled you, you had enough to put up with. When I hadn't even a home to take you to."

"You could have left me with them," she said bleakly, "When I was happy with them the most of my life. They could have brought me up and you could have just kept on coming to see me at Christmas and that."

"Brought you up! Brought you up to be fit to scrub floors or be a waitress in some café. Anny was a servant girl in her day, Patrick labours a few acres of land. People like that couldn't prepare you for the life you have to lead. In a few years time you'll be going off to the training college like me. Or maybe to university. Wouldn't you like to be a teacher, Eileen? Or a doctor, even? Wouldn't you like to go to Queen's, wouldn't it be great?"

Eileen shrugged, and hid herself carefully away behind her straight unsmiling face.

The woman lost her temper: "Have you no gratitude,

Eileen? Have you no feelings at all? What sort of a daughter are you? I was left on my own at twenty-one years of age with no one to depend on, I had to fight my corner every day for years to be able to do the best for you and you can't even . . . "

Gerald must have heard her shouting through the thin wall because he came in from his study, tall and grey and soothing: "Now now Margaret, of course the child's grateful. Of course she loves the pair of us, why wouldn't she? It was a bit of a shock to her that's all, it was a hard thing to hear, she hasn't right taken it in yet. Isn't that so, Eileen?"

Eileen agreed that that was so, and Gerald suggested they kneel and say a decade of the Rosary to ask for a blessing on all their futures. Eileen went off to boarding-school next day, feeling as bereft as she'd been the day Anny settled her in the front seat of the bus, and her mother dressed all in black had waved and waved from the square, and she'd gone away forever from the red-tiled kitchen and her father's songs and the walled garden with the chestnut trees and Anny hanging out clothes among the scented white roses.

"I'm not really her daughter, you know", she told Mitzi, "Mrs O'Neill can't have children, they adopted me when I was ten. Gerald made her adopt me because they saw me when they were on holidays in the country and he asked who was that beautiful sad child who never smiled and they told him I was a poor orphan with no mother or father. Gerald's a kind good-living man and he said he'd give me a good home and send me to the university and everything. My real parents were killed by a bomb. We used to live in a lovely big house and we had a maid called Anny. She wanted to adopt me too only they wouldn't let her, an old maid of nearly sixty, she was too old for it. It was in all the papers about my parents, they were famous, only I won't tell you their names so I won't."

"You're a liar, Eileen O'Neill, you're a friggin' wee liar, do you think I came up the Lagan on a banana boat or what?" Mitzi had been a boarder since she was six, because her parents were in and out of jail for years. At one time, Mitzi said, her father and mother and grandparents and aunts and uncles were scattered through seventeen prisons all over Britain. Mitzi was a heroine in the school. Before the Easter holidays she went round selling Easter Lily badges, and her leather pencil case with the picture of an Irish wolfhound burned into it had been made by her daddy in the prison workshop the last time he was in Crumlin Road. "I heard all about that bomb you're on about," she sniffed, "It's not something to go bragging about!"

Mitzi was two years older than Eileen. Her mother was a cousin of Gerald's first wife, and she sometimes came to the house. She lived at the top of the Donegal Road, not very far from Eileen.

When they quarrelled, Mitzi passed the adoption story round the dormitory and it got back to the nuns. Reverend Mother sent for Eileen and scolded her for making up such insulting stories about a good Catholic lady like her mother who'd had such a tragic experience in her life and who, Reverend Mother was sure, had always been the soul of kindness and affection to her daughter. "You live in a dream world," the nun dismissed her, "Come back to reality, Eileen, and stop seeing life as some big drama with you as the heroine. Read a bit less at your recreations, child, and learn to laugh and giggle like the other girls. You'll be healthier and happier for it!"

She told Teresa about her father when she was sixteen, the last Easter holidays she spent with Anny and Patrick.

But Teresa knew already, she'd always known. The whole country knew, Teresa said, meaning the people in that townland knew, through Anny. "He wasn't a *hero*, your oul' fella! He was an unfortunate poor eejit that couldn't leave the bottle alone. It's your mother was heroic," she said, "Many a one in her place would have just sat back and lived off assistance. And there'd have been no boarding-school for you, my lady, because you weren't brainy enough to get a scholarship like yours truly here and she couldn't have paid for you, you'd have ended up like your old Anny so you would! God I wonder how you manage to survive it in that convent without me there to do your homework for you!"

Teresa was a day-girl in the local secondary school. She was doing well and expected to go on to university.

"Could you not put on your spurs, darlin', and catch up with her?" Patrick asked, only half joking, "Agnes Quinn's daughter, I'd hate to see her getting the better of you, and you growing up in a houseful of teachers!"

At what point did the holidays begin to turn sour? At what point did Patrick begin to sidle out to greet her, when the pale blue Ulsterbus coach stopped at the foot of the pass, moving his shoulders nervously inside his old jacket, apologising for this wee oul' shanty of a place you have to pass your holidays in, darlin', after the way you're used to living with your mother and stepfather and the nuns. When she was thirteen, tall and blonde and straight-faced? Fourteen, a good head taller than either him or Anny?

Eileen was impatient, and embarrassed for them. "But I love coming here, sure I wouldn't come if I wasn't happy here! Don't I come to get *away* from my mother and stepfather and the bloomin' old nuns!"

And Anny instantly turned huffy: "I hope you're well enough reared to have come anyway, even if it was only out of sheer gratitude after all that was done for you here!"

The fifteen-year-old Eileen couldn't stop herself: "You looked after me for six years because you were well paid to. You wouldn't have looked after me for nothing, would you?"

The next few weeks were all cold sulks followed by sighs and tears and finally by awkward forgiveness. Why doesn't she give me a clout across the jaw, Eileen thought, why doesn't she march me to Confession, warn me about mending my ways, threaten me with hell-fire and wild dogs and weasels? Why have they disclaimed all responsibility for me, why are they trying to make a stranger of me? She backed away into herself, and never again said anything about being happy with them.

"And anyway they don't *have* to live in a poor wee shanty of a place," she said to Teresa, "Seeing that's the way they look at it. They could easily get a grant to improve their house, couldn't they? Ned Maginn did, and the Connors, everyone seems to be getting grants these days and building bungalows. And what's to stop them watching telly and finding out that it's the nineteen-sixties and that different accents and clothes and education don't really *mean* anything anymore?"

"They're old," Teresa said, "And they're just afraid they can't keep up with you. You *are* different, Eileen, since you moved to Belfast. Even if it's only the way you speak. But you should be patient with them. Or else don't come at all. Why *do* you come, you're always saying it's dead boring? You can't stand the fellows round about, you won't even go to the Youth Club or the Feis Ceoils, what do you come for? You'd have a far better time staying in Belfast for the holidays, God if only *I* was in your place! But since you do come, would you for Christ's sake try and be nice to the old things. Go to the odd dance, *I'm* not above going so what have *you* to be so snotty about? What prince are you waiting for, eh?"

And the summer she was sixteen she didn't go to see them, couldn't face the nervousness and the sulks, and having to go to the Youth Club dances and be grabbed and squeezed by the local teenage yobs so as not to offend Anny and Patrick, and Teresa Quinn as well. Feelings were so easily hurt in the townland. She got a holiday job instead, in a café near the university. Mitzi, who was starting Queen's in October, found her a tiny bedsit in the house up the Stranmillis road she was sharing with four friends. "I'll take a run down to see you at Christmas," she wrote to Anny, and Anny instead of replying had a stroke a few weeks later, and died.

Eileen, numb with sorrow and guilt, refused to go back to school or to live in the Falls Road house again. "I'm school-leaving age," she told her mother, "I have a job and a room, I can support myself. You have no legal right to force me to go home," she said, fingers crossed tightly behind her back. "If you try to force me, I'll just get on the boat and go to England and you'll never see me again. If you leave me alone I'll come home every other weekend, OK? I was never any good at school, you know that well. I don't take after you, Mother dear, I must be a throwback to the thick shopkeeping Campbell side."

"Don't hurt your mother," Gerald said gently, "Of course you can leave school if you're not happy there. But do come home often and see us, won't you? We're not enemies, you know. We're the best friends you have and you'll find that out in the long run."

"Don't you worry your head about Eileen," Chaz McCreesh told her mother when they went down to visit Patrick, "Joan and myself will keep a good eye on her. I have to be up in Belfast every week or so for my firm, she might listen to sense from me where she wouldn't heed her parents. I won't let her go astray on you, Mrs O'Neill!"

❧

Plouch'en is not one of those picturesque French villages huddled cosily around church, café and boulangerie, where every household is awakened deliciously at dawn by the smell of baking croissants. Plouch'en was originally just a straggling line of workers' cottages, built to house the servants from the two châteaux. The older houses still belonged to Jean-Hubert and the du Bois Fleuri family though, as the tenants had been sitting for two centuries, they could neither be turned out nor their rents raised enough to give either family a decent income from them. The butter on the Bourjois family's croissants came from those hovels where elderly couples had finally died off and their children moved to the housing estate. Jean-Hubert, clever enough to do absolutely no restoration work beyond tacking on rudimentary bathrooms and kitchenettes, was able to let the beaten earth floors and damp walls to a succession of English and German visitors as bits of authentic Breton folklore.

The rest of Plouch'en consisted of the vast housing estate and two rows of mass-produced pavillons built in mock-cottage style in the Sixties and Seventies by the more prosperous children of the hovels. It was in these pavillons that most of Uncle Vladimir's possessions had found homes.

While the old men in the hovels still raised their caps and addressed Jean-Hubert as 'Master', their sons and daughters in the new houses were aggressively socialist. Plouch'en had its own little revolution in the early Eighties. Blood was shed. Not much, and only from a broken nose and a few splintered teeth, but still blood. That was the time of the council elections when the du Bois Fleuri family suddenly found itself out of office for the first time in two centuries. In the electoral campaign Monsieur le Comte's supporters, hefty peasants all, set upon the upstart Socialist campaigners outside the polling booth. There were gendarmes everywhere, big embarrassed lumps of country lads in uniform not too sure how to conduct themselves in a fracas. Usually they were only called upon to cope with the half-dozen annual suicides, or the frequent domestic squabbles with shotguns, or to keep crowds of sightseers at bay when Monsieur le Comte was marrying off one of his daughters. He had seven daughters and four sons, all safely off his hands, the girls married into local manors, the boys scattered influentially through industry, armaments, banking, and the media. (The socialist victory was, finally, merely a cosmetic one.)

Madame la Comtesse gave great offence a few years after the election when she refused to be decorated with the Gold Medal of the Mothers of Plouch'en: an award given every ten years to the most prolific mother in the village. Rosalind, who was on a long visit to Hélène at the time, assumed her refusal was symbolic – a courageous denial of the stereotyped role imposed upon Woman – and prepared a feminist campaign around her.

Madame la Comtesse, cornered in her own courtyard by this blushing foreign trespasser in a jogging suit, graciously invited her in, offered her tea, and recommended the gynaecologist who had guided her smoothly through her own mid-life crisis. Rosalind was twenty-eight at the time and, ever afterwards, was inclined to see that as the real symbol: France's reaction to the womens' movement: calm the poor cow down and have her checked out for hormonal disturbance.

Madame la Comtesse refused the medal only because it was offered by the new working-class mayor and council who had ousted her husband and friends. She felt they were impertinently trying to drag her down to their level. As indeed they were, if one accepted that 'down' was the word, which even Jean-Hubert didn't. More like trying to make her feel at home in the new modern Plouch'en they were, and the gesture was a compliment to the old lady's genuine kindness to the villagers – no one, after all, would have dreamed of offering a medal of any kind to Tante Ruby, or to old Monsieur Vladimir in his day.

The Socialist council had done a lot for Plouch'en. They'd expropriated part of the du Bois Fleuri's land to build the housing development, and a bit of Jean-Hubert's woods for the Youth Club to ride their BMXs in. They put the graceful old eighteenth-century mairie on the market, and built a bungalow-style one with net curtains at the windows and vivid beds of salvia, petunia and lobelia spelling out "Plouch'en" in red, white and blue in front.

And they installed a lending library. This library opened at nine every morning, partly to give employment to a few retired schoolteachers, partly in a vain attempt to introduce the village housewives and the local unemployed to literature. Rosalind was the only woman in Plouch'en who would dream of doing anything as useless as borrowing books at the start of a good working day – or indeed at any other time: most of the library's clients were schoolchildren trudging wearily through an official reading list.

On that blue Breton morning Hélène walked down the empty street between two hedges of bustling houses – coloured blankets shaken vigorously out of windows, mats getting thumped savagely against walls, an energetic slash of soapy water against already spotless windowpanes – and wondered vaguely what they must all be thinking of her, strolling idly outside in the sun when she could be at home doing a nice bit of housework. Or did they see her as a lady of complete leisure because she lived in the Big House? Sitting endlessly on silk cushions reading books from the library? Surely not, in this day and age. After sixteen years she still had no idea at all of how the village people saw her: surely that was unnatural? What they thought of Rosalind was evident every time they mentioned her, every time they looked at her, but Hélène had taken care over the years to develop some sort of protective colouring. Scruffy friendly Rosalind, beaming fraternity at everyone she met, was still sardonically referred to as l'Anglaise; Hélène, perfectly groomed, her head held cool and high, had succeeded in having her foreignness forgotten. In having her humanity forgotten, she wondered? She wished she had some clue as to what feelings lay behind the faces of blank politeness the village turned towards her. What did they know of her, what did they suspect? Had Jean-Hubert's arrival in the château sixteen years ago with a foreign wife been food for gossip around every village dining-table? Had her every move been chronicled, his every move? Had their tongues pounced on his affair (his *affairs*) with glee, naming him as a chip off the block that had been old Vladimir? Or hadn't any of them cared? Was the life of the château so remote nowadays from their own lives that they had all simply shrugged their shoulders with Gallic cynicism and switched on the telly? But who had the woman been, who was the woman still, was the affair still going on, was it the talk of the place? And why hadn't she had an abortion, it would have been the obvious thing. If she hadn't an abortion it's that she was attached to Jean-Hubert, that she was expecting him to support her. *Does* he support her? Or maybe just that she's married, married to some peasant, some clerk, some workman. What can her husband be thinking, can he be so unobservant that he doesn't even notice that the child is. Where *is* the flamin' child, why have I only seen him twice in all these years? Bastard, fucking little frog bastard, Hélène shouted silently behind her straight aloof face, but the problem did not diminish itself. I should have taken the car, she thought, mad to let myself be tempted by a lovely summer morning, in the car I would have been safe and sheltered from the village.

Mujah and Din were tethered to the railings outside the mairie and, inside, among the fake mahogany and visible beams of the library, was Rosalind. She was moving the translation of *Guerrillas* from Third World Studies back to the N shelf in the novel section. She did this every time she came to the library, one more futile gesture against French racism. As soon as she'd gone, one of the librarians always shoved Naipaul back in again beside Che Guevara and Bernadette Devlin. A book called *Guerrilleros* by someone with a Hindu name couldn't possibly be literature, it could only be a freedom-fighter's journal. Or a terrorist handbook, depending on whether that day's retired schoolmistress had taught in the council school or the convent.

"Another bank robbery over in Seulbourg!" Rosalind called, waving a copy of *Ouest France*, "Same couple, middle-aged, anonymous, just walked into the Crédit Agricole, nobody thought of challenging them – another form of ageism, do you think? I mean just because they weren't teenagers in leather jackets . . . till they reached the counter and whipped out two revolvers. Sixty thousand francs this time, I bet the gendarmes are hopping. It's just a joke, isn't it?"

"Some joke! Lets hope they don't switch over to private houses when they've emptied all the local banks. One really doesn't feel safe nowadays, even in the country. Listen Rosalind, I must apologise about Saturday and . . . "

"Thus spake the landed proprietor! Come home and we'll drink that famous coffee together now and you can tell me all about this sudden longing for the Oul' Sod, and stop sounding so nouveau riche and adult. Actually I've just been in there reading up on the Breton feudal system for an article I might do, not that anybody buys my articles these days but still . . . Never say die, innit. I got the idea from that old rhino you've got staying with you yet again, do you never get sick of her? The Last of the Romanovs, Pierre calls her. Scared the daylights out of poor Mujah and Din she did. Came charging round the grounds in her birthday suit, talk about Elephant Man, did Clem tell you? Oh well, takes all sorts, dunnit! What I reckon she needs is a few sessions with Pierre, might straighten her out. Seeing as how there's no guillotine handy. What's she doing still here anyway, why isn't she away over there in St Petersburg flogging the serfs?"

"Oh she says she's giving Russia time to get its breath back before she does anything rash. Likes her comfort, does Tante Ruby. But she has got around to joining the Russian Nobles' Union, it's some new thing, some monarchist thing, a guy called Kolodvinov's just contacted her. Do you not think it's like a fairytale? You know, the big bad wolf gets killed and all the old grannies and grandas that you though were digested long ago start crawling out of its tum as large as life. I mean a Nobles' union, yet!"

"Yeah, I can see old Ruby on the shop floor all right. Flat on her back, as usual."

"Rosalind, really! She is Jean-Hubert's aunt, after all. She's not a Romanov, by the way – that was the old boy in St Briac."

Rosalind laughed, and they walked companionably back up the street in the sunshine.

"Wouldn't you think the plague had struck?" Rosalind said, "Not a soul in sight. If this was an English village, you know like where my mum lives, we'd keep bumping into neighbours wouldn't we and having nice little chats, and then we'd all go off and have coffee in someone's house. Or in some nice olde-worlde caff. I never went for that villagey scene when I was actually living in Nailsworth but I must say I could do with a touch of it now! Look at them, just look at them all peering out from behind their curtains at us. With scrubbing-brushes in their hands!"

Hélène looked, and sure enough they were. On every garden gate was a notice saying Chien Méchant: inside every gate an unsmiling German Shepherd stared out at them from its little slated kennel, and an unsmiling housewife stared out at them from her matching little slated bungalow. Hélène found it disquieting (and was that little boy's mother staring out at her, hating her?). She looked quickly away.

"You know my friends the Nairns in London?" Rosalind said, "Well they moved out to Hampton a while back and Eve only threw a dogs' birthday party for the whole street. They've got a King Charles themselves, and she says it worked wonders in getting to know the neighbours. They've got masses of friends now. They all dog-sit for one another when they want to go away for a weekend or whatever. Imagine if I tried it on here for the Afghans' birthday! Do you think they'd have me locked away? Never know though, people are funny, it might even work. Bit of a giggle, Pedigree Chum birthday cake to start with, then a few G and Ts for the owners and bob's your uncle, before you know it all these daft social barriers might well come tumbling down."

She'd been trying for years to knock down the barriers.

All those housewives scrubbing furiously away on a sunny July morning had been young girls running to the bal de samedi soir when Rosalind was au pair at the château. She'd talked to them about Germaine Greer and foreign travel and self-fulfilment and they'd listened to her with polite blank faces, then tapped their foreheads behind her back and rushed off to find themselves husbands who'd build them little bungalows to scrub. When she returned to France some years later and married Pierre, she set about organising coffee mornings and Tupperware afternoons and bring-and-buy sales for Ethiopia, to which nobody ever went but Hélène. All day the young wives waged their endless war against dirt, in the evenings they knitted nylon versions of lovely designer sweaters, knotted away at acrylic carpets, and perpetrated immense and hideous petit point copies of Old Masters to hang above their outsize télés.

"Don't even attempt it!" Hélène warned, "They *would* think you'd gone off your head at last. Dogs haven't the same significance for them as they have for you and me."

"Neither have people by the looks of it. They're all so stiff and pathetic aren't they, just no way of getting to know them! I've been trying for years literally and I still don't know anyone at all except you and my in-laws."

"Well who does, in the country? And why bother getting to know village housewives? You're a doctor's wife now, Rosalind, you've a position to keep up. I mean you can't frequent just *anyone*."

"Oh hark at her! And then they go on about the English class system! Listen, if Plouch'en was in England we'd all be in and out of one another's houses all day wouldn't we, organizing gymkhanas and charity runs and car boot sales and."

Maggy Connor leapt into Hélène's mind, sewing

companionably on the doorstep with Anny; Patrick and Ned and Jem and Paddy sharing their tasks and their implements and their gossip and their worries, all of them raking shamelessly into one another's difficulties and scandals and tragedies; Agnes Quinn going mad with loneliness and sexual frustration; Nancy Maginn's love life spread shockingly over the townland . . . Rosalind's memories of her Cotswold childhood seemed to be reduced to the commonplace banalities of everyday life, jumble sales and coffee mornings and the superficial matiness of the local teashop. Hélène found it hard to comprehend that there were millions of people who lived on that level of reality – every detail and emotion of whose whole past was not fixed there, as on a video recording that could be taken out of its box and played over and over at will.

"It sounds ghastly to me," she said, "We should count ourselves lucky we found a couple of frog princes prepared to marry us. Listen, if you absolutely must chat to a village housewife come along in here and help me engage Madame Le Borgne to cook for us. The Happy Pair only decamped at the weekend."

Rosalind turned unaccountably pink. "No, no I shouldn't think that's a good idea," she muttered, "And actually I've got to be getting back," but Hélène grabbed her arm and marched her firmly up the path to the Le Borgnes' cottage. "I need you for moral support," she said, "I'm still quite hopeless at engaging staff."

Michel Le Borgne was getting out of his van as they rang the doorbell. He gaped at them with what looked like amazed embarrassment and went hastily round the side of the grey stone house to the garden shed. He was a thin sleepy-looking man in his thirties who'd been Uncle Vladimir's gardener, and whom Hélène engaged part-time

for a bit of digging and hoeing. When he wasn't working at
the château, he drove round farmhouses and run-down
manors looking for old furniture and pictures for his
brother's antique shops. She supposed he only did the
gardening these days to give him a claim on the tied
cottage, because the antique business was apparently
thriving: Denis Le Borgne's shop in Rennes was one of the
places Jean-Hubert had started yearning into recently, and
she knew the prices were high. Michel was probably the dud
of the family, the one who hadn't had the wit to fly the nest.
No, hardly a dud – he was an efficient worker and really
quite presentable – but it didn't particularly please her to
think that in Rosalind's ideal English village he'd be calling
her Eileen and roping her in to make tea for the football
team.

He emerged from the shed, carrying what looked like a
rucksack and camping equipment and slung it into the back
of the van. Could they be preparing to go away for a few
days, she wondered, *did* that sort of people take camping
holidays? How little, finally, one ever knew about the
private lives of French villagers!

"Is your wife at home, Michel?" she called. He looked
even more embarrassed.

"I, well I'm not quite sure, madame," he stammered, "It
is possible that she has already gone out to the shops." He
jumped into the van and drove off.

"How rude!" Hélène said, "Rushing off like that. Must
be one of his days for ripping off all those poor death-duty
widows and orphans!" She rang the doorbell again. "Bet
that fat cow of a wife isn't even up yet!"

"Let's not wait," Rosalind said uneasily, "You can always
ring her up, can't you. These women never like being
dropped in on."

161

At that moment the door opened and Nathalie Le Borgne appeared. Hélène gaped, and Rosalind turned scarlet. "Crikey!" she muttered, "I'm off."

Crikey? Hélène, for an instant, was back in Anny's, turning the bellows wheel, her head buried in the *Beano* . . . She turned back to Nathalie, lady of the manor again, cool and straightfaced, supremely capable of dealing with any embarrassing situation that might confront her.

Part Four

❧

Les Guerets,
Plouch'en
3rd July

Dear Ruth,

Another of my village sagas! I was just talking about Nailsworth this morning actually, to Hélène, my snooty neighbour/ex-boss, so consider the Cotswolds honoured! I was comparing the nice cheerful English social life you lead with the stiff dreariness of Plouch'en — you never saw such a shower of long faces, all standing on their Gallic dignity and terrified to relax for one second in case someone pushes them off the rung of the ladder they imagine they're standing on. No, but basically there's roughly fifty-six million different social classes in France and not one of them will condescend to mix with any of the others. You'd think with Pierre being a doctor we'd be socializing like mad with all the other doctors, dinner parties and barbecues and all the rest but no, not a bit of it! The other local doctors, you see, are the sons and daughters of nice professional families and Pierre is the son of a peasant (as he will keep insisting!) so it's arm's length all round. Between his inferiority complex and their superiority one we're well away!

Sorry about the grumbles – I quite often feel isolated and browned off these days. If you were here I'd cry on your shoulder but I can't very well in a letter because as soon as you actually write something down it becomes all dramatic and real doesn't it! Well, just a hint – Big Bad First Wife is back in the district. She's bought a country cottage and is really flashing herself around – art exhibitions all over the place. I haven't actually *seen* her in flesh and blood but every shop window you look in has a reproduction of some crumbling old cowpat she's immortalised in watercolours. I think her stuff is a load of rubbish myself (can't stand aquarelles, can you?) but they seem to go for it big over here. I can't really compete with the star quality so as you can imagine I feel rather useless at times. Hence the grumbles! I mean I don't think Pierre's about to ditch me and go back to her but he's definitely feeling a bit nostalgic which doesn't make life any easier – we had a flaming row the other night. Admittedly we'd both been tanking ourselves up on the good old vin rouge (had the dreaded in-laws to dinner!) so it probably didn't mean much.

Oh well, enough of my troubles, I'm really writing to bring you up to date on the local gossip (those funny frogs!). No, seriously I had the weirdest experience this morning. You know that rather nice Seventies drop-out I've been telling you about, Michel the gardener? He's married to this absolute slut and kind of sublimates his frustration or whatever (I'm as bad as Pierre!) by having a long-standing crush on Hélène (his boss), oh all very pure, "She came from her palace grand, she came to my cottage door" sort of thing, I mean the guy even *looks* as if he was invented by Joan Baez or someone in the distant past. Anyway, this morning Hélène decides she wants to engage Nathalie (that's the wife) as a cook (see the beau monde I'm associating with!) and she dragged me round there with her. Well I've got my ear quite close to the ground, thanks to Pierre's village patients, so I'd heard over the weekend that Nathalie was only shacked up with some waiter from the hotel, they were saying she'd actually walked out on Michel publicly in the bistro on Saturday evening, I heard there were dramatic scenes, Michel crying into his pint etc.

So I wasn't too keen to go round there but as it was on my way home anyway. To cut a long story short we saw poor Michel (obviously just in the middle of moving out himself and so embarrassed in front of Hélène!) and then the Nathalie one opens the door practically naked I swear it (honestly these French!) in this sort of transparent black Lurex negligée that I didn't think was even manufactured any more, and the waiter fellow (he's quite a hunk actually) wrapped in a fluffy bath-towel sort of propping her up in his arms. Why they bothered to answer the door I don't know (probably expecting a delivery from one of the mail-order catalogues – everybody's big turn-on in rural France!), but I must say I didn't stay to join the orgy: I fled, leaving Hélène to it! Serve her right – if she didn't live in such an ivory tower she'd have known what was going on (honestly the Irish – they never seem to be in the real world do they?). Anyway with a bit of luck Michel will get a divorce now and go off and get a proper job somewhere, join the family firm or something – can't think why he ever tied himself to a yokel like Nathalie!

Otherwise, what's new? Oh yes, Pierre's finally fixed up with Jimmy Savage, his old boozing pal from Northern Ireland and we're definitely exchanging houses with them in September. I'm thrilled to bits as you can imagine – a whole month out of France, and Jimmy says you wouldn't even notice that there's anything going on in Ulster, quiet as anything where he lives. And we're taking a few days in London so I'll see you then.

Latest news is that Hélène wants to come with us, or rather use us as an alibi! I don't think she actually wants to be living in Carrickfergus with us, according to Pierre she's homesick and wants to look up all her old friends in Belfast, apparently she's been weeping on his shoulder! Funny – she's always seemed to me to be more French than the frogs themselves, *the* ultimate in mindless integration. Mid-life crisis do you think? Probably just wants time off from her awful husband and kids! The Clémence creature has gone all National Front, and Henri goes round strumming a guitar spouting what sounds to me suspiciously like IRA propaganda! Though frankly I don't think Hélène even notices – she's so remote and wrapped up in herself most of the time, oh I am bitchy this morning!

I do like her really, and she's literally the only woman I know that you can talk to. (Sisterhood isn't exactly thick on the ground here. Well you can imagine – they're all brought up from babyhood to think of themselves as primarily man-fodder so any other women can only be seen as a potential rival. Yuck!) So I have to make the most of Hélène. It would probably be easier if she was English – say what you like but it *is* a different mentality. Not *very* different, but enough to notice. I do miss England, you all seem to be having such fun, in spite of the recession and the sex crimes and all the mad Rottweilers, I mean it all seems so warm and cosy compared with here!

Well I'll love you and leave you and please reply soon. There's nothing like marrying a foreigner to make one appreciate the lost art of letter-writing! Lots of luv,

Rosalind.

Part Five

❧

Jean-Hubert was in the upstairs sitting-room listening with a bored face to France-Musique when Hélène got back from the village. He switched it off as she came in. "Le juif Mendelssohn!" he snarled, "A vacuum! A pleasant boring vacuum! And people pretend to think he's up there among the greats. Of course we all know who runs broadcasting don't we! Mozart exists, Bach exists, putain de bon dieu Beethoven exists! And they offer us the jew Mendelssohn at eleven o'clock in the morning. Quelle époque! Mais quelle miserable époque!"

Hélène could see that Tante Ruby and his racist Bourjois cousins were fighting for possession of his soul.

"You don't hurt the Jews when you say things like that," she remarked mildly, "You just make yourself sound like a pathetic little National Front skinhead."

"I don't want to hurt the Jews do I, what would I want to hurt the bloody Jews for? I just want to put a label on that sod Mendelssohn."

Jean-Hubert was not really racist; at least, he claimed, not more than most French people, but he was bored and required to be constantly entertained to make up, he said, for the drudgery of being a twentieth-century châtelain. He owned all these cottages around the village, several gîtes ruraux, and some office property over at Seulbourg, and he'd at first dreamed of settling down to the life of a cultivated country squire, strolling round his broad acres reading poetry, listening to music, exchanging ideas with other country gentlemen. Except that none of the local notables were cultivated, unless one counted Pierre. And Pierre had to work for his living.

Jean-Hubert and Hélène had to work too. They'd soon found that it was no longer as easy as just collecting rents. "We may not be the Duke of Westminster," Hélène told Rosalind, "But you wouldn't *credit* the amount of accounting we have to do!" And Rosalind giggled and stored it up to quote in one of her innumerable letters to her friends at home.

"I was born a hundred years too late!" Jean-Hubert moaned regularly.

He'd been working, or at any rate suffering, that morning while Hélène was in the village. No sooner had he got home from driving the twins to their lycée than the front doorbell rang. "Les locataires!" Tante Ruby screamed up the stairs at him, "And they look frantic. I bet they've burned the house down. Mon dieu, mon dieu, tenants coming to the front door like that! Ah if poor Vladimir was alive!"

On the front steps Jean-Hubert found the rather sinister Parisian couple who'd rented one of the gîtes for a month, complaining shrilly that there were about a million bees swarming in on their bedroom window when they woke up. What he found sinister about them he had no idea, except perhaps that they'd chosen to take their summer holidays in June and July instead of waiting till August like everyone else in France. Unnatural creatures, and the female one was not even attractive. Jean-Hubert had a horror of wasting his time talking to any woman who did not offer him at least the possibility of sexual excitement, and he had no intention of examining and apologising for this one's bee stings.

But, vaguely recalling an old rhyme of Clémence's about swarms of bees, he rang the captain of gendarmes in Seulbourg, who was a keen beekeeper, and suggested he come over when he was off duty and take the swarm. The captain could come right away so Jean-Hubert was obliged to go back to the gîte with them and reassure Madame that no, it wasn't the start of an epidemic, and that no she wasn't likely to wake up tonight again with bees crawling all over her. The only creature, in Jean-Hubert's opinion, who'd have the courage to crawl all over her in the night was her poor fool of a husband who was standing there with his stomach decanting itself out of his chain store jeans, making knowledgeable remarks about insects as he watched the captain and his colleague, heavily disguised in khaki shooting gear and gauze masks, working away around the bedroom window.

He recounted all this to Hélène, and Hélène, busy smoothing him down, pouring out coffee, telling him how clever and efficient he'd been, didn't look forward to confessing to him about her failure with Nathalie Le Borgne.

Such petty incidents occupied a large part of their life nowadays, she thought. They couldn't afford much in the way of help so they were constantly struggling to keep the château standing upright, cementing and plastering and fixing putty round windowpanes. In Amsterdam they'd let the squat crumble to pieces around them while they got on with living life, and it hadn't seemed to matter: it was scheduled for demolition anyhow. Après nous an underground station. Hélène thought it sad that she'd so lost touch with that part of her youth that she didn't even know if they'd actually built that station yet, or if, incredibly, the squat was still standing, with a less innocent generation of squatters than they'd been drifting fecklessly along the Amstel.

But the château needed to be kept on its feet, the rented-out cottages needed to be made at least rainproof. Vegetables, fruit and flowers had to be grown. Hélène hoed and weeded and planted, sometimes with the help of Michel Le Borgne, more usually alone. In a year or two she hoped to be able to open the garden to the public, which would mean more money but also more work. Even when they had help in the house she had to do the work of about six Victorian domestics, busy up on ladders with brooms and dusters. If she didn't, they'd soon have had to claw their way out through a thick curtain of cobwebs. At the other end of the village, Monsieur le Comte and Madame la Comtesse presumably led a similar life. It was never talked of openly. When the two couples met, formally, once a year, at each other's houses, none of the hard labour was allowed to be apparent; everything was accustomed, ceremonious, as if teams of well-trained servants had, for uncounted centuries, been gliding up and down the gleaming staircases meekly doing their masters' bidding.

So Hélène dreaded telling Jean-Hubert she'd failed to engage help for their party. "Euh . . . Know the latest?" she began brightly, "Nathalie Le Borgne's only brought her latest lover to live in the cottage, imagine! And of course with typical village indiscretion, they both answered the door practically naked, stinking of supermarket eau de toilette. So much for Tante Ruby's theory about the feelthy villagers keeping philodendrons in their bathtubs! And naturally poor Rosalind almost fainted away in my arms with embarrassment."

"*Tu l'as voulu, Georges Dandin,*" Jean-Hubert intoned, "*Tu l'as voulu!*"

"What? How do you mean, you asked for it George Dandin? Who's George Dandin when he's at home?"

"It is a literary quotation," Jean-Hubert said in the thin tired voice he always used when he wanted to pinpoint her lack of culture. She wondered if it was a national characteristic, this overdone weary tolerance of other people's ignorance?

"By coincidence," he continued reflectively, "I've just finished that story of Borges'. If I understand it correctly it means that every poor prick in the world will eventually get the chance to have written the Odyssey. One has only to wait one's turn. So, comme ça, I too one day will certainly take my turn at cuckolding Michel Le Borgne. What is she like, la petite Nathalie, naked?"

"Oh tu sais . . . I didn't take much notice . . . Pink. Damp. A bit sluttish. Go and see for yourself, she looks as if she'd be delighted. Anyway, much too wrecked with passion at the moment to come and work for us." She noticed that Jean-Hubert's face was taking on the intent rapacious expression that meant he was being turned on by the thought of the pair in their bathtub.

"You haven't the curse or anything? No? OK," he ordered, "Viens ici!"

Hélène could never imagine where the French had got their reputation for romance. Jean-Hubert made love whenever he needed to with no pretence whatever that it was out of an overwhelming passion for her big blue eyes and perfect body. He'd always been completely practical and down-to-earth about sex. But then, who did she have to compare him with? The kids in Amsterdam who'd fumbled around in psychedelic dreams? That nice Belfast boy she'd tried to console herself with, who always behaved as if the Pope and John Knox were frowning down upon their nakedness? The chaste reticence of Christopher Milton? Maybe there just wasn't any romance, anywhere? "And what if Tante Ruby walks in?"

"Oh she's gone, didn't I tell you the big news? Got a phone call half an hour ago from someone at TFI, to say Patrick Poivre d'Arvor wants to interview her. Some documentary he's doing on St Petersburg. So naturally she rushed off to Paris immediately. Actually I think she was just waiting for the excuse. The old thing was beginning to miss her pastrycook."

Tante Ruby's husband, Gustave Boulanger, known in the family as le Patissier, owned a chain of very select shops throughout France and Belgium. Not that he ran them personally or even visited them at all nowadays. He was invited to all the best parties because of Tante Ruby's name and she could dress to go to those parties because of his money, so they agreed very well. Only, sometimes now that her children were grown up and married, she became bored with being the companion of an ageing self-made millionaire whose body no longer held any mystery for her. A down-to-earth Frenchwoman with no interest in adolescent sweethearts or wild flower gardens, she compensated by offering herself a young lover from time to time and living out a brief but très grand passion in some secluded corner of Corsica or Tuscany. Being Tante Ruby, she took care to stay faithful to Le Patissier in July and August when all the secluded spots were invaded by the vulgar populace enjoying their paid holidays. When the affair ended she always fled in tears to her dead brother's home and ruled Jean-Hubert's life for a few weeks as she once ruled her brother Vladimir's.

"So we're all alone in the château," Jean-Hubert continued, "Normally at this hour we'd be rattling round the rooms after the Happy Pair. Or their predecessors. Or their successors, whoever they're going to be. Quelle aventure!" he murmured, unbuttoning her shirt, stroking her shoulders, "Do you realise, Hélène, that we're on our own for the first time since Amsterdam? That we're quite alone together for the very first time since our marriage? Like a suburban couple in their little villa! Let's make beautiful mid-morning love, chérie, like an unemployed suburban couple."

"We'd be more likely going through the small ads at this hour if we were unemployed," Hélène shrugged, "We'd have more on our mind, than sex."

"I always suspected the working classes were dreary," he sighed, plumping her down on the sofa like a cushion, depositing small neat kisses all over her, "And now you confirm it! If they have no work and no social life and no appearances to keep up I can't think why the poor slobs don't stay in bed all day and enjoy their Social Security benefit. Ah mais c'est bon," he continued, settling himself cosily on his elbows, "Mon dieu, ma chérie, qui c'est bon de baiser comme ça, tout seul dans un château!"

A small ghostly part of Hélène flew out the open window to join Christopher Milton under a tree of white blossom in a Belfast park, but the rest of her was suddenly overcome at the memory of Rosalind fleeing down the path dissolved in blushes and she laughed out loud.

"She burbled as she came," Jean-Hubert commented, "Citation littéraire: Jabberw – "

173

"I know, I know, I read it as a child, can't you lot even make a joke without giving chapter and verse?"

But she thought how nice it was after all that sex with Jean-Hubert was no big deal, you could laugh and chat all the way through, no big passion and no big drama. A friendly act. "As you say," she murmured, "How good it is to make love, mon chéri, all alone in a château."

Unfortunately, Jean-Hubert became a different man once he'd stepped back, satisfied, into the dignity of his clothes. "So you didn't succeed in finding help for our reception?" he accused sternly. "You will have to unearth someone, Hélène, we have one hundred and fifty people coming here next Saturday week: do you intend to prepare and serve the food yourself?"

"It's getting a bit late to find anyone decent now," she said, "Why don't we just get caterers in for this once? Do you want me to ring round a few places in Seulbourg?"

"*Caterers?*" Jean-Hubert seemed to swell in outrage, "Caterers for our guests? We are not organizing a peasant wedding, ma chère! Have you ever seen caterers in any of the houses we've been invited to? Nous sommes en Frrrawnce my dear Hélène, one would assume that after sixteen years you would have picked up some of the nuances!"

"Well, I could try the Le Moal girls. They might be glad of the pocket money."

"The Le Moal girls! Student teachers giving themselves airs. Roaring up the avenue on their motor-bikes, wanting to be treated as equals. The idea! No, I shall occupy myself of this. It is evident that Nathalie Le Borgne is the only answer. She is said to be an excellent cook and what is important, she *looks* the part of a servant. The Le Moal girls' legs are far too long. I sometimes wonder if Uncle Vladimir . . .

174

However. I will take every measure necessary to ascertain that the little Nathalie comes to us. You, ma chère épouse, will see that the garden is impeccable for our guests to walk in. That is where your talent lies, after all."

"Oh the garden," Hélène said sulkily, "I don't intend to bother too much about making it nice. A big crowd like that, they'll probably just trample all over the flowerbeds and crush out cigarettes in the urns."

"Hélène, my dear," Jean-Hubert sighed with heavy patience, "As I said before, we are talking about a civilised reception, not an Irish wedding. And besides, old General Blérot du Boisauvage, who hates going into Society, is doing us the great honour of coming here *expressly* to enjoy this white rose garden of yours that he heard so much about. *Personne comme les généraux pour aimer les roses.* Literary quotation," he explained thinly to her raised eyebrows, "Louis Ferdinand Céline. This rather tenuous contact we have with the general is very important to us. We must feed and water it, so to speak. He will be of the greatest use in getting Henri into St Cyr."

"But Henri doesn't want to be an army officer!" Hélène protested fiercely, visualising with horror her lively creative son brutalised into a robot in a posh military college, "He has the deepest contempt for the army. And you know perfectly well he intends going to Trinity after his Bac to do Celtic Studies. Henri's Irish roots are very important to him, Jean-Hubert, you mustn't – "

"We are no longer in the nineteen-seventies," Jean-Hubert interrupted crushingly, "Long-haired students learning Gaelic and Quechua and making love instead of war are hopelessly dépassé nowadays. You live in the past, darling Hélène – actually it is part of your charm, your little coté démodé. But confine it to your garden, I beg of you, to your pale rambling roses and repressed little hedges, and leave my children's future to me!"

Madame la Comtesse du Bois Fleuri spent Wednesday morning shopping and cleaning for old Laetitia Bedel, a retired servant of hers, bedridden after a stroke. Perched precariously on a set of kitchen steps, she squeaked a polishing cloth round and round the glass of the picture-window panes. Daily window cleaning was not something she had ever found necessary in her own home and she privately thought it a great waste of one's short precious life – how many actual years of poor Madame Bedel's eighty-five had been squandered on this mindless offensive against non-existent dirt? – but as a good Christian she was aware that one can be of no use whatever to those in need if one refuses to respect their little totems and taboos. And not so little either: people who for centuries had owned nothing *naturally* clutched on to pettinesses like obsessive cleanliness and obsessive respectability as the only luxuries they were able to offer themselves. The countess was committed to cleaning every one of the bungalow's wide windows every day until a full-time home help could be found, just as she was committed to sitting by Madame Bedel's bedside talking gently about God's will and helping the old woman to accept with resignation the cross He had in His wisdom asked her to bear. It was one of the duties that came with her position, this responsibility towards those who had served one faithfully for as long as they were able.

Standing on the ladder, she saw Hélène Bourjois strolling down the village street and later, while she was dusting the collection of pathetic pottery ornaments on the front room windowsill, she saw her strolling back again with her friend, the doctor's eccentric foreign wife. Hélène did not see her or, if she did, saw only the vague shape of a village housewife going about her dreary chores. People like Hélène, the countess reflected, never actually *saw* her fellow human beings as they went about the business of their lives; they saw villagers, peasants, shopkeepers, and seeing them thus labelled and filed away could have no proper sense of responsibility towards them. The countess told herself that she did not wish to be snobbish, she was only disappointed; she had, after all, once held such high hopes of Hélène – an Irish Catholic, therefore bound to be doubly spiritual, doubly imprinted with a sense of simple kindly standards of behaviour. It had seemed for a while that the little Madame Bourjois might become one of the caring few who continued to keep traditional values alive in the village. "Though indeed how could I have expected it?" Madame la Comtesse asked of the old woman's twisted uncomprehending face, "Married to a Ploudel de Medeu! The poor creature was bound to be swallowed up by them in the end and what, I demand of you, what could the Ploudel de Medeus possibly know of tradition? Empire nobility! There was a Jacques Ploudel guarding the cows for my great-great-great-great-grandfather, just before the Revolution. It is there in black and white, in our farm records!"

Madame Bedel responded to the tone and to the Ploudel de Medeu name; she nodded her old head in vicious agreement. Madame la Comtesse sat by the bedside until she was relieved by cheerful young Séverine Bourel, the roadmender's daughter (through she noticed he was calling himself a council employé nowadays), whose married sister Nathalie seemed to be turning out so very badly, really the stories the parish priest had to tell about her, disgusting quite disgusting, and if the unfortunate husband were to

find out . . . "Can't you do something, madame?" old Father
Plouer had requested, "Use your influence on the young
woman. " But really, thought the countess, one had so very
little influence nowadays and that was the truth. Among
the older villagers there were still many simple biddable
souls like poor Madame Bedel, who were grateful for any
little thing one could do for them, but sadly the younger
generation seemed to be coarser, more cynical . . .
Aggressive even. One had unfortunately very little power
left to do good among them. Socialism of course, the
countess thought distastefully, one could so easily trace the
village's decline back to that upstart Mitterrand's victory in
1981. It had encouraged people to get ridiculously above
themselves. One had seen it coming of course; since 1968
one had been aware, even in Plouch'en, of France's slow
deliberate slide down into chaos. It would not last: happily
there were signs of change. "The good God has shown His
power in eastern Europe," she told Madame Bedel, "And
He is not going to sit idly on His throne and let Evil
triumph. Even in France there are forces for good
preparing themselves at this very minute. The spirit of
Jeanne d'Arc is still alive in our midst, and Our Blessed
Lord will not allow this blasphemy that is Socialism to
prevail in the world!"

Séverine Bourel raised her eyes to heaven; old Madame
Bedel, who in late middle-age had been gripped by an
undying passion for Che Guevara, made a horrible face at
the countess which she knew the old lady would mistake for
a grimace of pain or of servile agreement.

"Hou la la!" sighed Séverine when the countess had
gone, "I thought that old skin was going to preach till
dinner-time! Listen madame, want to hear the big news?
Want me to recount you all the latest sizzling details about

Nathalie's big romance with Gabriel? You'll never believe what . . . "

When Madame la Comtesse arrived home, her femme de ménage had already left; the wing of the château they lived in was decently tidy, not that it was ever otherwise nowadays since the children had grown up and gone; the dining table was set for two with delicate old Sèvres plates and silver cutlery, and she knew there would be a large tin of moussaka decanted into a casserole dish ready to be heated up for lunch. Madame la Comtesse took her letters from the heavy silver tray in the hall where Madame Bourdais had arranged them, (she saw with delight that there was one from her daughter Beatrix in Paris), and went through into the kitchen. The label on the discarded tin said *Cuisine Sans Frontières*, which was a dreadful impertinence on the part of the manufacturers, playing as it did on the public's sympathy for Médécins Sans Frontières who did such wonderful work among famine victims. Really these people would be claiming to protect the ozone layer next: perhaps one ought to boycott their products? But, ever since her Greek honeymoon in the Forties, moussaka had been one of her favourite foods, and life was too short and too full of interesting activities to waste whole hours of it cooking, now that one could no longer afford to be served as one had been used to.

While they ate, she commented on Beatrix's letter, as her husband liked her to do. Since his eldest son's unpleasant divorce and remarriage he preferred to be warned in advance of any unexpected news his children might spring on him.

"I'm so pleased!" she cried, "She says they're coming to us next week. But oh dear, she asks me to find her a nurse for the babies, now who in the village might be suitable?

How very extraordinary, Joffroy, she says they came back from the theatre one evening last week with supper guests, only to find the English nanny curled up barefoot in the drawing-room reading Levi-Strauss!"

"*Wearing* Levi-Strauss she must mean," the count commented, "Don't you remember, dear, when the girls were young . . . "

"No no darling, *reading*, it's quite a different family. One of these new philosophers I believe. Or am I thinking of a different Levi? But imagine how embarrassing! Of course she sacked her straight away. I did warn her against engaging an English girl, it never works out. Do you remember that silly woman who turned up on the doorstep the time they wanted to give me their ridiculous medal? The most absurd ideas about equality . . . How I dislike that word, and one hears it everywhere nowadays! Even in the pulpit though not, thank heavens, when dear Father Plouer says Mass. It is quite a meaningless word: how *could* people possibly all be equal? Can they really be so insensitive as to have no perception of the natural superiority of some human groups over others? However. At least it means we are going to have the babies here rather sooner than we expected."

"We can bring Beatrix with us to Jean-Hubert's party," the old count said, "I am always afraid that she finds her visits to us boring, the quiet life we lead nowadays."

"Now Joffroy! I have already said that we are not setting foot at Ruby Boulanger's pretentious reception. We must not lower our standards to that extent."

"It's not Ruby's party, it's Jean-Hubert's, I've told him we'd be along. What have you got against the fellow anyway? His father and myself were perfectly good mates in the Resistance."

"He wants his daughter to marry Timothy, our own grandson, is that not enough?"

"But the girl doesn't want it, does she? Knows her place, the little Clémence. From what Timothy tell me she spends all her time at the lycée glued to the son of Delamotte the auctioneer, or whatever he is. Even in the classroom, under the teachers' noses."

"How disgusting! A child who was properly brought up would never dream of behaving in that way. She is exactly like Ruby and Elsie when they were girls. And look how *they* turned out!"

"Oh come now! Ruby married a millionaire, we must not be provincial. You heard Beatrix say the Boulangers are received everywhere, in Paris."

"In Paris! In Paris, do not forget, they beheaded our king and our ancestors before going on to elect a stationmaster's son to the Elysée Palace. Such a president, for a nation that once knew Charles de Gaulle! And no doubt you are going to tell me that the little Monsieur Mitterrand is received everywhere too! I am proud to be a provincial, if to be a Parisienne means that one can marry a grocer, and be applauded for it."

"Ah that poor little Ruby, how well I remember her at twenty. She was always so hungry during the Occupation; remember how hungry we all were? All the young people at the time. Rutabagas, wormy peas – how we dreamed and dreamed of food! Naturally the little one seized upon the occasion to have always enough to eat."

"As you say, mon ami, we were all hungry, but did *I* marry a grocer? I could have, you know, there were very many self-made men who would have been glad to marry a title and give respectability to their fortunes after the Liberation. But I am glad to say I chose a gentleman of my own class, of my own family. And if you, my cousin, had not been available, I would have been prepared to marry an impoverished squire, even some obscure *hobereau* whose château was falling to pieces around him, because I would have known at least that he'd been brought up with the same values and the same rituals and the same sense of duty and responsibility as myself. Order, continuity, decency, honour. A *grocer*, yet! Imagine being obliged to live in close intimacy with a man of coarse breeding. The shocks to which one must submit! The indelicacies! All that because Mademoiselle Ruby was obliged to be hungry for a little while. But, my dear, as you are so good at explaining, tell me now why her sister chose to marry a schoolmaster, the son of a peasant? Was she perhaps hoping to gorge herself at their pig-killing festivals?"

"I believe you know yourself that it was different for Elsie. She may have been hungry for glamour, for heroism. Do not forget that she had travelled abroad, that she was presented at the English court, that she rode to hounds, frequented courageous young men in scarlet coats, young English officers wearing swords and brilliant uniforms, and that at the age of twenty she returned to France and found . . . Well, we both know what she found in France after the Defeat. She did not, I think, see herself eloping with a schoolmaster; what Elsie eloped with was the handsome and gallant Resistance officer . . . "

"Nonsense! All that, mon pauvre ami, is perfect nonsense. I too was a spirited young girl. I too suffered shame at the defeat of France. But did I imagine I could find heroism by sleeping with a peasant? Rubbish! I joined the Resistance myself!"

"Yes, my dear. But twelve hundred years of faithfully handed-down tradition made it possible for you to become a heroine. Poor Ruby and Elsie's family had existed for only a century and a half at the time. "

"And that is precisely what I reproach them for! They ought *never* to have existed. Without that dreadful Revolution . . . In 1435, if you remember, our family was given the right to erect on our land a gibbet of six places. And, generation after generation, at least one of those places was occupied by a member of the Ploudel family. It is in all the records . . . "

"Yes yes my dear but we must live with our time," sighed the count, "The Ploudel de Medeus are no threat to us now, after all, and the young Bourjois couple are charming."

"They have introduced a couple of foreign homosexuals into their house, they are giving scandal to the whole parish, Father Plouer has spoken to me about it. What do they need servants for? *I* manage perfectly well with one cleaning woman."

"The Dutch couple left at the weekend. And Father Plouer is an old woman. As regards sinful couples, Augusta, do not forget that our own eldest son is living in sin with his mistress: the Church does not recognise divorce, you know. We must exercise charity and forbearance. The charitable thing will be to go to this reception, we need not stay very long, it would not be expected of us. And perhaps, my dear," he continued hesitantly, "If you would consent to engage a second domestic, we might not, perhaps, be obliged to eat so very many tins of this, euh, this meat and vegetable mixture. Excellent indeed though it is," he added, with the perfect courtesy that came of twelve centuries unsullied descent from Charlemagne.

Every French window on the ground floor opened into Hélène's garden. Lawns stretched out on three sides of the house, fading almost imperceptibly into green-white hedges of climbing roses whose flowers were discreet clusters of tiny eglantines. Cool pastel-coloured ghost flowers that looked best at twilight and in the early morning.

When they first came to the château, on a June evening, after five days travelling from Holland in a broken-down old van, five nights camping by roadsides and riversides, (the last dying convulsions of freedom, Hélène was to realize later), she'd been shaken and assaulted and horrified at the sight and the scents of Uncle Vladimir's rose garden that seemed about to hurl itself bloodily upon them as they stepped out, stiff and irritable, clutching two carrycots, into the reality of their new possessions.

What actually hurled herself upon them was Tante Ruby who grabbed hold of Jean-Hubert, planted great smacking kisses on both his cheeks, then stepped back coldly to survey her new niece before disappearing into the ugly nineteenth-century manor house, cooing alternately into the carrycots she'd grabbed out of their hands.

Jean-Hubert's mother, thin and elegant, already somewhat ravaged by the cancer that was to kill her, examined them first with icy eyes, then gathered them into a welcoming but equally icy embrace. "We learned from your solicitor," she enunciated, "From your solicitor, mon fils, that you'd acquired a family during your travels. And whom did you marry, so secretively, Jean-Hubert? Who is this lady who could not be presented to your mother?"

"Yes . . . yes . . . well actually, maman . . . " Jean-Hubert was stammering defensively, "I would like to . . . that is to say . . . I have the great honour to . . . to present Eileen to you now, I am sure that you will love her. My wife comes from an old Belfast family, a family of great intellectuals, one of her great-aunts was a heroine in the Resistance against the English, she is mentioned in all the history books . . . "

Eileen looked at him in amazement, whatever is he on about? What on earth is he making up all that for? *Intellectuals?* Her mother and Gerald? She noticed that he was almost babbling, like a small boy reciting a lesson he'd desperately learned to ward off punishment, and she took his hand supportively. "Autre pays, autre moeurs," his mother murmured with distaste, "In France we leave it to the gentlemen to become heroes; their wives have the discretion to stay at home and commemorate them in tapestries. The good ladies of Bayeux . . . Your family is Protestant, of course?"

"No. Oh no!" Eileen exclaimed, glad to have found something that would please this terrifying old lady. "I'm a Catholic. We got married in the loveliest old church in Amsterdam, we had a Nuptial Mass and everything. It's just that I couldn't *afford* a big traditional wedding with all the. My family wasn't there either."

"A Belfast Catholic. I see." The words formed themselves like icicles on her mother-in-law's lips and hung there, freezing them all. "I must welcome you into our family . . . Eileen. So Irish girls are still called Eileen! I used to go to Hunt Balls in Ireland long ago. Do you know the Brownes? The Breffnis? No? Then perhaps you've been to the Mountcharles place? Slane Castle?"

"It's a hotel now, they have folk concerts in the grounds," Eileen said, tactlessly grabbing on to something she'd heard, wounding her mother-in-law's lost girlhood.

The old lady turned to Jean-Hubert with a smile: "Chéri, your wife is charming, but I think you and I have many things to discuss alone. Perhaps if . . . Hélène . . . were to visit Uncle Vladimir's rose garden? It is famous throughout Brittany. Though not mentioned in the gardening histories," she added with another icy smile, beckoning to a tall thin youth in an embroidered smock and torn jeans who was sleepily trickling water over a bed of vivid crimson roses. Looking at him, his floppy straw-coloured hair tied back in a velvet ribbon, Hélène was torn with a sudden longing for Amsterdam and the squat and the similar dreamy young men who'd been her constant companions since she left Belfast and whom, she realized for the first time, she'd abandoned forever.

"Le Borgne," the old lady commanded, "You will show Madame, the wife of my son, around the garden for half an hour, then you will be good enough to bring her to us in the small green salon."

Taking Jean-Hubert firmly by the arm, she almost wheeled him in through the nearest door.

For half an hour Hélène trailed around massed beds of Chrysler Imperial and Papa Meilland, past climbers and shrubs in every shade of purple and crimson and orange that gripped pillars and pergolas, poured themselves into apple trees, snaked thornily across low walls. "William Lobb," Le Borgne murmured reverently, stroking the petals with long sensuous fingers, "Cérise Bouquet, La Belle Sultane, Roi de Siam, Madame Isaac Pereire . . . And here, madame," he announced, turning a corner into an isolated green space occupied by one hideous purplish shrub, "Here is Laetitia Ploudel, the rose that was especially created by the Meilland nurseries as a wedding present for Monsieur Vladimir's poor wife. It was delivered and planted, alas, on the very day of the tragedy."

"Tragedy?"

"Madame Laetitia was killed in a car accident just two weeks after the wedding," he announced with a face of sad circumstance, "They were still on their honeymoon. Monsieur Vladimir never got over it, and always refused to remarry. Though of course he had many mistresses," he added with a grin, "The old man was notorious. Though not mentioned in the Love Stories of French History."

Hélène looked at him, startled, and then laughed. She felt that at least she'd have one ally in this terrifying and unexpected place. Someone like herself. A possible friend.

"Jean-Hubert never told me it was going to be like this," she confided, "You are going to stay on and work for us, aren't you? Please?"

Le Borgne hesitated, "Well you see, madame, I'm not really . . . This is not really my . . . Oh well, yes. Yes, all right. Of course I will stay with you, madame, if you wish me to."

But by the time they'd finished the tour of the vast garden and he'd shown her the drawing-room entrance she'd almost forgotten his existence: she was irretrievably back in the past, eighteen years old, trembling with love and with panic, standing in a rose garden arguing with Chaz McCreesh.

Over the years she replaced the Chrysler Imperial with Iceberg and Candeur and Virgo. Low box hedges replaced the thorny walls. Into the trees climbed Wedding Day and Alberic Barbier and Thalia and New Dawn. Uncle Vladimir's garden, the garden of a passionate sensual old French rip, became her garden, cool and straight-faced and unimpassioned. Only Laetitia Ploudel resisted, her fierce thorns made her difficult to dislodge. Finally dug up, part of her roots stayed in the ground, to shoot up the following years as energetically as briars. In the end, Hélène gave up and there the great shrub still stood, balefully and defensively, hands on hips as it were, spitting out twice a year her great madder-crimson blossoms whose scent floated on the air like a memory of some riotous past. Laetitia Ploudel was the only red rose in the garden but luckily she was some distance from the house and Hélène had long since taken care to screen her from view with a thick hedge of pure white buddleia and syringa.

Hélène refused to have red roses in the garden; they were too mixed up in her memories. Red roses were too painful a part of her past. Spiralling back they could send her, down to that ridiculous year when she was still Eileen, not quite eighteen, and so very painfully in love.

The Turfstack's garden was, that long ago summer, a showground for some local nursery. Roses stood in straight lines or climbed pergolas, labelled. Eileen stared into the pointed insolence of deep red petals and knew for certain that she must not, that it would be the biggest mistake in her life to, leave that garden and walk with Chaz into the tobacco-scented thatched dimness where He was. Intruding on Him. His ironic eyes, the cool courtesy of His voice. His suave astonishment. "We'll go somewhere else," she pleaded, "There's a coffee place in the village. Or we could drive on into Lisburn."

But Chaz liked the look of the place and besides, he said, he needed his drink. That's what they were out for, wasn't it, a few jars and a good look at this fella of hers. "It was your idea," Chaz said, "God knows *I* never asked to play gooseberry but now that we're here," he said. Chaz said. His silly name. His Old Spice aftershave. His Christian Brothers schooling that would always stick out like chapped knuckles from under the back-slapping friendliness and the. She could still see Chaz sticking out like a chapped knuckle among the red McGredy roses. She knew she'd never again be able to look at a City of Belfast rose.

"You're not scared of the chappie, are you? Christ, I thought you were figuring to marry him. God it's a poor thing if you can't even face into the public house where he drinks!" Chaz disgracing her, as a parent might.

"There's no *question* of marrying him," she hissed in a whisper, as if the roses were attentively listening. As if the roses might be His spies. "I'm in love with him," she whispered, "I admire him more that anyone in the world. I've never in my life met anybody like him. He's not just some ordinary fellow out of a dancehall, Chaz, that I might be counting on *marrying*."

"Haw bejay!" Chaz said, "Haw bejay and what else might you be counting on doing with him? How far is this thing gone anyhow? Come on now inside here, I want to take a wee squint at this Protestant reporter of yours." Chaz, her friend, solid citizen. Solid Catholic citizen, upholding morality.

She dragged him farther down the alleyway of red roses. In case the thick pub walls might sprout concealed microphones? "It hasn't gone anywhere yet. Not as much as a kiss. He took my hand once, crossing over Botanic Avenue, and then he dropped it when we got to the other side. He takes me out, that's all, and we sit in pubs and places and talk. He's so witty, Chaz, if you knew! And he's been everywhere, he was in London for years, you could listen to him, you could just sit and listen to him."

"He's not queer is he? I bet you anything he's a bloody homo that's what it is, what age did you say he was again?"

"No he's not, it's just that fellows like that, men from that sort of, his mother was English you know, he grew up on the Malone Road and all, he was at Oxford, his dad was a British army officer you know, Christopher was born in India and everything, they're different, they don't lep on you

189

first thing, Chaz, fellows like that. I think they don't. In books they don't. They sort of get to know you first. They have to like you intellectually I think. Before they try any."

But he'd never kissed her. He'd been kind and friendly and interested, wanting to know all about her, dead keen to be introduced to her family and her student friends, but wasn't it odd that he didn't seem to fancy her at all? Even hold her hand or anything except that one time. The time he absentmindedly picked up her hand at the edge of the pavement she let it lie there in his like a frightened bird, afraid to move in case he noticed it was there and dropped it, electric shocks crackling up and down her body hoping he would absentmindedly let it stay there forever. It worried her that he didn't seem to fancy her. Even Chaz fancied her a bit, and Chaz was married and loved his wife. Chaz kissed her the first time they went out together though he never had the slightest intention of going any farther. He was really only keeping an eye on her for her mother the way Anny and Patrick had; he was just a continuation of Anny and Patrick. But he'd assumed she expected to be kissed. Any girl would, according to Chaz. Thinking back on it, she realized that Chaz must have been a right peasant underneath it all. She'd suspected it at the time, because he was so much older and yet he seemed not to have learned anything real from life, any of the things she sensed were there to be learned.

They were each other's alibis all that year, Chaz and Eileen. He loved his wife but he didn't want to look an eejit in front of the other salesmen on a Belfast trip, sitting like an innocent wee Child of Mary alone in the pictures. And his existence, his scandalous married presence in her life every few weeks, was Eileen's excuse for not going to stand like a wallflower at parochial dances. For refusing invitations to bottle parties where drunken young schoolmasters tried to get sly gropes in between stanzas of "A Nation Once Again."

Twenty years later she knew she would not have been a wallflower at the dances, and now that she was middle-aged, cool and confident, she knew that nobody needed an excuse to stay away from those dreary parties, nobody needed an alibi. But between seventeen and eighteen her life was a state of sheer panic. She had left home and school, Anny was dead, Patrick, alone on the farm, had taken to drink; she had no idea where she wanted to go. Where she was capable of going. Suddenly left without their hands to guide her she could sense the wild dogs waiting in the drain, weasels lurking in the ditch, the hundred-headed monsters, the hot leaping flames ready to devour . . . And she didn't know where to run for shelter.

That was the Sixties, the very end of the Sixties, in Belfast, just before things started falling apart. The old-fashioned bottle parties Mitzi and her crowd threw in their bed-sits round Queen's, with male virgin drunks trying to get a quick feel at one's own virginity in between singing patriotic songs. Or else the clerically-chaperoned dances her mother approved of, where shy student teachers with Pioneer pins plucked up courage to ask other shy student teachers to dance to harmless Val Doonican tunes. Eileen thought there must be more, surely there must be more than that? There must be Narnia, and Aslan the Lion, and gods and witches and a fabulous land. There must be magic. But they all assured her there wasn't. This is all there is, they told her, the grown-ups, the priests, the books she was advised to read; this is all there is, an ordinary decent Catholic life, what more do you want? Looking at the people around her – looking at Belfast, looking at Ireland –

she had a sensation of futility, of life not being lived, just being hacked away gracelessly at with blunt old chisels. She sat in her room alone and tried to write poetry and played Bob Dylan records.

It was all right, it was perfectly acceptable, to sit in a room playing Bob Dylan and trying to write poetry. Hundreds of people were doing it, all over the province; a few would become celebrated. But she didn't know that then. She took everyone's word for it that she was an oddity. She should have been out at the dances looking for a good Catholic husband. She used to cringe with shame because she couldn't bear to go out to the dances looking for a good Catholic husband.

So she waved poor Anny's nephew around the Falls Road and Bradbury Place and Stranmillis Road, like a red scandalous flag.

There was another Belfast she didn't even know existed. There were several other Belfasts that year. There was one where they sat in rooms talking about Civil Rights for Catholics; Mitzi's Belfast impinged on that one. There was one where they sat in rooms talking about running guns to defend Protestants. There was one where they knew all about the other two and thought maybe they could use them. Cash in on them. Launch themselves off them. (Some months later, all those Belfasts were to collide and become bloodily entangled for decades, but by then Eileen would be gone.)

Outside of all that, there was a Belfast where it was OK to listen to Bob Dylan and try to write poetry. She realised now that it had been Christopher Milton's Belfast but who was there around at the time to tell her that? He must have thought she already knew. She looked as if she knew. She sounded . . . But all she knew was Patrick and Anny and the townland and her mother and Gerald and Chaz, and the few things Chaz had taught her. How to order steak in a restaurant. How to let a man take off your coat, open a door, pay you a compliment. ("You're looking great, Eileen," "Thank you, Chaz." Instead of wilting and blushing like a typical Falls Road girl.) All that was a great help in fooling people. Making her look at ease in public places. All that would have made her a suitable wife for a Sales Manager. It didn't do her any harm with Jean-Hubert's people either. It had nothing much to do with Bob Dylan, or with Christopher Milton. Or with how to make Christopher love her.

More than twenty years on, among the white and cream and shell-pink nuances of her garden, she thought that probably, at the beginning, he'd been on the point of loving her. That she blew it all away, panicking, ignorant, impatient. That maybe, in Christopher Milton's Belfast, before the impatient ignorance of the bombs blew it away too, love and kindness, acceptance and rejection, were all a question of nuances that she, and everyone else, had been too thick to distinguish.

If she'd known enough to distinguish, of course, she would never have got the chance to walk in a château garden in France on a July morning. There was that. Most of the time there was that. Lurking behind that was a wise, battered-looking journalist in a beige Burberry who'd mysteriously given up a great job on a London paper to sit and drink Guinness in a thatched pub. What had he come home for? Why drop out of a promising career to trail contentedly round a shabby little city that was already, that year, beginning to show its cracks? The Irish Exile syndrome, Pierre told her it was. You have it yourself, Hélène, you're homesick. You're not pining for this

Christopher, you're just homesick, it's this Belfast of yours you're pining for. You think you ought to have stayed over there, Pierre said. You think it's your place. Well, go then, get it out of your system, Pierre said.

They'd gone into the pub, of course, she and Chaz. She'd let herself be bullied. And He was there, as she'd known He'd be, surrounded by a little group of working men drinking mugs of stout.

"What's he hanging round with that lot for?" Chaz wanted to knew when they'd slunk out, abashed, after drinking one drink. "A sophisticated chap like that, what does he want with a crowd of hard-faced navvies in Dunsher caps? I ask you!"

"He says they're authentic," she whispered wretchedly, "he always says men like that are far closer to the reality of life than."

"I tell you he's a homo, Eileen, that's your flamin' authentic!"

But she could tell Chaz didn't believe what he was saying. Chaz was blustering to hide his embarrassment, just as she was walking cool and quiet and straightfaced to the car to hide hers. The thing to have done, of course, was to have strolled smiling up to his table: "Oh Christopher, I was just suddenly longing to see you!" (Which was the exact truth. Which was why she'd suggested going there.) "And this is Chaz McCreesh, a nephew of Anny's. A nephew of that old nurse of mine." (Which was also the exact truth.) But, halfway to the table, she'd caught his coldly raised eyebrow, his quizzically contemptuous eye, and she knew he'd heard about Chaz, from Mitzi, from someone, heard the lying scarlet-woman version of Chaz she'd been using all year to keep decent Catholic mediocrity at bay. To guilt-edge her insecurities. Faced with that judging eye, all she could do was simper and giggle like some poor Falls Road yokel: "Well hi there, Chris, surprise surprise! Fancy meeting *you* here!"

He nodded, and the group of working men stared impassively from behind their broad decent Protestant faces, and she and Chaz made it to a table with their backs to him and ordered a drink and drank it, whispering: "Go you, Chaz, and ask him to join us."

"No, you. You go. You're supposed to be his friend,"

"I *can't.*"

But when at last she'd fought down her shyness and turned round, smiling at him, he was gone and his crowd of donkey-jacketed disciples with him. "Well, you've managed to spoil *their* little outing," Chaz said, "Not to mention mine!"

He was never on the doorstep again when she got back from work. He never rang the café or casually dropped in for lunch the way he sometimes had.

She bumped into him once, amazingly, in a Catholic dance-club and once, after Teresa came up to Queen's, they went to his flat to speak to him. She'd been thirsty to see him. Starving for months to see him. But that was a disaster.

Christopher thinks you're the dregs, Eileen, was what Mitzi said to her. You can forget Christopher, Eileen. But she hadn't, ever, quite forgotten him.

Hélène could not stay tending her garden all day, even though that was where her talent lay. According to Jean-Hubert. One had to cook lunch and eat it and clear away and then drive to Super U to do the shopping. But was that where her talent lay, she wondered, had she always been merely this well-groomed conventional lady who knew so well how to arrange a garden with taste? Had there not, once, been a promise? That year when she was between seventeen and eighteen, sitting in a room near the university, writing poetry and listening to Bob Dylan? So why had the promise never fulfilled itself? Had Christopher Milton destroyed it with his rejection of her? Had her parents? Anny and Patrick? Or had she destroyed it herself, because outside of that room she'd had no idea at all of how to go about living, had stumbled around blindly, not knowing the answers to any of the riddles? Had there ever, even, been a promise? She recalled, with some embarrassment, the beginning of one of her poems: 'That old woman by a June-bright gatepost, Showed me their photo in the Chronicle . . . " Hardly Seamus Heaney after all. The poem had been called "Roots", and the photo was of her Campbell grandparents and uncles and aunts, at the opening of a big new extension to their shop in Claghan. She hadn't yet met them at that stage, had not yet lived through that humiliating interview.

Still, how could it be that now, a grown-up lady, with two children to her credit, a marriage not perfect but perhaps as good as most after all, a house that functioned, happy holiday-makers in well-tended cottages, the money rolling in, growing respect from the local notables, how could it be that her husband believed her only talent lay in planting white roses in a garden? What lack was he seeing in her? Were they all seeing?

"You won't make it, Eileen," Yann said gently, crouched in the shadows beside her where he'd been painfully trying to spell out *Beautiful Losers* by the light of her candle stump, "Look at you, shit, look at you, babe!" Eileen was sitting up in her sleeping bag among the incense and the music, among the sighs and the groans of other people's love, distant and straight-faced, rubbing Helena Rubenstein into her clear straight undrugged skin as she did last thing every night. "You're not going to make it, Eileen. This isn't your scene. Go off and marry this Bourjois, live in a nice house in a French suburb, do a bit of gardening, look after your complexion, send your kids to the lycée." Said their hero, their strong chestnut-haired guru, demolishing her.

She'd noticed that people tended to make statements like that about her. Throughout her twenty-one years, one person after another had taken this tone of superior inside knowledge and sentenced her without appeal. "You can forget Christopher Milton," Mitzi spat at her that evening when dislike finally surfaced, the evening after she'd gone with Teresa to see him in his flat, "Christopher despises you. You haven't a hope. Christopher thinks you're the dregs, Eileen."

And Eileen, without trying further, had hopelessly moved away. Out of her little room up the Stranmillis Road, out of her job in the café, to cry for weeks in her mother's house, with Gerald helplessly making cups of tea, her mother telling her to snap out of it for heaven's sake, there were other fish in the sea, the man was only a Protestant and far too old for her, he might be nice enough in his own way but this was no time to go mixing with the other sort, and anyway there were far more important things going on now than boy friends and romance, could she not open her eyes and look around her, take a look at what was happening in Belfast for heaven's sake, happening to her own neighbours!

Eileen had looked dully out through the mist of her tears and seen strange stiff young men with scared eyes patrolling the street in uniform, armed. Mitzi had been preaching for years about Imperialism and British occupation and the insult of foreign troops upon our soil, but this was Eileen's first sight of a soldier of any kind, and their presence outside her home was totally irrelevant – they might as well have been stray dogs, or a flock of town pigeons – compared with the reality of her own broken heart.

Her mother and Gerald were constantly in and out, attending meetings, consulting with priests and social workers; in the end a burnt-out Catholic family was brought home to shelter for a while. "Till suitable accommodation can be found," her mother said, having quickly picked up the jargon, "And for heaven's sake show a bit of charity, Eileen. A bit of generosity." There they sat, six of them, endlessly weeping, smelling of sweat and poverty, imprinting their passive despair and their dim sense of eight centuries' oppression on the prim brown sitting-room, rubbing Eileen's nose in a grim reality she did not want to face. She suddenly put her things together one day and took the bus to Claghan, seeking out her more acceptable roots. That was dreadful: even now Eileen refused to dwell upon the coldness of the welcome that had driven her out of the tall bleak house after only two days to seek warmth among the foreign hippies squatting uncomfortably amid the strange yet familiar artifacts of an unvisited folk museum. (The museum, she realised, was exactly like Anny's house, but with the life drained out of it: too tidy, too complete in its period fittings.)

One of the hippies had been Yann. She told him her story and he listened without comment and then suggested she drop everything and leave Ireland along with them: Claghan was no longer a cool place to be. She had listlessly obeyed, having no other alternatives. Later, in Amsterdam: "You'll never make it, Eileen," he told her. "This isn't your scene," he said.

All their friends were making it back then, in the dead Seventies, were handcrafting their lives into some nostalgic fantasy of childhood innocence. Trailing clouds of glory up mountains and through deserts and into little lost hamlets with exotic names. Anneka and Kees were keeping sheep in the Pyrenees, Tamsin was cultivating edible seaweed in Connemara, John and Judy spreading their Jesus People gospel of peace and of love from a shack in the Sinai desert, Anita collecting rare herbs and unguents from remote Indian tribes.

But: "You're never going to make it," Yann advised, "You'd much better marry this bourgeois kid, this fils à papa, go on and marry your French daddy's boy," Yann said. Or Jan. She never even knew how his name was spelt.

He'd been across the Sahara in a landrover, Yann had, walked through Iran to Persepolis, to the peacock-feasting at Persepolis, had these blue angel's eyes under russet lashes, what was he: Swedish? Danish? Breton? She may have heard he was Danish. Until Jean-Hubert came along he sat with them every night, gentle and quiet and wise, in the squat on Weespersijde, "Suzanne" like rich heavy smoke on the air (Eileen said, trying to be clever, and he smiled and she felt stupid), the rich smoky wisdom of Leonard Cohen's voice, Yann sitting with them on the piled-up sleeping bags that were their sofa, in an abandoned grocer shop beside the, was it river or canal? Fish floated past the door on their backs in dead white shoals, poisoned even then by the waste from the factories higher up. It was the Amstel of course, they were all playing at being Suzanne in their rags and their feathers, squatting among the garbage of a decade that was already being polluted and poisoned though they didn't know it, thought it was going to go on forever.

Eileen was born slightly too late, she nearly missed out

on the lovely spoiled second childhood of the century. Nearly. The Sixties obligingly spilled over into the Seventies for her, only really coming to a stop when Jean-Hubert brought her to France and the respectable adult world. She married Jean-Hubert Bourjois out of sheer obedience to Yann, or out of laziness, or the need for shelter. Or out of a sense of her own inadequacy, ('What better do you think you'll find, Eileen, for heaven's sake? What prince are you waiting for?' In her mother's voice, in Anny's, in Teresa's.) Or in one more effort to wipe out Christopher Milton. She certainly wasn't in love with this French boy, tall and dark and elegant though he was, this beautiful cliché loping moodily along the Amstel, sowing his wild oats among the last of the hippies. Not as she remembered love from that Belfast summer. Yann was in love with him, hopelessly and jeeringly, obsessively matchmaking for Eileen out of his own frustration. Jan was less gentle and less wise when Jean-Hubert dropped in on the squat.

She didn't often think of Yann after they moved to France, in fact she never thought of Jan, he died like a nobody a year or so after they left: this wise free spirit, this omnipotent passer of judgements, died like any poor prick, of an overdose of heroin. Eileen had been counting on him, counting on his lifelong friendship, counting on years and volumes and trunkloads of wise and witty letters to guide her through the stony paths of exile. When she found out he was dead she went back to thinking about Christopher Milton instead.

She'd expected to go travelling with Jean-Hubert: he'd talked vaguely of Katmandou and of the Arizona desert, and of tilling the land in the Shetlands or in some outlandish part of Wales. Instead they went tamely to live in Brittany where there were no hippies, where the land was still being tilled by squat peasants in Gitane-blue boiler suits, perched glum-faced on top of their John Deere tractors.

"Mustn't look a gift house in the moat," Yann sneered when he heard of the unexpected inheritance.

Jean-Hubert laughed and coaxed the dismay out of Eileen's face: "Maybe just for a year, chick, it could be cool for a year, lord of the manor could be a fantastic trip, baby!" Jean-Hubert talked like that, back in the Seventies, unbelievable as it sounded to her now.

Old Maître Bourin, the family solicitor, had tracked Jean-Hubert down with difficulty to the new squat near the Concertgebouw, had taken in Eileen's existence with a sniff, and that of the twins with a sigh, and sat uneasily for an hour or two among the incense and the Afghan rugs and the remains of the takeaway rijstafel they'd hastily bought to be hospitable, telling them about l'oncle Vladimir's will.

"Vladimir!" Eileen gigged foolishly, to hide her dismay, "Wouldn't Estragon have been more Français? Was the old boy a Russian, then?"

"Not our kind of Russian," Jean-Hubert told her, and Maître Bourin sniffed again, "The other kind, the kind full of samovars and sables and sleigh bells in the snow, and exiled dukes driving taxis in Paris. One of my relations married into them a couple of generations ago and the family's never quite got over it."

The 'maybe a year, baby' didn't stand a chance. Hardly were they crossed over the frontier into France with twins and belongings bundled into an ancient Volkswagen van than the mantle of noblesse oblige dropped with a thump on to Jean-Hubert's shoulders and he'd been wearing himself out trying to grow into it ever since.

Hélène thought of the Seventies again that Wednesday afternoon in the supermarket. They started playing a

Leonard Cohen tape while she was wandering in the aisles pushing her trolley, consulting her shopping list. Suddenly among the golden oldies for the ladies with the shopping baskets, suddenly there he was, and how amazing, how utterly amazing, she hadn't heard him for years and years! Why had she not heard him? How had she not heard him? Where had he been? Could he possibly have been there all the time, wryly commenting on the years and the modes and the doings, gently and richly guiding other people's lives while she was wearing herself out, stumbling ineptly after Jean-Hubert through the labyrinth of Beethoven and Xenakis and Mozart? *Everybody knows the war is over,* Leonard Cohen was singing, and his voice was a thousand years older and a thousand years wearier, as she wheeled her trolley down endless avenues of tinned couscous and cassoulet, *Everybody knows the good guys lost,* but Hélène was, lullingly and anachronistically, still hearing *rags and feathers from Salvation Army counters,* Hélène in silk shirt and pleated skirt was picking up packets of Grandmère coffee beans and jars of Oxford marmalade and cartons of fresh cream and fromage frais, and escalopes in cellophane and Gruyère and Brie and Roquefort and mushrooms, and *Old Black Joe's still pickin cotton for your ribbons and bows,* but Eileen was wheeling her laden trolley through magical abundance, towards the mythical Chinese tea and Chinese oranges . . . *Everybody knows the boat is leaking,* he sang, *everybody knows the captain lied,* but Hélène, missing the point as Eileen never would have done, stopped dead in her tracks in disgust: Leonard Cohen had become a sales technique, an aid to relaxed consumerism, his golden voice was only there to make her buy and buy and buy . . . Leonard Cohen, the spirit of the long-dead Seventies, and Yann was dead and the squat was bulldozed out of existence and Christopher Milton, just another British tourist in a BMW, had walked away again and left her in tears again beside the statue of one of those dreary old French writers Jean-Hubert was never done quoting.

All those years had dithered by since the squat on the Amstel and there she was, in high-heeled Bally sandals and classically-pleated skirt, standing in an air-conditioned supermarket in France, nodding to the doctors' wives and the notaires' wives, (*not* nodding to, not even seeing, the lumpy anonymous village wives who did their shopping in nylon overalls and bedroom slippers: no nonsense about equality and fraternity in Plouch'en). She saw herself quite clearly for an instant, she gaped open-mouthed for a split second into the face of time, but what could she really do, only go on buying meat and fruit and salad and Ajax? She had a big house to run, tourist cottages to look after, and they were having old Maître Bourin to dinner the following evening. And they might as well have the Bouchons too while they were about it, now that old Ruby was out of the way for a few days. Pierre could casually bring up the idea of Carrickfergus for Jean-Hubert's approval, and poor lonesome Rosalind would be only too delighted to be asked up at the last minute to eat a meal at the château . . .

She paid, and packed her things into the car boot, and drove home remembering the squat, and beautiful gay Yann chastely sharing her sleeping bag, and Colleen and Carol and Patrick and Val, and Ian from Claghan going off every evening with his hair tied back in a velvet ribbon and his lock-picking tools in an embroidered bag, and Clodagh painting stolen bicycles in psychedelic colours to sell in the Flea Market.

"Do you steal too?" Jean-Hubert asked avidly the first time they shared a joint together in the Mellow Yellow. It was a big turn-on for him, being there with them. Cool that there was this whole street made of nothing but squats, that even their local café was a cracked house where they cooked hashish-cake and coffee with electricity tapped illegally from the street cables. Far-out, all those chicks with sweet unmade-up faces and fluffy hennaed hair and long trailing dresses from Salvation Army counters.

Jean-Hubert wanted to be Involved, Jean-Hubert wanted to Live. In May '68, aged sixteen, he'd torn up a paving-stone and hurled it vaguely in the direction of the Riot Police. From there (though he'd wisely finished his studies and got his degree first) the logical destination could only be a commune in Amsterdam and political protest and a decadent love affair with a gangster's moll.

"The mild-eyed melancholy lotus-eaters," Jean-Hubert called the kids in the squat, that first day when he walked in out of nowhere, vainly trying to interest them in a demo about Allende's death. "It is a literary quotation," he added kindly and they gaped, most of them, wondering vaguely from what Hermann Hesse, from what Ginsburg, what St Exupery . . . But, in any case, taking it as a compliment because Jean-Hubert's accent, when he spoke English, was so childishly touching, so charmingly innocent.

"Let us alone!" Eileen snapped, sensing the condescension, "What pleasure can we have/ To war with evil?", because Gerald was a great one for reciting Tennyson, and Jean-Hubert looked at her appreciatively and gave this funny nineteenth-century bow that went beautifully with his frilly shirt and embroidered jacket, and asked her to come and have a coffee in the Mellow Yellow. That was foreign and surprising and a delightful courtesy – it ought to have been a warning. Guys did not ask you out formally in those days. Asking a girl out was all part of the old patronising male-domination scene that was like, dead, man: what you did was, you drifted together by some gentle loving instinct and you trailed yourselves together in the sunshine along the banks of the Amstel and you subsided together on to a wooden bench along a scrubbed café table, hands touching or not touching, eyes meeting or not meeting, a future vaguely together or vaguely elsewhere. But Jean-Hubert looked her over and visibly summed her up as being the only chick in the squat that might be worth his while, and then he formally asked her out for a coffee.

"That should have warned me," she murmured to Michel Le Borgne the first day, the first half hour, wandering through Uncle Vladimir's garden, "Should have warned me that this whole incredible scene would eventually exist. Or some scene in the same genre . . . "

"I don't steal," Eileen said, "I haven't the talent, for one thing. And my ancestry forbids it, for another."

"Mine too!" he enthused, "I also have ancestors too arrogant to permit me to steal the bicycle of a Dutch worker. But I want to live differently, quand même, from these ancestors of mine. Not you?"

"Oh me too," she said fervently, thinking of her poor drunken daddy slumped into the back of his mate's van, with a bomb for a pillow, "In fact I am living differently. Though I think my family were expecting me to join the IRA, just to annoy them." She added that bit lightly, to hide the fact that her mother and Gerald had given up expecting anything much of her. In those days you could still talk lightly about the IRA: in spite of poor Mitzi and her flatmates being picked up and interned, in spite of Bloody Sunday and the horrific pub bombings, it still seemed a bit of bravado that would probably blow over in another six months or so. Like Jean-Hubert's famous May '68. And she was not living all that differently: the cement-floored squat, without electricity or running water, the easy-going hand-to-mouth quality of their days, bore a comforting resemblance to the life she'd led up to the age of ten, in Anny and Patrick's cottage in Ireland.

"And do you intend to stay here forever, smoking pot in Amsterdam?" Jean-Hubert asked her, gazing theatrically into her eyes in a way none of the men she'd known had ever gazed. In a way Christopher Milton had decidedly not gazed. "What do you live on, Eileen, if you don't steal?" Months later he told her that he'd been expecting to hear that she lived on prostitution: it would have seemed quite logical to him in the circumstances. He had no points of reference at all for people like Eileen. In Jean-Hubert's world there were nice conventional middle-class girls who dressed themselves with quiet chic and played tennis and studied for careers and went to nice conventional middle-class parties to find husbands exactly similar to their fathers and brothers. There were also the peasant girls he met when he stayed with Uncle Vladimir in the summer, daughters of the tenant farmers; great chaste lumps, he said, with woolly armpits, and many of them actually Uncle Vladimir's own daughters: very virile among the peasantry, l'oncle Vlad in his day. And finally there were 'les putes.' Surely a girl who lowered herself to accept lifts in strange cars, and wore second-hand clothes (so badly cut too!), and washed herself in the public baths, and slept in one room with a gang of thieves and drop-outs would not draw the line at turning an honest guilder on the streets? So reasoned Jean-Hubert.

"A prostitute!" Eileen yelled at him, "Me! You must have been crazy!"

He shrugged: "Only at first I thought it. It is a perfectly honourable profession, very well regarded in my country. It seemed as natural as anything else you might have been doing. If you had been, of course, I could not have married you."

"But in France there must be girls like me? Hippies? Freaks? Girls who've rejected boring middle-class values and choose to do their own thing?"

"In Frrrrawnce," said Jean-Hubert grandly, "En Frrrrawnce, my dear, we have quite different standards."

The arrogant way he rolled the "r" in "France" was very attractive to her then. She became accustomed to it over the years. Every rolled "r" taught her a useful lesson in becoming an acceptable French wife. At some point she found herself in such danger of being rolled into a doormat that she began longing, at odd moments, not for the squat or for Yann, but longing again for Christopher Milton whom she thought she'd forgotten, her first and only love.

In the beginning they lived in Amsterdam, in a luxury flat Ian cracked for them. Quite soon all the others from the squat moved in along with them, so marriage was just a continuation of the lovely carefree life on Weespersijde. When the twins were born they seemed to belong to everyone, the only sour note being when Jean-Hubert peremptorily rejected all the lovely gentle Hindu names that were floating about and insisted that they be christened Henri and Clémence. Family names. Names of their French ancestors. It was after the birth of the twins that Jean-Hubert began changing.

Christopher Milton made his first reappearance in her dreams the night they crossed the frontier into France and camped by a river near Mulhouse. Next morning she woke up crying, so noisily that it woke Jean-Hubert, who instantly rolled over and made love to her. Without asking what was wrong, but assuming that whatever her problem was his body would be sufficient to solve it. As it did solve it, for ten minutes or so. But when he looked at his watch and said: "They'll be awake and hungry soon," and crawled outside to light the camping gas, she remembered why she'd been crying and she sat up in the sleeping bag and couldn't stop talking.

"Do you know, Jean-Hubert," she said, "My very first lover was an Ulster Presbyterian, would you believe it? And so was the first man I was ever in love with. Two different guys of course. Picture," she said, "a big broad solemn-faced fanatic in a bowler hat, a dead ringer, say, for the Reverend Ian? Right? Now picture the exact opposite of that, the exact opposite of everything you've ever heard about awful Ulster protestants. Got it? Well, that's Richard. Now ditto, only about ten years older, and that's Christopher Milton. I slept with Richard because Christopher wouldn't have me! Oh not that I'm still pining," she said, "Only just I dreamed about Christopher last night and you know how when you dream about someone he invades you body and soul, he colonises you? Takes you over the whole day after and shatters you completely? Unless you manage to exorcise him first thing. Will you let me exorcise Christopher on you, Jean-Hubert?" She was sitting up in the sleeping bag, holding her knees, talking urgently out at him where he was bent over the camping gas stove. "Will you?"

He didn't answer, crouched over with his back to her, his silky black hair swinging over the saucepan of water where the twins' bottles were warming. The twins lay sleeping in their baskets, sucking not quite identical thumbs.

"Not a blow-by-blow account," she pleaded, "Just tell you this weird dream, this awful sort of . . ."

"I don't want to hear it," he enunciated coldly, with his back still turned, "I don't want to hear anything. Not dreams or sordid details. I don't want to hear a thing. You are my wife, therefore any squalid little adventures you may have had in your past do not interest me. Tu comprends ça, ou tu ne comprends pas?"

She understood. Vive la Frrrrawnce, she hooted glumly and silently, lying back again in the sleeping bag watching Jean-Hubert, that modern male, working away out there in the other compartment, warming his babies' bottles. She understood, well was beginning to understand, that Jean-Hubert, having fathered a family, inherited a château, was stepping back into some stiff ancestral armour. That he needed, for his own dignity, to pretend to himself that he'd created his own wife: that he'd written her, that he'd painted her, that he'd taken a piece of clay and fashioned her, that he and he alone was her author. Long-haired and bearded and jeaned as he was, some part of the Latin maleness deep within him needed to believe that his chosen bride, la mère de ses enfants, had come to him in well-bred holy purity, had brought him her priceless treasure still intact.

Treasure, she thought, treasure? For those three love-torn wandering years before she met him had some value; she had not, after all, sprung into existence when he shone his light upon her. She was there. She was real. She was making her way. Not walled up behind a thorn hedge waiting for some prince to free her. Kiss this prince, she thought, and he turned into a strait-laced old frog, corseted in Catholic tradition. I must remember that line, she thought, write it in a letter to Teresa. Or not. *I'm* the one who got away after all, she thought, alone on her back watching French sunlight filter blue through the canvas, her children asleep at her feet. *I'm* the one who refused to get bogged down in the misery of Belfast, who actually had the courage to roam off across the continent and meet an exotic foreign nobleman. I'm the lucky one.

Poor Teresa had written her a comic letter describing her own catastrophic wedding night, sitting up in bed in a Dublin bridal suite watching her Timothy carefully unroll and stretch every one of his precious begged, borrowed or stolen French letters to its full and useless length, utterly terrified to tell him how he *ought* to be doing it because then he'd know for certain, instead of just suspecting, that Teresa's precious treasure etcetera. Teresa's accounts of her chronically-pregnant marriage were comic, but why should Eileen make a victim of herself just to amuse a friend?

I'm not a victim, she thought, I'm a happy woman. This is the man, out of all other men, with whom I've chosen to spend the rest of my life. Only, since the twins were born, he'd turned into de Gaulle or someone, and she was beginning to suspect that this was the real Jean-Hubert. That the other, the moody dreamer who'd loped into her life and married her in that picturesque ceremony in a grey old Amsterdam church, had been only a sack of wild oats getting sown.

And then, the previous night, lying in the tent with Jean-Hubert beside her and the twins asleep in their baskets at her feet, she'd dreamed that Christopher Milton was dead, and when she woke her throat was sore from crying.

In the dream there was a country house, a cottage in the Mourne mountains. She lifted the latch and walked right in. There was no wolf, no kind wise grandmother, no strong commonsensical wood-cutter to restore her to life. There was a quantity of dust on shabby deserted-looking furniture. She waited for him with the anxious Mills and Boon heart-thumping dried-up mouth, sick stomach, there always had been while she waited for him. Then an inside door opened and a thin dark-suited man, a man with a holy Presbyterian face, a Twelfth of July face, entered the room, showing not the least surprise at seeing her there: "This is where he died, Mrs, this here is the room he died in."

The least she could do was fall in with his casual tone: she'd always been a great one for letting others set the tone, for pretending to more information than she actually possessed. So she silently took on herself the knowledge of Christopher's death.

"He was living here at the time?" she asked.

"Just at the end," the man said. "He moved back over to London, you know, when the Troubles started, and then he was in the States for a long time too. Recruiting."

"Recruiting for . . . ?"

"It's all in the Biography, Mrs, five pound fifty at the wee bookstall upstairs. But he came back here you see, to die. He was crippled in the latter end. Paralysed."

She thought: I could have come here sooner and found him alive. Crippled. "When did he?"

"A long time ago, Mrs, he's dead this brave wee while now."

In the man's voice she recognised the intonations, the Ulster country idioms that had turned into quiet comedy when Christopher touched them with his voice of cool privilege. (Though not comedy for her. Wounds quickly covered over with a sycophantic smile. The times she'd secretly bled to hear Anny's speech, Patrick's, the speech of her ignorant loved childhood world caricatured so beautifully and so cruelly in his ironic public-school voice.)

If she'd come back sooner she might have sat by his chair, by his bed, been allowed to hold his hand and explain herself, the bewildered self she'd hidden from him and from everyone behind the straight pale mask of her composed face, been allowed to smooth pillows, fetch glasses of water . . . (Glasses of *water*, for Christopher Milton? Even in the dream she'd seen the absurdity of that. And yet, would he have been allowed to die still sipping with his connoisseur's sip, his cultivated Protestant outsider's sip, at a pint mug of Irish working-man's stout? Would they have let him? They? Had even Christopher, at the end, been helpless in the hands of starched white anonymous Theys? That witty ironic lift of an eyebrow carelessly wiped off like old man's spittle by the back of a countrified nurse's hand? The quietly demolishing phrase, so expensively gift-wrapped in its quote-unquote inverted commas brackets careful absence of capitals, torn apart by empty cheerful bog-laughter: och aren't we the naughty boy the day Mister Milton, aren't we the shawkin man for the wee joke! Had it been like that, without dignity, his end in the cottage in the mountains?)

The clerical-suited guide (butler, minder, strongman? Lover?) led her around the three rooms, pointed with a straight face to The Works, bound in artificial leather on the shelves of an imitation-oak, imitation-Irish, dresser. (It's that should have put you wise, Pierre told her years later, all that imitation stuff. Did that not enlighten you a bit, he asked her, and she didn't know what he was talking about.)

She tried to manufacture some awed touristy remark and hide behind it away from the guide's knowing contemptuous eyes. Had he been there, unnoticed, years ago whenever she went out with Christopher: watching her, knowing her? Had he been one of the tough picturesque working-men drinking Guinness in that country pub? Recognising her? She could make no remark because she was crying. She woke up crying. Lying in the tent her throat was aching from sobs and Jean-Hubert, Henri, Clémence, her future in this pretty foreign country, existed only as the total absence of Christopher Milton. Her whole future was nothing but an absence of Christopher. She knew it would pass, it always had, but for a few hours she would be invaded, weakened with tenderness and loss and desire and hate. As the day advanced it would pass. She knew it would pass.

Christopher Milton was not dead. Not that she knew of. Though again, how could she know? For a long time after leaving Belfast she'd assumed that she would, somehow, know if he'd died. She had an idea that one day, far in the future, she would stop at a news-stand somewhere in Europe to buy *Vogue* or *Elle* or *Rolling Stone* and there, exceptionally, would be a week-old copy of the *Belfast Telegraph* and she would open it and read of his death and be finally cured of him. Quietly at his residence after a long illness, or victim of a pub bombing, or executed as a token Protestant. It never occurred to her that she might one day open a paper and see his name or photo in some happier context: smiling at an art exhibition, distributing prizes, leading a Peace March, marrying a celebrity. And yet. Anyone born and reared in a place as small as Northern Ireland has the habit of living next door to headlines. Her art teacher at the convent was moving up to become one of Ireland's top painters, a classmate emigrated and got strangled in Bayswater, King Creon in the school play had made it into politics, somebody else was a fashionable journalist. At least two of her primary-school companions had in the past year been tried for murder. Poor Mitzi, released from internment, had almost immediately started serving a life sentence in Armagh jail. And, to go farther back, a distant cousin of Gerald's first wife had actually made it into the history books.

She herself had not emerged into any limelight, nor did she keep in touch with those who had. Christopher Milton was conceivably doing very well, unknown to her, in whatever career he'd finally adopted, and in the dream he had indeed been a successful man. And a dead one. She never, after walking away from his contempt, pictured herself hearing of him in any role but that of distant unseen corpse, respectably buried and disposed of long before any reaction was expected of her, but this was the first time she'd actually dreamed him dead. This was the first time since she married Jean-Hubert that she'd dreamed of him at all. After she left Belfast she dreamed of him often, and during that first appallingly homesick year in Amsterdam he was the constant companion of her nights. Always rejecting, always contemptuous, turning his back on her at a party, looking out at her blankly from a passing car as she stood hitching at the side of some endless desert track, stepping into a plane as she hammered hopelessly at the glass wall of the locked departure lounge, standing with cold face at the edge of a dance floor as she jerked and twisted and wriggled under the changing lights, ever more fantastically, ever more grotesquely, pleading for his desire.

Always rejecting her and now, dead.

The babies' bottles were warm. In every woman's page and magazine that year, poor housebound mothers were plagued with snotty screaming babies. The twins were beautiful and rarely cried. She herself was certainly not housebound, moving as she did from squat to tent to borrowed flat. And now, in two or three days, to a Breton château. I dreamed of Chris, she thought, only because of the château. Because I'm worried sick about going to live in this château. Because it's going to be the Falls Road drawing-room all over again, a big strange house that's sure to reject me.

Try as she might, her new home and the role she would have to play in it refused to take on any possible shape in her imagination. Outside Maastricht, on their way down from Holland, they'd spent a night in a big bare castle whose eccentric owner had thrown it open as a refuge for hippies and artists. Castel Burgh. It hadn't been bad, not impressive or anything, just an overgrown cream-coloured house set back from the road up a little hill, with big empty rooms smelling comfortingly of incense and pot. "Is it going to be something like this, our château?" she'd asked hopefully, already dreaming of throwing it hospitably open to every fascinating wayfarer who might happen to pass by on the road.

Jean-Hubert looked contemptuously about him and snapped: "It certainly is not! Why should it be like this? In Frrrawnce, my dear, we know about architecture!"

I was happy in Amsterdam, she thought, I was happy and safe and protected just like I was in Anny's. I dreamed about Christopher because, once again, my life is about to change as radically as it did when Anny died and I left home and met him for the very first time.

Jean-Hubert handed a bottle in through the flap in silence. Silent dudgeon, she wondered uneasily, having already learned to be wary of his moods, or was it only that he was still half asleep? He picked Henri expertly from his basket and fed him outside on the grass. She took Clémence, arranged her comfortably in the crook of her arm, and set her drinking, imagining with tenderness that Christopher Milton would draw open the flap of the tent and sit beside her in gentle amused patience while she fed their baby. Then she wondered: if Jean-Hubert could read her thoughts, would he see himself as a cuckold, every Frenchman's nightmare? And was able to laugh at herself through her tears.

She was still called Eileen then. If she'd married into a

different milieu she could have kept her name. Among left-wing intellectuals, for example, it would have had romantic overtones of Joyce and O'Casey and the Abbey Theatre and oppressed nations. Oppressed nations had a certain chic in France in the Seventies. But Jean-Hubert's mother had visited Ireland before her marriage, staying in various Big Houses, where the servants were all called Eileen. Those that weren't called Anny and Patrick.

In spite of losing both her names, in spite of the initial chill of her welcome to the château, and in spite of Jean-Hubert's disquieting change of character, Hélène had settled contentedly into life in Plouch'en. She was soon accepted as a daughter-in-law and, by Tante Ruby, as a niece-in-law: after Maître Bourin's report they had been expecting much worse. And then, the ancestry her husband had invented for her was all in her favour. Jean-Hubert's father had been a Provençal schoolmaster who joined the Resistance and married into the safe château from which he'd operated but he'd been, after all, a very obscure hero. The first Mrs O'Neill's far-off cousin, whom Jean-Hubert adopted so defensively as a close in-law that first evening, was in all the Irish history books: the old-fashioned kind that called her either a martyr or a villain, depending on the author's allegiance, and later the revisionist sort that saw her as a victim of the puritanism of her time. Eileen's immediate family too was judged presentable. (Though not by Tante Ruby who was heard to mutter: Petit bourgeois! Another Ploudel de Medeu has married into the middle class. I'd have known where I was with Irish peasants!)

Anny was dead by then of course, and Patrick in a Home, but *They* put in an appearance. Her mother and Gerald. In Donegal tweed suits and careful Linguaphone French and an air of sweet parental reason: "We were scared stiff that she'd fall in with some riff-raff! But Jean-Hubert is a lovely boy, and such a nice Catholic family too!"

"Jean-Hubert was brought up by the Jesuits, of course," Tante Ruby replied with cold sweetness, making the distinction between château Catholics and the Falls Road kind. Fervent believers themselves, the Ploudel de Medeus were glad la petite Hélène had the gift of faith; socially though, they would have far preferred her to be an Irish Protestant . . .

When she got back from the supermarket, wallowing as she so often did in the bitter sweetness of memory Hélène, to her utter amazement, found Nathalie Le Borgne and her lover busy in the kitchen, clearing away the last vestiges of the weekend chaos. Jean-Hubert was leaning against a doorpost, a tall glass of lemon tea in his hand, instructing them where to put things, his eyes interestedly following Nathalie's rather large bottom as it rolled rhythmically between sink and dresser, She giggled rosily as she passed him with a loaded tray of cups and dropped what was almost a curtsey in his direction. She did indeed look like anyone's idea of the old-fashioned buxom serving wench, and in the nineteen-nineties too: vive la Frrrawnce!

Hélène wondered with a little pang of distaste exactly what methods Jean-Hubert had found necessary to persuade her.

"I told you I'd organise it!" he crowed triumphantly, "Nathalie has agreed to cook for us, Gabriel will assist you with the housework and service, on the evening of the party we will dress them both up in pretty uniforms to look after our guests. Oh and I've given them the Dutch couple's room in the meantime; we shall see how things turn out."

"You're crazy!" Hélène protested, dragging him out into the corridor, "You've lost your mind, Jean-Hubert, you can't

217

instal that pair here in the château! Not with Michel as our gardener. It's so cruel. And just when we were being accepted so nicely. Just when everyone was starting to forget about old Vladimir! What's the village going to think of us now?"

"Don't be so middle-class, darling," he said testily in English, "*We* don't have to worry what the village thinks of us!"

"We'll have Father Plouer up to us, you know what he's like. It's so sordid. It's revolting. And what about the twins?"

"The twins are seventeen, old enough I would have thought to accept the facts of life. Écoute, ma chérie, we have our style of living to keep up, n'est ce pas, and you will agree that domestic help is almost impossible to find. At least the kind we can afford is. I notice you did not worry what Father Plouer thought of the Dutch couple and their very evident gaiety!"

She looked at him in amazement: "But why should he have thought anything? They were not his parishioners, and even if they had been, their private lives wouldn't have been any of his business."

"I doubt if Nathalie and Gabriel spend much of their lives in Father Plouer's confessional so *their* private lives need not concern him either, Listen, my dear, this way everyone is going to be happy. We are happy, they are happy, our guests are going to be happy. The little one would not have agreed to come otherwise, her Gabriel c'est la grande passion at present. It cannot last of course, but with some luck and some encouragement it will see us through the summer. And if you knew how little I got off with paying them!"

"But . . . "

"These situations occur every day, Hélène, in the world

we inhabit. Wake up, my dear, this is France in the nineties, not your Irish townland of thirty years ago!"

"I don't think these situations occur in holy Catholic Breton villages. Not out in the open anyway . . . "

"Catholic! They ask Father Plouer to baptise them, to marry them, to bury them. It is all for show, it looks well. Outside of that they don't give a shit about your Catholicism. You are still such a foreigner, ma pauvre Hélène, you have not yet seized any of the nuances."

"I've lived here sixteen years. Longer that I've lived anywhere else. And the village church is crowded every Sunday, *and* they all go to Communion, that's hardly for show. And old Father Plouer's just as strict as any priest I knew in Ireland thirty years ago. Oh God, how can we ever invite him to lunch again, I'd die of shame! You just can't do this, Jean-Hubert. And poor Michel . . . The poor husband. What about poor Michel Le Borgne?"

"The husband?" Jean-Hubert repeated, "Eh bien, my dear, if you look out of that window tomorrow morning, I am sure you will see the husband quite happily cutting your grass as usual. We are in France, ma chère Hélène, nous sommes en Frrrrawnce ici!"

In high good humour he skipped down the steps and drove away to collect the twins from their music lesson.

Part Six

❧

"... and it is the school holidays, doctor, and no one will come to find him till the rentrée. He has no friends, you understand, none at all, and he allows me to have none, no one ever comes to the house to see us ... And then I will take his car and drive home to Loguivy and spend my summer among the rocks and the whins and I will find a little cottage and ..."

"Ah yes, madame, but you will not have long to enjoy your little cottage n'est ce pas? When they find his body at the rentrée ... Living in a prison cell could be even less amusing than living with your husband in the schoolhouse, madame!"

Snipping off the poor man's balls indeed, and leaving him to die: the human mind and all its ugly little labyrinths! Why hadn't he trained as a plumber like his father wanted, it might have been cleaner. Pierre wondered briefly what the Balavoines' sex life must be like, but forebore once again to mention it: doctor or no doctor he felt that at ten o'clock in the morning he would prefer not to be regaled with a detailed account of the activities of his old schoolmaster's disgusting zizi, thank you very much! He knew that he

220

ought, on some occasion, to bring up the subject, it might well be important. If he'd been a real psychiatrist . . . It was often, he knew, the key to all other difficulties. Though surely in this case . . . Even if old René Balavoine conducted his wife to the gates of Paradise three times a night, it still wouldn't make him any less of a tyrant to live with in the daytime, the problem wasn't there.

Pierre recalled his own childhood in the village school, with old Balavoine – younger and slimmer then – standing at the top of the classroom, his cold eyes darting from desk to desk choosing a victim, making ready to drown and dazzle and stupefy that victim with stentorian roars of insult. How did I survive? The endless pages of French history learned off by heart, century after century of thrilling adventure made bloodless and boring, the viciously twisted ear if you recited a word out of place. He could still remember whole useless passages: *Robespierre executed, the citizens of Paris assumed the Revolution was ended and staged an uprising which was firmly suppressed by a young general named Bonaparte* – Repeat me that word for word, boys, or I'll twist the ears off you! The long long hours of irregular verbs – fairytales and poems and nursery rhymes reduced to dry grammatical construction. The way the bastard stood menacingly behind you as he enunciated phrase after phrase of never-ending dictations: "Maître Corbeau sur un arbre perché . . ." Crunch of the ruler upon knuckles: "Perché, perché, perché . . . Are you an imbecile, Bouchon? Or merely an idiot? Is it a congenital defect, perhaps? Peasant inbreeding?" The brightest pupils reduced to stammering fools. Education itself reduced to the parroting of clichés, the systematic assassination of all natural curiosity, the production of generation after generation of dull obedient sheep. L'éducation française. Could that be the explanation, he wondered, of our shameful collaboration with the Nazis? Could it be as simple as that, the conduct that's had the whole world wondering about us for fifty years? A whole system of schoolmasters like Balavoine, from nursery school on up, so that by adulthood we're conditioned to ask no questions, utter no protest, just drop to our knees and lick any jackboot that presents itself? They've got this mill, he thought, and they feed in lions and swans and donkeys and ducks and racehorses and the miller turns the handle and out comes a string of dull identical sheep. You only escape if you're big enough, or small enough, to avoid being completely ground. Yes, but there's millers and millers . . . I'd chop the salaud to bits myself, he thought, and I only had three years with him, not a whole lifetime like this poor cow. He was amazed at the sudden wave of hate that caught him up and silently shook him: why are we all such prisoners of our childhood? Why can't we ever get over it? Madame Bourjois even, the other evening (and that was a turn-up for the book all right!) still endlessly living and re-living those long-gone years of rejection. Ready to go chasing after shadows that must be dust and ashes by now, he'd been in Belfast, oh la la! He'd been there all right, nostalgia hadn't a hope in that place, she'd be damn glad to come running back to Jean-Hubert . . . But this poor thing here. Twittering on regularly once a week. Her memories, her fears, her resentments, her fantasies of violence. It kept her going, she said.

"Not that I'd have the first idea of how to cut off anyone's balls, doctor! Actually I don't think there is a sharp enough pair of scissors in the house, I've never been a great one for the needlework. But as you say, doctor, we all need our little fantasies . . . "

He wondered if she was as mad as a hatter after all. If he

222

ought to recommend her to a psychiatrist? If he didn't send her to a shrink would he be in danger of ending up with some hideous village massacre on his conscience? The old dear charging round the beach one afternoon brandishing the garden shears? Snip-snip, aaiiiieee! No. What nonsense. Of course she wasn't mad. She was probably saner than most people. Forty years with old Balavoine and still fit for a joke and a giggle, you had to hand it to her. Rich inner life. Devotion to her children. Though . . . Well, Jean-Marc was a decent skin, never set the world on fire, she says she had ambitions for him, child genius etcetera, blames the old man. Yeah, well. Pinch of salt definitely called for there. And Magali. He remembered Magali as a kid, a few years younger than himself, timid little thing with scared eyes, always hanging about in the château woods. Playing with Jean-Hubert in the summer holidays. They kept him out of their games.

"Plouc! Peasant!" they used to sing out from up in the branches, Magali made brave by her Parisian hero, her knight of the high castle, "Your old mother stinks of garlic!"

Well that was true enough, she did. The shame of his mother in a big white apron sweating away over the huge Aga cookers in the château kitchens: "Come on up there with me today, Pierrot, put on your Sunday clothes, old Monsieur Vladimir invited you, now wasn't that kind of him? Your little friend Jean-Hubert arrived from Paris last night, be a bit of company for you n'est ce pas? Better than hanging round the market stalls with that little crook Denis Le Borgne, voyons!"

Poor maman! She'd pictured the young master and himself having long refined chats, about books perhaps, about Paris, about museums and theatres, had long destined him for a future far beyond the village school.

"Plouc! Dirty peasant! Sale petit péquenot!" They'd had unanswerable power, both of them. Nephew of the château, daughter of the schoolhouse. Did anyone ever really get over it? Jean-Hubert was neighbourly enough these days but. Never trust the château. Never trust the bourgeoisie. Whole generations and centuries of humiliation had ground it indelibly into him. And Magali he could not think of now without a certain disgust. A disgust that he knew was unfair and ridiculous in an enlightened man, in this day and age. Still there it was, que voulez vous, you never finally escaped the weight of the narrow generations gossiping scandal round the village pump . . .

She was rabbiting on about those little lost hamlets, only an hour or two by car but a century into the past. Plouha, Loguivy, Lanloup, Ploubazlanec. He pictured her as a child with Magali's scared eyes, running barefoot along the stone walls among the gorse bushes. Down the coast there, in the forties and fifties, when she was a young girl. The bleak hardship of their lives. He'd seen films about it, there'd been a whole rash of them recently. The fashion for nostalgia, ageing directors chewing away at the profitable cud of their deprived childhoods! Another country, it was. No château there, no bourgeoisie, no fat farms, no clever little ploucs destined to be doctors. Men away half the year in the fog and the cold, fishing up by Iceland and thereabouts, Pierre Loti stuff. *'Loguivy-de-la-mer/ Qui a vu mourir/ Ses derniers vrais marins,'* who was it who sang that? Paimpol, one rainy Sunday he'd gone down there with Rosy to a flower show. Drove slowly along the coast afterwards, Rosy jumping out of the car every few minutes to dig up great mucky clumps of pink campion and harebell, honestly the English! Strolling by the sea, the Isle of Brehat just across a strip of water, a sad lonesome mist chilling one's face, dismal foghorn. That must have been Loguivy. Gardens blue with ceanothus, honey scent in the rain, surfboarders, little boats with coloured sails hurrying home to roost. Yes, but that was all recent, there'd have been no gardens in Madame's day, no surfboarders. Just the raw scrape of poverty, smell of fish lingering in all their clothes, overworked mother with the hand permanently raised to strike, village empty of men, the last real sailors and fishermen living, dying, trailing their gnarled half-lives between Iceland and Brittany, she'd been lucky to catch a schoolmaster all the same . . .

"I was lucky, they all said I was lucky, doctor, they all envied me. Slim and dark and elegant he was then, when he came on his holidays to Loguivy. Not like the local boys, no rough talk, no coarseness with the girls. But very reserved. Shut in on himself, like the people around here. And then he was sent to Algeria. That marked him, the war marked him, doctor."

It marked the poor Algerians more, Pierre thought, glancing at his watch, have to cut her off soon, time for a little coffee perhaps before the next . . .

"He was just a nice quiet boy, doctor, before they sent him out there on his National Service. Lads of twenty! La honte. Seeing his comrades butchered. That wounded him, doctor, it was bound to. He can't stand Algerians. It's a mania with him, he's always . . . Tenez! On Saturday someone broke one of the windows in the new house. Just some vandal with a brick, but he swears it can only be those Arabs, that family that came a few years ago. He says Seulbourg was a nice quiet town till the Algerians came . . . You see how . . ." Her voice cracked into a sudden panic: "Doctor, I don't want to retire with him to Seulbourg. What would I do there? In that little villa alone with him all day long? Having to listen to his monologues, hear him going

225

on and on. The hate in his voice, doctor! You should hear the hate, he's eaten with it . . . Watching him clean and polish that revolver of his. His mania about being attacked. What would I *do*, in Seulbourg?"

Learn to swim, he thought tiredly, collect shells on the beach, catch lobsters, why do you all think I know the answers to your problems? What makes you think I can heal your inadequacies? A whole sick nation turned in on itself, frightened to move, frightened to smile, frightened to greet its neighbour, neurotically arming itself against attack. When did it start coming to this, the whole noble idea of France, land of enlightenment, home of the intellect, the bright laughing ideals of '68 . . . When did it start turning in on itself? Turning into an old man in a mass-produced villa, wounded by war, wounded by occupations, wounded by his own growing impotence, arming himself against the outsider, against the young, against the immigrants, against Europe, against anyone who might have brought a bit of enrichment to his stiff schoolmasterly culture. Arming himself against the future? France in the nineties, groping its way fearfully and suspiciously towards the millennium. And poor Rosalind wants to start a family! Bring children into what? For what? To do what with their lives? *Their* children hunting one another through the ruins with clubs . . . And it's the same everywhere, it's not only France. The great ideas are dead, Neil Armstrong's footprints have long since been blown off the moon's surface. No one dreams of exploring the sky any more, all one can dream about nowadays is darning it, sewing little patches of ozone over the holes, that's all that's left out of our glorious causes. The twentieth century and its optimism is crumbling away. And to tell you the truth, Pierre thought, I'm not feeling too great myself these days. A family! But try explaining all that to Rosy, she'd laugh her head off. No great intellectuals, the English, no grasp of a philosophy. Live from day to day, on the surface of life. Gardening, chatting, pert little jokes, no sense of a deeper meaning. Best let her blame it all on poor Loulou . . . Loulou has a broad back . . .

"Take up some outside interest, madame," he said, as he said to all of them, wearily taking up his pen to renew the prescription. Tranxene, Temesta, what's this she was on? "Learn a foreign language, explore a new culture, open yourself to the outside world. We Bretons are too turned in on ourselves . . ." And, when she looked at him enquiringly: "Enrol yourself at the university, bon dieu! Or take art lessons. Or go and spend the weekends with your daughter and your grandchild. Life is full of options, madame, even if one is married to René Balavoine!"

"The weekends it is difficult," she said humbly, "They like to be en famille, my little Magali and her Claude. And Sebastian. And then, he does not allow me to use the car . . . But I could, it is true, spend an afternoon with them from time to time. Tenez, there is a railway station at Seulbourg . . ."

Pierre suppressed a feeling of distaste, as he often had to at the thought of little Magali Balavoine en famille with her lover. Though why it should matter! Your male vanity is insulted, Rosy would say, Well, perhaps . . .

"The answer, madame, is to fill your life with interest. Let him live with these war wounds of his. They are part of him now. You cannot cure them and they do harm only to himself. Tell yourself that, madame. That your children are grown up, that he will be retired soon, that he can harm nobody now. That he has no power over anyone's life but his own. And start at last to live for yourself."

She pushed a hundred francs across the wide oak table and he took it, payment for the neatly-wrapped empty package he felt he'd been handing her for the past hour. But she thanked him and seemed satisfied and made an appointment for the following week. He saw her out of the surgery and went into the house with a feeling of release, to drink coffee with his nice solid uncomplicated Rosalind.

"Did you see that Arab waiting in the music prof's hall, Henri, when you came out from piano? He's learning the guitar he told me, we had a nice little chat, imagine, while I was waiting. Me, talking to an immigrant! Milo, he's called, bet he changed his name, bet he's really called Mohammed or something. Well, I nearly warned him only I couldn't be bothered, you know Maurice's cousin had it all planned to lure him into an alley last Saturday and beat him up? Poor little scrap, imagine, I mean he's our age and all. And you know, really nice, not thick or anything, not nearly as thick as Maurice's cousin. Only he must have twigged on to something at the last minute, he turned tail and ran just as they were all ready to close in on him, they were furious. Furax! They were hopping by the time Maurice and I came along. Cyril was so mad he heaved a brick through someone's window, through the window of one of those pathetic little holiday homes, well he'd been all worked up for an afternoon of violence . . . You can *imagine*!

"You don't mean you and your skinhead went along there on Saturday to help beat up some little Arab? You *didn't*! Honestly you're obscene, Clem!"

"Of course we didn't, we just went to Seulbourg for a swim. I didn't even know there was an Arab in Cyril's class, what do you think I am? Of *course* we didn't. Cyril's a great yob actually, he said you can never depend on *bicots*, not even to stand still and have their faces smashed in, all they're good for is running away, he said. He's quite disgusting,

Cyril is, revolting. A real plouc stinking of tobacco and beer, yuk!"

"So think of all the charming in-laws you're going to have, when you marry your skin. Imagine presenting the whole Delamotte clan to Tante Ruby!"

"Marry Maurice, you have to be joking. September, Henri, waaaow! Paris! New life! Adieu Maurice!"

"Christ, you're a callous little bitch, you've only being going out with him all year! Does he know?"

"Well I expect he must guess. Why, would *you* still want to drag on with some dreary yokel when we go to Paris? Your fat Irish tourist for example? We'll be meeting *real* people at Louis-Le-Grand, you know."

"Real National Front from your point of view! I suppose you think when your Glorious Leader in block capitals comes to call on Tante Ruby he's going to take you on his big fat knee like a nice little girl and feed you sweets or whatever! What do you see in that lot, Clem?"

"What do *you* see in your shitty Irish heritage? Think about it, Henri, that's exactly what *I* see in *them*. Something to give me an identity of my own, so I'm not just Papa's little daughter from the château. All right for them. All right for the parents. They had their May '68 and their civil rights and their peace and their love. What did they leave for us, tell me? What sort of world did they leave for us? Just look at them, just *look* at Papa and his whole futile generation! Speaking of which, here he comes to collect us. Dead on time, as usual. Does he think we'd go selling our pseudo-aristocratic little bodies on the Boulevard if he give us an extra ten minutes to breathe in?"

And then of course the drive home and Papa being all masculine with Henri, how futile he was, chuckling his dirty chuckle about the new servants he'd found, couple of

pathetic failures as usual. Like the Dutch actors. Tante Ruby
swears one of the actors was a woman in disguise. Drunken
old bitch. Just because she made a pass and he didn't get a.
God I *hate* my family! Well at least no more washing-up for
me. What do I see in them? I wouldn't say it out loud to
Henri but what I see in them . . . It disgusted me all that on
Saturday about beating up that little brown nerd. And
especially now since . . . When you see someone up close
and talk to them, well he was just a teenager wasn't he, just
the same as us. Standing there with his guitar. Took off his
Walkman to talk to me, bet he fancied me and all. He likes
the Guns, and Nirvana. A bit plouc really, all that . . . I'm
going to start listening to classical music when we go to
Tante Ruby's, Boulez and everything. And go to the ballet.
Bon chic bon genre, bet they all do at Louis-Le-Grand.
When I told Maurice I was enrolled there for September.
His face. He could see me moving away. Moving up. Away.
Suddenly realised the good old social hierarchy isn't just a
sick joke. Most prestigious lycée in France, he said, gaping
like a plouc, couldn't get over it. Well naturally he couldn't,
I mean it's even a great step up for him being at a private
school at all, first in his family not to be educated free by
the dear old State! That's why he tried to get me to sleep
with him on the beach, Saturday. Imagine. So I'll be
preparing the entrance exams for les grandes écoles, he
wanted to know. Polytechnique? Commerce?
Administration? I could see myself achieving prestige, no
longer the democratic little mate to wave banners with.
Sordid basically, is Maurice. Poor old Henri, all he wants,
his great big dream, is Trinity College, Dublin. Something
out of Maeve Binchy. *Nos Rêves De Castlebay*. All those jolly
country girls in flats. I suppose you want to go into politics,
he said, old Maurice, as if it was something beyond our

wildest expectations. Well, it's beyond his, little plouc from Plouch'en, politics for Maurice is a pack of louts waving baseball bats . . . He suddenly realised I was way up there in the ruling class, well near enough. That's why he wanted to make love behind the rocks. Nearly a year we've been going out, he said, and we've been playing together since we were twelve, don't you think it's time we. So romantic! I can't stand skinheads now. To touch. Imagine nice long silky hair. Guys with ponytails, painters and that. You don't ever see any at the meetings, all that revolting stubble. I could quite fancy Michel in the garden. If he wasn't so old. His wife . . . imagine! Can't wait to see this new butler or whatever. Not very nice for poor Michel, though. Trust Papa to be so crass! Expect Michel will be leaving now, Mother's going to have a fit . . . Think he fancies Mother, though, should see him blushing and muttering, Oui madame, non madame, comme vous voulez, madame, bit of an old wimp really. Mother never notices, Mother never notices anything about anyone. Except herself. Can't *stand* my family! As if it mattered how long, if I'd really been in love with Maurice I'd have made him do it the first week, it's me who decides, not him, who does he take himself for? His rotten cousin, petit merde, looking me up and down, il s'y croit, vraiment! Can't stand plebs! I should have warned the Arab. They're going to be waiting for him every time he goes out now, the whole holidays. Pounce on him some night and lure him up the alley behind those new houses, nobody up there except in August. Wish I hadn't forged that invitation to Loulou, frankly I don't give a shit if his old father marries her . . . Still, if he had the wit to escape from them last Saturday he'll hardly . . . Didn't *seem* stupid. They have no idea, they honestly have no idea. Monsieur Le Pen has never once, not in any of his speeches, said anything about beating up Arabs. He is above that, he wants to give France back some pride in itself and it's not by beating up immigrants that . . . It's not what I want either. Little local vandals. What I want is, I want something pure and clean and square-cut and French. Die sooner than say that to Henri. He's sleeping with that Irish girl in the gîte, how can he? Red hair and covered in freckles, a cliché. He's sleeping with his Irish roots, that's what. Wouldn't mind getting hold of some of old Michel's weedkiller and pouring it over *my* Irish roots, can't *stand* the things! It's mother, she's so mystical and gooey about it. If *I'd* grown up like that, in a cottage with a pair of peasants, I'd have the wit to keep quiet about it, God I cringe every time . . . Lucky she doesn't go on about my grandfather and the drink and the bomb, at least not in front of people, la honte! How am I supposed to have pride in myself! We're so ambiguous. So dispossessed, all of us. We're not anything really, are we? My mother's just basically a summer landlady, and Papa with his books and his music and his boring quotations, you'd think he was some great intellectual. When all he's got is a degree in English, anyone can have a degree in English, any waiter can speak English as well as Papa! Not that it matters about the gîtes, lots of people they're not rich, they take in lodgers rather than sell their châteaux, the Countess picks her own blackcurrants and sells them cheap round the restaurants, it's not that. It's just that it's so ambiguous. And if they knew I was born in a commune in Amsterdam, God such a joke place to be born. How could I ever face them at school? I've always felt so precarious among them, so afraid to open my mouth and say anything. Birth certificates. Amsterdam? Oh, was your papa working in the Embassy there? Or what? What is your papa actually? *Who* is he? Who is he related to? In Junior school, when Mummy spoke English at Open Days I used to pinch her hard till she stopped, I used to want to pretend she was dumb. Struck dumb in an accident. She bled, one day, her wrist. I wanted a French mother. Till I found out it was chic to be bi-lingual. I'm not even a real twin, even that's nothing, not something real and solid. Because Henri is a boy, because we are not identical, it's all so ambiguous. We're so mediocre. Every generation they've sort of married down, your family, haven't they? Laetitia Blérot de Boisauvage. I'd like to ask you to my party, she said, only you wouldn't really know anyone, my parents said you might feel out of things . . . I want to belong somewhere. I want to be told how to live, how to think, what to do. That's why . . . Maybe it'll be better in Paris, when I'm living in Paris with Tante Ruby and Uncle Gus. They're accepted, in Paris, it's not like the country, and they're millionaires and anyway everyone knows now, about Tante Ruby, she's Russian nobility. Can't stand the old bitch, but she'll be a background for me, nobody need even know I have an Irish mother. Irish *Catholic* mother, like those victims whinging on the telly and those tourist posters of people with no teeth playing the accordion, Merde, Merde, Merde, I'm never ever coming back to Plouch'en again!

On Thursday morning, Michel bought a baguette and a couple of croissants, and the baker's wife served him in silence. Silence too, or an embarrassed near-silence, had greeted his "Bonjour, tout le monde!" when he entered the shop. There had been a few more or less friendly grunts, a perceptible shuffle of feet, a break in the conversation. He had the impression they would have all preferred him to buy his bread elsewhere. Tomorrow morning he probably would. He foresaw that from now on he would be driven to buy an inferior loaf and doughy croissants in the forgiving anonymity of the supermarket. Another man would brave it out, another man would force a confrontation, oblige them to speak, to come to blows if that's what they were looking for. Another man would not be in his position to start with: the blows would all have been struck last Saturday evening and it's Gabriel who'd have been slinking around half-scared to buy a loaf of bread for his breakfast. Savoir-vivre in a rural setting, and it still made him cringe away in distaste.

Last night there had been three phone calls. Three different callers, men he had known since he was a child, with whom he'd often had a drink on a Saturday evening: did they seriously imagine he would not recognise their voices on the phone? The first time, he'd picked up the receiver and heard: "Cuckoo! Cuckoo, Michel!" Jean-Roch Plerin: he recognised the phlegmy little laugh at the end. The second time he wouldn't have answered except that he was expecting a call from Denis about a job. "Oh Michel," the second voice said, "I've got a load of second-hand balls in my attic; I've been hearing you need some." Joseph Lemoine, le salaud! And then, his parents' next door neighbour from the housing estate: "Monsieur Le Borgne? Plouch'en abattoir here. We could let you have a pair of horns cheap. Several pairs, in fact!" Rustic humour. They were probably folded in four laughing at their own wit. And that wouldn't be the end of it. It would go on and on. *They* would go on and on, dreaming up new little torments, trying to break him. He'd known it happen before. A man had been driven to suicide a few years back, after six months hostile teasing from his neighbours. There had been some story of . . . What was it? What had he done? Nothing very serious, Michel thought, or he wouldn't have forgotten it so easily. Some offence, in any case, against the strict village code. Committed by an outsider, of course. Real villagers, those who belonged, were protected by a sort of rural freemasonry. He'd not, up until now, considered himself an outsider. He'd been born in Plouch'en, in a family that had lived there for centuries. He had grown up there, played football, tasted his first beer with his uncle Hervé in the bistro, slept with his first girl after a Saturday night dance in the Salle de Fêtes. Like everyone. True, he had left to go to university at a time when few village boys did. He and Pierre Bouchon had been the only ones of that decade, the first decade of universal opportunity. Pierre had returned, a successful man, and been accepted with friendship and respect. He himself had returned after only two years, without qualifications, had moved into his parents' rented cottage, been satisfied with menial work, married one of the roadmender's daughters. In his own mind he had remained part of the village: his present life was just a continuation of his warm protected childhood, moving gently between cottage and château, uninspired by greed for money or power. He felt that he had achieved a lot simply by living his life with decency, by refusing to use violence against either human beings or animals, by conducting his relationships with warmth and gentleness. It was the spirit of his generation after all, the ideal of the Seventies. It was the way he had deliberately chosen to live. It was also the sin he'd committed against village morals and village traditions.

He did not see himself changing, even now. He could *not* imagine himself grabbing poor Gabriel by the lapels of his monkey suit and knocking him down. That's what they had all been waiting for on Saturday evening, that's what Gabriel himself had been waiting for. It had been so comical, all those slow brawny men leaning up against the counter waiting for him to be transfigured into John Rambo. That's what they couldn't forgive, that he had found the situation, and them, so comical. He'd let them down, he'd betrayed their common Latin maleness.

He supposed he could have bought back some of their goodwill if he'd forbidden Nathalie the door when she finally turned up on Monday morning. She'd come home expecting fight, expecting the traditional movements of outrage and offended dignity and he had reacted instead in a way that was totally foreign to her.

Even Rosalind Bouchon had been horrified at that: "You let the pair of them just move in? Listen, sunshine, have you gone completely out of your mind or what?"

"What else could I have done? One tries to live with some logic n'est ce pas, and that seemed the logical thing to do. They had nowhere else to go, you see. He is out of work, he can no longer pay for a hotel room, what else could I have done? I have nothing against Nathalie, you know. She has more courage than I have, that is all. You know very well, Rosalind, that I have been in love with someone else for years and years now and I am too scared to do anything about it. Scared she would just send me on my way, tell me she never even noticed I exist. You know sometimes I think she does not even see me, that is what I am scared of. That is why I have been prepared just to drift on with Nathalie as if . . . Now I am free, thanks to Nathalie and that guy. So I am not about to knock his head off and throw her out of the house just to prove I am a tough village man with the acceptable number of balls."

"You're going to have to *leave* your precious village though, aren't you? You've cut your throat in Plouch'en, mate. There's no way you can stay on here now. There's no way they'd let you have any sort of life, you'd probably end up as one of Pierre's basket cases if you even tried. Imagine explaining your logic to some of the big Breton males in the bistro!"

She *can't* have noticed I exist, he thought, getting into his van outside the baker's. If she even spared me a thought she wouldn't have Nat and Gabriel up working in her kitchen. If she did that, if she took on the pair of them like that, it's just that we're not on the same planet as her. It's that Uncle Herve's right, people like that probably just see the rest of us as cattle or . . . But his mind slid away sideways to a timid lovely woman silently asking him for his friendship in Monsieur Vladimir's garden. That had been true, he had not after all imagined that, that had existed all right, that magic half-hour when they'd been left alone together after all the old boring people had gone inside to talk business leaving them, the young innocent children, to play outside among the roses. We were two of a kind, he thought, that day sixteen years ago, we recognised each other straight away so what can . . .

"Cuckoo! Cuckoo!" a mocking voice darted out of Le Moal's field as he got out of his van. He looked around wildly: who? where? what bastard? It took him several seconds to understand that it had been a real live cuckoo calling to its mate in the château woods. I'm going paranoid, he thought, Plouch'en is getting to me. Rosalind is right, they are all right, this place is the pits, it is long past time I was getting out.

The future was suddenly there in front of him, new and untouched, as full of possibilities and adventure as it had been the day he decided to drop out of college and stay on in the village. Except that this time he was not going to be fool enough to walk empty-handed into life. This time he was going to have enough wit to base his future on something more substantial than a dream. As Denis said last week, the world was no longer in the sweet innocent aftermath of the Sixties: this was the nineteen-nineties and if you had any sense at all you reached out your hand and you grabbed anything you could get.

He made himself a coffee, ate his croissants, and began figuring out the best way to get back at the bastards and give himself a bit of an advantage as well. Half an hour later the postman heard him give one loud bellow of laughter and sped off in his little yellow van to spread the word that Yeah, that was it, the man was off his head, Michel le Cocu was sitting in his empty house at eleven in the morning laughing away to himself . . .

Part Seven

❦

"The Bouchons are coming, the Bouchons are coming!" Clémence sang out from a first-floor window, "The Reverend Freud is bursting out of his Sunday suit, Madame has left off her jogging clothes for once and is draped, literally draped my dear, in a sweet Laura Ashley print, with pink eyeliner to match her blushes. Oh she does resemble one of her own wildflower borders, n'est ce pas, mon cher Soleil?"

Rosalind recalled that Clémence, as a child, had gone through a Madame de Montespan phase and, with Henri in the role of Louis XIV, used to station herself at an open window overlooking the front entrance when there were people to dinner, making rude remarks about the less important guests when her parents were out of earshot. This was the first time she had done it for years, and the first time Rosalind herself had been chosen as a victim.

"Well, of course she's bound to have it in for me after Saturday, daft little cow, but she's not really very funny," Rosalind muttered, horribly embarrassed, escaping thankfully into the shelter of the stone-floored hall that was icy even in the middle of summer, its walls great bare damp slabs of granite. "Nineteenth century mock-feudal," she told Pierre who was looking uncomfortable, "Hardly Versailles, the little bitch needn't give herself such airs! And I intend to have a word with Hélène about her before we go home tonight."

"I expect she's guessed that," Pierre said, "and that's why she's being so nasty. Drop it, Rosy, it's not really our business, we have no right to interfere. People of this sort . . ."

He was being the cringing barefoot tenant again, Rosalind saw, and she squeezed his hand reassuringly as Hélène floated out on a thin distant cloud of Calandre, kissed them distantly on both cheeks, and led them off to another freezing room for drinks and dinner.

The other guest, old Maître Bourin, was an absent-minded retired notaire, who'd been asked to dinner for Tante Ruby's sake. They'd been childhood sweethearts and, according to village rumour, a lot more besides. He'd also been, during the Occupation, commandant of the Resistance group in which Jean-Hubert's father served. Hélène apologised for the old lady's absence but Maître Bourin didn't seem to notice and from time to time turned to address a remark to Tante Ruby's empty chair.

Gabriel served at table trying, and failing as far as Rosalind was concerned, to be anonymously Jeeves-like in a neat dark suit. While he was in the room she tried to keep her eyes firmly on her plate unable, when she caught sight of him, to see him as anything but naked and rippling under a fluffy white towel. Picturing with embarrassment, as she steadily ate her escalopes á la crême to the rhythm of Maître Bourin's voice, the incredible things he must have been doing to the body of Michel Le Borgne's wife in the bath, honestly the French . . . In desperation, to control her blushes, she cast her eyes round the panelled walls of the long dining-room. Pity in a way about the furniture, though the heavy modern pine table and dresser weren't bad – Hélène had taught herself from a book how to artificially age them and if you didn't know . . . She thought of the lovely oak table in Pierre's surgery and blushed again: it had been in this room for over a hundred years probably, honestly she'd near thrown a wobbly when Pierre told her, a good thing really his old dad was dead or she'd never have been able to face him again, knowing . . . Ancestors gaped down at her, their smug little mouths, gooseberry eyes, their silly eighteenth-century faces. Not Ploudel de Medeu ancestors: they didn't have any that went back that far. Or at least, she supposed, the ones they had would look more like Van Gogh's Potato Eaters . . . These were ancestors of people the Ploudel de Medeus had married into. Lawyers they'd married, merchants, the occasional younger daughter of an impoverished foreign noble, nothing very spectacular, Madame Ruby's famous Russian estate was probably nothing more grand than an oversized farm. Actually Hélène herself would fit in nicely among that crowd on the wall, with her pointed chin and long neck . . .

Gabriel's sexy brown hands refilled her glass with something chilled and golden and delicious. Say what you like about Jean-Hubert, but his wine was always worth drinking. The rare time you were invited up to drink it. *"I sometimes wonder"*, she recited casually, *"What the vintners buy, one half so precious as the goods they sell."*

Jean-Hubert raised an eyebrow. "Nursery rhymes of the Cotswolds?" he enquired mildly and she felt herself blushing again. "Oh just some poem we did at school," she muttered, kicking herself. Why couldn't she have stated confidently: "Literary quotation, you twit. Omar Khayyám . . ." As *he'd* certainly have done. She comforted herself with the thought that the English could afford to be modest and self-deprecating because they had every reason to be quietly confident of their own superiority, whereas these poor neurotic French needed to be constantly blowing their own trumpets, reassuring themselves and everyone else that they weren't the mere frivolous nonentities the whole world took them for.

She caught Pierre's eye and raised her eyebrows slightly, to remind him about mentioning Ireland. He responded by sitting up straighter in his chair and clearing his throat with an air of importance.

Hélène looked towards him expectantly. His suit was made to measure and fitted him perfectly, but the way he wore it suggested to her an imminent bursting-apart at the seams as if Pierre was about to surge out of it clad in some humiliating peasant garb, a blue boiler suit perhaps, or long johns, or even his own large well-padded bones. Tante Ruby would have a fit if she knew he was sitting here eating his dinner in her dead brother's dining-room. In *our* dining-room, she corrected herself, and I'll have who I damn well like to dinner.

"Eh listen, Jean-Hubert," Pierre's big broad voice cut abruptly through the dining-table murmurs, "Listen, you know this house exchange thing we're doing with that doctor in Carrickfergus?"

Hélène pictured the doctor in Carrickfergus, surely thin and distinguished and soft-spoken as Irish doctors tended to be. As their neighbours in the Falls Road had been. How on earth had he and Pierre managed to become such great chums?

"Well, we were thinking, Rosy and myself, we thought well why don't we ask you two to come along and share the house with us? Seeing the twins will have gone to Paris, empty nest syndrome and all that . . . Bags of room, five bedrooms, what do we want rattling around in five bedrooms? Or even Hélène on her own if you can't get away, I know you don't ever . . . Do her good to get back to her roots for a bit! Doctor's orders, ha ha! I'll even write out a prescription if you like!"

Jean-Hubert give the slightest of shudders and said firmly: "Non merci, non merci, non merci! Literary quotation," he added, "Edmond Rostand. Thank you, Pierre, but surely by now my wife's roots are firmly planted in the soil of France? And as for me, you know quite well I never leave home for a holiday. One lives through nine months of gales and tempests here every year just so that one can profit oneself of two or three months of Breton sunshine in the summer. Nothing would drag me to Ireland in September!"

"Jean-Hubert and his spouse have everything they could possibly wish for in la belle France," Maître Bourin put in sternly, "I cannot imagine why anyone should wish to go abroad. I myself have never willingly crossed over the borders of The Hexagon, and I am proud to say it! I have everything in my native land that a man could possibly desire, food and wine and landscape and culture, and the most beautiful women in the world. N'est ce pas, ma chère Ruby?" He leered towards the massive pine emptiness of the chair beside him. The chair said nothing and he looked taken aback for an instant, then turned quickly to Hélène on his other side: "L'Irlande, quelle turbulente pays! I fear she will end by cuckolding poor England the way Algeria cuckolded La France. Is it not so, Madame Bouchon?" he called across to Rosalind, "Would it not desolate you to lose the last of your colonies, madame?"

"Oh you know, me and the colonies!" Rosalind laughed

in embarrassment, dragged out of a tiny dream she'd being allowing herself, of a lover with a body like Gabriel's suddenly appearing at her side on a Brittany Ferries deck, slipping his hand into hers as they watched La Belle France drop below the horizon forever. "I'm not exactly a flag-waving John Bull, you know. Can't stand that sort of thing actually. All those daft films on Channel Four about India and the Falklands and the jolly old Blitz, not to mention the moth-eaten heroes they keep digging up, fit for nothing but rattling their balls and polishing their medals and forever retelling their old wars . . ."

Someone kicked her hard under the table, Hélène to judge by her stricken face, and when she looked over in puzzlement she noticed that old Maître Bourin, purple and trembling, was crunching up his napkin and obviously preparing to leave in a huff. Too late she recalled the endlessly told tales of his Resistance exploits, his daring escape from the Gestapo, his decorations . . . Well, serve the old bastard right, she thought defensively. Did no one ever teach these ill-mannered frogs that you don't talk politics at table?

Jean-Hubert, to divert him, said quickly: "Talking of my wife's roots, one of Hélène's ancestors, a certain Constance O'Donnell, was a beautiful sexy lady who didn't have balls to rattle, but she was a national heroine all the same, for a time. She was in all the Irish history books."

Maître Bourin allowed himself to be diverted. "Yes, Ruby has mentioned that connection several times, but I have never been quite clear what she actually did, the old lady your grandmother?"

Hélène sighed, wishing once again she'd never mentioned her stepfather's faded little scrap of history to Jean-Hubert. Having successfully used poor Gerald's thirty-first cousin-in-law to give his new wife a bit of pedigree with his family, he'd been wheeling her out ever since as a conversation piece to get them out of tight social corners.

"Oh well," she began, playing up to him, "It was some years after Irish independence and the Dublin government, having used the IRA to chase the English, was desperately trying to eliminate it before it might decide to chase *them* out as well. So one night this Constance O'Donnell (she wasn't an old lady by the way, she was only thirty and very very pretty), anyway she was arrested trying to force open the bedroom door of a top politician. With a knife in her hand."

"Ahh la la!" chortled Maître Bourin, "Let us drink to these mischievous little ladies, les coquines! Jeanne d'Arc! Charlotte Corday! Madame votre grandmère!"

"Well, the whole country wanted her sentenced to death for treason and attempted murder, though her lawyers swore there had been no knife and that she'd actually been coming *out* of the bedroom when she was surprised by the guards. They said she and the politician had been lovers for over a year. She taught Gaelic in a convent and the politician, who was a great friend of de Valera, used to go round the schools encouraging the kids to speak the language. That's how they met."

"Ah. Just a banal little histoire de fesses, alors, like our own president Felix Faure." Maître Bourin sounded very let-down indeed, "So the lady was acquitted?"

"Well, no" Hélène said, "Of course she wasn't! This was Ireland, not France. It was a far worse crime to sleep with a Catholic politician than to try and kill him. The whole country said she should be flogged to death as well as hanged, for attempting to bring dishonour on a good Irish husband and father whose sole aim in life was to restore his native language and folklore. Nobody believed her story because most of her family had fought fiercely beside de Valera in the war of Independence and they were considered to be capable of anything. So she got a life sentence and died a few years later in prison. Of pneumonia. Of course as soon as she died she became a martyr and a heroine."

"I do not comprehend," Maître Bourin said. "Why a heroine, if it was an *Irish* statesman she was trying to kill?"

"Oh you know, just the fact of attacking anyone in authority. And then the old boy wasn't really very popular in the end. Gaelic's not the most fascinating of languages," she added disastrously, "and everyone was going mad about the blues and the Charleston by then, didn't want to be fobbed off with dreary old native folklore, I mean dancing at the crossroads never really . . ."

Someone kicked her hard under the table, Jean-Hubert to judge by his stricken face, and Hélène noticed that Maître Bourin was turning purple again and starting to crunch up his napkin. She remembered too late that since his retirement his sole interest in life had been the restoration of Breton Gaelic and native folk music.

Jean-Hubert glowered across almost imperceptibly and took up the story with aristocratic calm: "The best of it was, of course, that in the liberated Seventies, when people had quite enough of redhanded Irish heroes, someone published about eight hundred pages of amorous correspondence between Constance and the old politician. Apparently they really had been having an affair."

"Oh the bastard!" breathed old Maître Bourin, diverted again, "Le salaud! He let his mistress die in prison! Le salaud! Just what I've been saying all along. France is the only civilised country to live in. In France we respect les passions sexuelles, n'est-ce pas, ma chère petite Ruby?"

This time Tante Ruby answered him. She'd stolen in silently and unexpectedly with a plate in her hand while Jean-Hubert was talking, and was making up for lost time, putting away her food with great swiftness and relish.

"Well, judging by what's going on at this very minute in my dead brother's kitchen," she announced quivering, "my nephew and his wife have the most enormous respect for les passions sexuelles!"

Hélène gaped at her for an instant, and realised they'd been finished their meat course well over twenty minutes and the vegetables had still not arrived. She hurried out to the kitchen, clearing her throat and clacking her heels noisily on the stone flags of the passage.

As she opened the door, Gabriel was unhurriedly strolling away towards the cooker and Nathalie was gathering herself, pink and giggling, into a sitting position on the low pine working table.

"What's happening here?" Hélène asked with stern foolishness. Nathalie giggled.

"There is no problem, madame," Gabriel reassured her, "It is finished, our little romantic interlude, we are ready to be at Madame's service once again." He turned coaxing brown eyes on her: "You must excuse us, Madame. The little Nathalie, you understand, she is so very much in love with me at present. One could say that we are actually on our honeymoon, Madame, here with you in your beautiful château, n'est-ce pas?"

EuroDisney, Hélène thought, Mickey Mouse, Donald Duck, Roger Rabbit, La Belle France . . . Whatever is this grotesque farce that Jean-Hubert has introduced into my life?

"We've been waiting twenty minutes for you to bring in the vegetables, Gabriel. It really isn't good enough."

"Ah bah dîtes donc, madame! You don't waste time on your food in the upper classes, do you? My old mum and dad they chew away right through the evening's telly."

"And don't talk to me like that please," Hélène protested, "You're being far too familiar."

"Oh écoutez madame, we're old friends from way back, you and me. I used to be top of your catechism class, remember? Love is God, remember you used to teach me that, madame?"

"God is love," Hélène corrected mechanically. While her mother-in-law was alive she used to make more of an effort to live up to her position, and that entailed teaching catechism to the village children on Wednesday afternoons, the spiritual equivalent of carrying cast-off clothes to their cottages. In Gabriel's parents' cottage, fuller than most of Uncle Vladimir's possessions, she'd once chatted desperately, in floods of tears, about the obligation of Sunday Mass while his mother, not even pretending to listen, endlessly chopped huge Breton onions on what looked like a priceless Louis Quinze table. She recalled Gabriel perfectly, an angel-faced boy of nine with big innocent eyes, who'd once asked her in bewilderment: "But what exactly did the Angel Gabriel do, madame, when he declared unto Mary?" What ever can I have told him, she wondered.

"Six veg. coming up for these messieurs-dames," he intoned with a smile that said he was only helping out as a favour to an old crony, "Et dîtes donc, madame la marquise, this table of yours is a bit shaky on its legs n'est-ce pas? *Deux Belges* catalogue? Thought so. Only listen, madame, I happen to know where there's this real genuine château table for sale, I could probably get them to make you a special price, madame, seeing as how."

"I wouldn't if I were you," Hélène smiled back, "my

husband might recognise it. He spent his holidays here when he was a child, remember?"

The meal continued smoothly after that. Nathalie's cooking was as excellent as a *Cordon Bleu* evening class could make it, and Gabriel, moving silently round the table, seemed to glow with discreet attentiveness.

"I must congratulate you, Jean-Hubert," Tante Ruby said, "for once you have succeeded in finding the perfect servant. This young man is a treasure. A veritable treasure," she repeated, her greedy black eyes following Gabriel's sinewy body as it glided out of the room.

"He was a waiter at the Hotel de la Poste," Jean-Hubert said, "say what you like about their, euh, morals," he added with a furtive little smile that left Hélène wondering, "but they make a good job of training their staff."

"Oh they do, they do," Maître Bourin agreed, "That is one of their former chefs, you know, the owner of Chez Ludovic over in Seulbourg. Rather an interesting little restaurant. My daughter took me out to dine there last week."

"Oh, what did you have?" Tante Ruby's eyes lit up again with the anticipation of hearing about good food.

"Well, unfortunately I was obliged to settle for the sole myself – my poor liver was letting me down again. But Antoinette chose the Petits Culs de Grenouilles au Sauce Framboise and she – "

"Little frog's bums in raspberry sauce!" Rosalind giggled, full of the delicious golden wine, "They really go to town on their titles, these chefs!"

"Ludovic would take a cleaver to you if he heard you," Hélène said, "daring to laugh at one of his precious creations!"

"Doesn't take much to make them reach for a cleaver,

those blokes," said Rosalind, "Neurotic as hell the lot of them. Remember the time I was a waitress in that ski place in Switzerland?"

Tante Ruby and Maître Bourin raised disbelieving eyes, then hastily pretended they hadn't heard.

"No, but I mean you'd waltz up quite innocently to hand in some poor customer's order, and next thing half the frying pans in the kitchen were whizzing round your head!"

"It is a classic reaction," Pierre pronounced, "These men are encouraged by the media to regard themselves as great artists. So naturally a waitress is the enemy because her sole raison d'être is to steal away all the masterpieces and bury them forever in someone's inglorious gut."

"Must be why Picasso was such a crotchety old bastard," Rosalind said, "When you think how many of *his* masterpieces ended up forever buried in the guts of millionaire collectors."

"Oh thank you very much, madame!" Tante Ruby retorted, tossing her head, "But Gustave and I are prepared to lend our Picasso to any gallery that asks for it, and all our friends do the same. Though perhaps waitresses do not have sufficient free time to go to exhibitions and find this out?"

"I suppose," Hélène leaped in tactfully, "I suppose if nobody ever ordered their food the poor chefs would end up cutting off their own ears and sending them round to their colleagues."

"Petites oreilles de cuisiniers . . ." Rosalind murmured in her rich Gloucestershire accent, and Jean-Hubert looked faintly disgusted.

While the others were having coffee in the drawing-room (with Tante Ruby pointedly ignoring Pierre's presence), Hélène and Rosalind ran up to the children's sitting-room where they were watching television after supper.

"What are you watching?" Rosalind asked, in reply to the bored silence that greeted the opening door.

"Advertisements, of course," Henri growled, "What else is it possible to look at on French télé?"

"Oh I do so agree," Rosalind was anxious to be friendly, "I've often wondered why they don't buy up a few good English serials. I really do miss *Coronation Street* and *Eastenders*, can't wait for Pierre to have this satellite dish installed."

"Different lifestyles," Hélène said, "Can you picture any French audience making head or tail of *Coronation Street*, they'd think it was a circus. All those gross old working-class couples!"

"That's what I mean," Rosalind said, "I've watched three different French serials this year and they were *all* about impoverished nobles trying to make ends meet in ancestral châteaux. Wouldn't mind if they were even meant to be funny, *To the Manor Born* or whatever, but you were actually meant to empathise with them! It was supposed to be real life!"

"It *is* real life," Clémence said coldly, examining the Laura Ashley from collar to hem, sniffing inaudibly at every frill and ruffle. "*We* are nobles and we live in an ancestral château and we are always trying to make ends meet. That's why we haven't got a satellite dish, only the petit-bourgeoisie can afford them. A lot of kids at school are the same. We don't know anyone who lives in *Coronation Street*, do we, Henri?"

"Euh . . . what?" Henri was leaning forward avidly, gazing at a half-naked bruised-looking wench lying on a river bank, evidently on the point of having oral sex with a wedge of cheese. Rosalind turned away, blushing.

"Oh, do you want to guess a riddle, Rosalind?"

Clémence asked sweetly, "Tell me, what would you call it if an Arab immigrant got drowned in the Seine?"

"Really Clem, I don't think . . ."

"You'd call it *pollution* of course! Now what would you call it if *all* the immigrants in France got drowned in the Seine? Give up, Rosalind? Give your tongue to the cat? Well, you'd call it The Solution ha ha ha ha! Got it, Roz?"

"Don't be so racist, darling," Hélène said vaguely, "And now, mon petit bouquet d'amour, you'd better run down and be sociable to poor Maître Bourin or he'll be thinking *you're* a pair of ill-bred immigrants!"

Clémence snorted and made a rude sign at Rosalind behind her mother's back. Rosalind felt that now was the moment to come out with her friendly warning about the National Front but was far too embarrassed to begin. How do you tell a presumably doting mum that one half of her little bouquet d'amour is fast turning into a great brassy thug? And hell's bells, if she wasn't such a dreamer she'd have noticed it for herself, Rosalind thought irritably, that woman's living on the moon half the time. She decided sex was easier. "Doesn't it worry you, Hélène," she said as they went back downstairs, "Knowing Henri and Clem are watching all that rubbish? I mean being so interested in sex at their age?"

"Weren't we all?" Hélène laughed, "Only they used to feel they had to beat it out of us. I'm convinced that every single person in my boarding-school thought she was the only human being to own a vagina, and that it was some sort of shameful deformity that she had to mention in Confession. It's a hell of a lot better like this, everything out in the open. And it's all so basically innocent, isn't it? I mean the opposite of Mary Whitehouse isn't necessarily Magdalen Blackbrothel. Have you noticed how there's far fewer sex crimes here than in your nice friendly prudish England? Do you not think it's because young fellows like Henri can grow up seeing sex as just a normal part of everyday life? Instead of all sneaky and hidden away? Not to mention that all the old sex maniacs must have themselves worn to an empty foreskin, wanking away in front of the washing-powder ads?"

"Or telling smutty stories to Pierre on the National Health. Be glad to get to Ireland all the same. Different atmosphere. I do hope Jean-Hubert lets you come, he was being a bit the heavy husband just now, did you notice?"

"Oh, he'll be all right when he gets used to the idea. He always says no to everything at first, to show who's head of the family. That's his Provençal ancestry coming out. One gets used to it, eventually."

But she thought how nice it would have been not to have to get used to it. Not to have to struggle for every tiny scrap of liberty. To have married a man who came from a culture where male supremacy no longer had any meaning . . . A man like Christopher Milton, quiet and wise and confident, a human being completely without neuroses. She crossed her fingers and lightly touched wood, praying that Jean-Hubert would say yes. Realising that she was longing, not just to see Christopher Milton again, but longing for a whole month in the cool chaste repose of an Ulster town. The whole château, upstairs and downstairs was, as Rosalind said, permeated with sex. Glancing casually towards the kitchen wing as they passed a landing window, they saw Gabriel at the side door, peeing into the yard with obvious enjoyment, then examining his precious treasure with an expression of tender gloating concern as if he'd just given birth to it, before tucking it away gently in its little cradle between his legs. The old order changeth with a vengeance, she thought, the village suddenly seems very much at its ease in the château this evening. And whatever would Uncle Vlad have to say about that, old snob that he was?

"The very loaves in the bread-bin are phallic symbols," Rosalind sighed.

"Yes but think," Hélène reminded her, "Think of a flat boring sandwich of Mother's Pride bread with a slice of bright yellow processed cheese in between."

"All the same," Rosalind said wistfully, "Cheese that's been advertised by a chaste green film of a meadow full of cows . . ."

Hélène promised herself a chaste green dream to lull herself to sleep, meeting Christopher Milton in one of those cool shaded Irish gardens they open to the public, in the grounds of a grey Palladian mansion without turrets or chimneys . . .

"I've never known you to be so tactless," Jean-Hubert scolded, "Insulting a guest at our own table! And the level of conversation at dinner! Like a fifth-rate suburban party. That peasant friend of yours wallowing in sordid reminiscences of her waitressing days . . . Tante Ruby was most displeased, and my poor mother and uncle must be turning in their tombs!"

"I'm sorry," Hélène said, "I can't think what came over me. I suppose I was rattled by the idea of that pair in the kitchen, I still think you were mad to engage them. If *anything* could make your old uncle turn in his tomb . . ."

"I despair of you, Hélène. After all these years there are a thousand nuances you have not picked up. When my Uncle Vladimir engaged staff he *saw* them as staff, nothing more. He certainly would not have wasted his time agonising over the finer feelings of a cuckolded gardener. You are still so petit-bourgeois, my dear!"

"Well, that's one nuance, thank heavens, I was brought up without! And speaking of which, I hate having to talk about Gerald's old cousin as if she was my nearest and dearest, I've been trying to tell you this for years, it's really terribly embarrassing for me. And hurtful. I mean if the French can't just accept me for what I am . . . I can't bear all these pointless little lies, oh all right not *lies* exactly, I'm not accusing you, only she wasn't even *related* to me, could we not just bury the poor old thing from now on and try to forget her?"

Jean-Hubert stared at her in amazement: "Ma chére Hélène, amid the total obscurity of your family you have the great good luck to possess one connection who need not be blushed for. One single forebear to rescue your family from mediocrity and make you worthy to take your place among the Ploudel de Medeus. And that ancestor is the one you would wish us to forget? At times, my dear, you are incomprehensible!" Jean-Hubert rose from the breakfast-table and strode out. Discussion closed.

On a table on one the upper landings there lay an immense book, brown with age, which when she first saw it Hélène had taken for a family Bible. In it were inscribed the names of all the important families in France, together with their Paris and country addresses, their coats of arms, and their marital connections with the Ploudel de Medeus. When they first came to the château, Jean-Hubert had thought the book a huge joke, especially when he learned from it that, through some tortuous labyrinth of intermarriages, he was a twenty-eighth cousin of General de Gaulle. As the General's mother was of Irish descent they'd decided to work out a fake pedigree linking Hélène's family to hers and write it up in the book, just to see if any guest ever opened the thing and commented. At some point Jean-Hubert decided it wasn't very amusing after all: in mid-laugh, as it were, Hélène had seen the burden of his heritage descend upon him, and he'd become increasingly preoccupied with status ever since. By the time his daughter was twelve, he'd earmarked one of the du Bois Fleuri grandsons as a suitable husband for her, and no doubt Hélène's step-cousin-in-law had her role to play in making Clémence's foreign mother seem less of a joker in the pack.

When she'd told Jean-Hubert, in Amsterdam, about Gerald's wife's notorious cousin whose eight hundred love letters had just been published, it was more of an attempt to at last exorcise her mother and stepfather by ridicule than to lay claim to a famous ancestor. Unfamiliar with upper-class obsessions, she had no way of knowing that he and his family would pounce on this practically non-existent connection as the only belonging of value she brought to them. She was to learn that the status-hungry, and very insecure, Ploudel de Medeus – too nouveau to have sacrificed either their sons' blood or the bodies of their beautiful women in the service of one of the Louis's – had over the generations made a point of hanging on tenaciously to the slightest thing that could add to their store of acceptable possessions. (Like Tante Ruby's faded Russian photograph.)

So Gerald's wife's very removed cousin, like the family jewels some better-heeled bride might have arrived with, had become one of the useful and decorative items stored away in the château's strongbox, to be taken down and used on appropriate occasions.

When he heard he'd been left a château and the remains of an estate, Jean-Hubert's first reaction had been laughter.

In spite of Uncle Vlad's interest in him, he'd never even remotely expected to inherit. It was one of those miraculous fairytale things that had seemed possible in the Seventies. A good trip. A fantastic trip. Before he came to Amsterdam, he and his parents had led a perfectly ordinary middle-class existence in a comfortable, though hardly chic, arrondissement of Paris. His only contact with the aristocratic side of his family had been six weeks with the eccentric old gentleman every summer from the age of eight onwards. If he'd thought about it at all, he would have assumed that the place would go to Tante Ruby, Vladimir's favourite sister who, though living in far grander style in Paris, still hankered nostalgically after the old family home in Plouch'en. Jean-Hubert's mother, deeply in love with her Provençal schoolmaster, had apparently no regrets at all for the milieu she'd abandoned, and refused to set foot in Plouch'en until Uncle Vladimir's death. She had however continued to exercise all the snobberies of her upbringing, and passed them on so successfully to her son that Jean-Hubert was quite incapable of eating an apple without the aid of a whole set of cutlery, and was inclined in all seriousness to judge the human worth of new acquaintances by whether they cut their bread with a knife or tore it apart correctly with their fingers. The world of the Ploudel de Medeus was perhaps after all not so different from one of those acid trips they used to go on, where the most frivolous details took on an immense significance, while the real dramas and dangers of life went unnoticed. Or so Hélène thought that morning when Jean-Hubert left the breakfast-room in dudgeon and Nathalie, giggling in happy embarrassment, came in to clear the table. Because surely this sluttish young woman's presence in their home with her lover was the real *faux pas*, beside which Rosalind's slight vulgarity and Hélène's tactless comment to Maître Bourin were of no importance whatever?

"Madame will have the kindness to command my ingredients for the reception?" Nathalie asked, "Monsieur has informed me that he himself has already ordered the champagne. For the rest, I have made Madame a list of what I shall need. Also a little menu to give an idea . . ."

Just reading the buffet menu was mouthwatering. The party that, after the Happy Pair decamped, had been hanging round Hélène's neck like a tough old inedible albatross now seemed possible, delicious, successful – if every bit as terrifying.

For years after they'd come to the château, Hélène and Jean-Hubert had lived there in a sort of well-behaved obscurity. The local notables watched them discreetly to see if they put a foot wrong, greeted them politely after Mass, summed them up bit by bit as a nice unassuming couple, not quite either of them descended from the choicest stock, but tolerable. After about ten years, Hélène began receiving invitations to charity teas at various small local manors; later both of them were invited to unimportant and fairly anonymous dinner parties in the same manors, then to weddings and finally, quite recently, to slightly more intimate dinner parties and grander receptions. Only the du Bois Fleuris held back, but in the end even they consented to come and drink tea once a year among Hélène's impeccable rosebushes, and to invite the young couple in return to a yearly glass of porto under the precarious old oak trees that had been planted by Louis the Fourteenth himself when he dropped in for a meal and a bed on his way home from inspecting some of Vauban's fortifications.

Don't rush things, Tante Ruby advised from the beginning. Take your time, work your way in gently, advised Jean-Hubert's mother. She proposed that Hélène assist the Countess in her Catechism classes, and on her death-bed was still counselling her on suitable voluntary work to engage in. Boat-people were fine, she said, everyone supported boat-people. Battered wives were good too, and young drug abusers who could be recuperated in Catholic-run clinics. Amnesty International was out of course – too much emphasis on right-wing tyrannies – but Solidarnosc was a champion: anti-communist and Catholic too, a real blessing! The Countess ran a regular truck service to Poland, bringing food and clothes to Monsignor Glemp's starving and presumably naked faithful.

"I could do the same for the dispossessed peasants of Brazil," Hélène suggested helpfully, and Tante Ruby began tearing her hair and moaning.

"Ma pauvre petite, you have understood nothing! But nothing! Rien de rien. Those peasants and their priests are simply a pack of reds. You will destroy everything I and my dead sister have worked for if you touch South America!"

So Hélène, as well as teaching Catechism to council school-children on their weekly half-holiday, began sending all her cast-off clothes to Poland. Even the children joined in with enthusiasm: little Clémence and Henri one Christmas presented Madame la Comtesse with seven soft toys, one each for Lech Walesa's seven poor children, and were rewarded with an invitation to come and play with the du Bois Fleuri grandchildren, one of whom Jean-Hubert shortly began dreaming of as a future son-in-law. Hélène hid her boredom behind a face of friendly but unsmiling composure, her clothes sense had always been perfect, soon she spoke French without a trace of a foreign accent, she was on her way to being accepted. After the little revolution in the mairie, the Countess decided to drop the Catechism classes – the villagers had shown such crass ingratitude in voting Socialist – and Hélène had her Wednesday afternoons free again. (Sometimes she imagined Christopher Milton nodding his head in approval of how far she'd come, at other times she pictured his cynically-raised eyebrow, his mock-Belfast accent: "Would yis get a load of her, but!")

Jean-Hubert talked of changing his name to Bourjois de Ploudel de Medeu, and Tante Ruby wisely counselled: not yet. But, when her St Petersburg heritage began to be known, she allowed them to consider this large party at which they would consolidate the various tentative acquaintanceships they'd made over the years, only advising them not to try and outdo the Count and Countess.

"Remember le malheureux Monsieur Fouquet and Louis Quatorze," she warned in all seriousness.

The whole idea of this party excited and terrified Hélène. Just be natural, Rosalind advised, be friendly and chatty and welcoming, lay on mountains of food and rivers of booze and you and everyone else might even enjoy the whole bash. But Hélène knew it did not work like that in polite French society. Being oneself would be about as socially acceptable as appearing at a party in one's underwear: appearance was everything. And then, Jean-Hubert was so fastidious. About the food and drink, which must be sumptuous without any hint of vulgarity. About the service, which must be discreet and efficient without evoking the horror of hired caterers and hotel banqueting rooms. About the protocol and the savoir vivre, and why it was imperative to remember for example that Madame d'Untel must be chatted to for exactly five minutes less than the Baronne de Machin. It was all a great worry . . . Parties were a great worry . . .

"I think Christopher's going to be able to make it after all," Mitzi announced one evening, "Are you not dying to meet him, Eileen? The famous Christopher Milton?"

"But I thought he was as old as the hills," Eileen said, "The poor guy will be like a fish out of water, will you not have to drag in a pack of oul' dolls to chat him up? Teachers and that? He's going to ruin your whole party so he is."

"D'you know, she lives in another world, this wee child!" Sheila looked disgusted, "Listen here, Chris may be thirty, he may be even more for all I know, nobody ever even *thinks* of his age, he's one of these fellas . . . Look, Christopher Milton could be ninety years of age and he could have just about everything from a cleft palate to a club foot and half of Queen's would still be dying to get their shoes under his bed. How did you coax him to come, Mitzi? He must get asked to a hundred parties a week, that fella."

"Oh it wasn't too hard," Mitzi said airily, "I think he quite fancies me actually. And I sort of let it slip in nicely that we were expecting Eamonn McCann and Michael Farrell to show up. Luckily I hadn't to promise him wee Gerry Fitt and all! Do you think he's maybe writing a book or something about the civil rights movement? He seems dead interested in everything. And he was a journalist, he knows Mary Holland and all them . . ."

"*Everyone's* dead interested in civil rights."

"Everyone except Eileen here. This child doesn't give one wee shite about civil rights do you Eileen? It scares her, even. She was near wettin' herself that time in Derry with the stones flyin', weren't you, Eileen?"

"Wee Eileen doesn't give a shite about nothin' except her American folk music. Joan Baez and Bob Dylan! *We* have folk music too, Eileen, did nobody ever tell you about that?

The Dubliners? The McPeakes? We have a tradition too. And a civil rights movement and everything, every bit as good as the blacks, you can't just stay standing on the sidelines so you can't, Eileen. Not these days."

"Aye well, you'll be coming to the party though, won't you, Eileen? I mean I hope you haven't got one of your big sinful dates on that night? With your Married Man? Your Commercial Traveller? Quote unquote, close the inverted commas, as Chris would say."

"She'll have to come," Sheila laughed, "We need her for that little touch of exoticism. Our teenage drop-out. Our own wee pet hippy. Just so Chris will see we're not all a clatter of wild Irish rebels."

"He's sort of Irish himself."

"You'd never think it though, would you? The Cosmopolitan Man . . . Better not to let on about your disreputable da, Eileen. Stick to peace and love and poetry and he won't be able to keep his hands off you. The rest of us won't get a look in."

They were joking, and Mitzi didn't like it one bit when he spent a solid hour talking to Eileen at the party. None of them liked it much. Queen's had discovered Christopher Milton, Queen's considered it owned him, and Eileen wasn't even a student.

But nobody owned Christopher. He came to Mitzi's party as he went to a hundred others, he stood with his glass in his hand, looking and listening and taking it all in with his quiet ironic smile, wrapped in watchful solitude (as Eileen wrote in a poem that night), sole owner of himself. He talked to Eileen for an hour, or rather he listened to Eileen. She, not yet in love, not yet having to fear rejection, was able to be natural and unconscious, she chatted away to him as if he was Mitzi. As if he was better than Mitzi:

Christopher Milton knew how to put himself at the complete disposal of his listeners, without giving any of himself away, he had a great talent for making the shyest of people burst into bloom. That's why they were so mad about him . . .

He said goodnight to her after the party and she thought well that's it, I've met the famous Christopher Milton and now I know why all the other fellows seem so raw and thick-witted. Regretting, for the first time, that she hadn't stayed on at school and done her A-levels, because there was no way that a wee waitress in a café could have anything serious to do with someone like Christopher Milton.

She started going to meetings at the Students' Union with Mitzi and them, and one night she spotted him standing at the back of the hall, his face lit with quiet amusement, while a man with a long sweet sheep's face and long black sheep's curls and an Afghan coat talked earnestly about something that was miles and miles above Eileen's head.

Then Christopher dropped in at the café one lunchtime to eat, and behaved with amused complicity as if her serving him his shepherd's pie was just a nice little joke they'd made up between them, as if she was playing at being a waitress and he playing at being her customer. Even the way he left a tip at the end had the same amused complicity about it, so that she wasn't at all embarrassed about the situation as she would have been with Chaz for example: she'd have *died* with embarrassment if she'd had to serve Chaz a meal. And big thick Chaz would have died too.

And then one evening, miraculously, he was standing on the doorstep when she got in from work . . .

He must have fancied me at the beginning, she thought, he must have liked me quite a bit, or why would he have bothered wasting his time on me. Because he did waste quite a few evenings on me, if you looked at it like that. A fellow like that could take his pick. So what went wrong? Did *Chaz* put me wrong? Was it that thick eejit's fault?

"Don't you ever say to any of your boyfriends that you write poetry!" Chaz warned her, "Don't ever let on to them that you read it, even. That you read *anything*. They wouldn't touch you with a forty-foot pole. It's no skin off my nose, but your average fellow doesn't like to think the bird he's going out with has to sit in her room with a book in the evenings like some poor spinster of a thing. They like to think you're worth more than that, it reflects on them, you see. Learn to flirt a bit, Eileen, you're far too serious altogether, you should have heard yourself just now, God I wish I had a tape-recorder! 'And have you read *Door into the Dark* yet, Chaz?' Jeee-z-us! I mean *I* don't mind but try asking any ordinary fellow, any single fellow, a thing like that when he's just sitting having a quiet drink, he'd be off out through the door like a bat out of hell so he would! You know . . . You want to giggle a bit, chat about normal things, make a fella feel he's important."

And when Christopher continued taking her out all that summer, but treating her as if she was some nice sexless comrade, she remembered Chaz's advice, and followed it. Chaz was a man, wasn't he, Chaz must know what he was talking about . . .

And so here she was, more than twenty years on, far from Belfast, far from Christopher, in a big loveless mansion with servants – the kind of house she used to read about, a house out of *Hetty Gray*, a house out of *Mansfield Park* – planning a party for the local aristocrats.

Well now at least she could stop worrying about the

food. She smiled at Nathalie, seeing her for the first time not as some great scarlet lump of sin but as a saviour.

"Did you sleep well?" she asked kindly, suddenly anxious that this treasure should find no excuse to leave before the party. Nathalie giggled, and Hélène found herself blushing. "I mean, is the room all right? It's a bit high up but the last people . . ." She stopped, remembering the last people. "I'd better warn you," she began, "My husband's aunt can be rather . . ." and trailed off again, quite unable to say: "For heaven's sake don't let Gabriel run any baths for her!" "Yes well, I'll get all you need next time I'm in the shops," she smiled, "I'm sure it will all go splendidly, Nathalie, I'm so glad you could come to us after all." And she escaped into the garden.

There of course she came upon the unfortunate husband who was already trailing around the flower-beds with a hoe, silent and dreamy, looking as if he'd been keeping vigil there all night. Poor man, she thought, what he must be suffering, and so pale and poetic-looking with it! But of course he's not really Nathalie's type, too refined and wimpish, *naturally* a peasant like Nathalie would prefer a big hunky cliché like Gabriel, he's well out of it if he but knew! But she'll have to go, no party's worth it, she'll just have to go. Poor Michel, after all.

Her Iceberg roses looked pure and restrained standing in tight little lines behind their low box hedges, but right over in the far corner behind the screen of syringa and buddleia, Madame Laetitia Ploudel had overnight broken into immense purplish blossoms and was embalming the garden with her passionate thorny scent. She'll have to go, Hélène thought again, not quite sure whether she meant Madame Ploudel or big Nathalie Nipples in the kitchen.

Tante Ruby stepped out on to the terrace, swinging her

bikini top in one hand, Ray-Bans sunglasses shoved in her hair, eyes wrinkled against the morning sun. Michel Le Borgne kept on hoeing minuscule weeds from around the roses. Exactly, kinder not to look, kinder to keep on with whatever. The postman's yellow van crept in off the avenue and stopped. Hélène recognised her mother's handwriting on top of the pile. She took the letter with a mixture of warmth, hate, irritation and relief. It was real and solid, the letter, it came from a world where old women still had dignity and did not stroll around in their skin under the eyes of postmen and gardeners. A world where the opposite of right was still wrong, where in spite of bombs and murders it was all straight and simple, the ten commandments where they always were, eternal fires stoked up hot and ready and waiting for you if you broke them. It was a life she'd fled from many years earlier, swearing never to return, but that morning with its overtones of adultery and decadence, the longing she'd felt since the Saturday in Arles became overwhelming. Her mother's letter with its straight inflexible handwriting fell like a lovely reminder of Ireland into her own ambiguous world where looking-glass people like Jean-Hubert and herself would go to any disgusting lengths to find servants to serve up the marshmallow pies rather than lose face before other looking-glass people like Tante Ruby and the Count and Countess and the assorted minor diplomats, retired generals and country squires who would come, probably reluctantly, to their party.

She kept her mother's letter to read under the drier at the hairdresser's and sat down on one of the terrace chairs to look through the weekly news magazines and keep herself up to date on the chaotic world outside Plouch'en. In Belfast peace talks and sectarian killings were uneasily jostling each other for space, the Balkans were still like a witch's cauldron, another bit of the old Soviet Union was bloodily insisting on its national identity, the Irish tourist couple found murdered near Arles were being claimed by the IRA as victims of an SAS murder gang. Gibraltar the Second was the headline.

In the squat long ago Jean-Hubert had made them listen to Daniel Viglietti singing about liberty and struggle and watering the land with the blood of the fallen. It had seemed perfectly possible, sitting listening to him there in the arrogant innocence of the early Seventies, that the world could one day change and be free and fraternal. The blood of the fallen, when buckets of the stuff are not being shoved up under your nose with every news bulletin, can seem painless and noble and even rather beautiful. She turned several pages quickly with a small sigh for the days when *Tien an Men* was just the brand name on the soy sauce bottle, and came on the photo of a long-time Soviet exile, home at last, complaining about his motherland's disgusting new tendency to wallow in the delights of Western decadence. Decidedly the fellow was never satisfied. Can he not look around him, she thought irritably, the people who are spreading terror are not decadent, they're pure and cold and as spiritual as even he could wish for. The IRA are not decadent. Neither are the Muslim fundamentalists. Hitler wasn't decadent. Tante Ruby's a decadent old slob but she doesn't do anyone a bit of harm. Does them good, more likely, lending out her old Picasso for parties of schoolchildren to gape at. And so am I decadent and so's Jean-Hubert and the twins for all I know, and so what? Decadence isn't the worst that can happen.

The little burst of irritation cheered her up, rid her for the moment of her longing for Ireland, brought her back to herself. "Nathalie," she called, "I'm just off to the hairdresser's. If you and Gabriel could get busy on the downstairs windows meanwhile . . ."

It's not that I approve of them being here, she thought, but seeing they are I might just as well get a bit of value out of them.

Part Eight

❦

"So he walks into the bistro, je te jure Marie-Annick, he walks into the bistro, Saturday evening that was, and straight up to Gabriel: 'What's this I hear', he says, 'What's this I hear?' I'm standing there wiping a glass, trying to make myself toute petite, well you can imagine. 'Ça y est,' my old man he says to me in a whisper, that's it, better ring the gendarmes ma vieille, there'll be murder done, le Borgne's going to smash up the whole. But no, nothing at all. Rien de rien! 'What's all this I've been hearing,' Michel says and Gabriel he just turns round, you know what he's like, sacré Gabriel! And he says, 'I'm screwing your wife, so what? Et alors?' That's what he says, le petit Gabriel, 'Je baise ta femme. Et alors?' And he lifts his glass to his mouth again. Nobody moves. Waiting. All of us waiting. There'll be blood spilled, I says to myself. But no, nothing at all. Michel he just laughs and then he turns and walks out. Je te jure! Just walks out the door laughing. Laughing! Le vrai cocu. Next thing we know they're installed in the château no less. All three of them. La belle vie, quoi! Decidedly, those people there, I'm talking about the château now, they're not like us, are they? Ils s'en foutent, ces salauds-là!

269

Run to Mass every Sunday, kids at school with the priests and nuns, I mean it's all very well being modern but. Remarque, *she's* a foreigner, they haven't the same decency have they, those people there? The English, hou la la, the English!"

"Chut!" The plump little hairdresser, all pink, threw a glance towards Hélène where she was waiting behind the screen of philodendrons, about to open her mother's letter. The wife of the bistro, busy handing up the perm-papers, noticed nothing. "Non, mais c'est vrai, quoi! It's true, what do they care? We're not people to them are we, you and me, what do *they* care about poor Michel Le Borgne? Decent quiet lad, good schooling and all, not that he made much of it between you and me, no ambition, odd-job man for those foreigners after his poor parents sacrificing themselves. Mind you it's her I blame, it's that Nathalie I blame, only for that tart he'd have left the village and bettered himself, and there she is, invited up now to do her little business in the château, was *I* ever asked up to cook for these gentlemen and ladies? *Cook?* Is that what they call it nowadays? You mark my words, Marie-Annick, it'll soon be just like old Monsieur Vladimir's time. Half the village cuckolded, half the kids bastards, Hou la la, les salauds!"

Possibly she knew Hélène was there and was making her little revolutionary gesture, having nothing at all to lose. Nobody from the château drank in the bistro. The hairdresser was suffering, Hélène could see, afraid she was going to lose a good client. Turning her letter in her hands, playing deaf, Hélène reassured her. In any case she didn't care, she quite agreed with the woman from the bistro, Uncle Vlad had been a disgusting old slob when you came right down to it, and for all she knew Jean-Hubert might be every bit as bad . . . But she wasn't at the moment caring.

She was somewhere else. She was someone else. Holding her mother's letter, preparing to read the pious well-turned schoolteaching sentences, she was not the lady from the château. She was not Hélène.

She was Eileen, and the postman came smiling up the pass on his bicycle, bringing the world to Anny and Patrick's small cottage. *Saint Anthony's Messenger* and *Time* and *Newsweek* and parcels and big fat letters with stripy edges. A photo came of Anny and Patrick's Yankee sisters. They had not seen them since they were young girls and now they would probably never see them. Four stout women with lipstick and waved hair and carefully corseted bodies beneath flowery splashy dresses like the ones in the press. They were passed from neighbour to neighbour; descriptions were read out of their houses, their husbands' jobs, their labour saving gadgets, their children's colleges. They had Italian names, and German: curiously none of them had done the usual thing and married an Irish emigrant. All were prosperous. The one christened Bridget, as soon as she stepped off the ship had changed her name to Lucy: "I couldn't stand her", Patrick said, "she was a weasel. I never could stick the sight of that one, God forgive me, when I was a wee gasson I used to hide in terror of her!" His gentle tired face turned hard with hate, recalling an elder sister's airs and graces, her selfishness, adolescent cruelty, unconcern for her parents. The long hard oul' jaw of her! Lucy was the one that never sent a dollar, lived in California, wrote long boastful letters. But in the photo she was no different from the rest, wore a dress with sequins, smiled at the camera, was just an elderly exile with waved hair.

Eileen had no one in America. But you have someone in England darlin', that sends you parcels and asks all about you in letters. And if you work hard at school you'll be able to write to her yourself in no time. And if you're good and learn them wee words there you'd never know what Santy might take you for Christmas!

Santy took her her mother. Anny was scrubbing the house for weeks, and baking, and sewing new curtains, but when the bus stopped at the end of the pass and a tall pretty woman got off with two big suitcases Eileen had no idea who she was and held back shyly holding Anny's apron.

"It's your mammy, won't you go to your mammy now Eileen, that's the surprise that Santy was taking you."

"It's not Christmas yet," Eileen said, totally unable to take a step towards this stranger who was standing holding out her arms on the side of the road while Patrick manoeuvred awkwardly with the suitcases.

"Well, that's a fine welcome to get after eight or nine months away. And have you no kisses at all for your mammy?"

The woman was bright and hard-edged like the teachers at school, her voice was not like the quiet blurred voices Eileen had got used to, but she recognised something, a humorous brisk impatience that brought back the high white kitchen with its red tiles, a perfumed arm thrown loosely about her, records scattered carelessly on a soft carpet, and she was beginning to move timidly forward when her mother shook herself and turned away sharply towards Patrick and the suitcases:

"Oh that's great, so it is! Oh that's exactly the welcome I've been looking forward to, slaving away over there, weekends and holidays and everything! Well I suppose if nothing else, Anny, we can at least get ourselves inside out of the cold. Patrick, be careful with that box would you, it's breakable."

Anny smoothed things over and said it's a tiring journey especially at this time of year darlin' and isn't it only natural for a wee child to make strange, eight or nine months must be like a whole lifetime to the creature, and her mother said she's blaming me, she's holding it against me for going away, that's what it is! And Anny said that's only your own conscience talking Margaret, you know as well as me what you should have done at the time, it would have been the natural thing for a daughter-in-law to do and them after losing their son the way they did. And her mother started crying and Eileen moved shyly over and stroked her arm the way Teresa did when her mother cried, and her mother turned and hugged her and said some day it's all going to be worth it, some day I'm going to be able to make a proper home for you, don't you worry.

There were dolls and dresses and picture-books, and the crib in the chapel smelled of pine cones and candles, and then on Boxing Day Agnes Quinn and Teresa came to their dinner, sure I had to ask them Margaret, the poor thing has no one and that man of hers, and Anny's voice trailed into an och-och-och-och of complaining whispers beside her mother's ear.

"It's *your* house, Anny," her mother said impatiently, "You can invite who you like into it."

Agnes Quinn drank a lot of sherry and giggled and wanted to talk and talk about London with Eileen's mother. But it seemed that Eileen's mother lived in a different London from the one Agnes Quinn knew and had no idea at all what Agnes was talking about.

"I didn't even know there *were* Irish clubs in Hammersmith, I mean I'm afraid that to me, Mrs Quinn, Hammersmith is just another boring station on the way into London!" And she had never been near Kilburn and the singing pubs or the Cricklewood dance-halls. "I'm living in Roehampton, actually," she said, and Teresa looked at Eileen in triumph: "Your oul mother knows nothing," she whispered, and Eileen was desperately ashamed because Teresa's mother was bright and loud and knew everything and her own mother was just muttering into her sherry glass and looking bored.

"That woman's as common as dirt," Eileen's mother said, "And mutton dressed as lamb with it, she must be at least forty! And is that the kind of neighbours you have?"

Anny said mildly that the poor creature was lonesome and unhappy and only trying to make the best of things and that Margaret might have been a bit kinder to her in the holy season of. And anyway the wee girl was company for Eileen.

"Queer company!" her mother said, "Still, in a year or so now I'll be able to make a home for her. With a bit of luck I'll be able to have her with me in London sooner than I expected."

"If you're thinking of dead women's shoes, troth I wouldn't if I was you, Margaret! That house belonged to your Aunt Catherine's husband and as sure as anything it'll go back to his people when she dies, it's the way they do things in your father's family."

Her mother was furious and said she hadn't been thinking anything of the kind, what was a great-aunt when all was said and done, she paid the old woman rent and board, she regarded her as a landlady that was all, but thanks be to God there was still a few pound left in the bank out of what her poor mother left, the little that wastrel didn't get his hands on, and she might just use it to find a flat for her and Eileen, and not have her growing up an ignorant wee yokel making friends with all the tramps in the country. Eileen fell asleep to their quarrelling and was carried to bed.

Life was on edge while her mother was there, the walks down the meadow were like a catechism, what's that called? And that? And what exactly are you learning in Infants? And I suppose you've completely forgotten your home in Clagan, well all right then go on, tell me, tell me what you remember? Chestnut candles and white roses and daddy singing in the snow and the smell of wax and lavender when Anny polished the landing. Funny memories, and is there nothing else in your head, am I not anywhere there in these wee memories of yours? You were clean mad about Lee Lawrence, Eileen said. God above, God above Eileen what made that stick in your head? Who mentioned anything to you about? It was that night, Anny, do you remember that was the night, we stayed playing records till all hours, I was after buying "The Green Glens of Antrim" and I played it over and over till they were all sick of it and he still hadn't come home and then. Give it over, Margaret, give it up now, the child remembers nothing, there was nothing ever mentioned, it was just some wee thing you said that stuck in her mind, children's minds is like that. You're started over now with a clean slate and don't ever forget it, don't try forcing your own regrets on that child whatever you do, let her settle down and live her own wee life.

In the house Patrick sat silent in the corner, there was no reading from the Yankee magazines, Anny moved here and there doing fussy unnecessary things, her mother polished her nails, plucked her eyebrows, mended a ladder in her stocking with varnish. Eileen sat on her stool, there were long silences broken thankfully by the rattle of cups on the table, the bustle of breadknife and teaspoon.

Anny and Patrick's sister came from Richill with her big

gawky children. The eldest boy, Chaz, was a salesman in Belfast, doing great his mother said, a salary and commission and everything and going steady with the loveliest wee girl, go on Chaz, show them the silver cigarette case and lighter Joan bought you for Christmas. The lighter and cigarette case were passed from hand to hand, do you see now Eileen, this is the way you light it, and Chaz, red-faced and smiling, took her on his knee and let her light his cigarette, she's a great wee girl isn't she, what age are you Eileen, and are you started school yet? He smelled of hair oil and aftershave, he always smelled of hair oil and after-shave. Twelve years later, standing in the garden of the Turfstack, she couldn't even smell the roses for the whiff off him . . .

"I'm sorry about that, Madame," Marie-Annick towel-dried Hélène's hair, sat her in front of the glass, got busy with combs and scissors. "She didn't mean anything, that old crow from the bistro. Just talking she was."

"All the same, the village probably thinks it odd . . ."

"Poor Nathalie," Marie-Annick sighed, "She never had much of a life with Michel Le Borgne. Too serious for her. She deserves a break is what I say."

"I've never really understood why she married him. I mean I never took much interest, he is only part-time with us, what he does is his own affair but I did hear she was a bit flighty, so why . . ."

"You should have seen her when she was seventeen, madame! Big backward lump that girl was. And shy! Good-looking mind you, but none too bright. I used to think she was a bit simple myself, though you can't really tell with these country girls. I don't think she ever had a chap till Le Borgne started asking her out so of course she jumped at the chance to get away from her parents. Out of the frying-pan. She didn't laugh every day with Michel, I can tell you that. And especially now since she slimmed down with WeightWatchers and all, she must have caught on to what she was missing. Best of luck to her, I say!"

"And him? I know he's not everyone's glass of wine, that poor Le Borgne but he's not bad-looking, whatever did he see in her? If she was such a big lump?"

Marie-Annick laughed. "Maybe she caught him on the rebound. Maybe he had some tragic love affair? Who knows what goes on in Michel's head? He's a decent fellow but he's not like the rest of us, madame, not like the village people, even if he did grow up here. An outsider. All I know is he never got much joy out of Nathalie. Soon as she slimmed down a bit and started looking decent, she was off. She and Gabriel have been eyeing each other for ages. I expect they'll be getting married now, as soon as she gets her divorce."

"Married?"

"People do, madame, hou la la they do! She's only four years older than Gabriel and doesn't look it at that, does she?"

Hélène's mind slowly adjusted to the idea that this might well be a genuine love affair rather than a dirty joke. What a snob I've become, she thought in amazement. I've got the exact same idea of the village people now as that old hag Ruby, how disgusting! And then came the uncomfortable realisation that her attitude had actually been closer to that of the old crow from the bistro than to Tante Ruby's. After all, neither Jean-Hubert nor his aunt had ever seen anything remotely sordid in the situation. Whereas she, from the start, had been thinking in terms of sin and shame, and of the old-fashioned comic trio: tart, gigolo and cuckold. The Falls Road sitting-room lurched into her mind with its velvet curtains and the Pope on the wall and her mother getting up petitions against Sex in the Cinema . . . She pushed it away, and asked: "And Michel Le Borgne? How do you mean he's not like the rest of the villagers? Is he a bit, well I mean I've never really had much to say to the poor man, is he maybe a bit simple?"

"Simple, madame!" Marie-Annick looked astounded, "Hou la la! Simple! Not on your life, madame! Should hear Nathalie going on about the books he has over there, couldn't stand them Nathalie couldn't, always at him to let her pack them away nice and tidy in the attic. Well it stands to reason, madame, she's the one had to keep the place nice, couldn't have the neighbours talking, nothing like books is there for making a room look neglected, I mean she was ashamed to take people into the living-room, shelves and shelves of them he has. And records! Want to hear his old records, she used to say! No, madame, since Michel spent those couple of years at the university he's not like the."

"University?" Hélène was dazed, "Michel Le?"

"Oh not that he got his degree, madame. What they call a drop-out. Un marginal, quoi! There was a lot of it about at the time. Back to nature. Manual labour. Peace and love. *I* don't know! And dope," she added in a hissing whisper, "Used to smoke pot too, oh years ago when no one in the village even heard of drugs, not like now eh, they're all at it now, put you off having kids is what I say!"

Hélène recalled her first sight of Michel Le Borgne with his long blond hair and embroidered shirt in the midst of Uncle Vladimir's roses, and remembered how he'd looked exactly like the kids in the squat. He didn't look like that now, but then of course who did? She summoned up a picture of him in her head and realised, with a small shock, that he looked like a blond version of her husband. No wonder old Vladimir was a legend! And his clothes. Washed-out polo shirts and worn Levis. Not, definitely not, the blue boiler suit of the French workman . . .

"Mon dieu!" she wailed, "Mon dieu, Marie-Annick, I've been talking to that man for years in words of one syllable!"

I could have been friends with him, she thought, I almost was friends with him that first day when he was showing me round the garden, I remember we had a nice little chat, I felt at home with him, we even sort of laughed a bit about old Vladimir and the Ploudel de Medeus. But then, straight away, I was taken over by the family and the house and the estate and making money, and somehow Michel got filed away with all the others, labelled and slotted into place: workmen, villagers, peasants, tenants, with *Us* standing on the other side of some great high barrier. I let myself be colonised, she thought, I just adapted totally, without question. But what on earth must that man have been thinking of me all these years, talking down to him as if he was the local idiot? Maybe he's been laughing up his sleeve at me the whole time, he must know I'm not the world's greatest intellectual, that I'm not exactly choking on silver spoons, Christ I practically told him my life story that first day, why couldn't he have said . . .

"All the same," she sighed, "I'm sure everyone in the village does think it a bit much. Having the three of them up there working for us, I mean. I mean I keep expecting Father Plouer and a band of witch hunters to arrive at any minute and stone us out of it."

"Oh I shouldn't worry, madame. He's seen worse, Father Plouer has. No disrespect, Madame Bourjois, but in old Monsieur Vladimir's time hou la la!"

Under the drier she read her mother's letter, noticing for the first time that it had a French stamp. "Surprise,

surprise!" she'd written, "I'm in Paris of all places, been here for a month, sightseeing like mad and absolutely worn out from wallowing in the delights of French culture! You can expect me in Plouch'en quite soon – and prepare yourself for a few surprises, I've lots of news for you. Don't worry, I'll make my own way down from Paris, no need to meet me or anything. Love, Mother."

God, she'll be here for the party, Hélène thought, she must have gone to Lourdes early, what on earth am I going to do with her? News? Surprises? Whatever could she mean? The letter didn't sound a bit like her. Maybe she'd decided to enter the convent or something? Surely she shouldn't be on holidays so soon, had she taken early retirement or something? Was she *ill*, was that the news? Cancer? Heart disease? No, if she was ill she wouldn't be gallivanting around Paris, she'd be lying in some hospital bed. Hélène felt vaguely unsafe, as if things were moving out of her control, escaping her grasp. As if life itself had suddenly wobbled on its pedestal.

As long as her mother was there, in Belfast, courageously teaching in her non-denominational school, doing her little bit towards peace and unity, Hélène could feel the world was standing solidly on its feet, to be kicked against, to be screamed at, to be thumped, to be leaned against for comfort. Not that comfort was what she ever particularly got, from her mother. Common sense was more like it, and an efficient dabbing of wounds with iodine. And a swift slap across the face for questionable conduct. Questionable conduct would be that pair working in the kitchen, while the wronged husband miserably pushed the lawnmower. Would be Tante Ruby wandering topless round the garden. Would be . . .

On that first Sunday morning in Belfast, her mother had

stood on the church steps after Mass collecting signatures on a petition that she later presented to the manager of the Broadway cinema in protest against the immoral film he was showing that week. The film was taken off and a John Wayne western shown in its place. Hélène could not remember what the immoral film had been. Probably she had never even known the title: when she went to live in the Falls Road house she began to be shielded from the realities of life in a way she had never been in Anny and Patrick's townland.

On the Monday she'd gone with her mother to the school in Mimosa Street, a bus ride down the Falls to a district where the houses were sooty and squat and had no gardens and no sitting-rooms. A district of gloom, only a bus ride but still a whole world away from Gerald's tall house with its neat shrubs in front. "Country gawk!" they'd called her, as her mother warned her they would. They made a ring around her in the narrow dusty yard chanting "Country Gawk!" till the two other teachers scattered them. Her mother did not interfere, but that evening she began giving her speech lessons, which Eileen accepted with straight-faced docility.

A few days later she heard her mother talking to one of the other teachers.

"It must be hard on her though," Miss O'Flaherty was saying, "Starting a new school halfway through the year when all the wee friendships are made."

Her mother sounded quite cross: "I could hardly have taken her to live with us straight after the wedding! Good heavens, Kathleen, Gerald and I may not be exactly a couple of teenagers but we *were* newly-weds, we needed time to get used to each other."

Her name had already been changed from Campbell to

O'Neill to save her embarrassment, but still word went round that she was an orphan out of a children's home.

"I'm not an orphan! The teacher's my mother, so she is!"

"If she's your mammy where were you all last term, why didn't you start here along with her? She got you from the Assistance, so she did!"

"I can't fight your battles for you," her mother said, "where would that leave you if I was forever sticking up for you, they'd only start saying you were the teacher's pet. You'll just have to stand on your own two feet, Eileen."

Eileen retreated into herself and looked out from behind her pale straight face at the jostling yelping children in their ugly clothes. Reality was not in this playground with its dirty brick walls, reality was in the meadow and the haggard and the sunny doorstep where Anny sewed lace, reality was the soft blurred voices of their neighbours and the whispers and the gossip. Reality was her friend Teresa. She stood straight-faced in the playground or sat in the cloakroom reading *The Wind in the Willows*, and ached for reality.

"Isn't she a composed wee thing," Miss Cowan said, "I suppose you hardly notice you have her in the house with you!"

But they did notice. "Eileen, please! You came down those stairs like a baby elephant. Poor Gerald has exam papers to mark." "Eileen, I know we can't provide whole acres of fields for you to run wild in, but all the same maybe you could find something to employ your hands with instead of just sitting there dreaming." Backside, Eileen would whisper silently, cows' tits, cat's shite, while she looked out, polite and obedient, from behind her straight face. In her head she made up long loving letters to Anny and Patrick, full of the jokes they used to share, full of descriptions of all she'd lost, full of longing to be back there, full of affectionate detailed enquiries about the townland and the neighbours. But, when her mother sat her down in front of a writing pad: "Dear Anny," she wrote painfully, "Dear Patrick, I hope you are keeping well. I am well myself and settling down. Mother and Gerald are very kind to me. I look forward to seeing you in the holidays. Love from Eileen."

And Anny replied, just as stiltedly, "Dear Eileen, I am glad you are well and happy. We all miss you but please God we'll see you soon. We are both doing the best. Teresa and her mother were asking for you. Love from Anny and Patrick."

With every letter the townland retreated slightly backwards, while her mother and Gerald did their best to fill up the empty spaces in her life. She longed for the holidays, as she longed now for Belfast, and for Christopher Milton, longed for the lost far-off paradise from which she was exiled.

"Is that all right, madame? That what you wanted?"

"It's lovely, Marie-Annick, thank you. Yes, I think you've got it exactly right."

Her pale beige hair was cut in a bell shape just below her ears; it looked sculptured and pure in repose, but when she moved her head in the mirror it danced voluptuously above her long neck and sloping shoulders: Hélène could look at her own face for hours nowadays and be absolutely delighted with it. Christopher Milton walked into the long pale drawing-room, brought to the party by some . . . diplomat? Some poet? She gave him her hand to kiss. "Mes hommages, madame."

"But we've already met, Christopher."

"We've met . . . ?"

"Yes, but that was in another country and besides . . ."

She shook the little dream out of her head, turned herself this way and that, admiring the way her hair shimmered in the glass.

"Yes, it's perfect, Marie-Annick."

If I don't daydream at all, she told herself, if I don't even think about him, he'll be there when I go to Belfast, he'll be there by chance in the Club Bar, in Gardiner's bookshop, he'll be there having a coffee if I drop into the Lilac Room some morning. He'll be there if I pluck up the courage to knock on his door. (Last time he answered a doorbell to me it was catastrophe. Yes, but that was Teresa's fault, bloody peasant Teresa dragging me over there, serves her damn well right now with her houseful of whining kids, why couldn't she have let things be?)

"A propos de Michel Le Borgne," Marie-Annick was saying, "The Le Moal girls were telling me he's great friends with the doctor's wife these days. No words of one syllable there, madame, standing chatting over the garden fence like a pair of old cronies it seems! Like two old countrymen leaning on a gate, that's what Christelle Le Moal says they reminded her of. You can see what she means and all, madame, l'Anglaise is not the most feminine of. But imagine if there was some big love story building up!"

Hélène felt bereft for an instant, felt shut out of a friendship that might have been hers. "Madame Bouchon is herself a keen gardener," she said with a touch of repressiveness. Marie-Annick, on occasion, hovered just barely on the right side of familiarity, it was often necessary to point out to her discreetly exactly where the limits lay. "Thank you, that's splendid, and now I'd like to make an appointment for . . ."

She walked home, smiling at the picture of Rosalind and

Michel having long committed chats about compost at the end of the avenue, Rosalind no doubt managing to sound both chirpy and cranky at the same time like one of those magazine articles about organic gardening, no wonder she'd never really managed to fit in, God she was bound to stick out a mile in a French village . . .

She'd discovered Rosalind sitting on the steps of the village church that first day they arrived in Plouch'en. Jean-Hubert had stopped the van beside the mairie. "Better check on a few essentials, babe," he said, "Just in case we actually decide to shack down in this old château of mine for keeps. We could try out the local croissants for a start . . ."

There didn't seen to be any shops at all in the depressing little village. "Tu parles!" Jean-Hubert said, "My uncle had everything delivered from Seulbourg. Though surely even the peasants must eat?" Like Mole finding his way home he sniffed the air, located a smell of yeast and followed it to its source, which turned out to be a glowering elderly couple standing behind a counter in what was otherwise a bungalow full of pot plants and fake rustic furniture. When the couple learned that they were not foreign hippies but Monsieur Vladimir's lawful heirs come at last to occupy the château, the glowers changed to respectfully bashful smiles and they began to address Jean-Hubert as "Our Master."

After the bakery, Jean-Hubert had to see if there was a public convenience he could use on Sundays while he was waiting for Eileen to come out of Mass. "But I haven't been to Mass for years!" Eileen protested and Jean-Hubert, dazzled with all the "notre Maîtres' that had come his way, pronounced grandly, "En Frrrawnce, ma chère épouse, the lady of the manor always goes to Mass on Sunday. It is her duty to set an example to the peasantry." "Well then, I can drive myself down and you can go to the loo at home if you really have to!" she said, planning to spend a touristy half-hour drinking Pernod in the village café instead and getting to know the locals, but Jean-Hubert said that as far as he remembered about French provincial society, it was the done thing for the husband to drive his wife to church and wait for her outside, chatting amiably to the old men playing at bowls with a twinkling of ancient heads. Literary quotation, he added smugly. Wrong, Eileen snapped irritably, it's cards and hands, not bowls and heads, we did it at school. So Jean-Hubert went off in dudgeon to find a WC he could use whenever he got an attack of Frenchman's bladder while she was at Mass and Eileen, resigned to following local customs, went to have a look around the church where she'd be expected to save not only her own soul but apparently half the country's as well. Amsterdam suddenly seemed far away . . .

When she came out, it was obvious that Jean-Hubert hadn't found a gents', he was peeing quite openly up against the side wall of the mairie. (To awaken them to a sense of their civic responsibilities, he explained later.)

"The cock is their national emblem," said a voice from somewhere around Eileen's feet, "And how!"

Startled, she looked down on a head of short dark curls and the body it belonged to, plumply encased in a red terylene skirt, white nylon blouse and high-heeled sandals.

"Hello," she said doubtfully, not being in the habit of speaking to boringly-dressed tourists, "Are you English?"

"Used to be," said the girl, "I'm sort of a citizen of the world right now. Have a bun." She held out a paper bag with *Mangez des Croissants* printed on it, and went on: "I'm living at the bakery actually and I'm looking for work. Heard you in there just now, all that Master and Mistress bit – aren't frogs a hoot! – and I said to myself they're going to need help, in this château of theirs, your luck's turned, Roz, I said, and I followed you out. So, have you got a job for me?"

"What sort of work do you do?" Eileen asked, "Typing?" (She had by this time picked up Jean-Hubert's way of dismissing all working-class girls as *têtes de dactylo*, and Rosalind in her tights and white elastomere sandals seemed the very essence of a typist-head.)

"Actually I'm a nanny," the girl said, "Or rather I was a nanny for a while. I ran away from home last year and I've been working my way round France. You mark my words, luv, it's not all it's cracked up to be, la belle F! Actually I'd been intending to take the boat from St Malo and go home to mum for the summer only some creep stole my handbag before I got there. Charwoman at the bakery, that's what I am now, at least I won't starve, they give me all the stale buns to eat, must think I'm about ten! But frankly, minding kids was what I was best at, really."

"How old *are* you?" Eileen asked.

"Between you and me, luv, I'm sixteen and a half. But I've been letting on I was twenty, if you see what I mean. Sophisticated woman of the world, that's what I was seeing myself as. But all they saw, every sleazy old *père de famille* that I worked for, all they saw was some sort of old-fashioned domestic that was just there to be pounced on, honestly the French! So I had to keep on running away from work as well as from home, all go innit! Well at least I've seen a bit of life, you can say that. Makes a change from Nailsworth and my bleedin O-levels, Christ! That's the village I come from, Nailsworth, it's in Gloucestershire."

"So didn't you have time to take your clothes with you when you ran?" asked Jean-Hubert, who'd joined them and was listening, fascinated, "Did you arrive in Plouch'en quite naked, and did the baker's old wife have to lend you those funny things you're wearing?"

"You've got a bleeding nerve!" she snapped, "I can dress how I want, I don't have to wear a uniform. And I may not be the sexiest thing around but at least I have enough self-confidence not to have to pull out everything I've got and examine it every five minutes like you lot do!"

And then, unexpectedly, she blushed, a touching childish blush that spread from under her Marks and Sparks blouse right up to the unfashionable curls, making her look like a shy but cheeky twelve-year-old, and Jean-Hubert, more fascinated than ever, said: "Right. You're hired. You see that van over there, well, there's two babies asleep in it, I can't really see *us* having much time to play the doting parents what with one thing and another so they're all yours until school age. Only don't show up till tomorrow, will you? I've still got to face my old mum this afternoon."

Rosalind settled in, in the château and in France, though in a grudgingly defiant sort of way. "Of *course* I like France," she used to protest, half-jokingly, "I like Simenon and Tintin and Jacques Brel and the Mona Lisa and Jane Birkin and crème anglaise and Redouté roses. Everything that makes France France, quoi!" She was exasperated at being called Mademoiselle all the time, by the need to be always on her best behaviour, by the difficulty of making friends of her own age. (The boys made instant passes, the girls laughed themselves sick at her feminism and her clothes. "I refuse to wear a uniform," she kept asserting, "Jeans are the most conformist thing I know of." And they laughed even louder: conformism was far from being a dirty word to the jeunes filles de village.)

Yet when she returned to England after the twins started school, and tried to live for a time in the friendly village where her divorced mum ran a crafts shop, she was exasperated by that too. She spent most of her energy trying to convince the Cotswold lads that French kissing was quite an enjoyable alternative to an evening's lager drinking, and the trendy local housewives that avocado dips and Quiche Lorraine weren't exactly the highest point of French cuisine. When the latest dishy fella asked her back to his place, but only to watch snooker on the telly, and her mother started serving fromage frais with everything from hummus to poppadums, Rosalind decided it was time to take off again. Or so she recounted it to Hélène, and Hélène was once again fascinated by her friend's ability to skate along happily on the very surface of life. She spent several years wandering through Europe, from job to job and love affair to love affair, sending back dotty travel articles to *She* magazine, dropping in on Hélène for long visits from time to time to keep her *au courant* with her life story, still cheerfully and expertly dodging ritual passes from Jean-Hubert as she'd done every day of the three years she'd worked at the château.

("'Tis a consummation devoutly to be wished," he often sighed, cornering her half-seriously in the laundry room.

"Merde! And likewise mon cul!" Rosalind would retort, "Literary quote, mate. Your old Rabelais I shouldn't wonder.")

Hélène's own life over those years had become more and more settled into a contented status-conscious routine of wife, mother, landlady and lady of the manor. Her corners were all rubbed off, she was assimilated. Two seas separated her from the wrenching sadness of her childhood, from the insecurities of her teens. Her regrets for Christopher Milton, though chronic, had not yet become acute, and she counted herself a happy woman. She began to be horrified at what seemed the dead-end chaos of Rosalind's happy-go-lucky existence.

"You're twenty-five, Roz!" she would protest, "You're twenty-six! Twenty-seven!"

But when Rosalind was twenty-eight, Pierre Bouchon was already installed in the village, pale and suffering and depressed, having thrown up his very successful Paris practice when his marriage failed, and set up surgery in his parents' old home. Hélène found a vocation in bringing together what she saw as a pair of lonely souls, and wrote to Teresa that she felt like Emma Woodhouse when they finally decided to marry. (Teresa, who couldn't stand Jean-Hubert, thought: yeah, boring Emma boringly settled down with boring Mr Knightly, but in the interests of friendship decided not to comment.)

Now, having heard about the chats with Michel Le Borgne, it occurred to Hélène that Rosalind as a married woman was probably very bored and lonely. She had her house and garden of course, and wrote the occasional "I Married a Frenchman" article, but that wasn't much for someone who'd spent twelve years roaming Europe. Pierre was usually in his surgery or out making home visits, and from the beginning he had put his foot down about letting Rosalind work as his receptionist fearing, rightly, that her thick foreign accent would scare off the xenophobic villagers. No wonder she was reduced to chatting up everything in Plouch'en, from haggish housewives to jobbing gardeners. I really ought to be more company for her, Hélène thought, take her shopping in Rennes, get her together with the other doctors' wives round about. But then, presumably, Rosalind had already met the other doctors' wives by now and been kept at arm's length by them, in true Breton fashion. After all, I can't live her life for her, Hélène thought irritably, she's been settled here as Pierre's wife for three years, wouldn't you think she'd have come to terms with the way people behave here and made some sort of life for herself in spite of it? But her conscience bothered her. I could at least advise her about her clothes, how does she expect to be taken seriously, trudging around in track suits, grinning at everyone like an English tourist, she sticks out a mile in any French setting.

Like my old mother's going to stick out, she though in dismay, what am I going to do, how am I going to cope with her? From her Lourdes pilgrimage and the Louvre and Versailles, hotfoot to our sinful château, wearing her stiff tweed skirts like sackcloth, piously touching her Pioneer pin every time she's offered a drink, breathing disapproval and penance and novenas, articulating all over Tante Ruby in her schoolmarm French . . . Maybe I could palm her off on Rosalind some of the time, Rosalind would be only too glad to get a chance to speak English, give her ghastly accent a rest. That's it, I'll get the pair of them together, let them hold hands and tell their beads or whatever . . .

On impulse she turned in on Rosalind's gate. The front door was open and so was the small green door at the end of the corridor, leading to the garden. She went right through. Michel Le Borgne was hunkered down on the grass, apparently tracing out a flowerbed with a length of hose pipe. Rosalind stood by, watching him. So that explains the famous chats across the gate, Hélène thought, and was surprised at the relief she felt. It wasn't a budding love affair, silly cow of a hairdresser, old Rosalind just needed a bit of help in the garden. As Hélène walked down the path towards them, Le Borgne turned up his face towards Rosalind, said something, and laughed. He looked totally different when he laughed, alive and young and incredibly happy. What's he got to be happy about, she thought sourly, if his wife's just left him? Rosalind laughed too. All very democratic and cosy, and why isn't he up there anyway weeding my roses?

"Bonjour Rosalind!" she called.

Le Borgne stopped laughing, looked awkward, and bent his head to measuring again.

Rosalind turned slowly. "Oh hi," she said, "It's you."

"I thought I'd drop in and cadge a coffee," Hélène smiled, "And show off my new haircut."

"Oh sure. Sure. It's super. Really suits you. I was just going to make coffee actually. Euh . . . Michel?"

"Almost through now," he said in his usual blank drawl, "No coffee, thanks Roz. Another time. I've finished that weeding, madame," he told Hélène, "I'll drop in this evening and give them a good watering."

Hélène followed Rosalind into the kitchen. "I need a bit of light relief," she said, "Jean-Hubert's in a mood this morning, thanks to your sparkling dinner-table conversation. And the house is full of Tante Ruby. The reason she came hot-footing it back apparently is that Gustave's gone to earth with some glamorous foreigner and can't be found. The rumour is that she's Irish and that he's eloped to Dublin with her. The Tout-Paris is agog, Tante Ruby doesn't know whether to laugh or cry. And I'm going berserk over the nouveau Happy Pair. Though I must say the wronged husband doesn't look about to hang himself, not today anyway. Listen, did *you* know that Le Borgne's quite educated, been to university and all?"

"Well yes. Of course I knew. Everyone knows. Why?"

"I didn't. I sort of thought he'd been here, man and boy, for whole generations. Grown gnarled in our service, as it were."

"Stop being so dismissive, Hélène. And you could hardly call the fellow gnarled, he's younger than you are."

"I suppose it's because I found him here the day we came, toiling away as if . . ."

"Summer job. Then, for some mad reason, he decided he didn't really want to study law after all, and he just stayed on and made his life in the village."

"Not much of a life though, is it, for someone who's been educated? Born under the elm, married under the elm, buried under the elm."

"There are no elms nowadays. And it was a free choice. He likes living here. There's people who don't want to spend their whole lives climbing and grabbing, you know."

"Very Sixties though, isn't it, all this simple living when he doesn't have to. Anyway, who cares . . . Listen, Rosalind, my mother's coming. She'll be here for the party."

"Isn't that super! She'll be a bit of moral support for you among all those snooty nobles."

"It is not super. You've met my mother. It's a bloody disaster. I thought we were safe till at least August."

"She's a pious Catholic schoolteacher. So what? She'll hardly turn up brandishing a bamboo cane. And she doesn't own you, Hélène, she's just coming for a friendly visit like she does every year. Why's that a disaster for God's sake? She's quite presentable. She doesn't spit in the soup, does she? And she doesn't walk about topless either. Or try to rape servants. Or answer the door in the middle of coitus non-interruptus. Listen here matey, I'd say you've got disasters aplenty up at that château, but I don't reckon your mum's going to be one of then, so stop *whining* at me, would you!"

"What's wrong with *you* all of a sudden? Snapping my head off. Have you got PMT or something?"

293

"Christ you ought to be married to Pierre, you deserve each other. I simply meant, yes I have met your mother. She's not a monster. Right, you don't love her, so what's wrong with that? I don't love my mum, I mean not like I did when I was four. She gives me the screaming habdabs sometimes, if you want to know. But I don't make a Greek tragedy out of it whenever the old dear says she's coming over for a few days. Honestly you Irish! It's melodrama all the way, no wonder you can't stop killing one another!"

"*I* didn't *know* my mother when I was four. That's why it's a tragedy. She gave me away."

"Pardon me, luv, she did not give you away. She had you looked after by two lovely old people while she set about making a living for you both. You had a happy childhood, or so you told me, running wild among the haystacks, she went to see you quite often and then, as soon as she was able to, she made a home for you. What's so tragic about that?"

"You have absolutely no idea what my childhood was like!"

"Of course I haven't, how could I? I'm just saying it's over now, you're married with kids of your own. And talking of kids, has it ever occurred to you that Clem and Henri might have problems too, and that they might just possibly be glad of a bit of attention from you whenever you can drag your mind away from weeping over the distant past. I've been meaning to mention to you about Clem, do you know what she's . . . "

"Well if anyone deserves Pierre it's you, Rosalind! Homespun psychoanalysis at cut rates, with childcare advice from the expert. I suppose you're going to prescribe me some Valium and a good rest. OK, thanks for the coffee. I'll ring you when I need some more pious advice."

"Oh come off it, Hélène, I'm just being neighbourly aren't I, I've never been a great one for all this frog discretion. Right OK, so Clem's none of my business, Pierre's being telling me that and all . . . OK, let your daughter do what she likes, she's no skin off my nose and thank God for that! But I think I do have a right to be peeved over the way you're treating poor Michel Le Borgne. He is our friend after all, he often comes in for a drink and . . ."

"Has he been whining to you? Is that what he was doing here just now? Complaining about us? Complaining about the way he's treated? Well I must say, democracy in this village . . ."

"Oh hark at old Ruby! Look Hélène, poor Michel Le Borgne thinks the sun shines out of you. The reason he stayed on working for you is that you practically begged him to, apparently, that first day you arrived here. The poor sod actually thought you needed him, he thought you needed a friend, he thought poor fragile little you looked lost among all those tough old aristos. Lost! I keep trying to tell him you found yourself pretty bloody quick and he needn't have bothered. He doesn't believe me, naturally. Love being apparently deaf, blind and stupid, he thinks that underneath it all you're still the poor sensitive little Irish exile dragged weeping from your sweet innocent commune! So just imagine how he's feeling now that you've only installed his cow of a wife in the château, and that lover of hers!"

"I never asked them. It was Jean-Hubert, I had nothing whatever to do with it, Rosalind, I was as shocked as you are."

"Yeah, well it's the same thing innit. They're there. And so is he and he's in a damn awkward position because if he gives in his notice your charming husband is going to grab his house away from him and all, he'll be left with nothing. And the whole village has stopped speaking to him, he keeps getting all these obscene phone calls. Good old simplistic French folklore, laugh yourself sick at the cuckold, honestly these people, it's like another century! Why don't you just sack them? I mean you're not totally helpless. You're not putty in Jean-Hubert's hands. Explain it to them. Send them on their way – On your bike, Nathalie! Piss off, Gabriel! It's easy, you're supposed to be the boss."

"I can't. We have this party next week . . ."

"A party! *I'll* come and cook for the party. I'll rope in my sister-in-law, anything's better than."

"This isn't England, Rosalind, imagine a doctor's wife handing round the sandwiches like a skivvy. That would be the end of Pierre's practice, his patients would never take him seriously again. Honestly you'll never learn!"

"Well do something. At least say something to poor Michel, you can't just let him . . ."

Being told that someone fancies you. Being told that someone threw his whole future away for you, because that's what it amounted to, just because he thought you looked lost and lonely. Because you were lost and lonely . . . She did vividly remember that first day, when everything in the château was strange and forbidding and unwelcoming, and Michel Le Borgne seemed the only warm familiar person in it. She had intended then making a friend of him, she'd seen him as a sort of successor to Yann. She recalled the first months in Brittany – her strangeness, her timidity, the way Jean-Hubert had been immediately swallowed up by a new and important life that had little connection with anything they'd lived together in Amsterdam.

"He's very together, that Michel Le Borgne," she'd commented, "Definitely one of us! Doesn't he remind you a bit of Yann? Why don't we ask him in for a drink one evening?"

"Le Borgne?" Jean-Hubert had been genuinely puzzled, "What Le Borgne? Are you talking about that boy who works in the garden? But he is one of the tenants, Hélène, he is Hervé Le Moal's nephew!" As if there could not possibly be human contact between them. And of course there hadn't been. Hélène, terrified of her mother-in-law's disapproval, Tante Ruby's sarcasms, Jean-Hubert's cold astonishment, had taken care to walk only on accepted paths. Life in the château was full of nuances that she'd gone to a lot of trouble to pick up. Nuances of speech, of opinion, of dress, of attitude to the village.

"I *was* lost," she told Rosalind, "That first day when I met Michel Le Borgne. And you're wrong, I never did find myself again. Not my Amsterdam self. Not my Belfast self."

And not the self who'd cried her eyes out for Christopher. Or the self who stood terrified in the Falls Road sitting-room, dragged brutally out of paradise.

"Oh if it's *paradise* you're looking for!" Rosalind laughed, "Many a one would think you'd found that all right, many a one would give their two eyes to be where you are, mate!"

Jean-Hubert came into the drawing-room all excitement that evening when she was doing a bit of hoovering before dinner.

"Switch that thing off and listen!" he crowed, "The old schoolmaster's gone off his head at last! You know Jean-Paul Seguin, the little plasterer from down the village? You know how his wife's a Jehovah's Witness? Well, old Balavoine only went mad yesterday and banned the two kids from school for proselytising."

"What were they doing, flogging *The Watchtower* round

the playground? That's what Mitzi nearly got slung out of the convent for, she used to sell *The United Irishman* in the dorm after lights out."

"We are in France," Jean-Hubert said mechanically, "No, nothing as simple as that. But it seems the mother, silly old hen, started sending the boy to school in a grey flannel suit and waistcoat and a tie, poor little sod, his hair oiled down in a middle parting, with his young sister trotting along beside him in a navy-blue two-piece and white shirt. Of course all the other kids rolled them in the mud every time they saw them, well wouldn't anyone? So Balavoine claimed they were a threat to school discipline and chucked them out."

"The Ralph Lauren look," Hélène murmured, "Perrier and Roquefort in their lunch boxes, no doubt."

"This is serious, Hélène! Old Balavoine claims that clothes like that can only be emblems of a religious sect and that they are insulting the proud traditions of the Education Nationale, all the ideals that generations of anticlerical schoolmasters devoted their dusty little lives to, and he says he won't let them back after the holidays unless they start dressing like everyone else. Non-denominational jeans and Nike T-shirts, no doubt. *And* he's been heard saying the school will soon be awash in chadors and Stars of David and pygmy loincloths if he doesn't put his foot down now. He actually said that out loud at a council meeting, before witnesses. So!" Jean-Hubert rubbed his hands in high glee, "So now we'll be able to take him for all he's got, under the Racism and Anti-Semitism laws!"

"Why on earth do you want to make a big cause of it? They're not Salman Rushdie for heaven's sake, just a couple of boring kids in boring clothes. It's no concern of ours anyway, the twins have always gone to private schools."

"I don't care about the *cause*, I want to get *him*. The old fool in person," Jean-Hubert said viciously, "I've had it in for Balavoine for years and years. That man has done most bitter wrong to some who are near my heart!"

"Literary quotation," Hélène said, happy to catch on for once, "William But – "

"What on earth are you talking about?" Jean-Hubert quelled her with an amazed stare, "You are being unpleasantly flippant this evening. I am speaking of serious matters, Hélène. The little Magali Balavoine, closest and dearest friend of my childhood, happens to be the daughter of that grotesque old tyrant. He has been treating her abominably for years now. D'ailleurs, he always did treat her abominably, even when she was a mere infant. When I was nine years old and she six, the poor thing used to run to me for comfort every day of the summer holidays. We would hide in Uncle Vladimir's garden, our little bodies pressed warmly together, our little souls drunk on the scent of his roses – those magnificent old roses that you have abolished – and I would console her as well as I was able. We swore then that we would love each other for ever, and that one day we would revenge ourselves together on that old dictator. Of course we never did, life turned out so differently for both of us. And so the old madman continues to tyrannise. When Magali was eighteen years old he forbade her ever to set foot in her home again and he will not, even now, allow her poor mother to visit her in Rennes where she is living with – "

"So that's the reason," Hélène said coldly, "That is the reason for your little weekly business trips to Rennes! Now that you are forty and she thirty-seven, you still feel the need to comfort the poor little thing?"

"Magali is living in Rennes with another woman," Jean-

299

Hubert said with dignity, "She is living with Claude, the little friend who replaced me in her affections as you, my dear, replaced her in mine. With a father like Balavoine, how could one expect the little Magali to grow up and form a loving relationship with a man? I did what I could but," he shrugged, "I saw her for only six weeks every summer. It was not long enough to undo her mistrust of men. So Magali has found another woman to love. And for that reason alone her father has disowned her, vieux salaud! She and her beautiful companion, Claude, live very happily indeed, in a most pretty apartment, with their little boy . . ."

"Their little boy? They have a child?"

"We are in France, ma chère Hélène. Such things are possible . . ."

"So talented, these Frenchwomen," Hélène murmured absently, then leaped to her feet in horror: "You bastard, Jean-Hubert! You've been comforting her all right, you've been sleeping with her, haven't you? It's your child, I've seen him! I've *seen* him here in the village with his grandmother."

"I needed to sleep with her only once," he said with some pride, "And that was almost ten years ago. Magali and Claude, seeing their thirties approach, realised that they desperately wanted a child of their own, to make their couple complete. For the purpose, naturally, they needed to choose a man who was handsome and intelligent, with a perfectly formed body, a mind plutôt civilisé, and who could be trusted not to make a nuisance of himself afterwards. Who better than the dear friend of Magali's childhood, himself happily married and with children of his own?"

"You could have told me! Surely this was something we could at least have discussed together? Wouldn't it have been more considerate to ask my approval?"

"But there was nothing to discuss, voyons! My body is my own property, to use as I wish, as your feminist friend Rosalind would put it. Magali took from me nothing that was of value to you. You do not want another child, Hélène. We have both agreed that the dear twins are sufficient joy to grace any hearth, however much the government tries to bribe us to have several more. So in fact, by bestowing a third child of mine in a good French Catholic home, one could say I was merely performing my patriotic duty. Doing my own small bit to keep France white and save our native population from being completely outnumbered by the immigrants."

"It's not a joke, Jean-Hubert. Surely it's a serious matter, in a marriage, to behave like that behind my back?"

"Nonsense, ma chère! I was not being unfaithful to you. Had my friend needed money I would naturally have lent it to her, had she been homeless I would have let her live in one of the cottages. In fact, all she needed to borrow was my body and that, I assure you, for only about ten seconds. She didn't exactly encourage me to linger voluptuously, you know. Especially as the beautiful Claude was hovering in the next room like a hawk, with the door ajar. And no doubt with a stopwatch clutched in her beak."

"You'd have discussed with me first about the money and the cottage."

"Only because I'd have known you'd agree. And I knew you would not agree if I told you I wanted to give a baby to the little friend of my childhood, what wife would? Let us be logical, my dear, it would not have been intelligent of me to ask your permission knowing in advance that you would not give it. And that, en plus, you would be terribly wounded and feel obliged to make me a boring scene."

"I'm terribly wounded anyway, I've been suffering for

301

months over this, that kid's flaunting himself all around the village. I tell you I've seen him, he's the image of you, the whole country must know you've been unfaithful to me."

"Not unfaithful," he repeated patiently, "And he comes to the village only one or two weekends a year, you would not surely deny his poor grandmother the right to see him? En Frrawnce we have a very developed sense of family."

"People must be gossiping."

"Rubbish. Half of Plouch'en looks like me, thanks to Uncle Vladimir."

"Dead right. They were going on about him at the hairdresser's this morning, the dirty old pig."

"Et alors? Surely that is what châtelains exist for, to make the lower orders gasp and stretch their eyes? And though my late uncle might have been a pig by fanatical Falls Road standards (and the whole world can see where *they* lead!), I would have you know that most civilised people regarded the old gentleman as the last of the great Latin lovers, a magnificent sensualist of gargantuan appetites. More dignified n'est ce pas? Not that any Frenchman objects to being called a cochon. We do tend to see it as a tribute to our insatiable virility: in every Frenchman worth his salt there is a sleeping pig waiting to be awakened. Don't shout, darling, you know I was only joking!"

He pulled her close to him, rubbing his cheek against her clean hair. She was glad she'd managed to grab Marie-Annick's arm as she reached for the lacquer spray. "Lovely new hairstyle! You didn't really suffer did you, Hélène, believing I'd been unfaithful to you? Have you been brooding away in some doomed Celtic twilight ever since you recognised the little Sebastian? They would insist on calling him Sebastian, I'm afraid. So petit-bourgeois."

"I'd honestly rather you'd been unfaithful," Hélène said

sullenly, "It would have seemed more natural. The sort of irresistible physical impulse that all these cochons of Frenchmen have. I'd have been able to forgive you quite easily for that. It's what they say about you lot, isn't it? Your vices are OK, one can live with your vices, it's your virtues that are so bloody off-putting. This thing sort of shuts me out, doesn't it? All this mystique of your long-lost château summers and the dear little friend of your childhood and all."

"And I?" he asked coldly, moving away from her, "Am I not being continually shut out of your mysterious Irish childhood? Your dead father, dead as only an Irishman can die! And your old nurse with her grotesque cliché of a whitewashed cottage and your murdering friend Mitzi and your famous lost loves. How can a mere pig of a Frenchman compete with all that melodrama? Even my poor uncle's roses, with all their precious memories of my boyhood, had to be torn out and sacrificed to make way for that chaste convent garden you've created out there from bits of your hang-ups. You are so complicated, ma pauvre Hélène. The little Magali at least is a simple healthy French girl, completely physical, one knows where one is . . ."

He left the room and, minutes later, Hélène heard him yelling with dramatic rage down the phone at some unfortunate secretary at the League against Racism. She felt far more unhappy than she'd done when she first saw the little boy in the village, but perhaps not quite, she realised, for the reasons she'd given Jean-Hubert. Because, she had to admit, it was admirable, it was in line with all her principles, to give a child to a couple of women who needed one. Though there again, couldn't they have managed to dig up someone single? Surely they knew some men, surely in this day and age they weren't condemned to live in some sad female ghetto? But no, it must have seemed natural to Magali to turn to Jean-Hubert, her little childhood protector. And safer too, *given* the day and age . . . It was all logical, well it would be wouldn't it, everything Jean-Hubert did would have to have a logical explanation, that's what he was like. That's what they were all like, from Descartes on down. And then, ten years ago when it happened, he too in spite of everything would still have had shreds of Amsterdam clinging to him . . . A good trip, he would have been thinking, cool, far-out, to give a baby to a lesbian couple. Though again, surely the Amsterdam Jean-Hubert would have discussed it with her first, would have at least told her about it afterwards? No, it was the French Jean-Hubert, the caricaturally-Latin Jean-Hubert, who felt that deceiving one's wife was a perfectly logical way of living. It was this logic of his that she disliked, and his talent for being always above reproach. Trust a Frenchman, she thought, to be able to actually transform adultery into a high moral duty. I don't much like the French, she thought, I don't much like Jean-Hubert if it comes to that . . . So what am I doing here anyway? What have I been doing for sixteen years? September, she thought, September will make it all well again. After September I'll be able to plan myself a future . . . She switched on the vacuum cleaner again and pushed it idly around the high gloomy drawing-room, dreaming about Belfast.

"But my dear child!" Tante Ruby's trumpeting tones rose above the purr of the Hoover, "Why are you inside cleaning the floors on a beautiful summer evening? We have servants now, had you forgotten?"

"They can't do everything. It's a huge house." It's all very well for Rosalind, she thought, but imagine having to tell Tante Ruby I want to sack the help just to spare the gardener's feelings . . .

"*I* have a huge house in Paris, not to mention Gustave's hunting lodge in Sologne, and I am happy to say that I do not even know how these cleaning machines work. The couple I have now know they'd better do everything and do it perfectly, or back they go on the first plane to be eaten by their cannibal king."

"I've heard," Hélène said, "I've heard that the old king is losing his grip over there. Better watch out, Tante Ruby, or your two will be defecting off home to enjoy the fruits of democracy!"

"Juste ciel, mon enfant! What is the world coming to? Is it not enough that le bon dieu should amuse himself answering our prayers for the destruction of the Berlin wall? Do not laugh, my child, it is evident that you have not lived through a world war and a German occupation! Is it not enough that those poor Generals, Pinochet and Stroessner, have fallen? But that a backward little kingdom that nobody's ever heard of should have the impertinence to look for democracy and leave us to fend for ourselves . . . No, I shall dismiss that pair instantly before they have a chance to hand in their notice, and I shall replace them with two strong young people from one of the depressed mining towns in Alsace. After all, why go to the trouble of aiding the Third World when so many of our own lower classes are without employment? Jean-Hubert did very well to engage villagers. Only I beg of you, my child, do not let them fall into idle ways so soon. A tight rein to start with, my dear, then later on they will be glad of any little mercies you may choose to grant them."

The continuing saga of Tante Ruby's domestics was like reading *Newsweek* from cover to cover across the decades. When Hélène first met her she was still being nostalgic about the efficient Chilean couple who, on the fall of

Allende, had defected to a left-wing family who made them throw away their aprons, dressed them up in ponchos and took them to parties to be introduced to Sartre and Yves Montand. The Greeks who replaced them suddenly heard of the fall of the Colonels in the middle of washing-up and rushed off to Roissy with sudsy hands to joyously repatriate themselves. After that had come Portuguese, Spanish, Argentines, Irish, Iranians, Poles, Filipinos, who'd one after another been snatched out of Tante Ruby's hands to be used as status symbols by fashionable intellectuals as dictators fell, caudillos died a lingering death, dissidents disappeared, Ayatollahs emerged from hiding, prisoners hunger-struck, widows replaced beauty queens, stout union leaders developed chic and breakfasted at Maxim's . . . She couldn't, all the same, let Tante Ruby dismiss the present couple. Without work permits, identity papers or national insurance they would be helpless at large in an unfriendly France, with nothing to hope for but deportation and the king's wrath. "I was only joking, the monarchy's as stable as ever it was. Good for another century at least."

"The wit of the Irish," Tante Ruby said icily, "Of course in the British Isles they do not have a servant problem, do they? The immigrants are so pampered over there that no one can afford to engage domestics nowadays. Poor Gustave was at a directors' lunch in London and the girl who cooked and served the food was only the daughter of a man who plays polo with Prince Charles. She slapped his face when he made a harmless little joking advance! Seigneur! Seigneur! Is it any wonder one distrusts the English? A country where people refuse to remain in the place where le bon dieu in His wisdom deigned to put them! You were lucky, my dear, to find a French husband . . ."

"I'm not English, Tante Ruby. One would expect, after

sixteen years, that you would have picked up some of the nuances! And you're right, it's much too nice an evening to waste cleaning Jean-Hubert's château. I'm off out to the garden."

I'm going to have a nice little chat with Michel Le Borgne, she thought, I'll just pick up the conversation where I dropped it sixteen years ago, he can only look at me with that blank politeness of his, he can't beat me to death . . . If what Rosalind says is true he'll be only too glad of a nice friendly chat. And after all, if Jean-Hubert can offer himself the luxury of a little village friend . . . The bastard. The cynical bastard. Though imagine, that's the first time in my life I've dared to be cheeky to old Ruby, thank *you*, little Sebastian! The first time I've been able to talk to a Ploudel de Medeu without feeling it owned me body and soul.

Her garden stretched around her, cool and pale and straight-faced, symbol of the order she'd tried to impose on this big alien place that had taken her over and colonised her from the beginning. It wasn't much, a garden of white roses . . . It was nothing at all really, because the château itself loomed above it, overshadowing it, an arrogant and now decrepit place of disorder and of values that had always been foreign to her. There had once in her life been a garden of white roses, with a clothes-line cutting it in two, and chestnut trees and butterflies: look at all the candles, Eileen, smell the lovely white roses darlin'. A garden she'd been homesick for her whole life long. And then she thought, am I seeing things, am I going mad or what?

Because there *was* Anny, there in her garden. Impossible. Anny striding tall and straight and uncompromising along the geometrical paths between the rose beds. An impossible vision of Anny, and Anny's virtues and Anny's values, approaching swiftly among the roses. But when she looked closer it was only Madame la Comtesse du Bois Fleuri, and that was exceptional enough, the countess dropping in on her. If you could put it like that. In actual fact the countess was striding furiously up some invisible warpath, marching towards her wearing a face of determined outrage.

"This is intolerable, Hélène! This is really the last straw! My conscience will no longer allow me to be silent. Already Father Plouer has spoken to me about this young woman, this hussy that you are sheltering in her sin! I held my tongue about the homosexual couple because they, at least, had the discretion to be foreigners, but this . . . this . . . You and your husband are blatantly encouraging the ignorant villagers in their slide towards perdition. Think of the scandal!"

"But, madame . . ."

"It is unpardonable of you, a woman in your position who has the duty to set an example. I know of course that you and Jean-Hubert have always seen yourselves as young and modern, I know that you belong to the generation of '68, I know that century after century the Ploudels have set themselves up as revolutionaries, I prefer to say nothing at all about your disgraceful uncle Vladimir! But frankly, Hélène, I expected far better things of you, an Irish Catholic!"

"Madame, it is not at all my . . . I was just intending to . . ."

"So I have taken matters into my own hands. For a start I have advised the unfortunate husband to give up his employment here and to leave the village. He has agreed to do so. You will not see him here again, I have lodged him in one of my own cottages in the meantime. And, naturally, neither my husband nor myself intend to be present at your reception next week. Our friends of course may decide for themselves whether they wish to come, but I have felt it my duty to inform them all of your . . ."

She hopped smartly to one side as Uncle Gustave's red Jaguar slid in silently off the avenue and stopped between the flower-beds. The tall bright hard-edged young woman who slipped gracefully out of the passenger seat and stood close beside Gustave, smiling expectantly at Hélène, was almost a stranger. Almost. Hélène took a step backwards but the woman was holding out her arms to be embraced: "Isn't your garden a picture, Eileen! All those lovely white roses! I was right to come over a bit early this year."

Hélène recovered her wits: "Madame," she turned to the countess, "Madame, may I present my mother?"

Then Tante Ruby came striding out of the French windows. "Gustave!" she commanded, with an outraged quiver in her voice, "Gustave, you poor fish! Come here to me at once and tell me what nonsense you've been getting up to this time!"

Uncle Gustave looked helplessly at Hélène's mother and at the Countess, started to say something, and then meekly walked over to join his wife on the terrace.

"I see." Madame Augusta du Bois Fleuri drew herself up and turned to go. "It would appear that I made a great mistake about Irish Catholicism, as well as about everything else. It is always best, after all, to stay among one's own kind. That way there are no problems and no disappointments. Keep it in mind, my dear!"

"Well to be sure he'll come back to me, Eileen, what nonsense are you talking? I keep telling you he came down here with me deliberately to ask that woman for a divorce, so he did."

"He came down here to be at her side at this party. She's the hostess of honour and she needs a host. It's the done thing, it's called savoir-vivre. Very very important to these people is savoir-vivre, let me tell you, Mum! There's no way he'd have let her down, not in front of the assembled nobility. If any of them turn up that is, Jesus that bigoted old du Bois Fleuri bitch! Mind you I suppose she was right, Jean-Hubert did go a bit far this time but . . ."

"Savoir-vivre's all very fine but he does want to marry me. He spent a wee fortune on me in Paris. Look at me, Eileen, do you not think it's an improvement? This here is not exactly a face-lift you know, they do it with lasers in about five minutes, like it's no big Nancy Reagan thing but it's taken years off me. What are you laughing at, Eileen, there's nothing to laugh at that I can see!"

"Of course there's not. You look great, you look like my young sister. But if you knew it all, Mother! If you only knew the things I've being living through, since this morning. The things I've being finding out, it's like Act Five in some big drama. Or in some wee farce is more like it. And now this! I think I'm going to proclaim today as Eileen Independence Day. Do you know, I used to be scared witless of you? In awe of you, like? You used to be like some big inaccessible monument to middle-class Irish Catholicism."

"Aye well you can go on being in awe of me so you can, I'm not exactly transformed into some wee bimbo, you know, it's not because I got my face lifted and had a few clothes bought for me that . . ."

"No, but it's because you want to marry old Uncle Gustave. I mean honestly mother, I've just realised . . . My father, Gerald, and now l'oncle Gus, it's one big cliché after another with you, isn't it. The dashing young drunk, the kind gentle family man, and now the original French seducer. I mean that man's been at it all his life, he and Tante Ruby were made for each other. And you fell for it. You!"

"You were waiting for years for this, weren't you, Eileen, it's a gift to you what happened, isn't it? You always were a hard-natured wee bitch. No matter how much was done for you . . ."

"No, I'm not being spiteful, Mother, I'm just talking to you as an equal for once in my life. As if you were just Rosalind or someone. Look, you had a nice time in Paris, well good luck to you, it's worked more miracles than Lourdes ever did. You were wined and dined and all the big production. Great! It's more than I ever was, I can tell you! But I wouldn't expect any more than that if I was you. You saw what happened just now with old Ruby, she only had to snap her fingers. She's got the old fellow on a leash, always had, he's always gone running back to her. And you're well out of it, Mother, I can tell you. Frenchmen of that generation . . . Of *any* generation! If you had any sense you'd run a mile. If you knew what Jean-Hubert's been confessing to . . . Did I say confessing? Boasting, more like it, the bastard's dead proud of himself. Look Mother, why don't we just go back to Belfast, the pair of us, after the party? *Before* the party if you like. Let's just drop the whole lot of them and run! And you can go back to that school of yours in September with your nice new face and all these lovely memories to look back on? You know, see it as one great big holiday romance?"

"Belfast? You're joking, I hope. And anyway I've given in my notice, Eileen, I've got no job to go back to."

"So what do you intend to do, for God's sake? Have you any money saved? Are you entitled to a pension or anything? Because you can't come and live here, I won't even *be* here after . . ."

"Quit blathering would you, Eileen. What do you *think* I intend to do? Sure isn't Gustave going to look after me?

We went into all this in detail before we left Paris. We knew it wouldn't be a piece of cake, getting a divorce, we realised that, I was sort of expecting what happened . . . So quit going on about Belfast. Anyone's better out of that place if they get half a chance."

"Well *I'm* going back there anyway, I've been deciding it for ages, I think I was always longing to go back, right from the time I left, only I was too proud to admit it. I'm leaving Jean-Hubert, Mother, I've had enough. Now that the twins are . . ."

"Are you mad? There's nothing for you to go back to in Belfast. You wouldn't even recognise the place after all this time. And *I* won't be there and there's nobody you know. Catch yourself on, Eileen, what . . . "

"I know Christopher Milton. *He'll* be there, won't he. I saw him only about ten days ago, mother. He was in Arles when we were down there for the weekend, I only just missed getting talking to him, I was that shy and that flabbergasted that I just turned tail and he didn't even see me, talk about daft! But anyhow I realized then that I have to face facts. Christopher is the only genuine thing that ever happened to me, he's the only real experience I've had in my life. You know? Everything else has been just synthetic . . . So I'm going over there to look him up. Oh I don't mean any big romantic thing, I mean I'm not going to throw myself in his arms, actually it's probably just to look *Belfast* up if you see what I mean. Work out where I went wrong with Christopher. And anyway, Ireland's the only place I've ever really been comfortable in, I intend going down to Cross too, to Anny's old place. And to the Campbells in Claghan, I mean they're my roots as well, whether they like it or not, and I mean it's time I faced up to my roots do you not think, at my age?"

"Were you drinking, Eileen, or what? What's wrong with you? Christopher Milton? Sure that man's gone from Belfast this years and years, he *had* to go, the boys were on to him, he'd have been got, he'd have been killed like Captain Nairac and all the rest. They just narrowly missed him, I heard, I mean there were even people said he was dead already, the way he disappeared from Queen's just from one day to the next. Are you *sure* it was him you saw?"

"What are you on about, mother? What boys? What do you mean? Do you mean the IRA? Whatever for? What would Christopher have to do with the IRA? And why did you not say, why did you not tell me at the time?"

"Well, I suppose I didn't see what interest you'd have. You were eejit enough to go out with him a few times but I thought that was long forgotten. You were a married woman with children, I thought that nonsense was all behind you. And I didn't see any point in letting you know that he was just using you to get information out of you, the way he used all the rest."

"Using me? What information are you talking about?"

"Why do you think your friend Mitzi and the others were lifted that first time? They weren't doing anything, were they? Except talking. And poor Mitzi had wit enough in the finish up to work out who it was they did all the talking to. And what about. I expect he latched on to *you* when he heard how your poor father died, you were never done blathering about it, making him out to be something he wasn't, I suppose Mister Milton thought he'd tumbled into a lovely wee nest of republicans! I mean the blackguard even spent a couple of evenings licking up to poor Gerald and myself. Before he caught on that you were no use to him, you were so wrapped up in yourself and your wee daydreams that you didn't even realise there was anything going on in Northern Ireland! And you're still wrapped up in them by the sound of it."

"He was a *spy*? MI5 and all that? Christopher? Give over, Mother, things like that just don't happen. I don't believe you, you're just making it all up to get at me."

"Oh you may believe me. As I say, he got out just in time, it was an open secret, there was no big mystery. I mean they were all over the place, fellows like him, in the Seventies, and the most of them stuck out a mile, the English never were exactly noted for being subtle. Captain Nairac speaking Irish in the pubs round South Armagh, he might as well have gone round with a label on him! They're a lot cleverer now . . . Anyway, your Christopher man concentrated mainly on students. Women students, that's why he lasted so long. Everyone wants to believe in love, don't they, Eileen. I might even have fancied him myself if he'd bothered to turn the old charm on me! Lucky for me all he saw that Sunday he came to the house was a Legion of Mary woman well over thirty, busy Doing Good among the Poor. And Gerald wasn't much of a talker, outside of Tennyson and Latin odes. So why don't you forget about Belfast and why don't the two of us just stick to our French aristos when we have the chance? Be a wee Flight of the Wild Geese all on our own, like. Och, come on Eileen, catch yourself on, would you! Quit taking things so tragically!"

"You're like a child, mother. And I don't believe anything like that went on in Belfast, not round Queen's, it's like some spy film, it was just some rumour you heard. God there was nothing more solid and genuine than Christopher Milton, things like that just don't *happen*."

But there had been the Turfstack and the hardfaced men in donkey jackets drinking so incongruously with Christopher. And there had been the time she spotted him dancing in the wee Shamrock Ballroom up the Falls and he'd not let on to see her and disappeared pretty sharp out the door while she was working her way round to him in the crowd. Mitzi hadn't believed it was him. "Christopher in a place like this! You're imagining things. You're obsessed, Eileen, you're seeing him everywhere."

And there had been, above all, the Saturday she went with Teresa to seek him out in his flat, her mouth dry, her heart thumping away like a mad thing. "Jesus, Eileen, he's only a fella, he won't take a bite out of us. Either he'll be glad to see you or he won't. Either way you'll know, won't you, I mean you could go on till you're sixty just hoping to bump into him somewhere."

The landlord let them in on the front door and they went along the corridor to his flat, and knocked. Voices stopped talking behind the door, and Christopher was there, standing in front of her, with a face like a marble statue. Behind him, Mitzi and Sheila and a few other students she knew, sitting around on the floor and the divan with glasses in their hands. Students who'd all ended up in Armagh jail within a few months. Coincidence?

"Yes?" Christopher asked, in a voice as flat and full of rejection as a closing door, and she knew he hadn't forgiven her turning up with Chaz at the Turfstack. Why else would he have shut her out like that?

"Colonel Blimp!" Teresa joked feebly as they walked out of the Crescent, "Well, that's that, Eileen. At least you know for sure now. You'll get over him, he's not all that fantastic anyway, an old man with eyes like a fish! Jesus, he'd freeze you with a look, that fella! You'd think he had something to hide, were they in the middle of an orgy or what?"

"Christopher thinks you're the dregs, Eileen," Mitzi said next evening in the flat, "You haven't a hope, Eileen, he thinks you're the dregs. It's me he likes, he says it was always me."

And Eileen moved away, out of her little room, out of Belfast. Mitzi and Sheila and a few others moved shortly afterwards too. To internment . . .

"The whole thing's grotesque," she said, "I don't believe it. I mean there he was in Arles last week with his mates on holiday, all so normal, just like any educated tourist looking at statues."

"There was an IRA couple murdered last week in Arles," her mother said, "Gibraltar the Second the papers called it. Someone must have followed them, someone must have known them. Pointed them out like. Eileen love, maybe it's just as lucky for you he *didn't* recognise you! Are you *sure* now he didn't?"

"I'm not going to swallow *that*!" Eileen snapped, "It's grotesque even to think of it! You're getting carried away, Mother, you're taking yourself for John Le Carré!"

Disneyland, she thought, clowns and monsters and cardboard castles and caricatures of evil, Sylvester the Cat creeping up to pounce, and plastic knights making plastic wars over plastic causes . . . But it was supposed to be *here*, Disneyland, she thought, it was supposed to be Tante Ruby and Uncle Gus the Disneyland characters, and Jean-Hubert and his château and his little snobberies and his little lecheries and his ghastly son called Sebastian . . . Belfast was supposed to be reality, wasn't it? Northern Ireland was supposed to be reality, it was supposed to be standing there, solid and real and truthful in the background of my life, with everything being exactly what it claimed to be. I never really saw it as the past, I always saw myself as just lent out on a long visit that I'd return from, I always secretly saw myself returning, after the good trips and the bad trips and the cardboard castles, and the foreign lifestyles and the foreign values. I saw myself going back to the meadow and the hagard and the lilac branches tapping on the window and the velvet curtains and the white roses and my room and Christopher Milton, I always . . .

"Oh, here's Gustave coming to look for me," her mother said happily. "Maybe you should stop crying, Eileen, and go and wash your face before someone sees you."

Part Nine

❧

So Hélène's imagined conversation with Christopher Milton in Arles had to be rethought, re-looked at. It was now unthinkable that they would have made their way self-consciously to a café table, awkward in their pleasure at finding each other again. Unthinkable that he would have brought up Chaz, and the evening in the Turfstack, unthinkable that she would have been allowed to explain herself. Unthinkable everything. Unthinkable especially that it had really been Chris, and that he had most probably been there, in Arles, on some hideous media-land mission. Unthinkable above all that to her mother there was nothing macabre or media-land at all about a mission like that: it was normal, it was everyday, it was the function in life of people like Christopher.

And if she had not panicked, if she had surged up in front of him recognising him: "Why hello, Christopher, we've met. In Belfast . . ." How would he have responded? How would he have coped with that one? Indeed, what incredible things might have happened if she had not had that instant of panic, if she had not reverted momentarily to the wee lost Eileen image of herself that she'd quite rightly laughed about later in Pierre's surgery? What if she'd

318

behaved like the cool self-possessed woman she'd been allowed to be for so many years now, well-dressed, well-spoken wife of Jean-Hubert Bourjois, blundering with exquisite drawing-room poise into the mad Disney world, the dungeon-and-oubliette world Christopher must surely now inhabit? "In Belfast, Chris . . . oh, years ago!" She had a vision of being lured, unbelievably, into the black BMW with the three unseen friends who were surely, unbelievably, what might be known as tough guys. Surely, (unbelievably to Hélène walking among her rose beds, smiling a greeting, shaking hands with her guests), surely what she sometimes came across in news magazines, surely SAS officers? Trained killers? Lured into the car and then dumped somewhere, dead? As an undesirable witness? She? Hélène? Because what would her small insignificant life have mattered to them, shadowy purveyors of British justice? Purveyors, where did I get that from, she wondered? A word from out of the past, painted above an old-fashioned shop doorway: *Campbell and Son, Select Grocer, Hardware and Furniture Merchant. Purveyors of Fine Teas, Wines, & Spirits.* Christopher Milton, Purveyor of British justice. The justice of Arles, the justice of Gibraltar. A useful product, Christopher in his commonsensical way would see it, securely packaged, proof against deterioration at the hands of incompetent policemen, appeal court decisions and the overturning of sentences . . . What had Mitzi meant to him, and all those parties she used to throw with the sole object of enticing him, and her very, very obvious adoration? What had Eileen meant? Nothing at all, if her mother was to be believed. *Was* she to be believed? Old people often go paranoid . . . No, her mother certainly wasn't that, you couldn't say she was paranoid, or half-cracked or any other comforting cliché of dismissal. Not watching her there, elegant and young and happy, standing on the lawn with Gustave and his friends. Being witty and successful and accepted, judging by their laughs. A happy woman, while Tante Ruby sulked, while Hélène walked about on the edge of emptiness. Because where can I go to now, she thought, I was counting on Belfast. Deep down for ages now I've been thinking the rest of my life was going to be there. And really of course I never knew a thing about the place, she thought, it always stayed as strange to me as it was that first evening they forced me to go and live with them. All these strange and violent patterns must have been weaving themselves into the fabric of the city the whole time I lived there and I noticed nothing, stumbling about behind my cool straight face longing for what I thought was home, always imagining home to be some place else, totally unable to guess the answers to any of the riddles that life amused itself asking me.

No one else seemed to be coming to the party, it was going to be a complete failure, thanks to Madame la Comtesse, thanks to Jean-Hubert, thanks to that wimp Michel . . . And that's what I ought to be worrying about, she thought, these are the things of my life that I ought to be worrying about at this minute, not wandering about lost in some make-believe past. I should be worrying that my husband and his aunt and the children and I myself are being disgraced, that we are being snubbed by everyone worth knowing, that our house is not a place that people want to come to. I should be worrying but it doesn't seem very important. I should be worrying about what we'll do with all that expensive food, I should be booting Nathalie and Gabriel out of the place, I should be wondering why my own children haven't seen fit to show their faces yet, they were supposed to be here helping, being charming, being Children of the Château, quoi! These things are the realities. Christopher, and even little Sebastian, and my mother are not part of my life now, they never were part of my life, they don't exist. Tell yourself that, she thought fiercely, just keep telling yourself they don't exist, that reality is something else. Only *what* is it? And where?

"Hélène! Crikey, *you're* looking gloomy, for a party!"

At least here's Rosalind and Pierre arrived at last, she thought, and a couple more of Tante Ruby's Parisians, well that'll keep me occupied for a while, shepherding them into the drawing-room, feeding them drinks . . .

"I expect you'll want to go with your own friends to watch the fireworks this year," his father said, and his voice conferred on Miloud for the first time the status of Man.

Can't I go with *you*, he wanted to ask, a small frightened child begging inside his head, begging for a protecting hand to cling to, can't we all go as a family like before?

But the tone of his father's voice made that impossible. "Don't tell me my son is a wet hen!" his father would have said, and Layla would have jeered and said, "It's because Miloud has no friends to go with!" And that would have been impossible to bear.

Layla would go with the parents, naturally. A young Muslim girl could not go out after dark, even through a lighted town to an official celebration at the mairie, with only friends of her own age to chaperon her. The lives of girls were simpler, Miloud thought, if less glorious. Layla has only her body, he was in the habit of taunting her, she hasn't got a soul! And Layla always retorted that she had a brain and a character and a personality and if that wasn't as good as a soul, what was? He didn't ever report her words to the parents, though he could have done, because au fond he didn't really want her to be beaten for blasphemy. Not that the parents ever beat her hard but they felt obliged to be strict with her, out of respect for the grandparents' advice, and out of genuine anxiety for her safety. He wished they had an equal anxiety about him and an equal desire to protect him from the dangers of an infidel country. But then, would being beaten to a pulp by the racist school bully and his mates rate in their eyes as a danger equal to loss of virginity or loss of faith?

It was only because his wits were quicker than Delamotte's that he'd managed to get away in time that Saturday, but he knew that it would be foolish to expect so easy an escape next time. A gang of toughs on motor-bikes were not going to be fooled twice by any quick wits, especially now that they knew he'd caught on to them. How had he ever allowed himself to be fooled, how had he been daft enough to mistake his desires for reality? Knowing Delamotte as he knew him. Knowing his own place as an Arab, son of immigrants. Knowing France . . .

He thought of inventing a sudden illness but could think of nothing convincing. And did he really *want* to spend the rest of his life, for that is what it amounted to, lurking at home playing his guitar and listening to his Walkman, scared to go out? He would have to go out sometime. To start with, he would have to go out tonight. There was no excuse at all that would convince his parents he'd better stay away from the Bastille Day celebrations. It was very important to them to join in all the rituals of French life, they were scared to do anything different in case the neighbours whispered behind their backs, or to their faces even, and condemned them as aliens. No, if he made any move to stay behind tonight they would simply shoo him out of the house in front of them and lock the door.

And, anyway, how would he feel himself, cowering in the house while the rest of the school and the family were enjoying themselves at the fireworks? I'd feel an awful lot better, he admitted, than I'm going to feel trudging right across town at night to the mairie, supposedly meeting imaginary friends so as not to disgrace myself in front of the parents and Layla. Not knowing who's tracking me, jumping with fright every time I hear a motor-bike. Wondering who, standing there in the shadows, is getting ready to pounce. Yes, I'd feel a whole lot better curled up on my bed with the Guns. But he knew he'd have to go out. His father had as good as proclaimed him a Man, an adult male responsible enough to be let out for an evening's amusement without his parents. And, when he thought closer about it, it mightn't be so bad, well it might be OK really, there'd be crowds, wouldn't there? There would be other kids from school who didn't belong to Delamotte's gang. He could latch on to someone, to some group. He wouldn't necessarily be on his own at the mercy of some . . . Yeah sure, there'd be crowds, the whole town would be crowded, why was he picturing empty dark streets with Them lurking round every corner? There wasn't only Them, the town didn't belong to them, did it, no point in turning into an old woman scared stiff to go out at night. But still . . . still . . . Anxiety nibbled shamefully away at him. "I'm the son of a gun," he sang softly to give himself courage, "I'm a gun of the sun . . . "

"Oh mon dieu, mon dieu!" Layla jeered, "C'est le fils d'un revolver, ce petit con! Pauvre petit macho, off out for a big night with the boys. Mind now that they don't take away your virginity, petit frère!"

Anguish. The letter A. Aggressions. Alzheimer's. Arabs. Acid rain. Africans. Aggressions. America. Arabs. Age. Age. Oh God, age. Anguish. In twelve months I shall have become archaic. An aged man. Living in this house. These three small rooms, kitchen and bathroom, central heating, small square of garden. Smaller square of sea and sky glimpsed between the tourist villas. One of those big houses on the Boulevard de la Mer, waking to the waves, to the wind, to the sea-spray splashing on your terrace, it's one of those I used to dream of, when I could still dream. One of those I should have bought. Your own meanness, she said. Years of dreaming and planning, you even had the big walled garden landscaped in your head, she said, and then . . . The mean impulse, she said. No, but a house like that would have cost me a fortune, I would have needed a mortgage. I've never been in debt in my life. To anyone, bank or shopkeeper. I wrote out a cheque from my savings, forty years of savings, forty years of teaching and that's all it amounts to. Three small rooms in a sidestreet . . . Two would have done, what do we want with a guest room? Who will ever come to sleep in it? Certainly not my children. Those mediocrities. After all I gave them. All the sacrifices. My time and my patience. Private lessons morning and evening, advanced mathematics, science, Latin. You're killing the poor things, she said, let them go out and play with their friends like everyone else, quit making oddities of them. Friends! Village trash. No return for it. Nothing to hope for now. Wallowing with that bitch, that perverted . . . My daughter. Nobody will come. There's nobody to come. Salon, cuisine, chambre congugale, that would have been enough. More than enough. Conjugale! Con, con, con! Conjugate. Conjugate the verb 'to retire.' Nobody has the right to grow old. Age. Anguish. Alzheimer's. Nobody should be asked to grow old . . .

Still, with only this narrow box in a sidestreet to pay rates on I'll be able to put something by from my pension. Later, years later, when I'm eighty or so, dragging myself fearfully through these streets of an evening . . . Aggressions. Arabs. Anguish. A Home. Old People's Home. I'll put it by for a Home. Hospice for retired teachers, couldn't trust that bitch to look after me when I'm. Bit of comfort, nice young nurses, everything done for me. The town outside. Safely shut outside. Fear is everywhere, outside and in. Anguish . . .

She wanted me to buy a cottage in Loguivy. It's the seaside too, she said, so what's the difference? I earned the money, that's the difference. Her family. Cream of the cream, I don't think. Sunday dinners in Loguivy with her decrepit old brothers, tu parles! I have no one left. No brothers or sisters. No one to mirror the way I'm falling apart. Except her. Vieille carne! I'm a man of sixty, in the force of his age. But, age . . . Count on yourself, René, who else is there to count on? Who'll there be to pay my pension when I'm ninety? It's all right planning, but will there be anyone? La France est foutue. It's finished. Invaded. The future is full of anguish. Our politicians are not fit to govern us. Sold out. I worked for forty years, I fought for our colonies when my turn came, and still there'll be nothing left in the till for my pension. All handed lavishly out in Benefit to the immigrants. Four wives each, breeding like rabbits, drawing family allowance . . . You want to get something for your nerves, she said, you can't go on like that. You're getting odder and odder, she said, last week when she heard about the. She should know. About oddness. The expert. Running every week to the doctor to recount her miseries, he must have a good laugh. Pierre Bouchon. Thick peasant lump when he was a lad in primary school, I hammered the knuckles off him. He came

far. Well, at least she has the sense to go to Bouchon. One
of our own. Those other two! Doctor Moreau and Doctor
Goldman! If you're looking for symptoms there they are:
France is diseased all right. The Moreau woman, time was
she'd have been content to be a doctor's wife, playing bridge
and arranging flowers, now they're liberated soi-disant and
she's a doctor herself. Salope! Dirty bitch! Examining men's
bodies . . . As for Goldman, haah! Only got to look at
Goldman. There's another one got baptised with the
secateurs, see the beak he's got on him? Time was you didn't
see any of those lads in Brittany, not a rich enough country
for them. They're everywhere now. Got back on their feet
quick enough after the. After their famous Holocaust, they
have the ears battered off us with their Holocaust! Every
time you turn on the telly . . . 'Only a detail of history',
that was a good one though, that put them in their place,
you have to hand it to Le Pen all right! Solid Breton wit,
always handy with the language . . . One of our own.
France! I fought for our colonies, much good it did me. We
fell apart with the loss of Algeria, that's where the disease
started, that's where . . .

I'd walk on the beach, bit of sea air, only it's the
thirteenth of July, tourists, kids off school for the summer,
all worked up for the fireworks tonight. Jostling and
shoving and screaming bad talk. Can just about stand them
sitting quiet in straight lines of desks. One more year to go.
I shouldn't have excluded those two kids from the school,
that was a mistake. End-of-term nerves. They are French
after all, even if their fool of a mother belongs to that
foreign sect . . . A reprimand might have been sufficient,
not as if they were those Muslims wearing chadors in the
classroom. Thin end of the wedge though. Shouldn't have
let myself get carried away at the council meeting either.

The way they all looked at me . . . Is it a symptom? Could it be a symptom? Aggression, after all. They say Alzheimer's starts with. Rubbish. There's nothing changed about me, I always did say straight out what I thought, I was respected for it all my life, nothing's changed. It's not me, it's those pups on the council. Liberals. I'm thinking too much, letting myself be intimidated. There's too much hypocrisy, too much pandering to the Left. Hah! That's the one bright spot, they've got it in the arse now all right, the Left! Next election the way things are going and the Socialists will be swept into the bin, nothing's more certain. Shower of crooks, murderers, made France the laughing-stock of the. Twelve years with their snouts in the trough. Twelve years of failure, of unemployment, the ruin of our farmers, of our fishermen, twelve years of immigrants sailing through our frontiers as the humour takes them, twelve years of shame. The lost honour of my poor country . . .

The pane of glass had been replaced, that was something, the French working man could still be depended on. From the front window he could just perceive the corner of silvery sea, a mass of grey rock. He was standing on his own floor after all, between his own walls, bought and paid for, looking out at the waves. That was something, that must stand for something. All his life he had longed for the sea. Growing up on the farm, herding the cows on monotonous flat inland fields, he had dreamed of those silver waves crashing on grey rocks. And now they were his. His but poisoned. Polluted. The town he'd dreamed of, beach he'd dreamed of with quiet elegant couples in deck-chairs, long-legged classy French girls like Catherine Deneuve striding out of the sea, all that was finished. Seulbourg, like most other towns, had become a kingdom of yobs. Of foreigners and yobs. There they came, another lot of them, blotting out his corner of silver sea, jostling and yelling, thumping one another, dropping beer cans in the gutter. Seulbourg was a slum. No, not quite a slum, he had to admit, but going that way fast. Not the quiet civilised town he'd been brought to once, on his First Communion day, and that he'd dreamed of for years afterwards, in the mud of the farm, in the barrack-like promiscuity of the Training College, in Algeria the year of his National Service. Especially in the dusty dazzling horror that had been Algeria he had longed to rest in this cool grey town by the Breton sea. Crawling on his scared twenty-one year old belly among the scrub and pebbles, with *them* lurking silent and brown and vicious, blending with the rocks, confounded with the burnt-up bushes, stones among the stones. Waiting. The thin dark arm strong as a rope around your throat, the knife . . . The anguish. It was as real to him now, he could summon up and lose himself even now in the sheer terror of those nights tracking them along the dried-up valley of the oued, up the narrow ravines, across the thirsty blond stony desert. Or were *they* tracking him? That was always the fear, those nights of sudden ambush. It was everyone's secret terror, sent out in groups to track down the fellagha . . . Behind the grossièrités, behind the bravado, behind the 'Merde! Enculés de bicots!' was always the silent anguished question: and what if the fellagha are all the time tracking us? If I get lost, stray from the group, fall out for a piss, what state will I be found in? What unspeakable mutilations will they have made me live through before I'm finally found, a poor slaughtered thing lying under the desert sun? And then, driving in the jeep through silent lost villages that were rotten with them, where the treacherous peasants had killed off all their dogs so their barking couldn't betray the murdering footsteps of the mujahedin, waiting as you drove down the slyly-sleeping street for the rifle-burst from the window-hole of some ugly flat-roofed shack. Worry, hate, the constant anxiety. You couldn't be expected to forget. All over France there were men of his age whose memories and whose nightmares would not ever allow them to forget. Who passed their lives in rancour, condemned to incessantly relive the humiliating terror of that year, the official end of their childhood, the year that put a final full stop to their innocence.

And now Algeria had followed him to his dreamed-of seaside town. People might talk of one respectable family, but he *knew*. Family meant something different to them, something infinitely more numerous. Family meant a clan, a tribe, a whole swarming village of brown hangdog faces, false smiles, expressions of sneaky humility with the knife sharpened ready . . . Family meant a horde of uncles aunts cousins nephews smuggled in through Spain, living up twenty to a room, stealing the bread of the French, waiting their hour. You couldn't trust them, not one of them, he'd seen for himself that year what they were like, what they were capable of doing . . . They're not the same as us, they'll never be the same as us. Their narrow starved beliefs, their abstinence, their cringing sideways smiles. They didn't fight the same way as us, back then . . . Anguish.

Tonight for the first time he would miss the fireworks in Plouch'en. He couldn't face it. Face the other men on the council, face the parents, face the sniggering pupils. Made a right fool of himself with those Jehovah's Witnesses. Related to half the village, the Séguins, got the whole place behind them, the priest, the château . . . The château reported him to the League against Racism, some busybody came nosing round yesterday, some Jew. Sent the bastard on his way all right with an earful. Maybe that was a mistake . . . I'm losing my touch, he thought. She'll go to the mairie on her own tonight, with Jean-Marc and his fool of a wife. They'll watch the fireworks, laugh and clap like yokels, be glad of my absence. Solitude and anguish, what was the point of a man marrying? She ought to be sitting there beside him, listening to him, agreeing with him, soothing his anguish. That was her job, that's what she took on forty years ago. She never agreed with him now, or else in a sly way laughing up her sleeve, that was Bouchon's fault. Encouraging her. Probably mad enough to be tied up, let alone running to tell tales to a doctor. All those pills she stuffed herself with. For depression, she claimed. As if we weren't all depressed. As if the whole country wasn't depressed, and with good cause . . .

He took his revolver out of its case, if he had the courage he'd put a bullet in himself, here in this polluted town of strangers, in this narrow house of retirement that was a betrayal of all his dreams. The house that spelled out the end of all hope, the beginning of death. A coffin-house. Anxiety. Anguish. An ageing man. Anachronism . . . The light was draining away, his square of sea was turning invisible, blending into the evening sky, the air full of voices and quiet sniggers. He would sit there by the darkening window as he did every Saturday, holding his revolver, the only one thing in his life he could count on now. The one sure protection he had against outside, against the gathering evil dark, against the beer-bottle smashing on the pavement, the menacing snarl of a motor-bike. Against the hushed giggles at his back, the mocking faces. Against the rustle of a dry desert bush that moved slightly without wind, against the sudden little rush of pebbles down the side of a ravine . . .

And they were there, Miloud realised, and they were after him, about ten of them running silently like wolves. They must have left their motorbikes on the boulevard when they saw him take off up the narrow alleys, through the small back gardens, and if only he could find someplace to hide! Only there was nowhere to hide, no door to knock on, and no one to let him in if he knocked. They were all out at the fireworks, all the sour shopkeepers, all the retired pensioners, all the tourists from the holiday villas, the doors, the windows and shutters were all securely locked against him. He'd always been a good little runner, it was the only sport he'd bothered with, but they were bigger than him and gaining. The whole town was empty of kind helpful adults, there was no mercy and no reason. There was only these wild things whose purpose was to hurt him, to maim him, to humiliate him, make nothing of him . . .

No but wait! No maybe there *was* one place. Yes there was, there *was* a place, and not so far away either, he could make it, he could get there and . . . There was one sure place after all that he could run to, where there was sure to be someone. Someone at home, someone awake. That daft old schoolmaster everyone gossiped about, the stout old man with his white hair and his old-fashioned sabots, who sat up every weekend guarding his property, they said, against the bikers and the vandals. He would be there sitting at his window as he always was now on a Saturday, hunched awake in his armchair gobbling sandwiches with his bottle of vin rouge on the windowsill, peering like a watchman out at the street. He would be sure to see, he missed nothing. He would help. It would be his duty to help, he was a grown-up. They said he was a schoolmaster in some village, so he would not be afraid of the Delamottes and the skins, he would have power to stop them in their

331

tracks. He, above all he, a schoolmaster, a man of authority
. . . To him, a strong stern old man after years in a
classroom, to him they would only be children to be
scolded. They wouldn't be monsters, they wouldn't be
Terror. Big Cyril Delamotte would only be a child to get his
ear clipped. The thought was warm and comforting and he
held it to him: For this man they would be nothing! This
grim-faced old watcher, solid in his window seat, was the
image of Reason, he stood for the whole of the adult world
and its wisdom, and he would look out and the pack and its
quarry would be nothing to him, a crowd of naughty
children . . . He, Miloud, would be just a smaller child to be
protected, to be comforted.

He doubled back quickly down the alleys towards the
Boulevard but another group of figures ran at him out of
the dusk, closer this lot. Calling to him: "Milo! Milo! Wait
for us, Milo!" Like shit he'd wait, he wasn't that much of an
imbecile. Their feet came thudding after him, he could hear
them yelling just behind him: "We're your *friends*, Milo!"
Merde merde merde, oh merde! He was done for. "Help!"
he would shout, if he could only get his breath back. "Au
secours!" he would call as he approached the little villa and
the old man would throw open his door, warm and
protective as a parent, and there would be no more fear. He
would stay there in the little house till the fireworks ended,
sharing the old man's sandwiches, and then the old man
would walk him home, au fond it would be a little
adventure to remember. Something to recount to Layla . . .

Closer, closer down the Boulevard and into the mouth of
the little street and they were gaining on him the second lot,
still calling his name. But it was there. The funny narrow
little house was there and the big bulky old man in the
window half asleep as they'd often seen him, comically

guarding his microscopic little property against the Delamottes and the . . .

"Au secours!" he called. "Au secours, monsieur!" he screamed, panting the last few metres to sanctuary.

René Balavoine woke, sitting cramped in his basket-chair by the open window and it still wasn't completely dark, these long summer evenings, or was it the moon, and for a second he wondered where he was: dozed off at home in his study above the school in Plouch'en and the wind crying and the pattering of autumn leaves in the playground? He groped, confused, and found the revolver wedged on his lap and he wasn't sitting at his desk at home, he was in Seulbourg. And it wasn't the moon but a streetlamp. And it wasn't the wind crying but voices, and the slap-slap patter of feet, a whole mob of feet, and suddenly he was wide awake. They were attacking him, he knew it, he had always known it would happen. They were making down the alley straight for his house, calling out something, whooping and screaming like wild things, like savages, it's what he'd always been waiting for. Their leader clear in the dusk, under the street lamp, hurtling towards the window, how could you mistake that face, that scrawny body? Nearly forty years shrivelled away and dissolved in front of him and he was back there, young and terrified, surrounded by them . . . The frizz of hair, dark bony features, the scared hangdog expression. Black eyes rolling wide with hate, arms wildly gesticulating, pointing out the house, the mouth wide in a yell of triumph. And close behind their leader the pack hunched and running, ready to crash in on his refuge, smash down his doors and windows, lay hold of him and mutilate him as they'd mutilated his two comrades back there one summer night in a gully outside the little hamlet, God don't let me miss this time, oh God God don't let me miss . . .

He lifted the revolver, aimed it and fired, and the leader danced in the air and fell, it was like a film on the telly, it was the war all over again, and the others stopped dead, froze together and waited. That put a stop to their gallop, he thought in awed satisfaction, if I can hold out now till . . . Till what? He groped anxiously in the fog of his thoughts: hold out till . . . ? But I'm not in Algeria, he thought. I'm not in Algeria, I'm not in a war. Algeria was another time, where am I? What have I just done? The fog lifted and he peered out again and they were only children, three or four children, one of them a girl, huddled scared under the street lamp watching him, the girl from the château, oh Jesus God what have I done, Bourjois' daughter watching him with her eyes and mouth wide open while Bourjois' son bent over a smaller darker child who lay bleeding and twitching in the middle of the road.

Je suis foutu, René Balavoine thought coldly, that's it, I'm done for now, the Arabs have finished me. He felt a terrible bleak nostalgia for his school and his wife and his lost retirement and the narrow little house that he wouldn't, now, be allowed to end his days in. They've done it at last, the bicots, and if I had the courage I'd. But he knew he wouldn't have the courage and he let the revolver slide out of his hand on to the floor and he got up off his chair and went out to confront them.

They spilled out of the long drawing-room on to the terrace, on to the lawn. Tante Ruby's friends, Uncle Gustave's friends. Parisians – and enough of them thank heavens, well *nearly* enough, to cover the absence of the local aristocracy. Hélène was aware that, with the exception of Rosalind and Pierre and old Maître Bourin, they themselves seemed to have no real friends worth talking about. They had useful acquaintances it was true, quite a number of useful acquaintances carefully cultivated by Jean-Hubert over the years. But the acquaintances by their very nature belonged, as precariously as they did themselves, to the camp of Madame la Comtesse and, because of that precariousness, could be depended upon to obey the old hag's every wish.

So: Rosalind and Pierre in their Sunday best looking exactly what they were, and old Maître Bourin, pink and already tipsy, clinging to Tante Ruby. (Or being clung to by Tante Ruby in her embarrassment at Gustave's defection? For defection there clearly was and Uncle Gustave, having had time to collect his wits, seemed unlikely to come scurrying to heel again if his wife was unwise enough to call him.) Finally, the Parisians in the tight little groups they were used to being in at parties, laughing and gossiping and obviously relieved at being left peacefully among themselves and not dragged away from one another's delightfully malicious company to be polite to a lot of rustic squires and their worthy ladies. Wondering though, from a remark or two Hélène overheard, why there *were* no local notabilities present – were Ruby's nephew and niece perhaps not quite all they ought to be . . . ? Not perfectly frequentable, perhaps? Was *Ruby*, in the country, not considered to be quite . . . euh, quite . . . ? But there was plenty to drink and the buffet-tables, glimpsed through the double doors of the dining room, looked more than promising, and the garden in the gathering dusk was quite eccentrically charming – only to be expected of course with an English hostess, oh all right, Irish, c'est la même chose, non? And as soon as this raout was over, as soon as one could decently take one's leave, they all intended to descend in a crowd on the du Bois Fleuris, because dear old Augusta and Joffroy lived just down the road after all and how very very odd that they weren't here . . . How odd that even Beatrix wasn't to be seen and Beatrix, they knew, was staying with her parents, and Beatrix had never yet been known to miss a party . . . So really there must be something, quelquechose qui clochait vraiment with this Bourjois couple. Never mind, Augusta and Joffroy would put them wise . . . And in the meantime, they were saying, frequentable or not let's make the most of them, chère amie, seeing that we're here anyway, and just *look* at old Ruby eyeing up that dishy butler! And can that be Gustave's latest mistress in the red Lacroix, he *can't* have brought her home to meet the family! No no, of course it isn't, even Gustave wouldn't . . . But yes, I swear! I saw them with my own eyes last week holding hands chez Lipp, I swear it's the same woman! No it's not possible my dear, would even a grocer have dared bring his mistress to the family château? The Irish *mother*? No really! You're mistaken, that can't be the mother, that woman can't be more than . . . How *old* are this Bourjois couple then? No no, *I* bet on the fancy piece and Ruby's treating herself to the butler in revenge. Russian morals my dear, and we all know Ruby! Catherine the Great in person, insatiable . . . But who, do tell me who's that extraordinary creature in the feather boa and the long velvet skirt who's just trotted across the lawn, my dear she's got half the Flea Market on her back, she can't possibly be French . . . no *that* must be the Irish mother and the other, the glamorous dark lady, must be . . .

"Madame Boujois? Oh pardon me, I hope I'm not disturbing you but I'm Mary-Lou Korrigan the painter, you sent me an invitation . . . I'm a bit late, I'm afraid but I do seem to have arrived at last, don't I, in every sense of the word ha ha! Received at the château, imagine! I'm *so* pleased you thought of me. Actually I brought a few of my Works along, just a few aquarelles, local scenes, I thought in case any of your guests might . . . The servants are hanging them over the buffet tables, you don't mind? Only I said to myself, with all this beau monde there's going to be at the reception, all rotten with cash, I couldn't resist, I said to myself . . ."

I invited *her*? Of course I didn't invite her, I've never met this scarecrow in my life, is she drunk? Hélène smiled and held out her hand, "I'm so glad you could come, madame!"

"Hou la la, I wouldn't have missed this for anything, I've been longing for years to see the old château again! I used to come here sketching every summer holidays you know, when we were all teenagers. The times we had, Pierrot, Jean-Hubert, his old uncle didn't know the half of what went on, he'd have had the dogs on us! I expect he's often talked about me, old Jean-Hub?"

Oh that explained it, Hélène thought sourly, another little friend of his childhood, he might have told me he was inviting her. And imagine bringing her pictures along, the cheek, what does she think it is anyway, a bloody auction? God, if that's supposed to be big sexy Loulou . . . "Come and have a drink and say hello to Jean-Hubert, won't you, madame."

"Sure! I'd love to see the old pet again, can't wait! Imagine me being here *legally* as it were, not hiding in the bushes, that's what comes of making a name for yourself! Only *look* . . . look isn't that my ex-husband standing over there? He *has* got fat! All that English cooking, oh dear, without me to look after him . . . Actually I wasn't sure if you meant me to bring a little boyfriend, madame? So I played safe and didn't, is that all right? Only I find boyfriends are always such an encumbrance at parties don't you? So it's just as well I didn't. I'm going to hurl myself upon my poor Pierrot, he doesn't look happy at all does he, madame? Won't he be pleased to see me turning up like this! Does he know you invited me? Oh good, big surprise then, I'll just drag him behind a rosebush and we'll have a great old giggle about our lost jeunesse! That's where we did all our courting, did he ever tell you? Over there behind Madame Laetitia Ploudel. Oh the whole village knows Laetitia, Hou la la if the old creature could talk!" She gave Hélène a meaningful nudge and Hélène, conscious of the sharp-eyed Parisians watching with interested sharp-lipped smiles, hastily led her over to Pierre. Better at least than the shame of having her hurl herself upon Jean-Hubert in public with heaven knows what indiscretions.

Rosalind was having a hard time with an elderly consular wife.

"But then you must have been in Chile all through Pinochet's time, was it dreadful, how did you survive? That ghastly man, oh the petitions we used to sign back home in Nailsworth! How ever did you manage?"

The consular wife took off her sunglasses to examine Rosalind more closely, what an odd little Englishwoman and such a funny dress!

"Dreadful? What can you mean, madame? The Pinochets were a delightful couple. Très très charmants!"

Rosalind felt crushed for an instant, then common sense came to her assistance: the woman's husband was a very minor official and at his age he didn't risk too many promotions, it was unlikely that they'd ever got close enough to the General to put his delightfulness to the test. Honestly these French, forever boasting. Still, I suppose they can't really help themselves, poor things, must feel terribly insecure deep down . . . She muttered something

vaguely polite and sidled off across the half-empty lawn.
You could count the nobles on one hand, Jean-Hubert must
be doing his nut and serve him bleedin' well right. Should I
pass on Michel's message to Hélène, she wondered, and risk
getting the head bitten off me? Maybe just better leave
things be, let him come looking for her himself. I mean if
he's got the almighty neck on him to do what he's planning
it should be no bother to him at all to come striding in
among this lot like Young Whatsisname come to claim his
lady love. Pierre's right, the poor mutt must be round the
twist if he thinks Hélène's going to . . . No, I won't say a
word to her, mind my own business for a change, if he
thinks Hélène's just going to drop everything and go off
with him! Hélène of all people. Hélène likes her home
comforts all right. Maybe he's *not* quite right in the head?
All those years of dumb devotion, maybe it's *done*
something to him, maybe the village is right, the postman
did say he caught him talking to himself . . . God, I near
threw a wobbly when he told me his plans. Could he have
been joking? Maybe he was joking, maybe that was it,
maybe he was having me on, he probably just wants to say
goodbye to her nice and privately . . . But all those bleedin'
keys he showed me, keys to all the new houses, he said. If I
could believe him . . . All I know is, he better not try
loading Pierre's old oak table into that removal van of his,
he'll rupture himself, be no good to Hélène or anyone!
Could he *possibly*? It's true they'll all be out at the fireworks,
the whole village, and it's true they've all been bastards to
him but imagine dreaming up a trick like that to play on
them! I mean you'd need to be a bit twisted. Or else he's
joking . . . Still, seeing as he's got hold of all the keys. Just
imagine the Countess owning keys to half the village
houses, honestly you'd think you were in the sixteenth

century, *Angélique* or whatever . . . Well I suppose if her son was the architect for all those bungalows. Trust them to be into everything. Imagine her keeping copies of all the keys though, and imagine her giving them to Michel Le Borgne. "But Rosalind, she knows that Monsieur Vladimir was my grandfather, it's quite logical, Madame la Comtesse has very old-fashioned ideas about justice." Well honestly these frogs! Justice? Poor sod will see his fill of justice when they clap him inside for the rest of his days. But of course he knows he's safe there, there's no way the villagers could report him to the gendarmes . . . Be quite obvious to the Old Bill where all the stolen antiques came from in the first place, they could hardly claim they'd ordered them from the Trois Suisses catalogue! God, he *could* do it I bet he's going to do it, I mean he's what they call an original, old Michel. I wouldn't actually mind going along and giving him a hand myself, be a bit of a lark . . . More of a lark than this lot anyway. But of course it's not me he wants, it's Hélène. Jesus, does he seriously picture Hélène helping him to heft a great vanload of Monsieur Vladimir's furniture out of the tenants' houses, and then *elope* with him? Pierre's right, he's round the twist OK. He's living in another age, is Michel. Still maybe I'd better go in and find Hélène. At least tell her he's there, waiting for her . . .

Hélène waved a little dismally at her mother and Uncle Gus as they drove discreetly away from the side entrance and were lost among the darkening chestnut trees. The odd explosion could be heard from down in the village, the fête organizers no doubt testing their fireworks. An occasional modest rocket slid up and died sparkling in the dusk.

"Make you feel at home, wouldn't it," her mother had joked sadly. Though why sadly for heavens sake, she'd got what she wanted, hadn't she? Could she be starting to feel homesick already, Hélène wondered, picturing the struggle that lay ahead for this ageing, if still beautiful, woman who was once again bravely moving on, pulling up roots, letting the dead past lie there withering unnoticed behind her. Moving on this time to a life where nobody would be exactly flinging wide their arms in welcome.

Not, Hélène supposed, that anyone ever had, particularly, flung open their arms for Mother. Not the Campbells of Claghan, not the old aunt in London who'd treated her as just another lodger, not Gerald's grown-up children. And not me, she thought guiltily, I never exactly tried to make anything easier for her, hiding away from her behind this smooth blank face that I cultivated. Like a foretaste of France I must have been, the France the poor cow's going to spend the rest of her life coping with.

At parties like this for a start, she thought, as she exchanged crisp meaningless smiles and meaningless hostess/guest phrases with a couple of Tante Ruby's cronies. People like this, they'll try and make mincemeat out of the poor old thing. Unless they'll be licking her boots, you never know, what with all l'oncle Gustave's millions? Oh I'd say she'll be fit for them all right, Hélène concluded with a smile of relief, recalling her mother's long tanned legs sliding so elegantly into the red Jag. No, I certainly don't have to feel guilty or worried or protective any more: adieu Irish mother! Who probably never existed, she thought, except in my imagination. They probably never do exist, the holy Irish mothers, it's a role they invent for themselves. Or we invent for them, to keep them at a discreet distance, to keep from having to have any real truck with them.

"Though indeed and it's less of a goodbye this time, Eileen," she'd said, "Sure we're only just up the road so to speak, a couple of hour's drive. And listen, no more nonsense about Belfast, do you hear? Stay here where you're well and comfortable!" A rocket down in the village drowned out her goodbyes and they were away. Mother had won, Mother had triumphed, vive l'Irlande!

And Tante Ruby, where was Tante Ruby? The poor thing, the arrogant old slob, Tante Ruby must be . . .

Tante Ruby was actually gliding off into the shadows between the climbing roses, tiptoeing along the outside paths out of sight of the guests. A little drunk, Tante Ruby was, a little excited, new adventures on the misty horizon, Gustave's betrayal for the moment forgotten. It wasn't the first time after all and he'd be back, she knew he'd be back, quelle idée, some hag of a foreign schoolteacher! Et moi, Ruby Boulanger de Ploudel de Medeu, non mais . . . ! A sixty-year-old schoolmistress and puis quoi encore! Oh Gustave would come back all right, he always had, she and Gustave understood each other perfectly. But in the meantime:

"Ze night is young," Tante Ruby sang softly, *"Le ciel est bleu* . . . Come Gabriel," she whispered, "It is not so far now, it is by here . . ."

Well honestly, could you be up to them! Heading off behind the buddleyia bushes with the hired help, away off to do her courting or whatever under the branches of that disgusting purple rose tree, exactly like the village maidens in old Vladimir's time . . . Life as a French farce! In-laws straight out of the Théatre du Boulevard! EuroDisney . . .

I'm jealous, Hélène thought, that's what it is. There they all are in their happy little couples and here I am bored and middle-aged in a boring middle-aged marriage that probably won't last much longer, why should it last, the twins are grown up, what's to hold it together? I bet Jean-Hubert's off with someone and all, one of the little friends of his childhood, he's probably created a whole dynasty of little Sebastians by now . . . And the twins. Certainly the twins, else why aren't they here, away off in couples too no doubt, in the backs of cars watching the fireworks. And good luck to them! What have I, she thought bitterly, twenty years of lying daydreams about a seedy old hypocrite that . . . Maybe it wasn't even him in Arles, maybe I don't even remember right what he looked like? Gibraltar the Second, no, my mother must be crazy! Life doesn't fall apart to that extent, I mean I'm not some victim in a documentary . . . I'm not even a victim. I wasn't even one of his victims. I was nowhere. Not a single instant that I spent with him was real, I can't trust one single memory from anywhere. I never could. Anny and Patrick, they were paid a weekly wage to look after me, they wouldn't have looked after me for nothing. *They* wouldn't have chosen me either . . .

"Oh Hélène, Hélène, there you are, I've been looking all over for you. I've got this message, now promise you won't bite my head off? Well listen, Michel Le Borgne wants to see you. Urgently he says. He's actually waiting halfway down the avenue if you could just spare . . . Yeah, I know you've got all these guests to look after. Well just point them at the food why don't you, they'll be so busy stuffing themselves they won't even notice you've slipped off, they're French, aren't they? Because he's leaving the village tonight, that's why, he's had enough so he's going. And he wants to see you before he goes, you're his great big hopeless love as I think I mentioned before. Troubadour stuff, Michel's the last of the great Romantics, so just try and be nice to him, it's the least you can . . . I mean don't laugh at the poor man no matter what he says, or put on your Home Counties boss act or anything. The guy's actually suffering, he may

343

sound a bit . . . But let him down gently, Hélène, eh? Oh Christ look, isn't that a hoot! Look at poor Pierre over there under that awful painting, wherever did you get it? God, he doesn't look too happy! D'you think I ought to go and rescue him from his feathered friend, what is the woman doing to him? Who is she anyway, doesn't look much like a noble to me, looks more like a walking haystack. The poor love's got his trapped look on again, do you think she's about to rape him? *Loulou?* What do you mean Hélène, that's never the famous Loulou? That apparition? And to think I was actually offering him a divorce so he could go off and. You were right all along, I needn't have worried need I? That thing's Loulou? Well he doesn't look overjoyed to see her does he? No I don't think I'll go and rescue him after all, let him get himself out of this one, teach him a lesson! Hasn't half got a cheek though has she, really these French . . ."

What an idea, Hélène was thinking in amazement as Rosalind went rabbiting on, what a daft Mills and Boon idea, has the woman gone completely mad? A part-time gardener, old Hervé Le Moal's nephew, imagine! Well, he's lurking down the avenue is what she's saying, just waiting for me to stroll down so he can pour out his soul to me. What do they all take me for, Tante Ruby creeping off behind the bushes with the butler or what? Well, the presumption of it. If he's all that attached to me he only had to stay in his job, nobody asked him to leave, did they? Just walking out like that, where does he think I'm going to find anyone now, the whole place needs a complete going-over this autumn if I'm ever going to have it ready to open to the public . . . Honestly they're all the same, Hélène thought irritably, surprising herself with her resemblance to Jean-Hubert. To Tante Ruby. Don't laugh at the poor man,

Rosalind was saying, don't put on your Home Counties boss act. What does she think it is, the nineteen-seventies? Does she imagine we're still the naïve wayfaring people, Jean-Hubert and me, who arrived in the village all those years ago stinking of patchouli, in our rusty old van, and picked her up on the church porch? Doesn't she realise the Eighties have happened in between and we're well into the Nineties and that if by any chance I, Hélène Bourjois, even deigned to notice a scruffy teenager eating stale buns in a church porch it would never even remotely enter my mind to engage her to bring up my kids. Nannies from Hell have happened since then, Roz, hard drugs have happened, crazy killers have arrived in every village, terrorists and death squads come in all shapes and sizes and people such as us, the happy few sitting cosily on our little oasis, we'd better cling on with our fingernails and toenails for just as long as we can manage. Your husband understands that, Roz, and so does my mother even. Jean-Hubert's family and the old Countess and all this lot milling about here drinking my booze and eating my food, they've always understood it. And look at me. If I was shunted off into the garden today by way of a welcome, while my husband and his mother and his aunt held a family council over me, well I wouldn't be very likely to go weeping on the gardener's shoulder would I? I wouldn't even notice him, I'd just stroll happily around the place saying this is mine, I married into this. I've got it made, I'd be thinking, and every little wimp of a student in Plouch'en could be drooling around the rosebushes falling in love with me and I wouldn't even see them. That's what I'm like now, she was thinking, that's what everyone's grown to be like. Even my mother's given up on peace and harmony, hasn't she, and she's gone off merrily with the first millionaire she ever bumped into. And good luck to her. Christopher Milton, *if* he's alive, is driving round the place with a crowd of thugs, doing his furtive little dark deeds. Yann, the poor fool, is *not* alive, he's dead. Dead of the Seventies. He would have been a successful businessman by now perhaps. In Brussels or The Hague or someplace. Travelling in Concorde instead of in worn-out sandals. Only he let himself die, didn't he. Didn't realise the scene would ever change. And there's Michel Le Borgne, sole and innocent survivor, waiting romantically among the chestnut trees, twenty years out of fashion. Waiting to say goodbye to me. To a girl in a flowery dress and Indian beads. He hasn't even the wit to realise she doesn't exist. That she only exists now as the woman who paid his wages. Hélène Bourjois, middle-aged matron, wife of Jean-Hubert. That if he'd had any sense he'd have hung on to his job, could have gaped at me every day and had a roof over his head as well. He won't find it so easy to get another one, this is hardly a time for impulsive gestures.

But try as she might to convince herself, she felt a mild nostalgia for the girl in the long skirt and untidy hair walking in bewilderment among the aggressive opulence of Uncle Vladimir's roses, and for the student in torn jeans and a velvet ribbon who'd seemed, for half an hour, like a comforting promise that the lovely carefree life of the Seventies was going to continue forever.

Maybe I *will* go and say goodbye to him, she thought as she absentmindedly replied to Rosalind's nonsense. It can't do any harm and what else have I to do after all? I was complaining about not being part of a couple at this awful party, so maybe I *could* be part of a couple for five minutes or so, exchanging gentle phrases of regret and gratitude. Maybe we could even keep in touch now sometimes, Michel and I. Christmas cards or whatever. As friends. As equals at any rate, now that he doesn't work for me any more. Maybe he could replace Christopher, as an ideal, as a regret? The only real survivor, after all, from that gentle carefree time?

And then the gendarmes drove into the courtyard in their blue Renault, and soon people were surrounding Hélène with faces of concerned sympathy. She found herself confusedly back in a time, perhaps not so carefree after all, not so gentle, when the twins had just been born and, lying there cradling them in the squat, she'd realised that never again would she be safe from worry, safe from panic. Every car driver had suddenly become a potential crazed killer, every road a minefield for toddling feet, every dog a vicious snarling carnivore, every teacher a possible perverter of innocence, every stranger a hideous masked abductor . . .

And now. The twins were in Seulbourg, being held at the gendarmerie, in a state of deep shock. Jean-Hubert, naturally, was nowhere to be found. "Not that he'd be the most sensitive person for them to see at a time like this. I mean things must be traumatic enough for the poor little loves without having *him* sweeping in with his sarcasm and his . . . Oh God, Rosalind, my poor little children, to have witnessed . . ."

Serve the little pests right, Rosalind thought, but was shocked speechless at the thought of the poor dead Arab. What *she'd* like to know was what had actually been Clémence's role in it all? Innocent witness my foot, Rosalind felt like saying, but was forced to admit that Clem could not possibly have any guilt in the killing – she'd surely be the last person to have any truck with the mad old schoolmaster? Or would she? After all, she seemed to have quite a thing about stout old fanatics this last while, the same little Clem . . .

"Would you mind coming along with me, Rosalind?" Hélène asked, "At this stage in a party I know better than to go hunting down Jean-Hubert."

"But he is their father!" The gendarme was scandalised, "He is the head of the family, madame!"

"Yes, well this is a two-headed family," Hélène retorted sweetly, and then spoiled it by bursting into tears.

"Yeah, sure I'll come with you," Rosalind said, "And so will Pierre, won't you luv? After all you must be used to this sort of . . . No Mrs Loulou, we *won't* be needing an official painter along to record the scene, thank you very much! On yer bike, mate!"

Michel Le Borgne, waiting in the shadow of an overhanging tree, saw with horror the gendarmes' little R4 heading for the château. A picture leaped clearly and coldly into his mind: Rosalind delivering his message and Madame Bourjois, *not* the gentle bewildered Hélène of his dreams, not the woman he'd been in love with for so long but suddenly la patronne, the châtelaine, the wife of Bourjois . . . Right, *that* Madame Bourjois listening aghast to Rosalind and then striding off to find her husband: "Oh Jean-Hubert chéri, the gardener has gone crazy, he wants me to run away with him, he is intending to steal your heritage!"

To steal your heritage? Would she speak like that? How would she speak? How would she react? He realised that, finally, he knew nothing at all about her. He'd never had a real conversation with her since that day sixteen years ago. And people change beyond recognition in sixteen years. He himself was living proof of that. Standing beneath the trees, waiting for her to appear, his life in the village had stretched behind him like a gentle luminous time, a way of existence that had once been as precious to him as a toy or a childhood dream and that now had as little relevance. Summer days unfolding among a hectare of trees and pale scented roses, winter evenings reading or listening to music by the open fire in his rustic old cottage, beloved home of his infancy, a whole village of friendly familiar faces. Years of illusion those had been. The roses had never belonged to him, nor had the trees. His wife had probably been driven away by his books and his music and the damp old-fashioned cottage she couldn't persuade him to move out of. As for the village, how many real friends had he ever had there? Laughing at him behind his back, no doubt, the most of them had been and now, thanks to Nathalie, laughing out loud to his face.

Once he'd recognised that, the future had become easy. Ahead of him, these past weeks, had stretched freedom, his own business, the chance to become rich, a life among beautiful objects that, this time, would belong to him, would work for him and bring him profit.

He'd had no regrets whatever, standing there waiting under the tree, no scruples. Get to the devil out of this cursed village, he'd thought savagely, and hit the bastards where it hurts before you go.

It would have been perfect if she'd come with him. He'd almost believed she would come. What else, in his dreams, could she have done? But that had apparently been an illusion more grotesque than all the others. An imaginary tune played on a plywood violin. And a dangerous illusion too, it seemed. She had called the gendarmes. It was finished.

He could not quite grasp that it was finished, that all his plans had fallen apart, that she had put a complete stop to his future. In fact he had no time to grasp it. He was cutting back swiftly and furtively through the trees to where he'd left the big removal van parked in the shelter of Uncle Hervé's cattle-track.

He got in, started the engine, drove back towards the avenue. Where the track joined it he was forced to stop, because the gendarmes' car was already coming back again, slowing down and stopping before turning out onto the main road. And there in the back were Pierre and Rosalind with Madame Bourjois, amazingly, between them crying her eyes out. So the gendarmes had nothing to do with him at all, he had lost his head quite foolishly. Nothing was lost, his future was still intact, to be reached out and taken, exactly as he'd planned.

Only what could be wrong at the château? An accident apparently. Perhaps Monsieur Gustave and the mother? They'd passed him some time ago, speeding down the avenue as only Parisians can speed. Or the twins? Or Monsieur Bourjois? Would he be expected to get out? Do something? Rosalind glanced up at him, expressionlessly, as he peered down from the cab of the van, then turned back to comforting Hélène. The gendarmes glanced at the van too, and looked away again without interest. When the road cleared they turned right off the avenue and drove away towards Seulbourg.

He found he was trembling with the relief of it, and unable really to care very much about Madame Bourjois and her problems. That was the past. It occurred to him that, outside of his dreams, he had never really expected her to come with him. Or even wanted her to. He had not once thought of her while he was busy working out the practical details of his future. For years now she had been no more than an ideal to keep him going, a dream-girl from a dead dream-time. He no longer needed an ideal – in an hour or so he would be in the very thick of reality, finished with dreams for good.

He sat in the van at the end of the track until it got really dark and the sky over the Mairie began to fizz with the first real fireworks, then he drove down the deserted village street and parked in the bit of waste ground behind the bungalows.

He'd visited, at one time or another, every one of the houses he was aiming at. He knew exactly what there was and where it was kept in each house. He'd known for years, ever since as a teenager he'd been invited in by his schoolfriends and shown with furtive glee the wealth their parents had carried away one night from the hated château. Through working with his brother he knew almost exactly how much every object was worth. And how much a van load of it would be worth to him when he got to Paris. And he knew that not one of his former neighbours would dare to report even the theft of a single teaspoon . . .

The party fell into place again after the gendarmes left. Few of the guests had even noticed their presence, or noticed that Hélène and the Bouchons were gone. When Jean-Hubert, returning from a harmless little flirt with Nathalie in the kitchen, enquired after her he was told by Loulou ("Tiens!" he thought, "How did *she* get here? And looking so sexy too.") that Hélène had gone off in a car "with my ex-husband and his fat little foreign wife."

Typical, thought Jean-Hubert furiously, Hélène has never had any real sense of les convenances. Of how to conduct herself decently. The Bouchons, he recalled, went every year to mingle with the unwashed villagers at their firework display; apparently his wife had foolishly allowed herself to be persuaded along. A reception at the château was too select for the Bouchons, he supposed, they missed the noise, they missed le gros rire, the vulgar jokes. But Hélène, tout de même . . . He had imagined she was trained in the ways of the family by now. Sixteen years of his example, of the example of his poor mother, of Tante Ruby . . . He had a small angry thought about silk purses and sows' ears: Perhaps in reality Hélène was not suited to this kind of life?

He remembered uneasily the democratic impulses of her early years in Plouch'en, the bizarre characters she had frequented in Amsterdam – well *he* had frequented them too but he was a man, after all, it was different. He recalled the squalid dinner party of a few weeks back with these same Bouchons, poor Maître Bourin had been grossly insulted. Surely she was not going to disgrace him, now that he was on the point of arriving at last? After all, this evening's party was just a beginning. Would she show herself to be inadequate when she had regularly to entertain the notabilities of the region? Breton society was so very straitlaced. They were lucky actually that so many nice people had turned up this evening, after the way Madame la Comtesse had . . . That had been a mistake, he was willing to admit, Nathalie and Gabriel would get their walking-papers tomorrow morning. No point in compromising himself any further, Hélène would just have to get by with a femme de ménage and some elbow grease. It was only thanks to Tante Ruby that anyone decent had bothered to come.

Where *was* poor Tante Ruby? He hadn't seen her for hours. Suffering perhaps? Locked in her room weeping? He'd been perfectly right to order Uncle Gustave and his mistress off the premises. Quand même, it was going a bit far, even for old Gustave. He hoped no one had realised that his belle-mère was the old man's mistress, though the way they were clinging to each other . . . Perhaps Hélène had taken offence, seeing her mother ordered out like a malpropre? Of course she hadn't *seen*, she hadn't been around, mooning off someplace as usual, just got back to say goodbye to them. Hope she gets back to say goodbye to our guests, that would be the . . . I'd better find Tante Ruby, he thought, just in case she doesn't get back. Tante Ruby at least knows how to conduct herself, she is a Ploudel de Medeu, after all.

Gabriel, meanwhile, beneath the immense spreading rosebush, was feeling like a small boy who's got drunk for the first time. Nothing in his adventures with the village girls, nothing in his passionate nights with Nathalie, had prepared him for the new, and extremely bizarre, experiences he was undergoing. Paris, he thought confusedly, this must be how the Parisiennes do it. They are more sophisticated than we. Or the Russians? *They* are more savage and what after all is the difference, in sex?

Not that he was given much time to think. Madame Ruby loomed above him or wriggled beneath him, kneading him, biting him, pinching him, moulding him into shapes he'd never before realised the human body could take. Her perfume ("*Opium*, mon petit Gabriel, it is called *Opium*") was all over him, drowning him, suffocating him, seeping into every pore of his skin, into his nostrils, into his ears, into . . . He'd have to wash for a week before he could face Nathalie. At this rate he'd have to go to confession before he could face Nathalie. He had an appalled vision of old Father Plouer's face listening agape through the grille. No, perhaps not confession . . .

He felt helpless, imprisoned naked in the web of the old lady's enthusiasm, his clothes and hers scattered le bon

Dieu knew where. Hours they'd been here, hours, Monsieur Bourjois would give him the sack. The party, the service, he was supposed to be serving the drinks up there at the château . . . And he was really feeling quite painful, painful in places that he hadn't even known existed. Would he be able to walk even, when she released him? *If* she released him. He had a nightmare feeling that never again would he be allowed to see the light of day, that never again would he perform ordinary little human gestures like pouring a drink, like driving a car. Like laughing even. Laughter was nowhere in what he was living here under the rosebush with this wicked witch out of one of the tales of his childhood, laughter did not exist. It did not exist in Hansel and Gretel, it did not exist in Baba Yaga, it did not exist with the aunt of his employer. La tante du patron! It ought to be a joke, anyone would laugh, but he did not believe that he, Gabriel, would ever be allowed to laugh again.

The ambitious little dream he'd been working on ever since he arrived at the château staggered painfully to its death. The old skin, walking around naked, obviously mad for it, being so grateful to him that she would willingly finance a little bungalow in the village where he would live happily with Nathalie and their future children, putting in the occasional hour's labour when his services were required. Like Hervé Le Moal he'd seen himself paying in man-hours for the lease of his home. A different kind of labour, of course. But this? Perhaps he was not fitted to be a gigolo after all? Gigolos were meant to be in control . . .

Above them both loomed the great archway of Madame Laetitia Ploudel, her long branches trailing thornily to the ground to make a claustrophobic cave-like shelter, and springing fiercely up again in spiny clumps where they'd taken root, her huge flowers intoxicating him with their perfume in the dark.

"In St Petersburg you will be my butler, Gabriel," Madame Ruby whispered, "I have now decided to take you away from this village. You have become indispensable to me, I will make you learn Russian. You will keep my household accounts. You alone will shop for my food and prepare it. You will see that my native servants do not cheat me or poison me. And you will have other duties too, bien sûr mon petit!"

She pulled him close and he pictured himself wading chilblained through sombre streets of Russian snow like some pathetic remnant of la Grande Armée, saw himself standing for hours in a sullen-faced queue of hefty square-bottomed housewives in headscarves to buy the daily ration of black bread and wormy beetroot, presiding over a servants' hall of savage-eyed serfs footless on vodka, submitting his fragile young body night after night to even more of the pleasures he was enduring now. The pinchings, the bitings, the chewings, the . . .

"Non," he groaned, "Non, non, madame, I cannot! I am too weak!" and in a final effort to get free he tore himself frantically out of the old lady's clutches and rolled away out of her reach. Over and over he rolled and scrambled, clawing desperately around for his clothes, until he caught his bare foot on a stump and tumbled heavily flat on his belly into the thickest thorniest clump of the big rose-tree's vicious branches.

A group of guests, bidding goodbye to Jean-Hubert in the courtyard, heard his screams and stood still, appalled, to listen.

"It sounds like some poor devil having his throat cut," whispered Monseigneur de Petitpied, "May the good God have mercy . . ."

"*Not* his throat," corrected old General Blérot de Bois Sauvage, "I think you can count upon me to recognise that particular quality of scream. Do not forget, my friends, that I myself presided over many of the interrogations in the Algerian war. I would say it is quite a different part of his anatomy, that!"

En masse they rushed courageously down the garden to the rescue, led by Nathalie who lit the way with two branched candlesticks she snatched up from the buffet tables. They arrived at the scene just as Tante Ruby, having managed to disentangle poor Gabriel from the rosebush, was attempting awkwardly with teeth and fingernails to remove dozens of immense barbed thorns from the delicate lacerated parts of his body.

"The Martyrdom of St Sebastian," Jean-Hubert giggled, then fell silent under the frozen stares of his guests. Nathalie, after a moment's shock, screamed loudly, hurled the candlesticks at Tante Ruby and fled.

Nobody there, in spite of many centuries of excellent breeding, could think of a single urbane remark to break the spell of embarrassment. They all trudged back silently up the garden in the dark. Jean-Hubert wondered briefly if he ought perhaps to stay and be of assistance to his aunt. What, in the circumstances, would be correct behaviour, what would be savoir-vivre? What exactly did noblesse oblige in a situation like this?

Not, he reflected finally, that noblesse risked playing any great role in his future existence. In a matter of minutes probably, the news would be winging its way from mobile phone to mobile phone, from manor to château, from hôtel particulière to Versailles villa and, most destructive of all, from gentleman's residence to Préfecture to Bishop's Palace in all the Departements of Brittany. It was the official and very public end of the Ploudel de Medeus. Never now would he and his family be accepted into the closed staid world of the good Catholic Breton aristocracy that had seemed, for a tantalizing few months, to be on the point of discreetly opening its doors to them. Never now would the twins be invited to débutante rallye or tennis party, never would Clémence be asked to pour tea for visiting Polish cardinals or to spend her Easter holidays carrying stretchers at Lourdes with all the jeunes filles de bonne famille, never now would Henri have a helping hand to push him through St Cyr . . .

And meanwhile where the devil was Hélène when he needed her? When, he realised with amazement, (and with an amused picture of his snarling Clémence meekly carrying stretchers anywhere) when what he really needed her for above all was so he could recount to her the whole episode in all its scandalous detail and have a bloody good laugh over it. Sacrée Tante Ruby, after all. The last real Ploudel de Medeu . . .

Part Ten

❧

Another summer, and another and yet another. Rosalind wheeled her sleeping baby up the village street, the toddler Anna trotting beside her. They could almost be Breton babies, stocky and light-haired and slightly tanned. They could almost be Pierre's babies.

Somewhere deep inside her she was aware that these were strangers' children, but she usually managed to keep the awareness buried. In any case it did not matter nearly as much as she'd feared it would all those months ago when Pierre confronted her with his decision. Her only terror was that her son and daughter might, some day in the future, in some now-unimaginable time of peace for their country, be justly but cruelly taken from her. They were not adopted. It had not been possible, in the confused circumstances, to legally adopt them. They were foster-children, guest children. Their futures, and Rosalind's peace of mind, were at the mercy of care agencies, social workers and, just possibly, tortuously-traced relatives.

Pierre was reassuring: who did she imagine would come and take them away? Who could possibly want them, and have a greater *right* to want them, than Pierre himself? The children, with a hundred others, had arrived in France and

358

been offered asylum at the end of a long dangerous journey, after being snatched haphazardly by UN troops out of the ruins of several bombed-out villages. Their parents were almost certainly dead. The war in their country, the chaos, the destruction of all civilized living, was far from over. Rather, it was now spreading like a toxic cloud beyond the frontiers, into prosperous little neighbouring states whose citizens had until now lived harmoniously and comfortably together with no particular sense of their tribal identities.

In his gloomier moments, and they were many, Pierre envisaged that war and all the other ethnic wars, all the local conflicts, joining up eventually, engulfing the rest of Europe. Engulfing France. Why should they not? Pierre reasoned. Another world war was the only logical destination, given the road the human race was travelling. Why did Rosalind imagine that she would be allowed to sit forever in front of the television knitting baby bonnets and watching other people's children being hacked to pieces? What was so special about France? Only fifty years, Rosy, since the German occupation, and that must have been unthinkable enough beforehand! I am not talking fantasies, Pierre said, I am being realistic now, I consider it the duty of every intelligent person to be as pessimistic as I am. Otherwise, he told her, one might as well imitate my poor sods of patients, swallowing their daily Prozac and grinning all the way to the abattoir. Quite depressing he could be, Pierre, when he put his mind to it. It was a relief that he so often seemed to get things wrong. Nice that people weren't always as sordid as his pathetic patients had him believing. All that nonsense he'd fed her about France going overboard for the National Front and then what actually happened? Even old Chirac had to practically turn Socialist, had to transform himself into a sort of Abbé Pierre, before they'd elect him President! The French were far more caring than Pierre would like her to think, he was far from being the One Just Man. Not that she'd dare say that to him, but it was nice to know, seeing she had to spend the rest of her life here.

Meanwhile they had the children. They were doing something really worthwhile in fostering the little Eric and Anna, something, he reminded her, that was far less egoistic than the mindless perpetuation of their own very imperfect genes, which is what Rosalind had been so thoughtlessly campaigning for. So she had better be content with the situation hadn't she, because that was all she was going to get.

Rosalind *was* reasonably content. She would have been completely happy if she'd not had occasional middle-of-the-night visions of a refugee camp somewhere in Europe where a distraught mother was going mad with grief.

"But there is nothing we can do about that, voyons!" Pierre said impatiently, "Be logical, Rosy, the only action in our power is to care for these children. Where is the sense in having nightmares?"

But if that distraught mother was miraculously traced? If she arrived here in Plouch'en, months or years hence, to claim her own?

"Well then," Pierre said, "In common humanity we should rejoice for her. There will always be sufficient children for us to foster. After all, there is no shortage of human evil to produce them."

And he insisted that they learn the language of the children's country so that they could bring them up bi-lingually. Just in case.

Rosalind, labouring through a *Methode Assimil* grammar in the evenings when the babies were asleep, wondered whether her husband was a saint or just an insensitive French lump with a head full of dreary Cartesian logic instead of nice ordinary human feelings. She was sharply conscious of the differences in their race and upbringing. With an Englishman she would have known . . . Yes, she thought, but with an Englishman I'd probably have been bored out of my mind by now.

She wheeled the pram out of the village in the direction of the château, pausing to say Bonjour to Madame Balavoine working happily away in the front garden of what used to be Michel Le Borgne's cottage. Poor Michel would have had a fit: the old dear had only torn out all his honeysuckle and clematis and rambling roses and planted straight lines of French marigolds and red salvia. Still, give her her due, she was surviving. Thriving, even. Monsieur Balavoine, after his token prison sentence, had broken down completely and was now in a mental home. The Seulbourg house was up for sale, and Jean-Hubert had rented the cottage to Madame. Magali, Claude and the little Sebastian often came to stay for weekends.

Rosalind passed by her own old home without much regret. It was a holiday cottage now: there was a Dutch family sunbathing in the front garden, with huge red thighs and great big mouthfuls of teeth. She waved happily at them and little Anna imitated her. The family waved back. It was nice and friendly having foreigners around. There were more of them than usual in the village this year, because of the château being a hotel now. You had to hand it to Jean-Hubert, and to Hélène too of course, they were both working like Trojans. Even if Jean-Hubert's idea of work was to stroll in a lordly way among the guests, quoting French literature and playing the châtelain. Though she had to admit, the guests lapped it up: after all, that's presumably what they were paying through their noses for. And both Jean-Hubert and Hélène were far friendlier than they used to be, not nearly so much nonsense about them . . . She was glad not to be living on their doorstep all the same. They had a habit of trying to rope you in. Not that she'd have minded, but what with the children and all . . . Today was OK, it was just cleaning silver and the kids could be having their nap. And it *was* a lovely day for a walk. But she wouldn't want to be doing it too often, it wasn't like the old days when she was longing for company and anything would have seemed like a nice change. She'd just have to tell Hélène straight out. You're letting them exploit you, Pierre kept saying, and we're not even *tenants* any more, we're not *serfs*, Rosy!

When Father Plouer died Pierre had bought the presbytery. It had a large garden for the children, and a field for Mujah and Din to rollick around in. Plouch'en shared a priest now with three other villages but it didn't really matter because only Madame la Comtesse and her relations bothered going to Mass any more. Even Hélène had dropped out, and most of the older parishioners had died off in the last few wet winters.

Pierre maintained that the village had undergone some fundamental change for the worse in the past three years. It wasn't just that the whole place had dropped their hard-won Socialist principles and voted for right-wing parties in the last election. The whole of France had done that, after all. No, it was as if their old schoolmaster's act of violence and Michel's pillaging of their stolen treasures had brought some deep disillusion to the people of Plouch'en. Neither the traditional dignity of l'Education Nationale nor the kindly innocent values of the generation of '68 had been able to resist the encroaching barbarity of fin de siècle France, and the shocked villagers had in consequence become more barbaric themselves. Rosalind couldn't see it at all. In her view the people of the village had always been as raw and barbaric as you could hope to meet. As for the old schoolmaster, hadn't Pierre himself often told her the guy was a complete nutcase? And Michel. Well it had been high time the man got a grip on himself and grew up, just a pity he hadn't the wit to do so twenty years earlier.

They'd had a long letter from Michel a week ago. With Monsieur Vladimir's things to sell, he'd taken a stall in an antiques market in Paris and apparently hadn't looked back since. He was moving into his own premises shortly, had a nice girlfriend and was thinking of settling down. Not much barbaric about that, Rosalind thought. But that was Pierre for you, all theories.

She wondered if she ought to tell Hélène about the letter, and then decided against it. Hélène was no longer someone who'd be interested in the past, or in the fortunes of a gardener she'd probably forgotten even existed.

Hélène, looking out of a window, unconsciously expected to see Mujah and Din bounding along destructively in front of the pudgy figure of Rosalind and was, as always nowadays, slightly stunned at being confronted instead by the pram and by the pathetic fairytale prettiness of the little Anna and Eric.

She could never approach these children with anything but an awed trepidation: what must be there, hidden inside their little blond heads, behind the shy pale charm of their smiles? What horrors must they have seen? What witnessed pain must forever be walled away there beneath whatever shell the years would construct around them?

She always felt slightly repelled by the matter-of-fact

jokiness with which Rosalind bounced the children around, dumped them giggling in cots, spooned carrots into them as if they were, well, just any ordinary unwounded babies. They seemed to thrive on it, Hélène had to admit, but surely there was a respect, a *distance*, owed to them? A recognition of their hidden fragility?

She realised she was very probably being foolish: where, after all, would awed trepidation have got her with the twins after they'd witnessed their own particular horror? All they'd wanted, there in the gendarmerie, had been a long tight hug and the chance to cry and cry and cry. And when all the unpleasantness was finally over and they were home again the thing that had probably, more than anything else, helped them back to normality was Jean-Hubert's bawdy account of the scandalous end both of the party and of his own aristocratic hopes, his description of the assembled notabilities, "including the *bishop*, mes enfants!" gazing horror-struck by candlelight on Tante Ruby's antics with Gabriel under the rosebush. And what had united them all in a great wave of sympathy and enthusiasm was his recognition that now finally, after two centuries' struggling, the Ploudel de Medeus were as good as finished socially so they could simply step off the uncomfortable tightrope they'd been balancing on and stride off on their own towards the year 2000.

When she thought about it, Hélène had to admit that that was probably the closest pleasantest family evening they'd ever spent. It hadn't lasted, of course. Jean-Hubert could not be expected to change his nature in any fundamental way, and whatever area of fragility the twins were carrying inside them they certainly didn't want to talk about it or cry about it any more. Or to be hugged again or cheered up again. They were as remote from her as they'd ever been, bright average young people home now from Trinity and from the Institut de Sciences Politique, swimming and riding their bikes and helping out charmingly in the hotel dining-room while they waited for their exam results. *Not* indulging in finer feelings or états d'âme about the past.

Nor did she herself lately have time or inclination for much soul-searching. Hélène could not remember when she'd last had a real daydream. The sort that used to fill every waking hour. The sort that were once more real than the life she'd been absentmindedly leading.

Nowadays, while she supervised the cleaning of a bedroom or personally set the long oak table for the special Dîner au Château the guests paid a fortune to eat, her mind was actually following the progress of the duster into corners, or registering the knife or fork or spoon her hands were laying down. Actively searching out missed specks of dust. Judging the suitability of one set of silver over another. Not, as in the past, sliding mistily off across the years and the wounds and the longings to a lovely aching dream world that had not so much been a refuge as an identity in the confusion of exile. *Not* recalling how that oak table once stood in Pierre's surgery and was a witness to her yearnings for Ireland and for Christopher Milton, that almost forgotten shadow from an irrelevant past.

One autumn, the autumn when guns were put back into holsters and Christopher himself had presumably become irrelevant, she'd made a last effort to seek out that past. Leaving Jean-Hubert at the château happily bossing the workmen who were transforming the place into a hotel, she travelled over with Rosalind and Pierre, shared their holiday house, spent increasingly bewildered days in Belfast and Claghan and Crossmaglen. She found no drama and very little to inspire nostalgia.

Belfast resembled any university city, Rennes or Caen or Nantes, the shop windows full of young fashionable clothes, impossibly childlike students slouching the streets: had Mitzi and Sheila and Bernadette Devlin and Eamonn McCann ever looked so new and so raw, so very recently minted? She found herself unexpectedly longing for Henri and Clémence. Love and dreams and heartbreak were their territory now, after all, no longer hers.

Her little café near Queen's no longer existed. The gloomy house where Christopher's flat had been now had a pink front door; a young woman with Botticelli hair came out tugging a pram across the step and looked curiously at Hélène when she offered a hand with the baby.

The Club Bar had been closed down years earlier. For drug-dealing, they told her in the place where she had her lunch. A place that she remembered as narrow shabby old Smoky Joe's and that was now a very up-market Italian restaurant. Smoky's grandchildren grown up and doing well for themselves? She felt a hundred years old. Even if the Club Bar had still existed she knew she would not have had the courage to wander in as she'd planned and order a Pimms in the brown and beige lounge and recapture that first evening with Christopher.

There was absolutely nowhere left in the city that echoed her teenage years and in the end she walked sadly to Great Victoria Street and took a bus south.

In Cross, a brisk and matronly Teresa was heavily involved in community projects, reluctantly taking time off from youth training to accompany Hélène on a tour of Anny's townland. No nostalgia there either. She was appalled by the flat fenced fields, the emptily anonymous space where Patrick's cottage used to stand, the prosperous suburban-looking bungalows lining either side of the murderously transformed road along which she and Teresa used to amble to school.

In Claghan she found her tyrannical grandmother sitting senile and diminished in a corner, two of her uncles already dead, one in the States. Her aunt Phyllis was an ageing schoolteacher anxious to be friendly, name-dropping like mad about some romantic novelist she'd been at school with. "Well now, isn't it a funny coincidence the both of you in Brittany," she gushed, "and the both of you ending up in châteaux as well!"

"Oh, we let the natives live in the ordinary houses," Hélène smiled and her aunt Phyllis looked at her blankly for a second and then laughed, too loudly. "No but all the same you should get in touch with her some time. Just write to her, why don't you, and say you're my niece, I'm sure she'd be delighted to see someone from home. We were always very great, myself and old Maureen . . . Mind you, that's going back a bit, there's none of us getting any younger is there?"

Phyllis had very little to say about Hélène's parents. "Och sure our Brian was that much older than me, twelve or thirteen years, isn't it a lifetime when you're kids? He was always away at boarding-school and then college, it seems he had it all planned to do his MA and everything. A real brainbox. They never quit boasting about him," she added sourly.

"And . . . ?" Hélène prompted.

"Well, and then he just suddenly threw it all up . . . I was never told exactly what happened. Dada went mad, I do remember that. Our house was sheer hell for a while, we didn't dare open our mouths us young ones. I never met your mother I don't think, only the once. We weren't let to the house, you see, and of course she never came here. Brian did, he took you here a couple of times when you were small. It was Dada pulled strings to get him the job in St Brendan's Grammar, only he never really . . . Well, I suppose I can say it out straight now, he drank, didn't he. What do you mean, Hélène, tell you something real about him? It must be near forty years ago, what details could I remember, I tell you I hardly knew our Brian at all . . . I mean I just wouldn't have a clue about his personality or the books he read or whatever. He was just an ordinary fella, I suppose. He broke his parents' hearts, I do know that."

Maybe he did, Hélène thought bitterly, but that didn't stop them getting on with it and making a great living for themselves, they didn't exactly rend their garments and lie prostrate in grief. Nothing to be had from the Campbells, she decided, now any more than back then, Anny was right.

And nothing to be had from the squat in Quarry Street where she'd started living life as an adult over twenty years ago when her grandmother turned her away. The house no longer even existed. Blown up, she was told, oh it must be ten years ago now. There was a traditional restaurant in its place called The Old Soup Kitchen, wafting bacon and cabbage deliciously over its plate-glass neighbours. No ghost of Yann or of Ian Lewis or of her teenage self drifted among the deal tables or dropped a few mischievous grains of cannabis into the cast-iron pots of Claghan Colcannon. The rest of the street looked newly and cheaply prosperous, video shops and souvenirs and a motor-bike showroom with a huge poster, Fifties style, of Marlon Brando on a Harley Davidson.

"Plenty of cash going to be injected into Claghan in the none too distant," she was told when she enquired about the frenzy of obviously new commerce, "Yank money, British money, European. Handouts to small businesses.

Any man with brains in his head has himself set up to qualify."

"We all believe it's going to last this time," they told her, "No going back to the bad old days. Sure who'd want to, now?"

And Hélène, who had never known the place in the bad old days, who had passed her life in a comfortable dream while people were murdering one another in her birthplace, wandered aghast through the newly peaceful battered town, searching in vain for something to give her an identity. Something that would say: "Eileen Campbell grew out of this place, her roots are here and always will be." She gave up eventually and with a half-acknowledged sense of relief went off to pass the rest of her holiday as the ordinary foreign tourist she finally admitted to herself she'd always been, driving with Rosalind and Pierre around the Giant's Causeway and Lough Neagh and the green glens of Antrim. *"The green glens of Antrim are calling to me,"* crooned an ancient drunk in a pub one evening and Hélène had a piercing instant of nostalgia – record sleeves scattered over a red carpet, the smells of scent and powder and nail polish, "I'm clean mad about Lee Lawrence!" giggled her pretty young mother, putting the '78 back once more on the turntable, the night her father died. That close and only that to a lost childhood.

"I can't stand these old drunks singing folk songs," she snapped to Rosalind, "Like a Third World beer commercial. Would any of us set foot in a place like this back home in France? It's not because we're on *holiday . . .*"

She no longer needed Ireland now, she no longer needed memories to give her a sense of who she was. She had her own identity, that of a competent woman of the Nineties, running a small but successful family business. When her mind did slide off from the chore she was performing, it usually slid to the possibility of roping in one or other of her acquaintances to lend a hand in the frequent emergencies that crop up in hotel life. Or it slid forward to a time when Jean-Hubert might possibly feel he could afford a team of more reliable workers and she would no longer be obliged to exploit her friendships in this way. Even Rosalind was beginning to sound a bit reluctant when she was called upon urgently yet again to save her old friend's life and reputation.

In her spare time Hélène worked on the details of her plan for transforming part of the large beautiful garden into a very chic sales area where the guests, if they wished, could buy rooted cuttings of the magnificent and historic Madame Laetitia Ploudel whose rich and riotous colour, whose passionate scent, so enchanted them on their pre-dinner strolls.

In spite of the recession there was no shortage of guests. English, of course, in search of la vieille France, but also Parisians, Americans and Japanese recommended by her mother and Uncle Gus, who came to stay themselves whenever their busy social life allowed them to.

Tante Ruby had never been to the hotel, nor had she yet been allowed to claim her inheritance in St Petersburg. "Tu parles!" sneered Pierre, "That place resisted Napoleon, it resisted Hitler, why should it fall so easily to Madame Ruby?" For years he expected to hear of her retreating home pathetically through the Russian snows like the remnant of a defeated army and he had still not given up hope in spite of the radically different retreats the old lady was making. After hanging around in the city for boring fruitless months waiting for property rights to be granted her, it seemed Tante Ruby had, amazingly, found God. She would have been hard put *not* to find God in St Petersburg, said Jean-Hubert, who read all the fashionable news magazines, it seems the whole place has been awash in evangelists and exotic sects ever since Communism fell; the Russians have taken to religion like a national sport now, faute de mieux.

She wrote to them once from an Orthodox monastery where she was undergoing a spiritual cure: "More like a luxury hotel than their real hotels," she said, "And as for the Director of Conscience, quel bel homme mes chers! What shoulders! He is built like a veritable Breton wardrobe, that man!"

In the office where she kept the hotel accounts, Hélène had a black-and-white framed photo of Anny making Carrickmacross lace in front of an open turf fire. Her mother had taken it years ago and Hélène had recently had it enlarged. She'd had one wall of the office decorated in lime-washed rough stone to echo the cottage wall. When people commented she would say: "Oh yes. Anny. That's old Anny Maguire. Une paysanne adorable who helped to bring me up."

And she meant it. Anny had been a peasant, and adorable. Hélène had loved her very much as a child. That was all. It was the past, in another country, where fathers could die with casual violence, where first loves could turn out to have been the most shadowy of monsters. A past whose few moments of charm could be preserved in a photo and a piece of kitsch decor, to be glanced at from time to time as Hélène moved forward confidently into the future.